PENGUIN ⊙ CLASSICS

THE PENGUIN BOOK OF MERMAIDS

CRISTINA BACCHILEGA is a professor and the graduate program director in the Department of English at the University of Hawai'i at Mānoa. Her published works include *Postmodern Fairy Tales: Gender and Narrative Strategies*; *Legendary Hawai'i and the Politics of Place: Tradition, Translation, and Tourism*; and *Fairy Tales Transformed? Twenty-First-Century Adaptations and the Politics of Wonder*. She has been awarded a Guggenheim Fellowship, the Chicago Folklore Prize, a Fulbright Teaching/Research Award, and the Distinguished Scholarship Award from the International Association for the Fantastic in the Arts.

MARIE ALOHALANI BROWN is an associate professor and the undergraduate chair in the Department of Religion at the University of Hawai'i at Mānoa. Her first book, *Facing the Spears of Change: The Life and Legacy of John Papa 'Ī'ī*, won the Palapala Po'okela Award for the best book on Hawaiian language, culture, and history.

The Penguin Book of Mermaids

Edited by
CRISTINA BACCHILEGA
and
MARIE ALOHALANI BROWN

PENGUIN BOOKS

PENGUIN BOOKS

An imprint of Penguin Random House LLC
penguinrandomhouse.com

First published in Penguin Books 2019

LIBRARY OF CONGRESS CATALOGING-IN-PUBLICATION DATA
Names: Bacchilega, Cristina, 1955– editor. | Brown, Marie Alohalani editor.
Title: The Penguin book of mermaids / edited by Cristina Bacchilega and Marie Alohalani Brown.
Other titles: Mermaids
Description: New York : Penguin Books, 2019. | Includes bibliographical references and index.
Identifiers: LCCN 2019017633 (print) | LCCN 2019020637 (ebook) |
ISBN 9780143133728 (paperback) | ISBN 9780525505570 (ebook)
Subjects: LCSH: Mermaids. | Fairy tales—History and criticism. | Symbolism in fairy tales. |
Women—Folklore. | Sex role—Folklore. | Human ecology. | Spirituality in literature.
Classification: LCC GR910 (ebook) | LCC GR910 .P34 2019 (print) | DDC 398.21—dc23
LC record available at https://lccn.loc.gov/2019017633

Printed in the United States of America

Set in Sabon LT Std

Contents

THE PENGUIN BOOK OF MERMAIDS

Water Deities and Sirens
from Olden Times

Mermaids and Other Merbeings
in Europe

Literary Tales

Merfolk and Water Spirits
Across Cultures

Introduction

The Stories We Tell About Mermaids and Other Water Spirits

> The loveliest maiden is sitting
> High-throned in yon blue air,
> Her golden jewels are shining,
> She combs her golden hair;
>
> She combs with a comb that is golden,
> And sings a weird refrain
> That steeps in a deadly enchantment
> The list'ner's ravished brain . . .

These stanzas of Heinrich Heine's poem "Die Lore-Ley" (1823), rendered here in Mark Twain's translation, "The Lorelei," encapsulate some of the most salient and lasting features of the mermaid as a beautiful and dangerous being who attracts men to their watery deaths. Evoking popular Western iconography, Lorelei, bejeweled and combing her golden hair with her golden comb, appears to sailors and sings them a tune, the sweetness of which is irresistible and fatally entrances them. By the end, "Lorelei's grewsome work" is done, and the water has engulfed "sailor and bark."[1]

Historically, Lorelei's tale emerged in the early nineteenth century as a local legend and cautionary tale connected with the dangerous waters and the echo heard in the vicinity of the tall cliff Loreley along the river Rhine in Germany. In a version that predates Heine's, the beautiful maiden, betrayed by her loved one and accused of witchcraft, throws herself down from the cliff into the mirrorlike waters of the Rhine, where the echo of her name continues to be heard.[2] Faced with the prospect of living without the one she loves, Lorelei desires to end her life, or eventually to be reunited with him in the water. But her backstory and act of romantic loyalty are forgotten in later musical and poetic compositions,[3] in which she becomes emblematic of a widespread trope of femininity: a mermaid of alluring beauty who uses her sirenlike song to draw men to her and to water.

Mermaids: What and who are they? What do they look like? How are they different from sirens? How are they related to other water beings around the world? What are the cultural, religious, and popular beliefs that sustain specific plots of human-merfolk encounters? Why do we continue to tell stories about eerie mermaids and other water spirits in the twenty-first century?

The Penguin Book of Mermaids does not pretend to provide a definitive answer to any of these questions, but its more than sixty tales from a wide range of cultures and time periods illuminate our fascination with mermaids today. Our choices aim to broaden readers' knowledge of European mermaids; to encourage considering today's popular-culture mermaid in relation to her merfolk kin in belief tales across the globe, past and present; and to foster appreciation of the cultural significance of the tales, since mermaids and other water spirits raise issues of gender, voice, and sexuality, as well as knowledge, ecology, and spirituality—especially but not only in Indigenous contexts. Our interest, in other words, is to provide an opportunity to enjoy and reflect on the diversity across place and time of human experiences with the mysterious, nonhuman, aquatic other.

The tales in *The Penguin Book of Mermaids* are of folkloric or literary provenance, and our short introductions help to situate them historically and culturally, as well as to underscore that those circulating in oral tradition are not necessarily confined to the past. The multiplicity of languages in which mermaid and other water-spirit narratives are found and the variety of modes in which they are experienced present a huge challenge for a print anthology in the English language. It goes without saying that such a collection cannot represent all cultures or do justice to the nuances of the innumerable stories, so we have chosen to take on the challenge in ways that expand our expectations of what mermaids are and what they mean across languages and cultures. Notably, twenty tales appear here for the first time in English—translated from Estonian, Greek, Hawaiian, Ilocano, Italian, Japanese, Khasi, Persian, and Spanish. Furthermore, since mermaid tales are often repurposed for specific audiences and contexts, we have included two contemporary literary adaptations of "The Little Mermaid," one from Japan and one from the United States.

Their Bodies, Our Anxieties

There is something deeply unsettling about a being whose form merges the human with the nonhuman. Whether they dwell in fresh or salt water, aquatic humanoids raise questions about what it is to be human and what lies beyond a human-centered world. Physically, they are both like and unlike us. They eat, sleep, and breathe in a realm that we can access only temporarily, but they can live among us, as they are often able to shed the nonhuman portion of their bodies and infiltrate the human world. And the shores and banks where we come across them, like the vessels on which we cross their waters, are thresholds between our world and theirs. We humans do not deal well with betwixt and between—liminality makes us anxious. We prefer our world organized into well-ordered and sharply defined categories, and we prefer to be in charge of it. Nonetheless, we are strangely drawn to the other who is in part a mirror image of us and appears within reach, even if mentally ungraspable.

Our anxieties about water beings are magnified by our attraction to them, and, even more so by the mermaid's seductiveness, which in many stories results in the human's loss of control, self, and even life. Embracing a water spirit can prove lethal. Will the mermaid drag us beneath the water to drown us or to give us a new life? If we were able, with the help of magic, to survive in the merfolk's watery world, would we be their prisoners or their partners? And if a mermaid or maiden of the sea marries a human, will the relationship last, or will her otherness prevail?

Our ambivalence toward mermaids and other water spirits finds its representation in their bodies, which are often alluring, but can also be frightening. Perhaps most powerful is the image of the mermaid's hybrid body—her fish-human, super-feminized, but strange form. Descriptions of the merbeing's fishy lower half tend to be generic, but there are a few notable exceptions. Water spirits with the lower half of an ocean-dwelling porpoise are found in Oceania; human mixed with freshwater dolphin (or porpoise), dugong, or manatee bodies are found in the Amazon region. Other merbeings and water spirits are partly reptilian—dragons or water snakes. This hybridity may be a sign of superhuman, divine powers, as in the case of the mythic Oannes; or of lack and subhuman bestiality, as exemplified in the "Feejee mermaid" hoax.

Whether it has religious significance or is bestialized, the human-fish or human-snake hybrid is all the more a monster because its element is water, which is both a life source and a mystery that humans are transported by but cannot fully inhabit. Our use of the word "monster" here reaches back to the Latin *monstrum*, a "portent" or prodigious being that defies what is commonly found in nature and thus elicits both fear and awe. In contemporary cultural theory, we are reminded that "a construct and a projection, the monster exists only to be read: the *monstrum* is etymologically 'That which reveals,' 'That which warns.'"[4] Biform water creatures are signs, then, that often serve both as admonition for humans not to cross borders and as incitement to do so.

Such admonition and incitement come in innumerable permutations across sexual, gendered, racial, species, ontological, and spiritual divides. For instance, reductive definitions of mythological Sirens as real-life "harlots outstanding in both instrumental music and sweetness of voice" who "reduced passers-by to beggary" already circulated in Greek and Roman antiquity;[5] and the appellation of prostitutes as "mermaids" in early modern British culture[6] likewise attests to how a woman who oversteps the boundaries of gender propriety has, over centuries, risked being defined as monstrous. In contrast, as shown in Odysseus's encounter with the Sirens, it is manly, in fact heroic, to engage with their seductive powers, as long as one does not fall prey to them. Stories of merfolk and other water spirits thus provoke us to think about gender and our expectations of differently gendered bodies.

The representation of mermaids' bodies seems to have a stable history, but when we consider the etymology of "mermaid" we find that, even confining ourselves to the mythologies of northern Europe, "maidens of the sea" come as undines, selkies or seals, nixies, and sea nymphs in many shapes and forms, some of which are not even described. Furthermore, mermaids have been represented as having a single fishtail, marking them as having some control over their bodies,[7] or as having two tails, perhaps suggesting sexual availability. In current iconography, the mermaid usually has one tail, a fishtail that in its long and scaly shape is only somewhat reminiscent of the serpent's tail in some medieval stories.[8] Iconically appearing upright and bare breasted with her piscine half hidden in the water, the mermaid's body is often read as a sign of her mutability and duplicitous nature. The striking reversal in René Magritte's painting "The Collective Invention" shows a mermaid lying on the beach, on her side, facing viewers; she has a fish's head and side fins, while her lower body is human and naked. Does Magritte's rearrangement of the mermaid's body parts show how dehumanizing a patriarchal "collective invention" of the mermaid can be?

While some mermaids, merfolk, and other water spirits unsettle the human-nonhuman divide by their ability to inhabit different bodies at the same time, others do so by shapeshifting, for instance, from seal or reptile to human. Hans Christian Andersen's Little Mermaid's transformation into a human is the outcome of her pact with the sea witch. For other merbeings, shape-shifting is a way of life: a seal woman may sun herself in either shape when she pleases. But her hybrid nature is more than skin deep: when access to her nonhuman body is taken away by a man who wishes to hold her on land, she is mutilated. As many tales about marriage between humans and merbeings suggest, interspecies romances are risky.

While some of the mermaids that real-life voyagers and explorers have reported seeing in their travels are not described as beautiful, in most narrative and visual accounts it is the beauty of the mermaid—in contrast to the siren's knowledge—that attracts men. In misogynist ways, such beauty is often connected with vanity, as the mermaid narcissistically holds a golden mirror while combing her long, flowing hair. Beauty can be a powerful weapon—a lure that draws us nearer, a temptation that we are unable to resist. It beckons us, whispering that it will give us what we want most, whether that be love, sex, or both. But what does our fascination with this dangerous yet desirable other suggest about us?

Answers to this question are found in the many tales that different peoples tell about water spirits. They reflect our fascination with and fear of female bodies and of water and our dread of predators or poisonous creatures that live in or near water. But such tales are also social and cultural commentaries about what it means to be human: they encapsulate our beliefs and mores, express our weaknesses and strengths, and expose our deepest fears and desires. Furthermore, stories of sirens, mermaids, and other water spirits consistently admonish humans for testing their place in the social and natural world by mingling with nonhuman or monstrous water beings.

Story Currents, Crosscurrents, and Genres

Since ancient times, humans have noted that stories from discrete cultures around the world can be remarkably similar, and have tried to account for why the same motifs and themes occur globally. This is true of stories about water beings. To explain this phenomenon, various theories explore the origin of traditional narratives, but they are difficult to verify. What bears keeping in mind is that the value of stories is not the degree to which they are authentically native, but the ways that they reflect the concerns or values of the group who tells and retells them.

The popularity of water-spirit tales also depends on the powerful material and symbolic role of water, without which life as we know it would be impossible. Given that everything we need to survive, in one way or another, depends on water, it is unsurprising that peoples across place and time have ascribed religious significance to water and developed water symbolism. But water is also a shape-shifter that is not easily grasped and that affects nearly everything it touches. Whether fresh, brackish, or salty, water holds a mystery that fascinates humans, has aesthetic qualities that delight our senses, and—like water spirits—is both attractive and destructive.

Stories move about in the world in ways that are comparable to ocean currents, following a course as they move. This is not to say that the flow of these story currents is a natural occurrence. While it is difficult to ascertain with certainty whether parallel stories are the product of diffusion, it is easy enough to imagine the historical forces behind the circulation of stories—human migration and dispersal throughout the ages, exploration, trade, the expansion of colonialism and empires, and our age-old fascination with humankind, which leads us to learn more about peoples and their cultures. The material and ideological forces of capitalism and colonialism, often in conjunction with sexist ideologies, may have caused localized and indigenous story streams across the world to dwindle and their currents to be diverted. Thus, mermaid and water spirit stories as a global phenomenon do not circulate in isolation from one another. Like the crosscurrents of rivers and oceans, they flow into and cut across one another; they cause whirlpools, run in overt resistance to a dominant current, or persist hidden under it.

All these forces come to bear on how a story is passed on. Thus the individuals who collected and recorded tales—and their culturally informed understandings of genre and the purpose of genre—have also impacted the circulation and appreciation of tales locally, nationally, and transnationally. Thinking of currents and crosscurrents of stories encourages us not to compare and contrast them as separate and innately different, but rather to think of them in dynamic relation to one another. The cross-cultural dynamics of water-spirit stories can help loosen the hold of the all-too-popular reading of the siren or mermaid across time as a symbol of dangerous femininity.

Part of the attraction that keeps us telling and retelling merfolk and other water spirit stories lies in the mystery of these beings' existence and the lasting question, "Are mermaids and other water beings real?" Already in the first century A.D., the Roman naturalist Pliny the Elder was writing in his book *Natural History* about sightings of the remains of nereids and tritons—sea nymphs covered in scales and fish-tailed men. Visual representations of mermaids in medieval bestiaries, or visual compendia of beasts, also offered an outlet for answers to this question. The small images introducing each section of this collection gesture to the varied ways in which we have imagined merfolk and other water beings over the centuries.[9]

Twenty-first-century people—whether in real life or through our imagination, as seen, for instance, in multiple *Little Mermaid* live-action films—continue to wonder. Thus, along with historical accounts of mermaid sightings, we have included some first-person accounts from recent or contemporary oral tradition of seeing or interacting with mermaids or other water spirits. Like any other narratives concerning one's personal interaction with the divine or the inexplicable, these tales are approached with respect, whether or not we share their sense of reality.

Mermaid stories did not emerge as fairy tales—that is, as fictions—but as myths and legends. Folklorists explain that, in different ways and in contrast to folk and fairy tales, myths and legends raise questions of belief—meaning not that every teller believes the events in the tale really happened, but that somewhere, at some point in time, people (not just one individual) believed or believe in the material and/or symbolic truth of the tale. Myths often narrate the beginning of all life, as well as human life, and attempt to explain how and why things are the way they are and who is accountable for what. These stories have religious, spiritual, and philosophical functions and meanings, and feature gods as well as humans, often interacting with one another. While myths make accounts of early history believable or at least memorable, legends are grounded in a more recent and localized history that tells us how certain features of a place originated, or that situates events and their superpowered human protagonists within specific places and historical times. Place names and realistic details seek to verify the truth value of legends; folk and fairy tales (often called wonder tales), on the other hand, bolster our suspension of disbelief by staying away from specifics and following a magical logic of their own. However, this belief versus fiction distinction is not universally applicable when we consider how stories are relevant to the social group or community within which they circulate.[10]

Plots, Gender, and Human-Nonhuman Relations

Whether they are historical accounts, myths, legends, or folktales, or they belong to other genres that unsettle these distinctions, we can identify three common plots in mermaid and merfolk tales: the first features a fleeting interspecies encounter, the second a mer(maid)-wife, and the third the abduction of a human into the water.[11]

Over the centuries, humans have reported encounters with "strange" water beings. These narratives do not tell of lasting relationships between humans and merfolk, but of their fleeting meetings, either in the water or at its edge. The portal between the two dimensions is wide open, but rather than crossing over into the other space to stay, merfolk and humans find themselves interacting temporarily in contact zones—what anthropologist and cultural critic Mary Louise Pratt described as "social spaces where cultures meet, clash, and grapple with each other, often in contexts of highly asymmetrical relations of power."[12] Mermaids and humans belong to different worlds, and an imbalance of power often informs these accounts. That said, when water spirits are approached with respect rather than being treated as bad omens, the encounter can have a positive outcome for the human. Some tales from Ulithi Atoll and Yap in the Caroline Islands, for example, feature female porpoises who remove their tails every night so they can come ashore as humans to watch islanders dance.[13] These kinds of interactions express an understanding that merfolk and water spirits are part of an animated universe, the powers of which are neither good nor evil but must be respected.

Such difference, power, and mystery also fire human desire for a lasting relationship, which all too often turns into a form of appropriation, the subject of the second common type of plot. Within a European context, mer-wife plots vary, but at the outset they often hint at or showcase the maiden's difference, and they rarely have a happy ending. At stake in these stories is the female merbeing's existence between worlds—her being and not being human; her living with humans while also participating in what we call a "supernatural" sphere; her ability to cross the threshold into the world of humans and "pass" there as human while never fully belonging. When she is a powerful water being, such as Mélusine, the maiden sets her own conditions for her marriage with a human and hides her difference of her own accord; but when she is a selkie or seal woman, a man marries her by stealing her animal skin or hood, thereby precluding her return to the water and her kin. In both cases, the mer-wife's difference remains hidden in the human everyday, and she proves to be a loyal wife and caring mother. And yet, it matters whether she keeps the secret of her identity, because it determines her agency in the tale and the power dynamics of her marriage. These tales speak to the discrepancy between men's longing for a woman unfettered by social mores and their attempt to control her by domesticating her. The mermaid is beautiful, and men yearn to possess her, but it must be on their terms and not the mermaid's.

In the plots where the mer-wife remains more than human, the union consistently fails due to the man's inability to keep his word, which in some stories is shown to amount to his sexual betrayal. When the wife is instead an "animal bride" transformed fully into a human, the marriage fails because her domestication as a human wife and mother does not succeed in eradicating her ties with her water kin, or her desire to be in her own skin and element. While these tales have in the past often cautioned men not to marry an outsider, they also may be read as narratives of violence against women, in which the mer-wife must be considered the victim of an abduction.

In the final most common plot—a reversal of the second—mermaids, mermen, and water spirits are the active protagonists of tales about humans being held captive underwater. In some cases, the water being's taking hold of a young human is the outcome of a parent's binding words, a curse, or a promise; in others, it happens by chance. Regardless of the action's premise, sympathies do not lie with the captors, even if they are owed a human's life. Demonlike, they cannot be trusted and act stealthily; their hybrid bodies and the fluid ways in which they move in and out of the water are interpreted as duplicity. In most of these captivity tales, nothing is said of the human's experience with the merbeing. When dwelling with the mermaid symbolizes the sexual bewitchment of a forbidden liaison or an extramarital affair, the experience is conveyed as the man's disappearance from the human world—the only proper social world—into an abyss that is not described. This silence in the narrative furthers the perception of the captivating mermaid as monstrous.

In European traditions, the focus in all of these common plots is on the relationship between a human and a (somewhat unsettling) water being, with an emphasis on the human's desire and well-being. In other words, regardless of who has more or less agency in the stories, the merbeing's perspective is rarely presented and instead basically assumed: this is what "they" do, and we do not understand it. These narratives, then, reflect an anthropocentric view of the world and universe, in which humans hold a place of honor in a hierarchy of beings. In most cases, the framework is strongly patriarchal, and in some, it is also heavily Christianized, so that the (water) serpent is reduced to a demonic symbol of evil.

When investigating water spirits from societies that hold an animistic or all-animate view of the world, on the other hand, it is important to keep water's life-giving and death-dealing properties in mind, because as a collective these water spirits embody most, if not all, of water's attributes. Hawaiian stories about romances between female *mo'o*—Hawaiian reptilian water deities—and human males offer a glimpse into this worldview. Just as sirens and mermaids are notorious for their seductive songs that drive sailors mad with longing, *mo'o* are renowned for their loveliness. Significantly, there are no tales of men who try to tame their *mo'o* partners, because the *mo'o*, like the features of water they embody, cannot be contained or domesticated. Thus, the confluence of anthropocentrism and misogyny often found in the European tales is absent. The *mo'o* is, as in European tales, the ultimate dangerous but desirable other, and stories about *mo'o* seducing men are cautionary tales. But these accounts warn men to control their desires, to keep their wits about them in the presence of a "supernatural" beauty that represents, at the same time, the power of nature. Rather than cautioning men against the dangerous power of powerful female beings in the European tales, these tales enjoin respect for nonhuman life and divine power.

In other cases, stories are not concerned with sexual or romantic human–water spirit relations at all, but are transformation narratives in which a human becomes a water spirit as a punishment or as the result of love, or because a powerful water spirit wishes to have more helpers. And in other narratives, such as the Native American tale "The Woman Who Married the Merman," the significant interaction is between family members across species: the woman who is turning into a whale and her human brothers, whom she wants to support with food in exchange for arrows. In all of these tales, our place as humans in the world is negotiated within a set of social relations that are not limited to sexual or gendered dynamics, and encourage reciprocity and humility when interacting with other species and nature.

Water spirits, like water, are powerful, unpredictable, and

awe inspiring—that is, both terrifying and wonderful. In stories across cultures, they may seduce, punish, or reward humans, though their actions are ultimately outside of human grasp. Like water, they are shape-shifters that resist being contained.

Mermaids Among Us Today

Cultural assumptions and beliefs about who and what we as humans are, should not be, and could be—or what our place might be in relation to other humans as well as nonhuman animate beings—are presented, tested, and transformed in these stories. So it is not surprising that reimagining mermaids and water spirits more generally is a global and vibrant phenomenon in contemporary culture. In the late twentieth century, riding the second wave of Western feminism, Andersen's Little Mermaid became Disney's Ariel, and her voice and songs memorably asserted her double betweenness as an adolescent mermaid. The much-anticipated twenty-first-century Disney live-action remake has other cultural waves and currents with which to contend. Nowadays, we find in North America alone thousands of professional mermaids as well as women and men mermaiding (i.e., wearing a monofin or costume mermaid tail to perform, swim, be photographed, have fun), and academia as well as popular culture is contributing to what some have called a "mermaid economy."[14]

This contemporary fascination with mermaids is not new, and the stories selected for this book suggest the range and depth of the ways in which this preoccupation has been adapted from folklore and religion for various artistic and entertainment media. However, the increased popularity of Coney Island's Mermaid Parade,[15] of the March of Mermaids in Brighton, England, of mermaid Halloween costumes, of celebrities wearing mermaid fashion, and of mermaid blogs focusing on spirituality, conservation, and mermaiding, all attest to the fact that these new embodiments of our fascination with mermaids breathe new life and possibilities into the stories. The reimagined figure of the mermaid resonates for many today as fluid feminine self-possession or playful queerness. If the mermaid's overstepping the boundaries of gender or sexual propriety is transgressive, it is embraced as such, and not punished. And the exposure to new currents across cultures promises further unpredictable shape-shifting.

CRISTINA BACCHILEGA *and*
MARIE ALOHALANI BROWN

Notes

1. From Mark Twain's "The Lorelei" in *A Tramp Abroad* (Hartford, CT: American Publishing Company, 1880), chapter XVI. There are variant spellings in German (*Lore Lay, Lore-Ley, Loreley*) and English (Lorelei, sometimes Loreley). We will consistently refer to this mermaid as Lorelei.

2. This is in the ballad by German Romantic Clemens Brentano, thanks to whom Lorelei's tale came into being just a couple of decades before Heine's poem was published.

3. The legend of Lorelei is now part of a local tourist attraction on the Rhine, but it also has its own resonant echo in globalized popular culture—as seen in "The Lorelei Signal," an episode from the first season of *Star Trek: The Animated Series* (1973). In this episode, Captain Kirk and the other male members of the *Enterprise*'s crew are attracted by a mysterious signal to a planet where they are held captive by a group of women who keep them under their spell in order to take over the men's life energy. Notably, the *Star Trek* enchantresses stand on two legs, but then nothing is said in Heine's poem about whether Lorelei has a fishtail.

4. Jeffrey Jerome Cohen, "Monster Culture (Seven Theses)," in *Monster Theory: Reading Culture* (Minneapolis: University of Minnesota Press, 1996), 4.

5. These passages—one from Heraclitus in approximately the third century BCE and the other from "Servius's commentary on

Vergil, compiled soon after 400 CE"—are quoted in Leofranc Holford-Streven's "Sirens in Antiquity and the Middle Ages," in *Music of the Sirens* (Bloomington: Indiana University Press, 2006), 24.

6. Tara E. Pederson, *Mermaids and the Production of Knowledge in Early Modern England* (Burlington, VT: Ashgate Publishing Company, 2015), 25.

7. Misty Urban, "How the Dragon Ate the Woman: The Fate of Melusine in English," in *Melusine's Footprint,* eds. Misty Urban, Deva Kemmis and Melissa Ridley Elmes (Leiden, Germany, and Boston: Brill, 2017), 368–87.

8. See Frederika Bain, "The Tail of Melusine: Hybridity, Mutability, and the Accessible Other," in *Melusine's Footprint,* 17–35.

9. See Pliny the Elder's *Natural History* (1855 English-language edition) as well as John Cherry's *Mythical Beasts* (1995) and Arthur Waugh's "The Folklore of the Merfolk" (1960).

10. See Thomas King's *The Truth About Stories: A Native Narrative* (Minneapolis: University of Minnesota Press, 2008), Leanne Simpson's *Dancing on Our Turtle's Back: Stories of Nishnaabeg Re-Creation* (Winnipeg: Arbeiter Ring Publishing, 2011), and Marie Alohalani Brown, *Facing the Spears of Change: The Life and Legacy of John Papa ʻĪʻī* (Honolulu: University of Hawaiʻi Press, 2016), 15–20, 27–29. Examples of how history and belief are conveyed through wonder abound in the "Merfolk and Water Spirits Across the Globe" section of this book, and the discussion of *moʻolelo* as a genre that straddles the belief/fiction distinction in Hawaiian culture furthers this point.

11. Strikingly, Hans Christian Andersen's "The Little Mermaid," currently the most popular mermaid tale, elaborates the interspecies sighting in a romantic way that does not fit either of the other two scenarios.

12. Mary Louise Pratt, "Arts of the Contact Zone," in *Professing in the Contact Zone: Bringing Theory and Practice Together,* ed. Janice M. Wolff (Urbana, IL: National Council of Teachers of English, 2002), 4.

13. William A. Lessa, *Tales from Ulithi Atoll: A Comparative Study of Oceanic Folklore* (Berkeley: University of California Press, 1961).

14. Elizabeth Segran, "Inside the Mermaid Economy," *Fast Company,* September 9, 2015, www.fastcompany.com/3050847/inside -the-mermaid-economy-2. Segran notes: "If you're suddenly seeing fish tails everywhere, you're not imagining things."

15. Information about the parade on the Coney Island USA website reads: "The MERMAID PARADE specifically was founded in 1983 with 3 goals: it brings mythology to life for local residents who live on streets named Mermaid and Neptune; it creates self-esteem in a district that is often disregarded as 'entertainment'; and it lets artistic New Yorkers find self-expression in public," www.coneyisland.com/mermaid-parade-faq.

Suggestions for Further Reading

Almqvist, Bo. "The Mélusine Legend in the Context of Irish Folk Tradition." *Béaloideas* 67 (1999): 13–69.

Austern, Linda Phyllis and Inna Naroditskaya, eds. *Music of the Sirens*. Bloomington: Indiana University Press, 2006.

Bacchilega, Cristina and Jennifer Orme, eds. *Wonder Tales in the 21st Century: Inviting Interruption*. Detroit: Wayne State University Press, 2020.

Bain, Frederika. "The Tail of Melusine: Hybridity, Mutability, and the Accessible Other." In *Melusine's Footprint: Tracing the Legacy of a Medieval Myth*, edited by Misty Urban, Deva Kemmis, and Melissa Ridley Elmes, 17–35. Leiden and Boston: Brill, 2017.

Barnum, Phineas Taylor. *The Life of P. T. Barnum Written by Himself*. New York: Refield, 1855.

Bendix, Regina. "Seashell Bra and Happy End: Disney's Transformations of 'The Little Mermaid.'" *Fabula* 34 (1993): 280–90.

Benwell, Gwen and Arthur Waugh. *Sea Enchantress: The Tale of the Mermaid and Her Kin*. London: Hutchinson and Co., 1961.

Bernardini, Silvio. *The Serpent and the Siren: Sacred and Enigmatic Images in Tuscan Rural Churches*. Translated by Kate Singleton. Siena: San Quirico d'Oricia, 2000.

Bottrell, William. *Traditions and Hearthside Stories of West Cornwall*, Second Series. Penzance: Beare and Son, 1873.

Braham, Persephone, Nettrice R. Gaskins, Philip Hayward, Sarah Keith, Sung-Ae Lee, Lisa Milner, Manal Shalaby, and Pan Wang. *Scaled for Success: The Internationalisation of the Mermaid*. Edited by Philip Hayward. Bloomington: Indiana University Press and John Libbey Publishing, 2018.

Bronzini, Giovanni B. "Giuseppe Gigli Scrittore di Folklore." *Lares* 68, no. 2 (2002): 301–11.

Brown, Marie Alohalani. *Facing the Spears of Change: The Life and*

Legacy of John Papa 'Ī'ī. Honolulu: University of Hawai'i Press, 2016.

Calvino, Italo. *Italian Folktales*. New York: Pantheon, 1980.

Carlson, Amy. "Kissing the Mermaid: Resistance, Adaptation, Popular Cultural Memory, and Maya Kern's Webcomic *How to be a Mermaid*." *Marvels & Tales: Journal of Fairy-Tale Studies* 33, no. 1 (2019): 60–79.

Carlson, Patricia Ann, ed. *Literature and the Lore of the Sea*. Amsterdam: Rodopi, 1986.

Cherry, John, ed. *Mythical Beasts*. London: British Museum Press, 1995.

Chesnutt, Michael. "The Three Laughs: A Celtic-Norse Tale in Oral Tradition and Medieval Literature." In *Islanders and Water-Dwellers. Proceedings of the Celtic-Nordic-Baltic Folklore Symposium held at University College Dublin (16–19 June 1996)*, edited by Patricia Lysaght, Séamas Ó Catháin, and Dáithí Ó hÓgáin, 37–49. Dublin: DBA Publications Ltd., 1999.

Christiansen, Reidar Th. *The Migratory Legends. A Proposed List of Types with a Systematic Catalogue of the Norwegian Variants*. Folklore Fellows' Communications No. 175. Helsinki: Academia Scientiarum Fennica, 1958.

Cohen, Jeffrey Jerome. "Monster Culture (Seven Theses)." In *Monster Theory: Reading Culture*, 3–25. Minneapolis: University of Minnesota Press, 1996.

Croker, Thomas Crofton. *Fairy Legends and Traditions of the South of Ireland*. London: Murray, 1828.

Darwin, Gregory. "On Mermaids, Meroveus, and Mélusine: Reading the Irish Seal Woman and Mélusine as Origin Legend." *Folklore* 126, no. 2 (2015): 123–41.

Drewal, Henry John. "Performing the Other: Mami Wata Worship in Africa." *TDR: The Drama Review* 32, no. 2 (Summer 1988): 160–85.

——— with Charles Gore and Michelle Kisliuk. "Siren Serenades: Music for Mami Wata and Other Water Spirits in Africa." In *Music of the Sirens*, edited by Linda Phyllis Austern and Inna Naroditskaya, 294–316. Bloomington: Indiana University Press, 2006.

Eliade, Mircea. *Patterns in Comparative Religion*. Translated by Rosemary Sheed. New York: Sheed & Ward, 1958.

Fraser, Lucy. *The Pleasures of Metamorphosis: Japanese and English Fairy Tale Transformations of "The Little Mermaid."* Detroit: Wayne State University, 2017.

Hamilton, Virginia. *Her Stories: African American Folktales, Fairy Tales, and True Tales.* New York: Blue Sky Press, 1995.

Heiner, Heidi Anne, ed. *Mermaids and Other Water Spirit Tales from Around the World.* Nashville: SurLaLune Press, 2011.

Hurley, Nat. "The Little Transgender Mermaid: A Shape-Shifting Tale." In *Seriality and Texts for Young People*, edited by Mavis Reimer et al., 258–80. London: Palgrave Macmillan, 2014.

Jarvis, Shawn C. "Mermaid." In *Folktales and Fairy Tales: Traditions and Texts from Around the World*, edited by Anne E. Duggan and Donald Haase, with Helen J. Callow, 2nd edition, 646–47. Santa Barbara, CA: Greenwood ABC-Clio, 2016.

Jorgensen, Marilyn A. "The Legends of Sirena and Santa Marian Camalin: Guåhananian Cultural Oppositions." In *Monsters with Iron Teeth: Perspectives on Contemporary Legends*, vol. 3, edited by Gillian Bennet and Paul Smith. Sheffield, UK: Sheffield Academic Press, 1988.

Kabwasa, Angèle Kadima-Nzuji. *Song of the Mermaid and Other Folk Tales from the Congo.* Bloomington, IN: AuthorHouse, 2008.

King, Thomas. *The Truth About Stories: A Native Narrative.* Minneapolis: University of Minnesota Press, 2008.

Lao, Meri. *Sirens: Symbols of Seduction.* Rochester, VT: Park Street Press, 1998.

Lessa, William A. *Tales from Ulithi Atoll: A Comparative Study in Oceanic Folklore.* Berkeley: University of California Press, 1961.

Levi, Steven C. "P. T. Barnum and the Feejee Mermaid." *Western Folklore* 36, no. 2 (1977): 149–54.

Murai, Mayako. *From Dog Bridegroom to Wolf Girl: Contemporary Japanese Fairy-Tale Adaptations in Conversation with the West.* Detroit, MI: Wayne State University Press, 2015.

Ogunleye, Adetunbi Richard. "Cultural Identity in the Throes of Modernity: An Appraisal of Yemoja Among the Yoruba in Nigeria." *Inkaniyiso: The Journal of Humanities and Social Sciences* 7, no. 1 (2015): 61–68.

Otero, Solimar and Toyin Falola. *Yemoja: Gender, Sexuality, and Creativity in the Latina/o and Afro-Atlantic Diasporas.* New York: State University of New York Press, 2013.

Paracelsus. "A Book on Nymphs, Sylphs, Pygmies, and Salamanders, and on the Other Spirits." Translated by Henry E. Sigerist. In *Four Treatises of Theophrastus von Hohenheim, Called Paracelsus*, edited by Henry E. Sigerist, 223–53. Baltimore, MD: Johns Hopkins University Press, 1941.

Pedersen, Tara E. *Mermaids and the Production of Knowledge in Early Modern England*. Burlington, VT: Ashgate Publishing Company, 2015.

Phillpotts, Beatrice. *Mermaids*. New York: Ballantine, 1980.

Pitrè, Giuseppe. "La Leggenda di Cola Pesce." In *Studi di Leggende Popolari in Sicilia*, 1–173. Torino: Carlo Clausen, 1904.

Pliny the Elder. "The Forms of the Tritons and Nereids. The Forms of Sea Elephants." In *The Natural History*, edited by John Bostock and Henry T. Riley. London, H. G. Bohn, 1855.

Plonien, Klaus. "'Germany's River, but Not Germany's Border': The Rhine as a National Myth in Early 19th Century German Literature." *National Identities* 2, no. 1 (2000): 81–86.

Pratt, Mary Louise. "Arts of the Contact Zone." *Profession* (January 1991): 33–40. Reprinted in *Professing in the Contact Zone: Bringing Theory and Practice Together*, edited by Janice M. Wolff, 1-18. Urbana, IL: National Council of Teachers of English, 2002.

Pukui, Mary Kawena with Laura C. S. Green, collected and translated. *Folktales of Hawai'i: He mau Ka'ao Hawai'i*. Honolulu: Bishop Museum Press, 2008.

Quintana, Bernardo Mansilla. "Pincoy." Chiloé Mitológico. http://chiloemitologico.cl/los-mitos-de-chiloe/mitos-acuaticos/la-pincoya.

Sajadpoor, Farzaneh and Ebrahim Jamali. "Fairies in the Folklore of Booshehr." *Anthropology of the Contemporary Middle East and Central Eurasia* 3, no. 1 (2015): 36–42.

Segran, Elizabeth. "Inside the Mermaid Economy." *Fast Company*. September 9, 2015. www.fastcompany.com/3050847/inside-the-mermaid-economy-2.

Simpson, Leanne. *Dancing on Our Turtle's Back: Stories of Nishnaabeg Re-Creation, Resurgence, and a New Emergence*. Winnipeg: Arbeiter Ring Publishing, 2011.

Skye, Alexander, ed. *Mermaids: The Myths, Legends, and Lore*. Avon, MA: Adams Media, 2012.

Tvedt, Terje and Terje Oestigaard. "A History of the Ideas of Water: Deconstructing Nature and Constructing Society." In *Ideas of Water from Ancient Societies to the Modern World*, edited by Terje Tvedt and Terje Oestigaard, Series II, vol. 1. London and New York; I.B. Tauris, 1–39.

Urban, Misty, Deva Kemmis, and Melissa Ridley Elmes, eds. *Melusine's Footprint: Tracing the Legacy of a Medieval Myth*. Leiden and Boston: Brill, 2017.

Valk, Ülo. "The Guises of Estonian Water-Spirits in Relation to the Plot and Function of Legend." In *Islanders and Water-Dwellers. Proceedings of the Celtic-Nordic-Baltic Folklore Symposium Held at University College Dublin (16–19 June 1996)*, edited by Patricia Lysaght, Séamas Ó Catháin, and Dáithi Ó hÓgáin, 337–48. Dublin: DBA Publications Ltd., 1999.

Warner, Marina. *Fantastic Metamorphoses, Other Worlds*. Oxford: Oxford University Press, 2002.

———. *From the Beast to the Blonde: On Fairy Tales and Their Tellers*. New York: Farrar, Straus and Giroux, 1994.

Waugh, Arthur. "The Folklore of the Merfolk." *Folklore* 71.2 (1960): 73–84.

Yant, Christie. "Author Spotlight Genevieve Valentine," *Lightspeed* 33. February 2013. Accessed August 14, 2018. www.lightspeed magazine.com/nonfiction/author-spotlight-genevieve-valentine-4.

Yolen, Jane and Shulamith Oppenheim. *The Fish Prince and Other Stories: Mermen Folk Tales*. New York: Interlink Books, 2001.

Zipes, Jack, ed. and trans. *Catarina the Wise and Other Wondrous Sicilian Folk & Fairy Tales*. Illustrated by Adeetje Bouma. Chicago: University of Chicago Press, 2017.

Acknowledgments

Any anthology, and especially those collecting folkloric texts across cultures, will benefit from collaboration. Aiming to foreground place-based scholarship, we were especially fortunate to enlist several scholars who agreed to share their knowledge by authoring the introductions to tales from their respective regions and area studies. It is our pleasure to thank Charity Bagatsing and Regie Barcelona Villanueva, Margaret Lyngdoh, Ulrich Marzolph and Moḥammad ʻJaʻfari Qanavāti, Mayako Murai, Marilena Papachristophorou, and Ülo Valk, who contributed their scholarly expertise, local knowledge, and/or translation skills to enable the publication of texts, whether oral or in print, from the Philippines, Northeast India, Iran, Japan, Greece, and Estonia that were previously unavailable in English. Combining these scholars' and our own competence in multiple languages has been crucial to further diversify readers' exposure to mermaid and water-spirit tales. We are also grateful to Erika Charola, Laurel Fantauzzo and Katherine Diaz, Cynthia Franklin, Terry Adrian Gunnell, kuʻualoha hoʻomanawanui, Maria Natividad Karaan, Jesse Knutson, Bianca Lazzaro, Jing Li, Laura Lyons, Qiu Xiaoqing, John Rieder, Noenoe K. Silva, Gretchen Schmid, and Jack Zipes, who in different ways helped us navigate as we explored the fascinating storyworlds of mermaids, merfolk, and other water spirits. And finally, as coeditors we acknowledge each other's expertise, willingness to cooperate, and good humor throughout the process.

The Penguin Book of
Mermaids

WATER DEITIES AND SIRENS FROM OLDEN TIMES

Oannes[1]

Male and female water beings who are much more powerful
than mermaids feature prominently in myths. They may be
divine—as in the case of Poseidon and others—or at the very
least have extraordinary powers.

The description of Oannes that follows comes from the writ-
ings of Berossus (also spelled Berosus), a third-century priest and
historian of Babylonia, as processed through nineteenth-century
English-language accounts. Oannes is fish shaped, but he also has
features that allow him to exist on land and interact with humans:
a man's head and feet and the ability to speak human language.
Whether he was a fish god or merely a messenger of the ancient
water god Ea, Oannes has been connected with the Mesopota-
mian god Dagon and the Syrian goddess Atargatis, who in turn,
according to some ancient Greek writers, was also associated
with Aphrodite or Venus, the Greco-Roman goddess born of the
sea. Because at nightfall Oannes plunged back into the waters of
what is now the Persian Gulf, some see him as a solar deity.

It is significant that Oannes educates humans: this resonates
with the mythological understanding that, as also seen in the
Sirens of the Odyssey, *hybrid creatures associated with the sea*
are holders of knowledge.

At Babylon there was (in these times) a great resort of people
of various nations, who inhabited Chaldea, and lived without
rule and order, like the beasts of the field.

In the first year there made its appearance, from a part of
the Erythræan sea[2] which bordered upon Babylonia, an animal endowed with reason, who was called Oannes. (According to the account of Apollodorus) the whole body of the

animal was like that of a fish; and had under a fish's head another head, and also feet below, similar to those of a man, subjoined to the fish's tail. His voice, too, and language was articulate and human; and a representation of him is preserved even to this day.

This Being, in the day-time, used to converse with men; but took no food at that season; and he gave them an insight into letters, and sciences, and every kind of art. He taught them to construct houses, to found temples, to compile laws, and explained to them the principles of geometrical knowledge. He made them distinguish the seeds of the earth, and showed them how to collect fruits. In short, he instructed them in everything which could tend to soften manners and humanise mankind. From that time, so universal were his instructions, nothing material has been added by way of improvement. When the sun set it was the custom of this Being to plunge again into the sea, and abide all night in the deep; for he was amphibious.

Kāliya, the Snake[1]

Drawn from the sacred Sanskrit text Bhagavata Purana, the story of Krishna defeating the Naga (great snake) Kāliya is famous in the Hindu tradition not only as a depiction of young Krishna's power, but because he does not kill the Naga, and allows the snake and his family instead to move away from the river and out into the ocean. Krishna thus helps the people living near the river Yamuna, which had been polluted with the snake's venom, while acknowledging the Naga's place in creation.

The description of the serpent king and his water-snake entourage aligns with those of other mythological sea "monsters" that are portrayed as dangerous. Homer tells us of Scylla's six long necks and multiple rows of powerful teeth in each mouth; along with Charybdis, Scylla challenges Odysseus just after his encounter with the Sirens, in the area that we now identify as close to the Messina Strait in Sicily. But like other water deities in myth, the Naga is also an important symbol of transformation, an object of worship, and a significant living tradition.

Serpent worship is among the world's oldest and most widespread religious practices. Whether major or minor divinities, water serpents' interactions with humans run the gamut from benevolent to malevolent. Like other water beings, water snakes embody the life-giving and death-dealing aspects of water. As cosmic forces, they may symbolize creation and order or destruction and chaos—and at times, these opposing influences merge, when destruction becomes the catalyst for creation.

Moreover, in many cultures past and present, snakes—especially those associated with water—are phallic symbols. As benign entities, serpents may be tutelary spirits associated

with healing, knowledge and arts, or fertility; or progenitors of
certain lineages or entire peoples. As destructive beings, they
may be predators, sexual or otherwise, or the origin of diseases
and afflictions.

Once Kṛṣṇa went into Vṛndāvana unaccompanied by Rāma.
Radiant with a garland of forest flowers, he roved about in the
company of cowherds. Then he came upon the river Yamunā,
whose waves were tossing about as if she were laughing,
throwing patches of foam on the banks. But in the water he
saw a dreadful sight—it was the hideous pool of the snake
Kāliya, whose water was mixed with a fiery poison! The trees
on the bank nearby, splashed by the burning poison, had been
scorched while the birds were singed by sprays of that poi-
soned water tossed aloft in the wind.

Witnessing this sight, horrible as the maw of death, Madhusūdana thought to himself, "This must be the dwelling place
of the evil-souled Kāliya, whose weapon is poison, that wicked
serpent who abandoned the ocean when I defeated him there
once before. Now the entire Yamunā is polluted by him, all the
way to the sea, so that neither cows nor men suffering from
thirst are able to use it. I must tame this king of snakes so that
the inhabitants of Vraja can move around happily, without
fear. I have descended into the world for this purpose, to pacify those hard-souled ones whose domain is evil. Let me now
climb this broad-branched *kadamba* tree nearby and fall into
the pool of this snake who feeds on the wind!" So thinking, and
tightly tucking up his garment, Kṛṣṇa dived at once into the
pool of the serpent king.

So roiled up by the force of Kṛṣṇa's fall was the vast pool
that it flooded even huge trees growing far away. They burst at
once into flame, smitten by the wind that carried water burning with that snake's evil fiery poison; and that holocaust filled
all of space.

Then, in the serpent's pool, Kṛṣṇa slapped his arm defiantly.
Hearing the sound, the serpent king rapidly approached, his

eyes coppery-red with rage. He was surrounded by other venomous wind-feeding snakes with mouths full of fiery poison, accompanied by their snake wives by the hundreds adorned with fetching necklaces, who were beautiful with jangling bracelets that trembled when their bodies moved.

Then the snakes encircled Kṛṣṇa, making fetters of their coils, and bit him with their poison-filled mouths. When the cowherds saw that he had fallen into the pool and was being crushed by the serpents' coils, they fled to Vraja. Wholly overcome with grief, they cried aloud, "Kṛṣṇa, distracted, has gone and fallen into Kāliya's pool where he is being eaten alive by the snake king! Come and see him!"

The cowherds and their wives, thunderstruck at these words, hurried immediately to the pool, with Yaśodā ahead of them. "Oh oh, where is he?" cried the agitated crowd of cowherd women as they hastened, confused and stumbling, along with Yaśodā. The cowherds Nanda and Rāma, of wondrous valor, also sped to the Yamunā determined to see Kṛṣṇa. There they saw him at the mercy of the serpent king, rendered powerless, wrapped in the coils of the snake. Staring at the face of his son, the cowherd Nanda was immobilized, excellent seer, and so was the lady Yaśodā. The other cowherds, too, disheartened with grief, looked on weeping while, stammering with fear, they beseeched Keśava with love. . . .

When Kṛṣṇa was called to mind by the cowherds, the petals of his lips blossomed into a smile, and he split open that snake, freeing his own body from the coils. Using his two hands to bend over the middle head of that serpent with curving hoods, the wide-striding Kṛṣṇa mounted that head and began to dance on it. The serpent's hood expanded with his life's breath as it was pounded by Kṛṣṇa's feet. Wherever the snake's head swelled up, Kṛṣṇa trod it down again. Squeezed in this manner by Kṛṣṇa, the snake fainted away with a quiver, vomiting blood because of the blows of Kṛṣṇa's staff.

When his wives saw the serpent king with his neck and head arched over the blood streaming from his mouth, they went to Madhusūdana and said piteously, "Overlord of the gods, you are known to be omniscient, without equal, the ineffable light supernal of which the supreme lord is but a portion. You are he whom the gods themselves are not able to praise. How then can I, a mere woman, describe you? . . . Since silly women and miserable creatures are to be pitied by the virtuous, please forgive this wretched creature, you who are eminent among the forgiving! You are the support of the whole world; this is but a feeble snake. Crushed by your foot, he will soon die! How can this weak, lowly snake compare with you, the refuge of all beings? Both hate and love are within the province of the superior, O imperishable one. Therefore be gracious to this snake who is sinking fast, O master of the world. Our husband is dying! O lord of creation, grant us his life as alms!" . . .

[Then Kāliya himself begged for mercy:] "I am not capable of honoring nor of praising you, overlord of the gods, but please take pity on me, O god whose sole thought is compassion! The race of snakes into which I was born is a cruel one; this is its proper nature. But I am not at fault in this matter, Acyuta, for it is you who pour forth and absorb the whole world; classes, forms and natures have all been assigned by you, the creator. . . . Now I am powerless, having lost my poison. You have subdued me, Acyuta; now spare my life! Tell me what to do!"

"Leave the waters of the Yamunā, snake, and return to the ocean, along with your children and your retinue. And in the sea, O serpent, when Garuḍa, enemy of snakes, sees my footprints on your head, he will not harm you." So speaking, lord Hari released the serpent king, who bowed to Kṛṣṇa and returned to the ocean of milk.

In the sight of all creatures, Kāliya abandoned his pool, along with his dependents, his children and all his wives. When the snake had gone, the cowherds embraced Kṛṣṇa like one returned from the dead and lovingly drenched his head with tears. Other happy cowherds, with minds amazed, sang praises to Kṛṣṇa, who is unwearied by action, when they saw the river water safe. Hymned by the cowherd women and praised by the cowherd men for the fine deed he had done, Kṛṣṇa returned to Vraja.

Odysseus and the Sirens[1]

Nowadays Sirens and mermaids are both symbols of dangerous femininity, but they emerged from different waters and
cultures. Sirens, as their visual representations on ancient
Greek vases and funerary monuments show us, had human
heads, wings, and chicken feet or the talons of birds of prey.
But as they became conflated with the mermaids of northern
European folklore, sirens began to be represented as part flying
fish and part human female.[2] It is the power of their song and
music—rather than their appearance—that characterizes them
across time. This means that the Sirens' hybrid bodies morphed
into human-piscine shapes based on the power that, in stories,
Sirens share with mermaids.[3] Like mermaids, Sirens seduce:
lead astray, divert, lead elsewhere, persuade to desert one's al-
legiance, corrupt. But while the sexual connotation of seduction is now prevalent, there was no such connotation in the
Latin seducere or in English before the 1550s. Thus, the lure
and knowledge the Sirens held in antiquity had to do with life
and death, or knowing the future beyond human ability—not
so much with sexuality.

This episode of Homer's Odyssey captures the power of Sirens in classic mythology. A twenty-four-book epic poem probably composed in the eighth century BC, The Odyssey follows
Odysseus and his crew as they make their way home to Ithaca
from the Trojan War, encountering storms, monstrous beings,
and tests of all sorts along the way. The poem has been canon-
ized for its artful narrative and poetic form as well as its reflec-
tions on heroism, hospitality, and the aspirations and limits of
human nature.

Odysseus and his men encounter the Sirens in book 12. He
is ready for them thanks to the goddess Circe, who has warned

him and suggested how he and his men can pass them un-
scathed. As perpetuated in future traditions, the Sirens' song
is their deathly lure. While the crewmen—with wax stuffed in
their ears—do the physical work of rowing to get the ship past
the Sirens' shore, Odysseus is tightly roped to the ship's mast.
Thus immobilized, he alone is privileged to hear, in Alexan-
der Pope's translation, the "celestial music" of the "sweet de-
luders."

    Odysseus is subject to erotic temptation more than once in
the course of his homecoming, but the Sirens' lure is of a differ-
ent kind. Homer's Sirens sing a song that promises knowledge—
a wisdom that bridges worlds—instead of pleasure. While their
appearance differs from that of the mermaids with whom they
are later conflated, the Sirens' music is still a portal that draws
humans into a different dimension. This tempting song would
perhaps have had even further intensity in oral performances
of the Homeric poem.

The friendly goddess stretch'd the swelling sails;
We drop our oars; at ease the pilot guides;
The vessel light along the level glides.
When, rising sad and slow, with pensive look,
Thus to the melancholy train I spoke:

"'O friends, oh ever partners of my woes,
Attend while I what Heaven foredooms disclose.
Hear all! Fate hangs o'er all; on you it lies
To live or perish! to be safe, be wise!

"'In flowery meads the sportive Sirens play,
Touch the soft lyre, and tune the vocal lay;
Me, me alone, with fetters firmly bound,
The gods allow to hear the dangerous sound.
Hear and obey; if freedom I demand,
Be every fetter strain'd, be added band to band.'

"While yet I speak the winged galley flies,
And lo! the Siren shores like mists arise.
Sunk were at once the winds; the air above,
And waves below, at once forgot to move;
Some demon calm'd the air and smooth'd the deep,
Hush'd the loud winds, and charm'd the waves to sleep.
Now every sail we furl, each oar we ply;
Lash'd by the stroke, the frothy waters fly.
The ductile wax with busy hands I mould,
And cleft in fragments, and the fragments roll'd;
The aerial region now grew warm with day,
The wax dissolved beneath the burning ray;
Then every ear I barr'd against the strain,
And from access of frenzy lock'd the brain.
Now round the masts my mates the fetters roll'd,
And bound me limb by limb with fold on fold.
Then bending to the stroke, the active train
Plunge all at once their oars, and cleave the main.

"While to the shore the rapid vessel flies,
Our swift approach the Siren choir descries;
Celestial music warbles from their tongue,
And thus the sweet deluders tune the song:

"'Oh stay, O pride of Greece! Ulysses, stay!
Oh cease thy course, and listen to our lay!
Blest is the man ordain'd our voice to hear,
The song instructs the soul, and charms the ear.
Approach! thy soul shall into raptures rise!
Approach! and learn new wisdom from the wise!
We know whate'er the kings of mighty name
Achieved at Ilion in the field of fame;
Whate'er beneath the sun's bright journey lies.
Oh stay, and learn new wisdom from the wise!'

"Thus the sweet charmers warbled o'er the main;
My soul takes wing to meet the heavenly strain;

I give the sign, and struggle to be free;
Swift row my mates, and shoot along the sea;
New chains they add, and rapid urge the way,
Till, dying off, the distant sounds decay;
Then scudding swiftly from the dangerous ground,
The deafen'd ear unlock'd, the chains unbound."

The Tuna (Eel) of
Lake Vaihiria[1,2]

*The male-centric view of the female water spirit as a dangerous
"other" is reversed in this mythological tale. A high-ranking
young woman is promised to a king who, unbeknownst to her,
is an eel. ("Tuna"—or its linguistic cognates, like "duna,"
"funa," and "kuna"—denotes freshwater eel in several Pacific
Island languages, including Samoan, Tongan, Māori, Niuean,
Tahitian, Tuamotuan, Cook Islander, Rapa, Fijian, Rotuman,
and Hawaiian.) She is repulsed by him, but he aggressively
pursues her. She escapes with the help of Māui, a pan-
Polynesian cultural hero who kills the eel and gives her its
head, telling her it will provide her with valuable resources. In
the end, it grows into a coconut tree.*

A supernatural eel who may sometimes appear as a man figures prominently in a number of Polynesian tales about the origin of the coconut, an important plant for Pacific Islanders,
who use every part of it: the tree's trunk is carved into drums;
its long, wide fronds are used to cover roofs and walls, and to
make mats, bowls, hats, and brooms; the hard shell of its large,
round seeds is used to make bowls, cups, spoons, combs, and
fishhooks; the fibrous husk is used to make sennit; and the
inner part of the seed provides coconut meat and water.

In this Tahitian variant of the coconut's origin story, the female protagonist is named Hina.[3] Elsewhere, she is known as
Sina (Sāmoa), Heina (Tonga), Hine (Aotearoa), and Ina (Cook
Islands). Hina-Sina-Heina-Hine-Ina is usually of high rank,
and sometimes semidivine. Depending on the version, she may
either fall in love with the eel or find him repulsive. With their
long, sinuous bodies, eels are phallic symbols. Indeed, in a Samoan variant, Sina is scorned because the eel takes her virgin-
ity as she swims in the pool where it makes his home.

There was once a beautiful young princess of Papeuriri, Tahiti, of the highest lineage, whose celestial patrons, the sun and moon, had named her Hina (Gray). When this young girl had reached the stature of womanhood and was becoming much admired for her beauty—flashes of light emanating from her person restricted her to a very select circle—the sun and moon espoused her to the king of Lake Vaihiria, before she had any personal acquaintance with him or her even seen him. The king's name was Fa'arava'ai-anu (Cause-to-fish-in-the-cold), and as her parents agreed to the marriage Hina felt no doubt of the suitableness of the match and entered happily into all the preparations for her wedding. Hina chose for her maids of honor, two childhood companions, named Varua (Spirit) and Te-roro (Brain), and when at last the marriage day arrived they were attractively dressed in white tapa gracefully wound around their persons, with garlands of maire fern interwoven with red *fara* strobile tips and snow-white *tiare*, and in their flowing raven hair they entwined similar wreaths. The bride also wore, in token of her rank, a necklet and girdle of rich red and yellow *'ura* (parrakeet feathers).

At length the bridal party set out to meet the bridegroom, accompanied with the measured beat of the drum and the soft notes of the bamboo flute and other primitive musical instruments, and they had gone half way up the valley to Lake Vaihiria, when, lo, the bridegroom was seen descending the declivity to meet them. And there in the distance Hina saw to her great horror, an immense eel, as great and long as the trunk of a tall coconut tree; this was Fa'arava'ai-anu, king of Lake Vaihiria, the intended bridegroom for the beautiful Hina!

Terror-stricken, she turned to her parents and exclaimed: "It is indeed this, O my parents? Do you wish me to be wedded to a monster and not a person? O how cruel of you! And now I shall seek my own salvation!" And she fled out of the valley to her home.

On arriving there, the people were surprised to see her and enquired what had happened. On knowing her grief and disappointment, sorrow and sympathy filled their hearts towards her.

"And now," she said, "farewell. I must seek my salvation quickly away from here. If all be well, I shall return again; but meanwhile, my dear friends, I entrust all my treasures to your care. If I live, I shall return to my own district, to be with you, my dearly loved ones."

Willing hands quickly prepared a swift canoe, and just as the moon was rising in its full glory, Hina, with trusted retainers, set off for Vairao, Taiarapu, to seek the aid and protection of the great Mâ-û-i who had noosed and controlled the sun, and there they arrived just before daybreak.

On entering his cave, Hina found Mâ-û-i was out, but she was kindly received by his wife. Shortly afterwards he came in and enquired of his wife what caused the brilliant flashes of light in their dark abode, and she replied:

"'This is Hina of the 'ura girdle, Hina of lightning flashes in the east, Hina, child of the sun and moon; her wind is the northeast trade wind."

Then Mâ-û-i welcomed Hina, and kindly addressed her saying, "O Hina, beloved daughter of Mataiea, what is your errand, my Princess?"

"O Mâ-û-i," she exclaimed, "save me from the hideous monster, the king of Vaihiria, who will be coming here to claim me as his wife! Have pity on me, behold now outside, and what is the wind? It is possessed, darkness is overshadowing the land, and the sea is foaming so that the ocean beyond cannot be seen?" And then, while Hina told her sad story, they saw the eel king breaking an entrance passage in the reef.

Mâ-û-i was horrified, and he hastened to place his two stone gods upon the cliffs and to sharpen his axe and make ready his fishhook for action. Then, as the eel was approaching the shore, Mâ-û-i placed some tempting bait upon the fishhook and secured it with Hina's hair.

As soon as the eel saw him, he roared out in a thundering voice, "Mâ-û-i, deliver me my bride!"

And Mâ-û-i cast his fishhook into the sea, saying, "This is I, Mâ-û-i the brave! No king can escape me here in my heritage; he will become food for my images."

Then the eel, perceiving the food, opened wide his mouth and swallowed the fishhook and bait, and soon Mâ-û-i drew him up on to the shore. He chopped off his great head, which he wrapped in tapa, and presented it to Hina, saying:

"Hold this, and put it not down an instant until you arrive home; then take and plant it in the center of your marae ground. This eel's head contains for you great treasures; from it you will have material to build and complete your house, besides food to eat and water to drink. But remember my warning, that you lose not your valuable property by putting it down before you reach home. Then you will ever be remembered as Hina-vahine-e-anapa-te-uira-i-te-Hiti'a-o-te-ra (Hina-of-lightning-flashes-in-the-east)."

So Hina took the great bundle, which became light by magic, and sending on her canoe along the coast, she and an attendant maid preferred walking a few miles. So they went on their way rejoicing, and arrived at a place called Pani (To-close), where they saw a nice deep stream of water, at which they stopped to drink. In doing this, Hina thoughtlessly put down her bundle. Soon the two girls made up their minds to take a bath. So in they plunged and dove first upwards in the stream and then downwards, when Hina all at once remembered her eel's head and left the water quickly to go and take it up again. But lo, as she approached it, she found the tapa removed, and there the head stood erect, rooted to the ground and sprouting! It had become a young coconut tree. Then Hina saw and understood why Mâ-û-i had told her only to put it down at her own marae, and she wept bitterly.

Just then a woman of the people, but of good standing in the land, came along and enquired of the girl her trouble, and when Hina told her, the woman whose name was Rû-roa (Great-haste), said comfortingly:

"Be not troubled for this land is ours; come and sojourn with me so as to watch the growth of your new tree, which shall always be yours."

Hina, comforted, accepted the woman's kind invitation, and after sending her companion on to the canoe with word for her people to return home, she committed herself to the care of her new friend, who soon made her very comfortable in her home not far off.

After partaking of a hearty breakfast, Hina threw herself down upon a mat, and fell asleep, which rest she needed, and towards evening as she awoke, she heard voices outside not far from the house. Looking out she perceived two handsome young men, sons of Rû-roa, who had been out fishing; and she heard them enquire of their mother as to the cause of flashes of lightning that they saw coming out of their dwelling, to which she replied:

"It is Hina, princess of Papeuriri, and child of the sun and moon. She has a young coconut tree growing yonder, which she is staying here to watch until it matures."

Awe-struck, the young men would not enter the house but remained outside. The younger brother went to see the new tree, and found it loaded with coconuts. So he picked one and husked it and took it to his mother and brother, and while they were examining and admiring it, Hina, wishing to place them all at ease in her presence, called to them to come in. She said to the elder brother:

"Your name must be Mahana-e-anapa-i-te-po'ipo'i" (Sun-that-flashes-in-the-morning). And to the younger brother she said: "You must be called Ava'e-e-hiti-i-te-ahiahi" (Moon-that-rises-in-the-evening).

By giving them these names, which plebeians never dared to adopt in times of yore, she created them nobles, an act which also gave rank to their mother. Thus united in bonds of friendship, they all lived happily together, the family being charmed with the beautiful and affable Hina, and they enjoyed eating the coconuts, which had become the admiration of all Tai'arapu.

Hina and Mahana-e-anapa-i-te-po'ipo'i became much attached to each other, and they were married, and in due time she had a daughter whom they named Te-ipo-o-te-marama (Pet-of-the-moon). But to her great sorrow Hina's husband soon died. She afterwards married the younger brother, who reminded her much of her deceased husband, and by him she had another daughter, whom they named Te-ipo-o-te-here (Pet-who-loved).

One day, as each child held a matured coconut in her hand, they were caught up by the gods on to a rainbow, by which they were conducted to Taka-horo, in the atoll of Ana (Chain Island), in the Tuamotus. The younger sister, finding that her coconut was without water, changed it for that of her elder sister, unbeknown to her, which displeased the gods; and causing her to drop the coconut, which was sprouting, they carried her away in the clouds, and she was never seen again. So Te-ipo-o-te-marama became the sole owner of this, the first coconut tree that grew at Ana, from which were produced all the coconut trees that have spread throughout the group and have developed into many varieties. The tree stood, towering high above all other trees of the group, until the cyclone of February 8, 1906, broke it off in three pieces, which were washed away by the sea.

Hina lived long and happily with her husband, sometimes in Tai'arapu, sometimes in Pape'uriri, and she had numerous issue.

MERMAIDS AND OTHER MERBEINGS IN EUROPE

MERFOLK IN THE WATERS
OF GREENLAND AND
ICELAND

*There have been accounts of human-merfolk encounters on
these northern islands ever since they were settled. Set in the
waters of Greenland, the account we include here, "The Marvels of the Waters About Greenland," comes from the translation of a Norwegian manuscript dating back to approximately
1250. In it, mermen and mermaids are referred to as "monsters" and "prodigies"—that is, amazing beings that are not
ordinarily found in nature—and as omens of possibly fatal sea
storms. More generally, in another Icelandic account from the
twelfth century the* marmennill (merman) *is consulted for his
power to foretell the future.*[1]

*In addition to these accounts, which were presented as non-
fiction, we have merfolk legends and folktales in Iceland dating
back to the fourteenth century. In those narratives, the merman (also called a* marbendill) *is a seer who makes use of his
superior knowledge to poke fun at human ignorance and regain his freedom. In the version included here, "The Merman,"
the unenlightened man gets a happy ending, but in other versions, things don't turn out so well for him.*[2]

The Marvels of the Waters
About Greenland[1]

It is reported that the waters about Greenland are infested with monsters, though I do not believe that they have been seen very frequently. Still, people have stories to tell about them, so men must have seen or caught sight of them. It is reported that the monster called merman is found in the seas of Greenland. This monster is tall and of great size and rises straight out of the water. It appears to have shoulders, neck and head, eyes and mouth, and nose and chin like those of a human being; but above the eyes and the eyebrows it looks more like a man with a peaked helmet on his head. It has shoulders like a man's but no hands. Its body apparently grows narrower from the shoulders down, so that the lower down it has been observed, the more slender it has seemed to be. But no one has ever seen how the lower end is shaped, whether it terminates in a fin like a fish or is pointed like a pole. The form of this prodigy has, therefore, looked much like an icicle. No one has ever observed it closely enough to determine whether its body has scales like a fish or skin like a man. Whenever the monster has shown itself, men have always been sure that a storm would follow. They have also noted how it has turned when about to plunge into the waves and in what direction it has fallen; if it has turned toward the ship and has plunged in that direction, the sailors have felt sure that lives would be lost on that ship; but whenever it has turned away from the vessel and has plunged in that direction, they have felt confident that their lives would be spared, even though they should encounter rough waters and severe storms.

Another prodigy called mermaid[2] has also been seen there. This appears to have the form of a woman from the waist upward, for it has large nipples on its breast like a woman, long hands and heavy hair, and its neck and head are formed in every respect like those of a human being. The monster is said to have large hands and its fingers are not parted but bound together by a web like that which joins the toes of water fowls. Below the waist line it has the shape of a fish with scales and tail and fins. It is said to have this in common with the one mentioned before, that it rarely appears except before violent storms. Its behavior is often somewhat like this: it will plunge into the waves and will always reappear with fish in its hands; if it then turns toward the ship, playing with the fishes or throwing them at the ship, the men have fears that they will suffer great loss of life. The monster is described as having a large and terrifying face, a sloping forehead and wide brows, a large mouth and wrinkled cheeks. But if it eats the fishes or throws them into the sea away from the ship, the crews have good hopes that their lives will be spared, even though they should meet severe storms.

The Merman[1]

Long ago a farmer lived at Vogar, who was a mighty fisherman, and, of all the farms round about, not one was so well
situated with regard to the fisheries as his.

One day, according to custom, he had gone out fishing, and
having cast down his line from the boat, and waited awhile,
found it very hard to pull up again, as if there were something
very heavy at the end of it. Imagine his astonishment when he
found that what he had caught was a great fish, with a man's
head and body! When he saw that this creature was alive, he
addressed it and said, "Who and whence are you?"

"A merman from the bottom of the sea," was the reply.

The farmer then asked him what he had been doing when
the hook caught his flesh.

The other replied, "I was turning the cowl of my mother's
chimney-pot, to suit it to the wind. So let me go again, will you?"

"Not for the present," said the fisherman. "You shall serve
me awhile first."

So without more words he dragged him into the boat and
rowed to shore with him.

When they got to the boat-house, the fisherman's dog came
to him and greeted him joyfully, barking and fawning on him,
and wagging his tail. But his master's temper being none of the
best, he struck the poor animal; whereupon the merman
laughed for the first time.

Having fastened the boat, he went towards his house, dragging his prize with him, over the fields, and stumbling over a
hillock, which lay in his way, cursed it heartily; whereupon the
merman laughed for the second time.

When the fisherman arrived at the farm, his wife came out
to receive him, and embraced him affectionately, and he re-

ceived her salutations with pleasure; whereupon the merman laughed for the third time.

Then said the farmer to the merman, "You have laughed three times, and I am curious to know *why* you have laughed. Tell me, therefore."

"Never will I tell you," replied the merman, "unless you promise to take me to the same place in the sea wherefrom you caught me, and there to let me go free again." So the farmer made him the promise.

"Well," said the merman, "I laughed the first time because you struck your dog, whose joy at meeting you was real and sincere. The second time, because you cursed the mound over which you stumbled, which is full of golden ducats. And the third time, because you received with pleasure your wife's empty and flattering embrace, who is faithless to you, and a hypocrite. And now be an honest man and take me out to the sea whence you have brought me."

The farmer replied: "Two things that you have told me I have no means of proving, namely, the faithfulness of my dog and the faithlessness of my wife. But the third I will try the truth of, and if the hillock contain gold, then I will believe the rest."

Accordingly he went to the hillock, and having dug it up, found therein a great treasure of golden ducats, as the merman had told him. After this the farmer took the merman down to the boat, and to that place in the sea whence he had caught him. Before he put him in, the latter said to him:

"Farmer, you have been an honest man, and I will reward you for restoring me to my mother, if only you have skill enough to take possession of property that I shall throw in your way. Be happy and prosper."

Then the farmer put the merman into the sea, and he sank out of sight.

It happened that not long after, seven sea-grey cows were seen on the beach, close to the farmer's land. These cows appeared to be very unruly, and ran away directly the farmer approached them. So he took a stick and ran after them, possessed with the fancy that if he could burst the bladder

which he saw on the nose of each of them, they would belong
to him. He contrived to hit out the bladder on the nose of one
cow, which then became so tame that he could easily catch it,
while the others leaped into the sea and disappeared. The
farmer was convinced that this was the gift of the merman.
And a very useful gift it was, for better cow was never seen nor
milked in all the land, and she was the mother of the race of
grey cows so much esteemed now.

And the farmer prospered exceedingly, but never caught any
more mermen. As for his wife, nothing further is told about
her, so we can repeat nothing.

TWO MERMAIDS AND
A SELKIE FROM THE
SCOTTISH HIGHLANDS

Story has it that the cold waters surrounding the Scottish Highlands and the Hebrides and Orkney Islands are populated with merfolk.[1] Two of the three tales that follow were collected from Scottish fishermen and peasants in the first half of the twentieth century; the third one is extracted from a volume of Gaelic lore, Carmina Gadelica.

In "The Mermaid of Kessock," which is clearly related to tales about Irish mermaid or selkie wives, the trick to keep the mermaid from returning to the water is to pull a few scales from her tail. Like Mélusine and the Irish sea maidens also represented in this volume, once married, the mermaid of Kessock is a good mother, but she is clearly not happy in her human life and form. Her beauty is described in detail, and she has golden hair, which is common in literary accounts but is often green or dark in oral tradition.

Selkie or selchie refers to sealfolk, and "The Grey Selchie of Sule Skerrie" recounts the tale of a woman who marries a seal man; like the mermaid of Kessock, he disappears to return to the sea, but then returns for his son. In another version, the seal foretells his own and his son's death.

"The Mermaid's Grave" is presented not as a legend, but as a report of islanders in the Hebrides encountering a mermaid and carelessly causing her death. Notably, she is a small being, the size of a child, but with a woman's breasts; she has a fish-

tail, but no scales. A time frame for the mermaid's appearance—the 1830s—and the existence of her grave, seen by many, give credence to the account. But in the words of Ronald Macdonald Robertson, who published the other two tales, readers are "free to draw [their] own inferences from the tales; with regard to responsibility for their accuracy, the writer can only say—'Ma's breug bh' uam e, is breug dhomh e' ('If it be a lie as told by me, it was a lie as told to me')."

The Mermaid of Kessock[1]

A Legend from the Black Isle

A man named Paterson was once walking along the shore near Kessock Ferry, when he saw, "'na suidhe air an aigein dhorcha" (sitting on the dark misty deep), a mermaid, whom he tried to detain by wading into the water and pulling some of the scales from her tail, in obedience to the old belief that if even part of her fish-tail was removed, a mermaid was compelled to assume human form. Before his eyes the transformation took place, and the sea-maiden stood up before him, tall and fair. She had long, silky hair that was as yellow as gold and soft as the curling foam of the sea; her eyes were wide and clear and blue as the sky; her lips were as red as winter berries and as tempting as fruits of summer—and in place of the fish-tail she had slim white feet.

Paterson fell desperately in love with the sea-maiden and took her home as his bride. The scales he carefully hid in an outhouse.

He lived in a cottage by the shore; and "nuallan nan tonn" (the raging noise of the waves), which sounded night and day at the foot of the cottage garden, filled his mermaid bride with longing to return to her home in the land-under-the-waves where she had been "nursed by the ocean and rocked by the storms." She used to plead with her husband to let her go, promising that if he did so their family would always be blessed with a plentiful supply of fish, and that no members of it would ever be drowned at Kessock Ferry; but he remained adamant.

One day one of the children, named Kenneth, discovered

the scales in the outhouse and took them to his mother, who straightway made for the shore and became a mermaid again.

Not since that day has the mermaid of Kessock been seen; but there are still local people who firmly believe in her existence, and declare that she still watches over her descendants and keeps them from peril at sea.

The Grey Selchie of
Sule Skerrie[1]

The rocky islet of "Sule Skerry" (skerry of the solan goose) some twenty-five miles west of Hoy Head in Orkney, is to this day the resort of thousands of seals—or "selchies" as they are called in Orkney. There is a very old Orcadian ballad with the above title which tells of a maiden who dwelt in Norway who fell in love with and married a seal-man called "Hein Mailer." Shortly after their marriage he disappeared, and the maiden was left to weep as she rocked her infant son on her knee.

One day as she sat by the shore, a "good grey selchie" came and sat down by her feet. The seal addressed her in human speech and said:—

> "I am a man upon the land,
> I am a selchie in the sea;
> And when I'm far frae every strand,
> My dwelling is in Sule Skerrie."

On hearing this, the girl realised that she was looking on none other than her husband, transformed once more into a grey seal. The "selchie" disappeared as suddenly as it had come. At the end of seven years he returned—this time as a man—and put a gold chain round the neck of his son, who thereafter followed him on his journeyings.

With the passage of the years, the woman forgot her seal-husband and married "a gunner good" who went out one May morning and shot two—an old grey seal and a younger one. Round the neck of the younger animal he found a gold chain; and when he brought it to his wife, she realised that her son had perished, and gave vent to her grief:—

"Alas! alas" this woeful fate!
        This weary fate that's been laid for me!
And once or twice she sobbed and sighed,
        And her tender heart did break in three."

The Mermaid's Grave[1]

Some seventy years ago, people were cutting seaweed at Sgeir na duchadh, Grimnis, Benbecula. Before putting on her stockings, one of the women went to the lower end of the reef to wash her feet. While doing so she heard a splash in the calm sea, and looking up she saw a creature in the form of a woman in miniature, some few feet away. Alarmed, the woman called to her friends, and all the people present rushed to the place.

The creature made somersaults and turned about in various directions. Some men waded into the water to seize her, but she moved beyond their reach. Some boys threw stones at her, one of which struck her in the back. A few days afterwards, this strange creature was found dead at Cuile, Nunton, nearly two miles away.

The upper portion of the creature was about the size of a well-fed child of three or four years of age, with an abnormally developed breast. The hair was long, dark, and glossy, while the skin was white, soft, and tender. The lower part of the body was like a salmon, but without scales. Crowds of people, some from long distances, came to see this strange animal, and all were unanimous in the opinion that they had gazed on the mermaid at last.

Mr. Duncan Shaw, factor for Clanranald, baron-bailie and sheriff of the district, ordered a coffin and shroud to be made for the mermaid. This was done, and the body was buried in the presence of many people, a short distance above the shore where it was found. There are persons still living who saw and touched this curious creature, and who give graphic descriptions of its appearance.

A SEAL WOMAN OR
MAIDEN OF THE SEA
FROM IRELAND

*This tale is set in a specific location, names a human protago-
nist, and connects to local history, so it is no surprise that folklorists have classified it not as a folktale, but as a legend—a
migratory one that has been circulating in Iceland, the Scottish
Highlands, the Orkney and Shetland Islands, Sweden, Den-
mark, and especially Ireland, where it is very popular.[1] The tale
is also reminiscent of folktales about the swan maiden, another
animal bride with whom the seal woman shares the ability to
shape-shift; in both cases, a man domesticates them by thwart-
ing their ability to move across species, but eventually they
escape.*

*While the version included here identifies the "supernatural"
wife as a seal woman, in Ireland she is most often referred to as
maighdean mhara ("maiden of the sea"), or mermaid. This
maiden is presented from the start as possessing special powers, but she is in no position to pose conditions for her marriage with Tom Moore: he has her hood, and this makes her his
captive.[2] Like the mermaid of Kessock, this seal woman is a
good wife and mother. When she retrieves her hood, however,
the sea calls her back, in the form of her brother's loud seal
roar. In some versions, she drowns her husband and children in
order to take them with her; in this version, she leaves behind a
well-kept house and kisses her children good-bye.*

The message of this interspecies encounter seems to be that marrying an outsider can work, but only temporarily. However, the children and their descendants maintain a connection to their mother, which is either marked on the body—webbed fingers and toes—or, in other versions, signaled by special swimming or fishing abilities. These markers also function as a warning to fishermen not to hunt seals.

Tom Moore and the Seal Woman[1]

In the village of Kilshanig, two miles north-east of Castlegreg-ory, there lived at one time a fine, brave young man named Tom Moore, a good dancer and singer. 'Tis often he was heard singing among the cliffs and in the fields of a night.

Tom's father and mother died and he was alone in the house and in need of a wife. One morning early, when he was at work near the strand, he saw the finest woman ever seen in that part of the kingdom, sitting on a rock, fast asleep. The tide was gone from the rocks then, and Tom was curious to know who was she or what brought her, so he walked toward the rock.

"Wake up!" cried Tom to the woman; "if the tide comes 'twill drown you."

She raised her head and only laughed. Tom left her there, but as he was going he turned every minute to look at the woman. When he came back he caught the spade, but couldn't work; he had to look at the beautiful woman on the rock. At last the tide swept over the rock. He threw the spade down and away to the strand with him, but she slipped into the sea and he saw no more of her that time.

Tom spent the day cursing himself for not taking the woman from the rock when it was God that sent her to him. He couldn't work out the day. He went home.

Tom could not sleep a wink all that night. He was up early next morning and went to the rock. The woman was there. He called to her.

No answer. He went up to the rock. "You may as well come home with me now," said Tom. Not a word from the woman. Tom took the hood from her head and said, "I'll have this!"

The moment he did that she cried: "Give back my hood, Tom Moore!"

"Indeed I will not, for 'twas God sent you to me, and now that you have speech I'm well satisfied!" And taking her by the arm he led her to the house. The woman cooked breakfast, and they sat down together to eat it.

"Now," said Tom, "in the name of God you and I'll go to the priest and get married, for the neighbours around here are very watchful; they'd be talking." So after breakfast they went to the priest, and Tom asked him to marry them.

"Where did you get the wife?" asked the priest.

Tom told the whole story. When the priest saw Tom was so anxious to marry he charged £5, and Tom paid the money. He took the wife home with him, and she was good a woman as ever went into a man's house. She lived with Tom seven years, and had three sons and two daughters.

One day Tom was ploughing, and some part of the plough rigging broke. He thought there were bolts on the loft at home, so he climbed up to get them. He threw down bags and ropes while he was looking for the bolts, and what should he throw down but the hood which he took from the wife seven years before. She saw it the moment it fell, picked it up, and hid it. At that time people heard a great seal roaring out in the sea.

"Ah," said Tom's wife, "that's my brother looking for me."

Some men who were hunting killed three seals that day. All the women of the village ran down to the strand to look at the seals, and Tom's wife with others. She began to moan, and going up to the dead seals she spoke some words to each and then cried out, "Oh, the murder!"

When they saw her crying the men said: "We'll have nothing more to do with these seals." So they dug a great hole, and the three seals were put into it and covered. But some thought in the night: "'Tis a great shame to bury those seals, after all the trouble in taking them." Those men went with shovels and dug up the earth, but found no trace of the seals.

All this time the big seal in the sea was roaring. Next day when Tom was at work his wife swept the house, put everything in order, washed the children and combed their hair; then, taking them one by one, she kissed each. She went next to the rock, and, putting the hood on her head, gave a plunge.

That moment the big seal rose and roared so that people ten miles away could hear him.

Tom's wife went away with the seal swimming in the sea. All the five children that she left had webs between their fingers and toes, half-way to the tips.

The descendants of Tom Moore and the seal woman are living near Castlegregory to this day, and the webs are not gone yet from between their fingers and toes, though decreasing with each generation.

DANGEROUS MERMAIDS
IN TWO CHILD BALLADS

Francis James Child (1825–1896) published The English and Scottish Popular Ballads *from 1882 to 1898. As narrative poems that are often episodic and filled with repetition or refrains, ballads move across media and cultures, straddling orality and print as well as folklore and literature. In these two popular ballads, "Clark Colven" and "The Mermaid,"[1] we encounter the mermaid as a femme fatale who brings doom to men. This is not surprising in a ballad, a poetic form that often features themes of loss and violent death, and that in its repetitive structure often figures the lure of adventure as bewitchment.*

These ballads, which continue to circulate in contemporary folk performances and recordings, epitomize the association of mermaids with sex and death; however, they also raise questions of the men's accountability, bearing in mind that in early modern England "mermaid" meant "prostitute." In the case of "Clark Colven," the man is warned to stay faithful, but he is inconstant, betraying his land wife and the mermaid both.[2] In contrast, in "The Mermaid," the men are simply unfortunate. Just seeing the beauty at sea who holds a comb and mirror in her hand is enough to signal to the sailors that their ship will sink and they won't return to their families. Several versions of this ballad begin with the captain and sailors setting sail on a Friday, which is already bad luck in many belief traditions.

Clark Colven, Child 42A[1]

Clark Colven and his gay ladie,
    As they walked to yon garden green,
A belt about her middle gimp,
    Which cost Clark Colven crowns fifteen:

'O hearken weel now, my good lord,
    O hearken weel to what I say;
When ye gang to the wall o Stream,
    O gang nae neer the well-fared may.'

'O haud your tongue, my gay ladie,
    Tak nae sic care o me;
For I nae saw a fair woman
    I like so well as thee.'

He mounted on his berry-brown steed,
    And merry, merry rade he on,
Till he came to the wall o Stream,
    And there he saw the mermaiden.

'Ye wash, ye wash, ye bonny may,
    And ay's ye wash your sark o silk:'
'It's a' for you, ye gentle knight,
    My skin is whiter than the milk.'

He's taen her by the milk-white hand,
    He's taen her by the sleeve sae green,

And he's forgotten his gay ladie,
  And away with the fair maiden.

* * * * *

'Ohon, alas!' says Clark Colven,
  'And aye sae sair's I mean my head!'
And merrily leugh the mermaiden,
  'O win on till you be dead.

'But out ye tak your little pen-knife,
  And frae my sark ye shear a gare;
Row that about your lovely head,
  And the pain ye'll never feel nae mair.'

Out he has taen his little pen-knife,
  And frae her sark he's shorn a gare,
Rowed that about his lovely head,
  But the pain increased mair and mair.

'Ohon, alas!' says Clark Colven,
  'An aye sae sair's I mean my head!'
And merrily laughd the mermaiden,
  'It will ay be war till ye be dead.'

Then out he drew his trusty blade,
  And thought wi it to be her dead,
But she's become a fish again,
  And merrily sprang into the fleed.

He's mounted on his berry-brown steed,
  And dowy, dowy rade he home,
And heavily, heavily lighted down
  When to his ladie's bower-door he came.

'Oh, mither, mither, mak my bed,
  And, gentle ladie, lay me down;
Oh, brither, brither, unbend my bow,
  'T will never be bent by me again.'

His mither she has made his bed,
  His gentle ladie laid him down,
His brither he has unbent his bow,
  'T was never bent by him again.

The Mermaid, Child 289B[1]

One Friday morn when we set sail,
  Not very far from land,
We there did espy a fair pretty maid
  With a comb and a glass in her hand, her
      hand, her hand,
  With a comb and a glass in her hand.
    While the raging seas did roar,
        And the stormy winds did blow,
    While we jolly sailor-boys were up into
      the top,
        And the land-lubbers lying down below,
          below, below,
        And the land-lubbers lying down below.

Then up starts the captain of our gallant ship,
  And a brave young man was he:
'I've a wife and a child in fair Bristol town,
  But a widow I fear she will be.'
    For the raging seas, etc.

Then up starts the mate of our gallant ship,
  And a bold young man was he:
'Oh! I have a wife in fair Portsmouth town,
  But a widow I fear she will be.'
    For the raging seas, etc.

Then up starts the cook of our gallant ship,
  And a gruff old soul was he:
'Oh! I have a wife in fair Plymouth town,
  But a widow I fear she will be.'

And then up spoke the little cabin-boy,
    And a pretty little boy was he;
'Oh! I am more grievd for my daddy and my mammy
    Than you for your wives all three.'

Then three times round went our gallant ship,
    And three times round went she;
For the want of a life-boat they all went down,
    And she sank to the bottom of the sea.

A BAVARIAN
FRESHWATER MERMAN

This tale, taken from Franz Xaver von Schönwerth's (1810–1886) archive of Bavarian stories, has the markings of legend. No location is specified for the village and lake in which the story takes place, but the final line inserts the story's events in history by offering them as an explanation for the present state of things in the area.[1]

The lake's water seems to have magical qualities at first, attracting young women to it with the promise of beauty enhancement. But this works only for the local maidens who are already beautiful and who, unbeknownst to all, have established ties with the lake's powerful merman. We are not told of these ties, or their possible kinship, only of its consequences. The bridegrooms in Schönwerth's legend discover their brides' "fish scales" on the wedding night, and the social verdict is death by fire. The "gatelike" quality of the merman's jaw in the story turns the title's image of captivity into the possibility of renewed life in the lake's waters for the young women who already have fish scales. But the all-human girls' verdict is unequivocal: no makeover is worth becoming merfolk.

In the Jaws of
the Merman[1]

There was once a village near a large body of water, and many beautiful girls lived there. The more often they swam in the lake, the more lovely they became. Everyone adored them. Girls living in other places heard about them. They came in from many different regions to swim there. But since many were ugly and couldn't stay underwater as long as the girls in the village, they did not become prettier. In fact, many of them drowned.

Girls stopped traveling there, but suitors from all four points of the compass came courting. All the girls in the village were married on one day. The morning after, there was an enormous uproar. Everyone was running, and the grooms had grabbed their wives by the hair and were pushing and shoving them to the point of exhaustion, and then they raced away.

It turned out that there was something not quite right with the girls—they had fish scales. A judge appeared on the scene with his officials, took a look at the brides, and ordered all of them to be burned at the stake at once. As the flames were licking the stake, tall waves rose up and washed into the village, and a huge head emerged from the waters. It spewed water like a whale and put out the fire. The brides all walked across an arc of water as if it were a bridge leading from the woodpile back to the water and then into the gatelike jaws of the merman. Since that time girls no longer swim in that lake.

A FRESHWATER MERMAID
IN GRIMMS' FAIRY TALES

*German philologists and librarians Jacob and Wilhelm Grimm
are best known for their collection* Children's and Household
Tales, *often retitled* Grimms' Fairy Tales, *of which they published
seven different editions during their lifetimes. While merfolk do
not appear in these stories, water sprites or nixies do appear in
two, "The Water Nixie" and "The Nixie in the Pond."[1]*

*In the first tale, which we have not included, the nixie captures
two children, a brother and sister who fell into the water while
playing near a well, and puts them to work. In the second, the
nixie promises a miller renewed prosperity in exchange for "what
has just been born" in his house, which turns out to be the man's
son. In both tales, humans experience only temporary captivity.
The children in "The Water Nixie" simply run away, taking advantage of the nixie's absence—she goes to church! They escape
in a typical "magical flight" sequence, in which the little girl
throws her brush, comb, and mirror behind her, and they transform into mountains that slow the nixie's pursuit and eventually
enable the children's escape. In "The Nixie in the Pond," the
miller's son is captured as an already married adult, and his loving wife is the one to save him, with the help of an old woman's
gifts to lure the nixie. The man literally flies or jumps eagerly to
rejoin the human world and marriage, but the husband and wife
undergo further trials before their final happy reunion, thematiz-
ing perhaps how difficult it is to overcome the problem of his
other life underwater. Memory and music, often associated with
water beings, play a role in reuniting them.*

The Nixie in the Pond[1]

A FRESHWATER MERMAID
IN GRIMMS' FAIRY TALES

Once upon a time there was a miller who led a pleasant life
with his wife. They had money and property, and their prosperity increased from year to year. Calamity, however, can
strike overnight. Just as their wealth had increased rapidly, it
also began to decrease each year until the miller could hardly
call the mill that he inhabited his own. His problems weighed
heavily on him, and when he lay down in bed after working all
day, he could not rest. Instead he tossed and turned and wor-
ried himself sick. One morning he got up before daybreak,
went outside into the open air, and hoped that this would ease
his heart. As he walked over the dam of the mill the first rays
of the sun burst forth, and he heard a rushing sound in the
pond. When he turned around, he caught sight of a beautiful
woman, who was rising slowly out of the water. Her long hair,
which she clasped by her tender hands over her shoulders,
flowed down both sides and covered her white body. He realized that this was the nixie of the millpond and became so
frightened that he did not know whether to go or stay. But the
nixie raised her soft voice, called him by his name, and asked
him why he was so sad. At first the miller was distrustful, but
when he heard her speak in such a friendly way, he summoned
his courage and told her that he had formerly lived in happiness and wealth but was now so poor that he did not know
what to do.

"Calm yourself," responded the nixie. "I shall make you
richer and happier than you ever were before. But you must
promise to give me what has just been born in your house."

That can be nothing but a puppy or a kitten, thought the
miller, and he agreed to give her what she desired. The nixie
descended into the water again, and he rushed back to his mill

feeling consoled and in good spirits. Just as he was about to enter the mill, the maid stepped out of his house and shouted that he should rejoice, for his wife had just given birth to a little boy. The miller stood still, as if struck by lightning. He realized that the sly nixie had known this and had deceived him. So he bowed his head and went to his wife's bedside, and when she asked him, "Why aren't you happy about our fine little boy?" he told her what had happened to him and what he had promised the nixie. "What good are happiness and wealth," he added, "if I must lose my child? But what can I do?" Even the relatives, who had come to visit and wish them happiness, did not know what advice to give him.

In the meantime, prosperity returned to the house of the miller. Whatever he undertook turned into a success. It was as if the coffers and chests filled themselves of their own accord, and the money kept multiplying overnight in the closet. It did not take long before his wealth was greater than it had ever been before. But he could not rejoice about this with an easy conscience. The consent that he had given to the nixie tortured his heart. Whenever he walked by the millpond, he feared that she might surface and remind him about his debt. He never let his son go near the water. "Be careful," he said to him. "If you just touch the water, she will grab your hand and drag you under." However, as the years passed, and the nixie did not reappear, the miller began to relax.

When his boy became a young man, he was given to a huntsman as an apprentice. Once he had learned everything and had become an able huntsman, the lord of the village took him into his service. In the village there was a beautiful and true-hearted maiden who had won the hunter's affection, and when the lord became aware of this, he gave the young man a small house. So the maiden and the huntsman were married, lived peacefully and happily, and loved each other with all their hearts.

Once when the huntsman was pursuing a deer, the animal turned out of the forest and into the open field. The huntsman followed it and finally killed it with one shot. He did not realize that he was close to the dangerous millpond, and after he had skinned and gutted the animal, he went to the water to wash his hands that were covered with blood. No sooner did he dip his hands into the water than the nixie rose up and embraced him laughingly with her sopping wet arms. Then she dragged him down into the water so quickly that only the clapping of the waves above him could be heard.

When evening fell, and the huntsman did not return home, his wife became anxious. She went outside to search for him, and since he had often told her that he had to beware of the nixie's snares and that he was never to venture close to the millpond, she already suspected what had happened. She rushed to the water, and when she found his hunting bag lying on the bank of the pond, she could no longer have any doubts about her husband's misfortune. She wrung her hands and uttered a loud groan. She called her beloved by his name, but it was all in vain. Then she rushed to the other side of the millpond and called him again. She scolded the nixie with harsh words, but she received no response. The water's surface remained as calm as a mirror. Only the face of the half-moon returned her gaze in stillness.

The poor woman did not leave the pond. Time and again she paced around it with quick steps, never resting for a moment. Sometimes she was quiet. Other times she whimpered softly. Finally, she lost her strength, sank to the ground, and fell into a deep sleep. Soon she was seized by a dream.

She was anxiously climbing up a mountain between two huge cliffs. Thorns and briers pricked at her feet. Rain slapped her face, and the wind whipped through her long hair. When she reached the peak, there was an entirely different view. The sky was blue; the air, mild. The ground sloped gently downward, and a neat little hut stood on a green meadow covered by flowers. She went toward the hut and opened the door. There sat an old woman with white hair, who beckoned to her in a friendly way.

At that very moment the poor young woman woke up. The day had already dawned, and she decided to let herself be guided by the dream. So she struggled up the mountain, and everything was exactly as she had seen it in the night. The old woman received her in a friendly way and showed her a chair where she was to sit. "You must have had a terrible experience," the woman said, "for you to have searched out my lonely hut."

The young woman cried as she told her what had happened to her. Then the old woman said, "Console yourself, for I shall help you. Here is a golden comb. Wait until the full moon has risen. Then go to the millpond, sit down on the bank, and comb your long black hair with this comb. When you're finished, set it down on the bank, and you'll see what happens."

The woman returned home, but she felt that the full moon was very slow in coming. Finally, it appeared in the sky. So she went out to the millpond, sat down, and combed her long black hair with the golden comb. And, when she was finished, she set it down on the edge of the water. Soon after, a bubbling from the depths could be heard, and a wave rose up, rolled to the shore, and took the comb away with it. The comb sank to the bottom in no time. Then the surface of the water parted, and the head of the huntsman emerged in the air. He did not speak, but with a sad look he glanced at his wife. At that very moment a second wave rushed toward the man and covered his head. Everything disappeared. The millpond was as peaceful as before, and only the face of the full moon shone upon it.

The young woman returned home disheartened. However, the dream came back to her and showed her the old woman's hut. The next morning she set out on her way once again and related her woes to the wise woman, who gave her a golden flute and said, "Wait until the full moon comes again. Then take this flute, sit down on the bank, play a beautiful tune, and after you're done, lay it down on the sand, and you'll see what happens."

The huntsman's wife did what the old woman told her to do. Just as she set the flute on the sand, there was a sudden bubbling from the depths. A wave rose up, moved toward the bank, and took the flute away with it. Soon after, the water parted, and not only the head of the man became visible but also half his body. He stretched out his arms toward her yearningly, but just as he did this, a second wave rolled by, covered him, and dragged him down into the water again.

"Oh, what's the use!" exclaimed the unfortunate woman. "I'm given glimpses of my dearest only to lose him again!" Grief filled her heart anew, but the dream showed her the old woman's hut for a third time. So she set upon her way again, and the wise woman comforted her, gave her a golden spinning wheel, and said, "Not everything has been completed yet. Wait until the full moon comes, then take the spinning wheel, sit down on the bank, and spin until the spool is full. When you're finished, place the spinning wheel near the water, and you'll see what happens."

The young woman followed the instructions exactly as she had been told. As soon as the full moon appeared, she carried the golden spinning wheel to the bank and spun diligently until there was no more flax left and the spool was completely full of thread. But, no sooner was the spinning wheel standing on the bank than the water bubbled in the depths more violently than ever before. A powerful wave rushed to the shore and carried the spinning wheel away with it. Soon after, the head and entire body of the man rose up high like a water geyser. Quickly he jumped to the shore, took his wife by the hand, and fled. But they had gone barely a short distance when the entire millpond rose up with a horrible bubbling and flowed over the wide fields with such force that it tore everything along with it. The two escapees could already picture their death. Then, in her fear, the wife called to the old woman to help them, and at that very moment they were transformed; she into a toad, he into a frog. When the flood swept over them, it could not kill them, but it did tear them apart from each other and carry them far away.

After the flood had run its course, and both had touched down on dry land, they regained their human shape. But neither one knew where the other was. They found themselves among strange people, who did not know where their homeland was. High mountains and deep valleys lay between them. In order to earn a living, both had to tend sheep. For many years they drove their flocks through fields and forests and were full of sadness and longing.

One day, when spring had made its appearance on earth again, they both set out with their flocks, and as chance would have it, they began moving toward each other. When the huntsman caught sight of another flock on a distant mountain slope, he drove his sheep in that direction. They came together in a valley, but they did not recognize each other. However, they were glad to have each other's company in such a lonely place. From then on they drove their flocks side by side every day. They did not speak much, but they felt comforted. One evening, when the full moon appeared in the sky and the sheep had already retired for the night, the shepherd took a flute from his pocket and played a beautiful but sad tune. When he was finished, he noticed that the shepherdess was weeping bitterly. "Why are you crying?" he asked.

"Oh," she answered, "the full moon was shining just like this when I last played that tune on a flute, and the head of my beloved rose out of the water."

He looked at her, and it was as if a veil had fallen from his eyes, for he recognized his dearest wife. And when she looked at him and the light of the moon fell on his face, she recognized him as well. They embraced and kissed each other. And nobody need ask whether they lived in bliss thereafter.

THREE ESTONIAN
WATER SPIRITS

Water spirits thrived in Estonia until the modernization of its traditional rural society at the end of the nineteenth century. Since then, thousands of legends about them have been collected and textualized. As in many other countries, water spirits in Estonia were sometimes considered to be the offspring of angels who had been hurled down from the heavens because they had joined Lucifer's forces in his rebellion against the Christian God. According to another folk etiology, these water spirits (and seals) were born from the warriors of the pharaoh's army who perished in the Red Sea. A third explanation is that people who have drowned often return as water spirits who lure the living into the water and cause new tragedies.

Thousands of lakes and rivers and the long coastline of the Baltic Sea form the natural environment of Estonian water spirits, commonly called näkks. As demonic shape-shifters, they take different guises, but they prefer human forms, such as those of a young woman, an old man, or a child. Animal forms, such as an ox, horse, or dog, are also common. Typically in stories, witnessing the näkk is a bad omen that predicts that somebody will soon drown. Sometimes, the näkk is actively luring the victims to their deaths—as in stories where a water horse invites children to take a ride and carries them under the water, or a beautiful maiden seduces a young man.

The three Estonian legends selected here are told as true stories, indicating the locations of the described events. Somewhat untypically, all also include dialogue between a human *and a water spirit who appears more benevolent than usual, granting or offering something to the human. In the first story, the woman, who is obviously heading to Tallinn, the capital city of Estonia, sees the water spirit and addresses her as "mistress of water" (vee-emand), which sounds more respectful than the somewhat pejorative näkk, with its demonic connotations. The second episode in the same story, about a man riding a horse, is a version of the migratory legend "River Claiming Its Due," which is widely spread in north European folklore.*[1] *The first two Estonian legends have been recorded in the inland from the country people, but the third story represents maritime folklore of fishermen. All stories express a sense of amazement and mystery—a fascinating and perilous other world is so near, and yet beyond reach.*

—ÜLO VALK, *University of Tartu, Estonia*

Three Tales (Untitled)

As told in 1929 by Emilie Kruuspak, a forty-two-year-old woman, to Rudolf Põldmäe, a professional folklorist, on his field trip to Harju-Jaani parish in northern Estonia.[1]

My great-grandmother was on her way to town. Near the bridge of Saula, she saw a woman washing her breasts in the river. The woman had yellow hair and broad hips. She was standing with her back toward my great-grandmother, who shouted, "Good morning, mistress of water!" The strange woman responded through her nose, "In the name of God, let your grandchildren have a happy life until the fourth and fifth generation. They will not die a watery death." This happened in the summertime at dawn.

In the evening, great-grandmother returned from town and heard that in the same place where the water spirit had been, a girl had drowned while washing sheep. The unlucky girl had also had long yellow hair.

After two weeks, in the same place, a voice was heard saying, "The hour is approaching but not the man!" This was repeated several times. Then a man came from the direction of Vaida to bathe his horse. On the way, people warned him not to go. The man took no notice of this. He drew the horse into the river in the same place where the voice had been heard. Suddenly the horse fell over, and the man fell into the river and drowned in the blink of an eye.

The narrator's grandmother, the daughter of the woman who had seen the water spirit, always told her grandchildren, "You don't need to be afraid of a watery death." And until today, nobody from their family has encountered death by water, although they have often lived near water and have been quite close to drowning several times.

*As recorded in 1898 in Kadrina parish, northern Estonia, by
Johannes Schhneier, from an unknown storyteller.*[2]

A man was once driving by Jäneda Lake (in the Ambla parish)
when he saw a young gentleman standing on the lakeshore. He
did not pay attention to him and kept on driving quietly. But
when he passed him, the young gentleman said, "Man, where
are you driving? Will you pass Viitna Lake (in the Kadrina
parish)?" The man was rather surprised because he was indeed
planning to travel by the lake that the young gentleman had
mentioned. He replied, "Yes, fair gentleman, I was planning to
drive in that direction." "It's good that you are driving there,
because I wanted to send greetings to the maidens of Viitna
Lake. Be so kind as to go to the shore of Viitna Lake and
shout, 'The young gentlemen of Jäneda Lake are sending their
love to the maidens of Viitna Lake,'" the young gentleman
said, and disappeared.

On the next day the man reached the tavern of Viitna. He
went to the lake to deliver the regards. On the shore of the
lake, the man shouted, "Young gentlemen of Jäneda Lake are
sending a lot of love to the maidens of Viitna Lake!" Immediately, the beautiful long arm of a woman appeared above the
water and threw a big pike fish in front of the man on the
shore. This was a gift from the water nymphs to the man in
thanks for the regards he had delivered.

As recorded in 1932 in Jämaja parish in Saaremaa, the biggest Estonian island in the Baltic Sea, by Andrei Kuldsaar, from an unknown storyteller.[3]

Long ago, some men were fishing in the sea near Pöide. One old man had taken his daughter with him. She was sitting in the prow and looking eagerly into the water as the ship was sliding up and down the waves. In the prow, there was also a pail of root beer that the fishermen had taken with them to slake their thirst. When they reached their ordinary fishing place, the old man who was steering the boat shouted to his daughter, "Girl, bring me the pail with root beer!" As the girl did not hear him, the old man had to repeat it several times.

Suddenly, a girl with black hair appeared from the sea in front of the ship, holding a pail with frothing beer in her hand, and offered it to the fishermen. They drank it and thanked her for the fine beer. The girl who had appeared from the sea said, "Why do you cast your net in front of our door? There are no fish here. Cast your nets a bit further, and you will get a lot of fish." Then she took her empty pail and disappeared into the bottom of the sea. The fishermen followed her advice, and caught many fish every time thereafter.

TWO GREEK MERMAIDS

The two tales presented here are quite representative of Greece's oral traditions about mermaids, who—according to Nicolaos Politis, the founder of folklore studies in Greece—are the only marine deities surviving in modern Greece's mythology: in the modern Greek imagination, mermaids are malevolent sea monsters, half fish, half women, who draw their traits from ancient Greek myths about the Sirens.[1] In legends about the past, mermaids are either associated with King Alexander III of Macedon, commonly referred to as Alexander the Great, or represented interchangeably with other sea monsters. In their modern Greek cultural contexts, mermaids appear in several genres of oral literature—primarily in legends, but also in songs, folktales, and in shadow theater plots (Karaghiozis).

The first story, from the island of Crete, entitled "New Tunes," was published by Politis, who considered it to be part of the legendary cycles connected with Alexander the Great.[2] The mermaid here is Alexander's forever-living desperate sister, while other motifs, such as the Cyanean Rocks, the water of immortality, or the fairies teaching music to humans, recall either Greek mythology or modern Greek traditions.

The second story, "The Mermaid," is an oral tale recorded in the local idiom of the island of Skiathos during the first half of the twentieth century. It is part of the considerable Greek corpus of tales that, like "The Nixie in the Pond," involve a miraculously born child who is promised to some (aquatic) demon; having reached puberty, the youth in this story has to overcome the demon's powers in order to save his own life.

—MARILENA PAPACHRISTOPHOROU,
University of Ioannina, Greece

New Tunes[1]

King Alexander, having fought and conquered all kingdoms on Earth and having the whole world in fear of him, summoned the magicians and asked them, "Tell me, you who know what's written in destiny, what can I do to live many years and enjoy the world which I have made entirely my own?" "Venerable King, your power is great," replied the magicians, "but what is written in destiny cannot be unwritten. There is only one thing that can make you enjoy your realms and your glory and become immortal, and live as long as the mountains. But it is difficult, too difficult." "I am not asking you whether it's difficult or not, but only what it is," said Alexander. "Then, if you please, my King, it's the water of immortality; if you drink it, you will have no fear of death. But if you are to reach it, you must cross two mountains that constantly clash against each other and not even a flying bird has time to pass through. Countless famous young princes and noblemen have perished at that formidable trap! If you make it past the mountains, there is a never-sleeping dragon who guards the water of immortality. You kill the dragon and take it."

At once Alexander sends for his horse, Bucephalus, that had no wings but flew like a bird.[2] He mounts his steed and goes. With a single flick of his whip he crossed the passage; he killed the sleepless dragon and took the glass jar with the water of immortality.

But when the blessed king reached the palace he failed to keep the water safe! His sister saw it, and unaware of what it was she threw it out. By chance the water fell on a wild onion, which is why these plants never wilt.

After a while Alexander sought to drink the water of immortality but couldn't find it. He asked his sister, and she told him that she didn't know what it was and had poured it out.

The king was beside himself with anger and frustration, and cursed her to become a fish from the waist down and forever be tormented, as long as the world stands, in the middle of the sea.

God heard this, and since then the ships that travel see her wandering in the waves. Still, she has no hatred for Alexander, and when she spots a ship she asks, "Is Alexander alive?" If the captain is uninformed and replies, "He is dead," the maiden in her sorrow starts beating the sea with her arms and her unbraided blond hair, and sinks the ship. But those in the know reply, "He lives and reigns," and then the wretched maiden, reassured, happily sings sweet songs.

That's where sailors learn new tunes and bring them to the world.

The Mermaid[1]

Narrated by Athanassios K. Trakosas, age seventy.

Once upon a time, there was a couple who had no children. They were very sad about it. The man was a captain with his own ship. He traveled a lot. Once, on a journey, he and his crew were sailing past a headland. They had a tailwind and were traveling just fine. Suddenly, the ship stopped dead, not moving an inch. They looked this way and that to see why the ship wouldn't move, if they had hit a shoal or anything, but couldn't see anything.

The captain looks down the prow and sees a Mermaid in the sea, with one arm against the bow of the ship to stop it from moving.[2] A Mermaid is a woman from the waist up and a fish from the waist down. The captain says to her, "What wrong did we do to you that you won't let us move on?" "You did nothing wrong," says the Mermaid. "Only, I heard you don't have a child, and I came to ask you: do you want to have a child? "I do," said the captain. And the Mermaid says, "Take this bone and give it to your wife to eat, and she'll get pregnant and you'll have a boy. On this condition: when the child turns fifteen, you'll bring him here to me. You'll leave him out there on that headland, and I'll come to fetch him." "All right," he said. The Mermaid dove into the sea and was gone. The ship moved again and continued on its journey.

Once the journey was over, the captain went home and gave the bone to his wife to eat. And then she got pregnant. The child was born, a handsome lad. He grew up and was baptized—Yannakis, they called him. Then they sent him to school, and he was very good at it. He was very clever.

The child grew. The more he grew, the greater his parent's heartbreak, because they'd have to take him to the Mermaid and lose him. And then he turned fifteen. It was time to take him to the Mermaid. What else could the poor father do? He was about to leave on a journey, and took the child aboard to leave him where he had seen the Mermaid. They sailed off, and in a few days they reached that headland. Then the captain says, "Let's go out on the boat to gather some limpets." Three or four sailors got into the boat, along with the captain and the lad. They took along a barrel of water and a basket of rusks. "Why do we need the water and rusks?" asked the child. The father lied to him so that he wouldn't get suspicious. "There is an old hermit who lives over here behind the headland, and we sailors have a habit of offering him something from the ship when we alight here, whatever we have on board."

They disembarked, unloaded the water and the rusks, and scattered around the rocky beach to look for limpets. At one point, the lad went behind a rock and bent down to collect limpets. Then the others took the boat, returned to the ship, and sailed off. After a while, the child raised his head from his work, looked around, and saw no one. He called out to his father, the crew. . . . No one. He turned to look at the ship, and saw it far off in the distance, sailing away. The poor thing could not understand why his father had left him behind in that desolate place. It was getting dark, and the poor kid got up and started going up the mountain in search of that hermit his father had spoken about.

On the way, he comes across two ants fighting over a dead worm. He takes out his knife, cuts the worm in two, and shares it between the two ants. He puts his knife away and gets up to leave. The ants call him back, saying, "Don't go. Open your mouth, and we'll give you our powers," they say. "What kind of powers do you have?" asks the boy. "Well, we have our own powers, too, you know." The boy opens his mouth, and the first ant spits right into it. And so does the second ant. Then they say, "If you ever need to become little, you say, 'A man I am, an ant let me be'; and if you want to go back to being a man, say, 'An ant I am, a man let me be.'" "Fine," said Yannakis as he got up and left.

On his way he comes across two eagles fighting over a carcass. "Hold it," he says. "Why fight?" He takes out his knife, cuts the carcass in two, and gives a piece to each one of them. Then the two eagles say, "You shall have our powers." "What powers do you have?" said Yannakis. "Open your mouth," the eagles said. The boy opens his mouth, and first one, and then the other eagle spit into it, and then they tell him, "If you ever need to reach some place fast, say, 'A man I am, an eagle let me be'; and if you want to go back to being a man, you say, 'An eagle I am, a man let me be.'"

Yannakis gets up and goes on his way. After a while, he finds two lions fighting over a carcass. Yannakis takes out his knife again and shares the carcass between the two. Then the lions say, "Open your mouth," they spit into it, and tell him, "If you ever need to be strong, say, 'A man I am, a lion let me be'; and if you want to go back to being a man, you say 'A lion I am, a man let me be.'" "Fine," said Yannakis and got up to leave.

He walked and walked, went around the whole mountain, but found no monk, nothing. He walked back, the poor thing, and reached the beach where they'd been collecting limpets. He was hungry, too, so he took a rusk out of the basket, soaked it with water from the barrel, and sat on a rock to eat it. That's when the Mermaid appeared in the sea. The boy was scared. She said, "Come down and pull me out." The boy was afraid and didn't want to go. "I can't get close to the sea," he said, "or I'll fall down the rocks." "Come," she kept saying. And in order to trick him, she says, "Your father sent me to fetch you." The boy goes down the rocks near her, and says, "A man I am, a lion let me be." He becomes a lion, grabs the Mermaid by the throat, pulls her out of the water, and drops her, face up on the rocks. Then he says, "A lion I am, an eagle let me be." He becomes an eagle, flies away, and lands in a distant place.

But as the Mermaid was on her back, she could see which way the eagle had flown. Once Yannakis was far from the sea, he became human again and went on his way.

As he was walking, he saw a bonfire in the distance. He

headed toward it, but there was no one there. He warmed him-self a little and left. Further on, there was a house. He walks in, and . . . what a sight! People with cut ears, cut noses, cut legs, cut fingers. "Why do you all have your ears cut, your noses cut, your legs cut, your fingers cut?" They say, "There is this princess down in the town, and she's black. She wants us to get the milk to her while it's still warm every morning, so that she can wash herself and whiten her complexion. But the town is far and we can't do it, so she has our ears cut off, or our noses, legs, or fingers cut off." Yannakis says, "Tomor-row, I'll take the milk to her myself."

At dawn, the shepherd milked the goats, poured the milk in a wooden bucket, and gave it to Yannakis. Yannakis took it, walked away, out of sight, and said, "A man I am, an eagle let me be." He turns into an eagle, picks up the bucket with his talons, and takes off. When he got close to the princess's pal-ace, he landed and said, "An eagle I am, a man let me be." Be-coming a man, he picks up the bucket with his hands and takes it in to the princess. The milk was still frothing. "How come the milk is warm today?" says the princess. "How would I know?" he says. "I ran all the way and brought it warm." "Make sure you're the one who brings it tomorrow," says the princess. "Fine, I will." The princess emptied the milk and gave him back the bucket. He took it, walked out, and said again, "A man I am, an eagle let me be." He turned into an eagle, picked up the bucket with his talons, and flew off. When he got close to the house, he said, "An eagle I am, a man let me be," picked up the bucket with his hand, and walked in. "Why aren't you maimed?" they asked him. "I am not maimed be-cause I brought the milk warm to her." Then the shepherd made Yannakis his son.

The next day dawned. Yannakis's father milked the goats, poured the milk into the jug, and gave it to him to take to the princess. Yannakis took it, walked down the road, turned into an eagle, and got it to the princess warm again. From then on, it was Yannakis who took the milk to the princess every day. But every day she asked him how he managed to bring it warm to her. At first, Yannakis didn't want to betray his secret, but little by little, she made him tell her the whole story about his ability to turn into an eagle, lion, and ant. The princess fell in love with Yannakis, and Yannakis with her.

At first they kept it a secret from her father, the king. Every night Yannakis turned into an eagle, landed outside the palace, and said, "An eagle I am, an ant let me be." As an ant, he entered the princess's room through a crack. Then again, he said, "An ant I am, a man let me be," became a man, and spent the whole night with the princess. At dawn he would turn into an ant again and leave the room through the crack. That went on regularly.

After a time, another king sent to ask for the princess as a bride for his son, the prince. Her father tells her, "Prince So-and-So has asked for your hand." But the princess said to her father, "It's Yannakis I'll have as a husband. I want no one else." Her father didn't like this, and said, "You, a princess, marry a shepherd?" But she was firm: "I love him, so I must marry him." "If you do, I'll disown you." But when the king saw that he couldn't change his daughter's mind, he let her have Yannakis. He married them one night, built a hut for them, and sent them to live there.

The other king, the one who had asked for the princess in marriage for his son, took offense and declared war against her father. What could the princess's father do? He began to prepare his own army for war. Those conscripted in the cavalry were told to go to the stables and get a horse and then go to the warehouses for their weapons. Yannakis was to be in the cavalry, so he went to the stable and chose a lame horse, then went to the warehouse and picked up a rusty sword, and then joined the cavalry. His father-in-law saw him and said, "Look at him, going to fight like this!"

When the two armies met, Yannakis dismounted and said, "A man I am, a lion let me be." He turned into a lion, picked a sword, too, rushed into the enemy lines, and started cutting up his foes left and right, with both sword and teeth, without any pause. His wife, the princess, and her father, the king, were watching the battle from a hilltop. The king then realized how worthy Yannakis was and regretted not wanting him as a son-in-law. Before long, he had destroyed the whole army. Not one enemy was left. Then Yannakis said, "A lion I am, a man let me be." He turned into a man, and since he was covered in blood, he went to the sea to wash it off. The Mermaid comes out, grabs Yannakis, and devours him. The princess saw all this from up high—she saw the Mermaid eat Yannakis and was devastated. She kept crying and wailing, no matter how much her father tried to console her.

The king, to put an end to her crying, found another soldier who looked the same as Yannakis and brought him to her as her husband. "This is not my husband. I saw with my own eyes my husband being eaten by the Mermaid. Father, just build me a crystal tower in the sea, and give me three golden apples." Her father built the crystal tower in the sea for her, gave her three golden apples, and sent her in a boat to the tower.

Once she was in the tower, she started playing with the golden apples. Then the Mermaid comes up and says, "What do you need three apples for? Give one to me." "I'll give it to you if you let Yannakis, whom you swallowed, stick his head out of your mouth, down to his neck, so I can see him." She gave the apple to the Mermaid, who ate it and then let Yannakis stick his head and neck out.

Then the princess started playing with the two apples. The Mermaid says again, "Give me one more apple." "I will, if you let Yannakis out down to his waist, so that I can see him." The Mermaid let Yannakis out to his waist; he was unconscious and didn't know where he was. The Mermaid took the second apple from the princess and ate it.

Then, as the princess played with the one apple in her hands, the Mermaid says, "Give me that apple, too—what will you do with it?" "I will, if you let Yannakis out to stand on your mouth." The Mermaid took the apple and let Yannakis out to stand on her mouth. The princess said, "Yannakis, remember the past." Yannakis says, "A man I am, an eagle let me be." At once, he became an eagle and flew away. The Mermaid was taken by surprise. While she was trying to see where Yannakis had gone, the princess jumped into the boat and went ashore. She went to meet Yannakis, whom she had thus won back from the Mermaid. They went back to her father's palace and lived happily ever after.

MERFOLK FROM
THE SOUTH OF ITALY

By the nineteenth century, mermaids in a narrative from Puglia—the heel of Italy, which in ancient times had been colonized by Greeks—had evolved from the Sirens of The Odyssey. *Certainly, the hybrid beings of the Italian imagination sang celestial songs just like their ancient Greek predecessors, but unlike Homer's bird women, these mermaids belonged in the water. Further south, in Sicily, merfolk such as Cola Pesce enjoyed swimming but, like humans, had to hold their breath under water.*

The first tale is drawn from a late nineteenth-century collection whose title translates as Superstitions, Prejudices and Traditions from the Land of Otranto, *and it alludes to local beliefs in fairies, as well as mermaids. The collector, Giuseppe Gigli (1862–1921), ascribes its origins to the people of the coastal town of Taranto in Puglia who, according to him, believed that women with unhappy love stories became mermaids.*[1]

The legend of "Cola Pisci" or "Cola Pesce" centers on a portentous being who was famous in Sicily for swimming like a fish, or, in many accounts, for being both human and piscine. (Aptly, his name consists of an abbreviated form of "Nicola," the Italian version of "Nicholas," plus the Sicilian or Italian word for fish.) In most versions, the king or queen orders Cola Pesce either to retrieve a precious object for them or to find out what lies under the sea to support the island. Cola Pesce complies, diving deeper and deeper even though it means risking his life, and eventually dies. The short version translated here is somewhat subversively open ended, leaving Cola Pesce's fate unclear.

The second Sicilian tale, "The Sailor and the Mermaid of the Sea," is in some ways the counterpart to "Cola Pesce": here, too, a human asks too much of a hybrid sea being, but the scale of the drama is much more intimate, suggesting a love story gone awry. Both stories, however, call out the cruel disregard of humans who hold power over others, whether that power is political or emotional.[2]

A Mermaid's Story[1]

She was a beautiful woman, around twenty-five, with hair and eyes as black as ink and skin as white as milk. Once when her husband, a seaman, was traveling in faraway regions and she was tempted by a handsome young nobleman, she gave in and was unfaithful.

But soon afterward she was filled with regret and, right away when her husband returned, she went down on her knees in front of him to confess her mistake and ask his forgiveness.

The sailor did not, however, give in to her pleas and decided, even though he loved his wife very much, to punish her.

"Prepare to die," he said to her.

Tearing her hair, the terrified woman begged forgiveness again, implored, cried. . . .

Her promises were to no avail. . . . Sailors keep their word!

That same day, accompanied only by his unfaithful wife, he set sail on his ship.

And when they were far from land and the water was deep, he suddenly grabbed her by the waist and threw her into the waves.

"I've had my vengeance now," he said, and sailed sadly back to the harbor.

But the mermaids had pity on the beautiful drowned woman and embraced her, taking her into their care.

The sight of beauty gives rise to compassion, and it was unacceptable for a woman like her to end her life as fish food.

So the mermaids took her in and led her to their enchanted palaces, where other beautiful women and charming young men were eager to welcome her: some combed her long and lustrous hair, while others applied perfume to her hands and bosom, adorned her slender neck with a red coral necklace, slipped big shiny rings onto her dainty fingers. . . .

And they gave her a name: Sea Foam.

Amazed at such riches and kindnesses, she somewhat let go of her past misfortunes.

But only a few days later, sorrow for having betrayed her beloved husband returned to torture her soul. Suddenly pale and unable to smile, she was sad and taciturn.

Distressed, the mermaids taught her to sing their sweet songs in the hopes of consoling her. This was a sign of how special she was to them, since only sirens know how to sing sweetly enough to lure unwary sailors into their nets. The woman thus took her place in the chorus of beautiful sirens.

But because she liked being alone she did not always join the charming group above water, preferring to wander here and there on her own.

One night, when the full moon brightened both sea and sky, she spotted a ship approaching, full sail.

The sirens said, "Come with us, come and sing with us. . . ."

And from below the ship, the sweetest music ever began to rise. . . .

Right then, a man was seen throwing himself over the ship's wooden railing and into the sea: lured by their song, he had fallen prey to the charms of these marine beings.

But Sea Foam recognized him in the moonlight: that man was her husband.

So she begged and implored the mermaids not to kill him, not to transform him into red coral or white crystal. She wanted to try out on him a magical transformation of her own . . . if they would only let him live for at least another twenty-four hours.

Moved to pity by her words, the mermaids consented.

Once alone, she approached the white palace in which her husband was kept and started to sing ever so sweetly.

Here are the words of her song:

I knew you in life, and I was ungrateful; you loved me, taking me from my maiden's nest to love's bridal chamber; I betrayed you; many tears, many tears I have cried over my unfaithfulness! Recognize me now; I am your wife, who can no longer return to land. To prove my love, I'm here to save you, and I will save you!

The unhappy prisoner heard the song and was amazed. Who was it singing so? Could it really be his wife?
The song continued:

To save you, I will be put to death, as the mermaids will punish me for freeing one who was destined to die. For you I will die blissfully! Now listen to me. The mermaids are frolicking not far from here, and it's getting late. The sun is about to rise, and as you know, mermaids rest in daytime and charm sailors into their nets at night. This evening, when the mermaids are far away, I'll come for you. Embrace me tight and let me take you. Farewell for now, my song ends here.

The day went by and evening came.
The seaman waited, anxiously and still doubtful, for his rescuer to come.
And indeed she did arrive, radiant with joy, and taking him with her, she swam and swam for many hours, until they were close to a big ship.
"Call for these sailors' help," said the woman. And the seaman called out three times. They lowered a rowboat from the ship into the water and rescued the man at sea.
But once he'd returned home, the man felt unhappy. His love for his wife had been reawakened and was now mingled with gratitude.
And so he decided to save his wife in turn, or die at sea himself.
He went far into a forest and sat down under a chestnut tree where fairies were known to gather.
He waited and waited. Suddenly, he noticed an ugly old woman next to him. She was smiling.
"Who are you?" asked the strange hag.
"I am an unhappy man," the melancholy sailor exclaimed.
"Let's hear about what causes your unhappiness. . . ."
The man realized she was a fairy who could help him out of

his predicament and so, opening up his heart to her, he told the fairy about his life.

"Well," said the old woman, having heard him out, "you seem like a fine young man and I want to help you get your wife back. But there is a condition. Do you agree?"

"I will do whatever you say."

"Come back here deep at night and leave under this tree the flower that can only be found in one of the mermaids' palaces, which is called 'il più bello'—the most beautiful."

"But how can I, just a wretched man, take such a flower from the bottom of the sea?"

"If you want to be reunited with your wife, you must deliver that flower here."

"All right, I'll try," said the man. And off he went to his magnificent ship and set sail.

When he was out at sea, he called to his wife. The beautiful woman answered him right away.

"My love," he said, "I want to save you."

"But how?" asked the poor woman, moved by his words.

"If you are able to give me a flower that is found in one of the mermaids' palaces and is called 'il più bello'—'the most beautiful'—you will be free to return home with me."

"Ah, this is impossible. There is such a flower, and its scent is heavenly, but it was once stolen from the fairies, and on the day when it is returned to them, one hundred mermaids will die. I would surely be among them."

"You won't die," the sailor reassured her, "because the fairies would save you."

"Come back tomorrow, and I will give you an answer."

The sailor returned the next day.

"Well?" he asked his wife.

And she answered, "In order for me to bring you the flower, you must agree to a sacrifice. . . ."

"What will it be?"

"You must sell all your belongings and use the money to buy all the most beautiful jewels that goldsmiths have in the main cities of the kingdom. Attracted by such fine jewelry, the mermaids will leave their palace, and I will be able to steal the flower."

"All right," the husband replied and went back to town.

Within just a few days he'd sold all his belongings; he then bought the most splendid jewels in the kingdom. With these, he sailed, and once he was out at sea he exhibited them in the sunlight.

A multitude of mermaids started to follow the ship, begging him for jewels.

While this was happening, there was a sudden and deep rumble, and the sea water rose to immense heights.

The mermaids understood. . . .

One hundred of them died.

And one could see, high up in the sky, a fairy riding her broomstick and carrying away the beautiful woman, the sailor's wife, and with her the stolen flower. . . .

Cola Pesce[1]

Cola Pesce was a great swimmer from Torre Faro, half fish,
half man: from the belly up, he was a human like us and could
come out of the water; from the belly down he was a fish and
never came out of the water. He would swim around under
water most of the time and dive down to the bottom of the sea.
When he came to shore, people would ask him, "Why don't
you come out of the water? Why is it that you can't be on
land?" And he would answer, "Can't you see what kind of a
creature I am? And anyway, underwater there are many sharks
and ferocious beasts that fear me, and thus do not damage
your fishnets. But the biggest fish is the conger eel, whose tail
is in the west while its head is in the east."

Once, at the king's request, he descended to the bottom of the
sea and never returned, and perhaps he is still on his journey.[2]

The Sailor and the
Mermaid of the Sea[1]

Once, it is said, that a sailor became friendly with the Mermaid of the sea, and that he wagered I don't know what that she would not be able to touch the bottom of the sea and retrieve a ring. This sailor knew that the Mermaid could not remain long underwater without having trouble breathing; this is something the Mermaid had told him once in confidence. They made their bet, and the Mermaid said to the sailor, "I am about to dive underwater, and if in half an hour's time you don't see me coming back, and in my place some blood drops rise to the surface, I will be dead, and you should go."

And so the sailor took a ring off his finger and threw it in the water and the Mermaid dove down into the depths of the sea; but she was not to be seen again. A half hour later the water turned reddish, and the sailor understood.[2]

LITERARY TALES

Legend of Melusina[1]

Jean d'Arras produced the first literary version of Mélusine, or Melusina, at the end of the fourteenth century, and it remains one of the most well-known mermaid stories.[2] Summarized here in Thomas Keightley's nineteenth-century account, this French medieval romance emphasizes how deeply taken Raymondin (Raymond in this translation) is with Mélusine's beauty when he first meets her at a fountain in the forest. He marries her and cares for her to the point that, when he first discovers her snake tail, he is not horrified but only saddened. Like the Sirens in the Odyssey, Mélusine, with her serpent tail, is not originally represented as a mermaid. A fairy who has been cursed with turning into a half snake, half woman every Saturday, she keeps her secret hidden, and makes it a condition of their marriage that Raymondin must not see her on Saturdays. Overall, she is presented as powerful and noble, as she makes Raymondin wealthy and magically builds him a castle. When he breaks his promise, she leaves, flying away in her winged-snake or dragon form; however, she continues to appear to her descendants, reasserting her ghostly presence in the castle. While in other folkloric and literary Mélusine tales, the husband immediately denounces her shape as demonic, d'Arras allows for more complexity in the couple's relationship—both by making Mélusine's snake tail the result of a curse and by depicting her as a good wife and mother.

Mélusine's tale is part of the category of mermaid stories that focuses on a water being's life in the human social world. Other animal brides, like the selkie wives, when married to humans have human bodies, but Mélusine continues to shapeshift on Saturdays. She is not a captive, having made a pact with her husband. More generally, the nature of her hybridity fluctuates: in illustrations, her dragonlike or serpentine tail

gives way over time to a mermaid's tail, and eventually to two
fishtails. This transformation from a half snake, half woman
into a mermaid may be tied to d'Arras's situating her near
water—a fountain and her bath—and to the fact that dragons
and serpents have scales, just like fish. In a Christian frame-
work, this transformation also helps to make her a more posi-
tive character, since fish and water hold a redemptive symbolism,
while dragons are more demonic. Starting in the nineteenth
century, a version of this story became part of Luxembourg's
foundational national myth, featuring the split-tailed Mélusine
with the nation's founder, Siegfroid, in the part of Raymondin.

Elinas, king of Albania, to divert his grief for the death of
his wife, amused himself with hunting. One day, at the chase,
he went to a fountain to quench his thirst: as he approached
it he heard the voice of a woman singing, and on coming to it
he found there the beautiful Fay Pressina.

After some time the Fay bestowed her hand upon him, on
the condition that he should never visit her at the time of her
lying-in. She had three daughters at a birth: Melusina, Melior,
and Palatina. Nathas, the king's son by a former wife, hastened to convey the joyful tidings to his father, who, without
reflection, flew to the chamber of the queen, and entered as she
was bathing her daughters. Pressina, on seeing him, cried out
that he had broken his word, and she must depart; and taking
up her three daughters, she disappeared.

She retired to the Lost Island;[3] so called because it was only
by chance any, even those who had repeatedly visited it, could
find it. Here she reared her children, taking them every morning to a high mountain, whence Albania might be seen, and
telling them that but for their father's breach of promise they
might have lived happily in the distant land which they beheld.
When they were fifteen years of age, Melusina asked her
mother particularly of what their father had been guilty. On
being informed of it, she conceived the design of being re-
venged on him. Engaging her sisters to join in her plans, they

set out for Albania: arrived there, they took the king and all his wealth, and, by a charm, inclosed him in a high mountain, called Brandelois. On telling their mother what they had done, she, to punish them for the unnatural action, condemned Melusina to become every Saturday a serpent, from the waist downwards, till she should meet a man who would marry her under the condition of never seeing her on a Saturday, and should keep his promise. She inflicted other judgements on her two sisters, less severe in proportion to their guilt. Melusina now went roaming through the world in search of the man who was to deliver her. She passed through the Black Forest, and that of Ardennes, and at last she arrived in the forest of Colombiers, in Poitou, where all the Fays of the neighbourhood came before her, telling her they had been waiting for her to reign in that place.

Raymond having accidentally killed the count, his uncle, by the glancing aside of his boar-spear, was wandering by night in the forest of Colombiers. He arrived at a fountain that rose at the foot of a high rock. This fountain was called by the people the Fountain of Thirst, or the Fountain of the Fays,[4] on account of the many marvellous things which had happened at it. At the time, when Raymond arrived at the fountain, three ladies were diverting themselves there by the light of the moon, the principal of whom was Melusina. Her beauty and her amiable manners quickly won his love: she soothed him, concealed the deed he had done, and married him, he promising on his oath never to desire to see her on a Saturday. She assured him that a breach of his oath would for ever deprive him of her whom he so much loved, and be followed by the unhappiness of both for life. Out of her great wealth, she built for him, in the neighbourhood of the Fountain of Thirst, where he first saw her, the castle of Lusignan. She also built La Rochelle, Cloitre Malliers, Mersent, and other places.

But destiny, that would have Melusina single, was incensed against her. The marriage was made unhappy by the deformity of the children born of one that was enchanted; but still Raymond's love for the beauty that ravished both heart and eyes remained unshaken. Destiny now renewed her attacks.

Raymond's cousin had excited him to jealousy and to secret concealment, by malicious suggestions of the purport of the Saturday retirement of the countess. He hid himself; and then saw how the lovely form of Melusina ended below in a snake, gray and sky-blue, mixed with white. But it was not horror that seized him at the sight, it was infinite anguish at the reflection that through his breach of faith he might lose his lovely wife for ever. Yet this misfortune had not speedily come on him, were it not that his son, Geoffroi with the tooth,[5] had burned his brother Freimund, who would stay in the abbey of Malliers, with the abbot and a hundred monks. At which the afflicted father, count Raymond, when his wife Melusina was entering his closet to comfort him, broke out into these words against her, before all the courtiers who attended her:—"Out of my sight, thou pernicious snake and odious serpent! thou contaminator of my race!"

Melusina's former anxiety was now verified, and the evil that had lain so long in ambush had now fearfully sprung on him and her. At these reproaches she fainted away; and when at length she revived, full of the profoundest grief, she declared to him that she must now depart from him, and, in obedience to a decree of destiny, fleet about the earth in pain and suffering, as a spectre, until the day of doom; and that only when one of her race was to die at Lusignan would she become visible.

Her words at parting were these:

"But one thing will I say unto thee before I part, that thou, and those who for more than a hundred years shall succeed thee, shall know that whenever I am seen to hover over the fair castle of Lusignan, then will it be certain that in that very year the castle will get a new lord; and though people may not perceive me in the air, yet they will see me by the Fountain of Thirst; and thus shall it be so long as the castle stands in honour and flourishing—especially on the Friday before the lord of the castle shall die." Immediately, with wailing and loud lamentation, she left the castle of Lusignan,[6] and has ever since existed as a spectre of the night. Raymond died as a hermit on Monserrat.

Fortunio and
the Siren[1,2]

The Pleasant Nights, *a collection of tales by Giovan Francesco Straparola (1550–1553), includes a few tales that are recognizably fairy tales, though such a genre had not been named yet.*

"Fortunio and the Siren" intertwines popular fairy-tale motifs and events: the unpromising hero, grateful animals, a bride contest, and a supernatural abduction. The hero's encounter with the sirena (the Italian word sirena is the equivalent of both "Siren" and "mermaid" in English) appears to be serendipitous, but it results from his adoptive mother's curse—that is, his own bad fortune. The mermaid's song, somewhat reminiscent of Homer's Sirens, seduces Fortunio, obliging him to spend several years with her in the depths of the ocean, but we have no details about her undersea world or their time together. As his name suggests, in the end, good fortune is on his side and brings him success. Fortunio is rescued by his bold and loyal wife, who brings their son as well as precious objects to aid her in her quest. As Fortunio is quick to demonstrate his desire to return to his wife, she stands in contrast to both his mother and the mermaid.

As the earliest known printed version of this tale, "Fortunio and the Siren" offers an entry point into thinking about mermaids in the European literary and fairy-tale traditions. Versions of "The Mermaid in the Pond," Fortunio's tale type, were later collected from the oral tradition in Europe in the nineteenth century, and we also find literary adaptations in French and German. While the tale is not well known in our times, it used to be popular, and we have included in this volume two other versions, the Grimms' tale "The Nixie in the Pond" and "The Mermaid" from Greek oral tradition. Good or bad

*fortune does not play much of a role in these later versions; for
instance, in the Grimms' tale, the pact between the miller and
the nixie points to how the family is indebted to the nixie: while
this gains her no sympathy in the storyworld, the boy is owed
to her.*

There was once a man named Bernio, who lived in the outer
regions of Lombardy. Though fortune had not been kind to
him, he had a good heart and good head on his shoulders. One
day he married a valiant and gracious woman named Alchia.
Though she was of low origin, she was nevertheless endowed
with brains and commendable manners and loved her husband
as dearly as any woman could. They desired very much to have
children, but God did not grant them this gift perhaps because
man does not know what will be best for him when he asks for
things. Still, they both continued to want a child, and since
fortune kept going against them, they decided at last to adopt
a child whom they would nurture and raise as their own legitimate son.

So, early one morning they went to a place where young
children who had been abandoned by their parents were left,
and seeing one that appeared more handsome and charming
than the others, they took him home with them, named him
Fortunio, and brought him up with utmost diligence and disci-
pline. Now, it so happened—in accordance with the wishes
and will of He who rules the universe and tempers and modifies everything—that Alchia became pregnant, and when the
time of delivery arrived, she gave birth to a boy who completely resembled his father. As a result, both the mother and
the father were incredibly happy and gave their son the name
of Valentino.

The boy was well nurtured and educated, and he grew up
with good manners and qualities. Moreover, he loved his
brother, Fortunio, so much that he despaired whenever he was
not with him. But discord, the enemy of everything good, became aware of their warm and fervid friendship, and not being

able to tolerate their affection for one another, it intervened and worked its evil so effectively that the brothers soon began to taste its bitter fruits.

One day, as they were fooling around with one another, as boys are apt to do, their play became heated, and Valentino, who could not bear that Fortunio was better in their game, exploded with such anger and fury that he called Fortunio a bastard several times and the son of a vile woman. When Fortunio heard those words, he was very astonished and disturbed, and turning to Valentino, he said, "What do you mean, I'm a bastard?"

In reply, Valentino muttered angrily between his teeth and repeated what he had said. Consequently, Fortunio was so disturbed that he stopped playing and left. He went straight to his so-called mother and politely asked her whether he was the son of Bernio and herself. Alchia responded with a yes, and once she learned that Valentino had insulted Fortunio with vicious words, she scolded the latter soundly and swore that she would punish him severely if he ever did something like that again. But the words that Alchia spoke only aroused suspicion in Fortunio, and he thus became certain that he was not her legitimate son. Indeed, he often sought to test her to see whether he really was her son and to know the truth. Seeing how obstinate Fortunio was and not being able to resist his pleas, Alchia finally told him that he was not her true son, but that he had been adopted and raised in their house for the love of God and to alleviate the faults of her and her husband. Upon hearing these words, Fortunio felt as if he had been stabbed in the heart many times, and he was tormented all the more. He could barely endure the grief, but he could also not bring himself to use violence and to kill himself. So, he decided to leave Bernio's house and to wander around the world to see if fortune would treat him more favorably in time.

When Alchia saw that Fortunio's desire to leave grew stronger each day and that she could not find any way to prevent him from carrying out his plans, she became enraged, cursed him, and prayed to God that if he should ever take a journey by sea, he would be swallowed up by sirens just as ships are by the stormy and high waves. But Fortunio, driven by the impetuous wind of indignation and wrath, did not care about the maternal curse, and without saying farewell to his parents, he departed and set out in the direction of the west.

As he journeyed, he passed lakes, valleys, mountains, and other wild places. Finally, early one morning, he came upon a densely covered forest. As soon as he entered, he found a wolf, an eagle, and an ant quarreling over the body of a dead stag because they could not agree on how to divide the meat among themselves. After Fortunio had come unexpectedly upon the three animals in midst of their hard dispute and none of them willing to yield to the others, they agreed after a while that the young man should resolve their argument and give each one of them some part of the meat that he thought would be most suitable. They also promised to be content with his final decision and not seek to contradict it, even though it might seem unjust. Then Fortunio undertook the task, and after he carefully investigated everything, he divided the prey among them in the following manner. To the wolf, who was a voracious animal with sharp teeth, he gave all the bones of the deer and all the lean flesh as reward for his hard work. To the eagle, a rapacious bird without teeth, he gave the entrails and all the fat lying around the lean parts and the bones. To the granivorous and diligent ant, which lacked the strength that nature had bestowed upon the wolf and the eagle, he gave the soft brains as her reward for her arduous work. Each one of the animals was very content with this just and reasonable decision, and they thanked Fortunio as best they knew and could for the favor that he had done for them. And since ingratitude is the most reprehensible of all the vices, the three animals agreed that the young man should not depart until they had rewarded him extremely well for the service he had done them. Thus, after acknowledging the decision, the wolf said, "My brother, I'm going to give you a certain power so that, if at any time you want to become a wolf, all you have to say is: 'If only I were a wolf.' And you will immediately be transformed into a wolf. At the same time you will be able to return to your former shape whenever you so desire."

Both the eagle and the ant rewarded him with the same power to assume their shapes whenever he wanted. Then Fortunio, extremely pleased by their gifts, thanked the animals as best he knew how and could and took his leave. He continued his journey until he finally arrived in Polonia, a noble and populous city, which was at that time under the rule of Odescalco, a powerful and valorous king who had only one child, a daughter named Doralice. Now, since the king was eager to arrange an honorable marriage for this princess, he had proclaimed throughout his kingdom that a great tournament was to take place and the winner in the jousts was to receive Princess Doralice as his bride. Many dukes, counts, and other powerful nobles from all over had already gathered in Polonia to contend for this precious prize. The first day of the tournament had already passed, and the jousting was won by a foul Saracen, who was deformed and strange and had a face as black as pitch. When the king's daughter saw the warped and filthy figure of the Saracen, she was extremely upset that he had carried away the honors of the day. Burying her face, crimson with shame, in her tender and delicate hands, she wept and bemoaned her hard and cruel fate, longing to die rather than to marry the deformed Saracen.

In the meantime, Fortunio entered the city and saw the splendid pomp and the grand competition of the contestants, and when he learned why this glorious tournament was being held, he ardently desired to show his valor in the jousts. But when he realized that he lacked all the equipment necessary for such competition, he lamented his situation. While he was contemplating his predicament, he raised his eyes to the sky and caught sight of Princess Doralice, who was leaning out of one of the large windows of the palace. She was surrounded by a group of lovely and noble dames and damsels and stood out among them like the radiant clear sun does among the lesser lights of heaven.

When it eventually became dark and all the ladies had retired to their apartments, Doralice, sad and alone, went to a small and beautifully decorated chamber. While she was standing by her open window, Fortunio was there below her.

As soon as he saw her, he said to himself, "If only I were an eagle!" No sooner did he utter these words than he became an eagle and flew through the window of her chamber, where he became a man again. When he stepped toward Doralice with a light and joyful air to present himself, she was completely bewildered and began to shout in a loud voice as if she were being torn apart by hungry dogs. The king, who was in a nearby apartment, heard her cries and ran to help her. She told him that there was a young man in the room, and he ordered the servants to search every corner. When nothing was found, they all went back to bed. Indeed, Fortunio had changed himself back into an eagle and had flown out of the chamber. However, no sooner had the father returned to his room to rest than the maiden began to shout once more because Fortunio had come back. This time, when the young man heard the girl's cries he feared for his life, changed himself into an ant, and hid himself beneath the blond tresses of the lovely maiden's hair. When King Odescalco heard his daughter's shouts, he ran to her again, but when he found nothing a second time, he was greatly disturbed and threatened her with harsh words that if she were to cry out again, he would play some joke on her that would not be to her liking. Thus he left her in an angry mood and thought that she had imagined seeing one or another of the contestants who, out of love for her, had been killed in the tournament. Fortunio had listened closely to what the king had told his daughter, and when he saw him leave, he discarded the shape of the ant and returned to his own form. As soon as Doralice saw him, she wanted to jump out of bed and scream, but Fortunio prevented her from doing this by placing one of his hands on her lips and whispering, "My lady, I have not come here to dishonor you or steal your virtue. I have come rather to comfort you and to declare myself your most humble servant. But if you cry out, one or two things will happen. Either your reputation and fair name will be tarnished, or you will be the cause of your death and mine. Therefore, oh lady of my heart, do not stain your honor and simultaneously endanger our lives."

While Fortunio was saying these words, Doralice was shedding a flood of tears. She could barely stand this fearful assault. But Fortunio realized how disturbed the lady was, and he kept talking to her with the sweetest of words that would have melted a heart of stone. Finally Doralice's stubborn will softened, and she was conquered by his tender way, which pacified her. When she also saw how handsome the young man's face was, and how strong and well-built his body was in comparison to the ugly, deformed Saracen, she began to feel tormented again by the thought that the Saracen as victor might soon possess her. While she was contemplating her lamentable situation, the young man said to her, "Dear lady, if I had some way, I would gladly enter the tournament, and I would win the heart that belongs to the victor."

"If this were to happen, my lord," she replied, "there is indeed none other to whom I would give myself but you."

Recognizing how ardent and how well disposed he was to her, the princess gave him a great deal of jewels and money, which Fortunio accepted with all his heart. Then he asked her what garment she wished him to wear in the tournament, and she said, "Dress in white satin," and he intended to do as she requested.

On the following day, Fortunio was dressed in polished armor covered by a coat of white satin that was hand-carved and embroidered with the finest gold. He mounted a powerful and fiery steed, decked in the same colors that he wore. Then he rode into the piazza unknown to anyone there. The people in the crowd had already gathered to watch the grand spectacle, and when they saw the gallant unknown knight with lance in hand ready for the joust, everyone stared and marveled at him. Indeed, they began asking, "Who could this brave and glorious knight be who has entered the tournament? Does anyone know him?"

In the meantime, Fortunio had joined the lists and called upon his rival to advance. Then the knights lowered the points of their knotty lances and charged at each other like two lions let loose upon one another. Fortunio dealt such a grave below to the head of the Saracen that the latter was knocked out of the saddle of his horse and crashed to the ground as if he had been broken like glass thrown against a wall. No matter what contestant he met that day, Fortunio came away the victor. The princess was very happy and watched Fortunio intently with the deepest admiration. She thanked God in her heart for having delivered her from the bonds of the Saracen and prayed to Him to let Fortunio win all the laurels.

When night arrived, Doralice was summoned to dinner, but she did not want to go. So she commanded the servants to bring her some delicious food and precious wine to her chamber, pretending that she did not have much appetite at present but perhaps she would eat later on. After locking herself alone in her chamber, she opened the window and watched with ardent desire for the arrival of her lover. When Fortunio returned like the previous night, they dined together with great joy. Then he asked her how she would like him to dress for the tournament the next day, and she replied, "I would like you to wear green satin embroidered with the finest threads of silver and gold, and your horse is to be decked in the same way."

On the following morning Fortunio appeared just as Doralice had requested. He presented himself in the piazza at the appointed time and demonstrated his valor as he had done on the day before and even more. And everyone shouted that he deserved to win the lovely princess.

When evening came, the princess was very cheerful and happy. She used the same pretext to excuse herself from dinner as she had done the previous day. After locking the door of her chamber and opening the window, she waited for the valorous Fortunio and had a pleasant meal with him. When he asked once more what color he should wear the following day, she answered, "I would like you to wear crimson satin embroidered with gold and pearls, and I would like your horse to be decked in the same fashion because I myself shall be wearing the same colors."

"Lady," replied Fortunio, "if by some chance, I should be somewhat late in making my entry into the lists, do not be astonished, for I shall not be late without good reason."

When the third day came and the tournament began, the spectators awaited the outcome of the glorious contest with great joy, but because of the indomitable power of the gallant unknown knight, none of the contestants wanted to enter the lists against him. Meanwhile, his own whereabouts were not known, and the princess began to suspect something, especially since she did not know where he was. Indeed, she was overcome by so much torment that she fainted and fell to the ground. But as soon as she heard that the unknown knight was approaching the large piazza, her failing spirits began to revive.

Fortunio was clad in rich and sumptuous garments, and his horse was decked with the finest cloth, embroidered with shining rubies, emeralds, sapphires, and large pearls that, according to everyone present, were worth a kingdom. Once the brave Fortunio arrived at the piazza, the people all cried out, "Long live the unknown knight!" and applauded vigorously by clapping their hands. Then Fortunio entered the lists and fought so valiantly that he sent all his opponents to the ground and triumphed in glory. After he had dismounted from his powerful horse, the leading men of the city hoisted him on their shoulders and carried him to the king amid the sound of trumpets and other musical instruments and loud shouts that went up to the heavens. When they had taken off his helmet and shining armor, the king saw a charming young man. Then he summoned his daughter and had them wed. The marriage was celebrated with the greatest pomp, and the party went on for an entire month.

After Fortunio had lived some time with his beloved wife, it appeared to him improper and somewhat deplorable to be so idle, merely counting the hours as they passed like those fools who make nothing out of their lives. Therefore, he decided to depart and go to places where he could demonstrate his valor. So, he prepared a ship and took a large treasure which his father-in-law had given him. Then he took leave of his wife and King Odescalco and embarked on a voyage. Prospering from gentle and favorable winds, he sailed until he reached the Atlantic Ocean. But before he had gone more than ten leagues, the most beautiful siren that had ever been seen appeared at the side of the ship and began singing softly. Fortunio leaned over the side of the ship to listen to her song, and soon he fell asleep. While he was dozing, the siren drew him gently into her arms and plunged with him deep into the ocean. The sailors were not able to save him and broke out into loud cries of sorrow. Grief-stricken and disconsolate, they decked the ship with black cloth and returned to the unfortunate and unhappy Odescalco to tell him about the horrible and lamentable accident they had had at sea.

When King Odescalco, Doralice, and the entire city heard about this, they were overcome with grief and began dressing themselves in black. Soon thereafter, Doralice, who had been pregnant, gave birth to a beautiful boy, who was gently and carefully raised until he was two. At this time, the sad and tormented Doralice, who kept thinking about her beloved and dear husband, began to abandon hope of ever seeing him again. But noble and brave as she was, she decided to test her fortune and to go and search for him on the deep seas, even if her father would not consent to let her depart. She ordered a ship to be prepared for her voyage, and it was well equipped and well armed. She also took with her three apples, marvelously wrought, one made out of brass, another out of silver, and the last out of the finest gold. Then, after she took leave of her father the king, she embarked with her son and sailed into the open sea with a propitious wind.

As the sad lady sailed over a calm sea, she asked the sailors to take her to the very spot where her husband had been snared by the siren, and they carried out her orders. When the ship reached this spot, the child began to shed a flood of tears, and the mother was completely unable to pacify him. So, she took the apple made of brass and gave it to the boy. While he was playing with the apple, the siren noticed him and approached the ship. After she lifted her head out of the foamy waves, she said to Doralice, "Lady, give me that apple, for I'm very much taken by it."

But the princess answered she would not give it to her because it was her child's toy.

"If you will give it to me," the siren said. "I shall show you your husband up to his breast."

When Doralice heard these words, she gave the siren the apple because she desired to see her husband. The siren rewarded her for the precious gift and did as she had promised and showed the husband up to his breast. Then she plunged with him into the depths of the ocean and disappeared from sight.

As Doralice watched everything attentively, she longed to see her husband even more. Not knowing what to do or what to say, she sought comfort with her child, and when the little one began to cry once more, the mother gave him the silver apple. But once again the siren saw the apple and asked Doralice to give it to her. But the princess shrugged her shoulders and said that the apple was her child's toy and could not be given away. Thereupon, the siren said, "If you will give me this apple, which is far more beautiful than the other, I promise to show you your husband down to his knees."

Poor Doralice, who desired to see her husband more than ever, put the love of her husband before that of her son and cheerfully handed the apple to the siren, who kept her promise and then plunged back into the sea with Fortunio. Meanwhile, Doralice watched in silence and uncertainty, and she had no idea how to free her husband. She picked up her child in her arms, tried to comfort herself with him and to still his weeping. Remembering the apple with which he had been playing, the child continued crying so that mother gave him the golden apple to appease him. When the greedy siren caught sight of his apple and saw that it was more beautiful than the other two, she demanded it at once as a gift from Doralice. She insisted so much that the mother conceded against her will and took it away from her son. In return the siren promised that she would show her husband in his entirely, and in order to carry out her promise, the siren came close to the ship carrying Fortunio on her back. Then she rose somewhat above the surface of the water to reveal him from head to foot. However, as soon as Fortunio felt that he was above the water and resting free on the back of the siren, he was filled with joy, and without hesitating a moment, he cried out, "Oh, if only I were an eagle!"

As soon as he said this, he was immediately transformed into an eagle, and he flew to the mast of the ship. All the sailors watched him as he then descended to the main deck and returned to his proper shape. Then he kissed and embraced his wife and his child and all the sailors. Together they all celebrated Fortunio's rescue, and they sailed back to King Odescalco's kingdom. No sooner did they enter the harbor than they began to play their trumpets, drums, castanets, and other instruments that they had with them. When the king heard the music, he was very much astonished and waited with suspense to learn what all this meant. Soon a herald came to announce to the king that his dear daughter had arrived with her husband, Fortunio. When they had disembarked from the ship, they all went to the palace, where they were welcomed with a grand and glorious celebration.

After some days had passed, Fortunio returned to his old home and changed himself into a wolf. Then he devoured Alchia, his wicked mother, and Valentino, his brother, in revenge for the harm that they had done to him. Afterward, he returned to his natural form, mounted his horse, and rode back to his father-in-law's kingdom, where he lived in peace with Doralice, his dear and beloved wife, for many years to the great delight of them both.

The Day after the Wedding,
from *Undine*[1]

A German writer of French ancestry, Friedrich de la Motte
Fouqué (1777–1843) published his novella Undine in 1811,
which George MacDonald, Scottish author of fantasy literature and Christian minister, identified as the "most beautiful"
of fairy tales in his essay "The Fantastic Imagination" (1893).
This is perhaps not surprising given the role that Christianity
plays in Undine.

Undine, a bubbly beauty who was adopted as a child by a
fisherman and his wife, marries a knight named Huldbrand.
She loves him, and after the wedding she reveals to him she is
really a water princess who, thanks to their marriage, now has
a soul. Entranced by her beauty, Huldbrand accepts her somewhat extravagant behavior. Unfortunately, some time later,
Huldbrand's heart begins to turn from Undine to his fellow
mortal Bertalda, whom Undine has been treating like a sister.
After a number of twists and turns that include Undine's pre-
sumed death and the wedding of Huldbrand and Bertalda, the
tale ends with Huldbrand's death and Undine's transformation
into a body of water surrounding his grave.

Undine's influence on Hans Christian Andersen's well-
known tale "The Little Mermaid" is clear and acknowledged.
In both stories, a beautiful mermaid is loyal to her human love
object and inspired by the prospect of acquiring a soul. Genre,
however, makes a difference in how the two stories approach
the soulless mermaid's desire to be human and be loved by one.
In Andersen's fairy tale for children, the little mermaid trades
with the sea witch, but remains otherwise childlike and innocent. In La Motte Fouqué's gothic fairy-tale novella, the water
princess Undine, in spite of her absolute loyalty, is accused of

being a "witch, who has intercourse with evil spirits." Unlike Andersen's mute heroine, Undine also delivers a number of significant speeches, one of them in the chapter that follows, in which Undine reveals to Huldbrand that he married a water princess in search of a soul.

The fresh light of the morning awoke the young married pair. Wonderful and horrible dreams had disturbed Huldbrand's rest; he had been haunted by spectres, who, grinning at him by stealth, had tried to disguise themselves as beautiful women, and from beautiful women they all at once assumed the faces of dragons, and when he started up from these hideous visions, the moonlight shone pale and cold into the room; terrified he looked at Undine, who still lay in unaltered beauty and grace. Then he would press a light kiss upon her rosy lips, and would fall asleep again only to be awakened by new terrors. After he had reflected on all this, now that he was fully awake, he reproached himself for any doubt that could have led him into error with regard to his beautiful wife. He begged her to forgive him for the injustice he had done her, but she only held out to him her fair hand, sighed deeply and remained silent. But a glance of exquisite fervour beamed from her eyes such as he had never seen before, carrying with it the full assurance that Undine bore him no ill-will. He then rose cheerfully and left her, to join his friends in the common apartment.

He found the three sitting round the hearth, with an air of anxiety about them, as if they dared not venture to speak aloud. The priest seemed to be praying in his inmost spirit that all evil might be averted. When, however, they saw the young husband come forth so cheerfully, the careworn expression of their faces vanished.

The old fisherman even began to jest with the knight, so pleasantly, that the aged wife smiled good-humouredly as she listened to them. Undine at length made her appearance. All rose to meet her, and all stood still with surprize, for the young wife seemed so strange to them and yet the same. The priest was the first to advance towards her, with paternal affection beaming in his face, and, as he raised his hand to bless her, the beautiful woman sank reverently on her knees before him. With a few humble and gracious words, she begged him to forgive her for any foolish things she might have said the evening before, and entreated him in an agitated tone to pray for the welfare of her soul. She then rose, kissed her foster-parents, and thanking them for all the goodness they had shewn her, she exclaimed: "Oh! I now feel in my innermost heart, how much, how infinitely much, you have done for me, dear, kind people!" She could not at first desist from her caresses, but scarcely had she perceived that the old woman was busy in preparing breakfast, than she went to the hearth, cooked and arranged the meal, and would not suffer the good old mother to take the least trouble.

She continued thus throughout the whole day, quiet, kind, and attentive, — at once a little matron and a tender bashful girl. The three who had known her longest, expected every moment to see some whimsical vagary of her capricious spirit burst forth. But they waited in vain for it. Undine remained as mild and gentle as an angel. The holy father could not take his eyes from her, and he said repeatedly to the bridegroom: "The goodness of heaven, sir, has entrusted a treasure to you yesterday through me, unworthy as I am; cherish it as you ought, and it will promote your temporal and eternal welfare."

Towards evening, Undine was hanging on the knight's arm with humble tenderness, and drew him gently out of the door, where the declining sun was shining pleasantly on the fresh grass, and upon the tall slender stems of the trees. The eyes of the young wife were moist, as with the dew of sadness and love, and a tender and fearful secret seemed hovering on her lips, which however was only disclosed by scarcely audible sighs. She led her husband onward and onward in silence; when he spoke, she only answered him with looks, in which, it is true, there lay no direct reply to his enquiries, but a whole heaven of love and timid devotion. Thus they reached the edge of the swollen forest-stream, and the knight was astonished to see it rippling along in gentle waves, without a trace of its former wildness and swell. "By the morning, it will be quite dry," said the beautiful wife, in a regretful tone, "and you can then travel away wherever you will, without anything to hinder you." "Not without you, my little Undine," replied the knight, laughing; "remember, even if I wished to desert you, the church, and the spiritual powers, and the emperor, and the empire, would interpose and bring the fugitive back again." "All depends upon you, all depends upon you," whispered his wife, half weeping, and half smiling. "I think, however, nevertheless, that you will keep me with you; I love you so heartily. Now carry me across to that little island, that lies before us. The matter shall be decided there. I could easily indeed glide through the rippling waves, but it is so restful in your arms, and if you were to cast me off, I shall have sweetly rested in them once more for the last time." Huldbrand, full as he was of strange fear and emotion, knew not what to reply. He took her in his arms and carried her across, remembering now for the first time that this was the same little island from which he had borne her back to the old fisherman on that first night. On the farther side, he put her down on the soft grass and was on the point of placing himself lovingly near his beautiful burden, when she said: "No, there, opposite to me! I will read my sentence in your eyes, before your lips speak; now, listen attentively to what I will relate to you." And she began:

"You must know, my loved one, that there are beings in the elements which almost appear like mortals, and which rarely allow themselves to become visible to your race. Wonderful salamanders glitter and sport in the flames; lean and malicious gnomes dwell deep within the earth; spirits, belonging to the air, wander through the forests; and a vast family of water spirits live in the lakes and streams and brooks. In resounding domes of crystal, through which the sky looks in with its sun and stars, these latter spirits find their beautiful abode; lofty trees of coral with blue and crimson fruits gleam in their gardens; they wander over the pure sand of the sea, and among lovely variegated shells, and amid all exquisite treasures of the old world, which the present is no longer worthy to enjoy; all these the floods have covered with their secret veils of silver, and the noble monuments sparkle below, stately and solemn, and bedewed by the loving waters which allure from them many a beautiful moss-flower and entwining cluster of sea grass. Those, however, who dwell there, are very fair and lovely to behold, and for the most part, are more beautiful than human beings. Many a fisherman has been so fortunate as to surprise some tender mermaid, as she rose above the waters and sang. He would then tell afar of her beauty, and such wonderful beings have been given the name of Undines. You, however, are now actually beholding an Undine."

The knight tried to persuade himself that his beautiful wife was under the spell of one of her strange humours, and that she was taking pleasure in teazing him with one of her extravagant inventions. But repeatedly as he said this to himself, he could not believe it for a moment; a strange shudder passed through him; unable to utter a word, he stared at the beautiful narrator with an immoveable gaze. Undine shook her head sorrowfully, drew a deep sigh, and then proceeded as follows:

"Our condition would be far superior to that of other human beings, — for human beings we call ourselves, being similar to them in form and culture, — but there is one evil peculiar to us. We and our like in the other elements, vanish into dust, and pass away, body and spirit, so that not a vestige of us remains behind; and when you mortals hereafter awake to a purer life, we remain with the sand and the sparks and the wind and the waves. Hence we have also no souls; the element moves us, and is often obedient to us while we live, though it scatters us to dust when we die; and we are merry, without having aught to grieve us, — merry as the nightingales and little gold-fishes and other pretty children of nature. But all beings aspire to be higher than they are. Thus my father, who is a powerful water-prince in the Mediterranean Sea, desired that his only daughter should become possessed of a soul, even though she must then endure many of the sufferings of those thus endowed. Such as we are, however, can only obtain a soul by the closest union of affection with one of your human race. I am now possessed of a soul, and my soul thanks you, my inexpressibly beloved one, and it will ever thank you, if you do

not make my whole life miserable. For what is to become of
me, if you avoid and reject me? Still I would not retain you by
deceit. And if you mean to reject me, do so now, and return
alone to the shore. I will dive into this brook, which is my
uncle; and here in the forest, far removed from other friends,
he passes his strange and solitary life. He is however powerful,
and is esteemed and beloved by many great streams; and as he
brought me hither to the fisherman, a light-hearted laughing
child, he will take me back again to my parents, a loving, suffering, and soul-endowed woman."

She was about to say still more, but Huldbrand embraced
her with the most heartfelt emotion and love, and bore her
back again to the shore. It was not till he reached it, that he
swore amid tears and kisses, never to forsake his sweet wife,
calling himself more happy than the Greek Pygmalion, whose
beautiful statue received life from Venus and became his loved
one. In endearing confidence, Undine walked back to the cottage, leaning on his arm; feeling now for the first time with all
her heart, how little she ought to regret the forsaken crystal
palaces of her mysterious father.

The Little Mermaid[1]

In 1837, Hans Christian Andersen (1805–1875) published "The Little Mermaid" in Danish; its first English-language translation appeared in 1846. "The Little Mermaid" is now Andersen's most popular fairy tale, thanks in part to the 1989 Disney animated film adaptation that gave it a new interpretation and ending.

A literary tale that was possibly inspired by one of Andersen's unhappy love experiences, "The Little Mermaid" draws on a web of stories in which the mermaid comes into the human world to marry, rather than seducing humans into her realm. The other best-known stories in this tradition are the medieval tale of the fairy Mélusine and Friedrich de La Motte Fouqué's German novella about Undine. In contrast to both Mélusine and Undine, various aspects of Andersen's tale conspire to represent the mermaid as "little": she is the youngest of six sea-princesses; she has just turned fifteen when she catches sight of her human love interest; the prince calls her "his little foundling" and loves her "just as one loves a dear, good child"; and in the end she becomes one of the "children of the air." Like her story ancestors, the Sirens, this little mermaid has the most beautiful singing voice, but she trades it for legs so she can be with the prince in the human world, and entertains him by dancing. Her two legs perhaps symbolically signal her sexual maturity, but the sharp physical pain in her legs when she walks and dances is a constant reminder of how she does not belong at the prince's court. Her love for the prince, like Mélusine's and Undine's, ends unhappily, but unlike them, the little mermaid never has a name or an actual romance. As she dissolves into an air spirit, her final transformation brings her closer to having a soul, thus exemplifying self-sacrifice as a form of self-fulfillment.

Andersen's little mermaid acquired a name in the Disney film—Ariel, which resonates with spirit and aria—and regained her voice, a powerful agent of her happy ending.[2]

Far out at sea, the water is as blue as the prettiest cornflowers, and as clear as the purest crystal. But it is very deep—so deep, indeed, that no rope can fathom it; and many church steeples need be piled one upon the other to reach from the bottom to the surface. It is there that the sea-folk dwell.

Nor must it be imagined that there is nothing but a bare, white, sandy ground below. No, indeed! The soil produces the most curious trees and flowers, whose leaves and stems are so flexible that the slightest motion of the waters seems to fluster them as if they were living creatures. Fishes, great and small, glide through the branches as birds fly through the trees here upon earth. In the deepest spot of all stands the sea-king's palace; its walls are of coral, and its tall pointed windows of the clearest amber, while the roof is made of mussel shells, that open and shut according to the tide. And beautiful they look, for in each shell lies a pearl, any one of which would be worthy to be placed in a queen's crown.

The sea-king had been a widower for many years, so his aged mother kept house for him. She was a very wise woman, but extremely proud of her noble birth, which entitled her to wear twelve oyster shells on her tail, while other well-born persons might only wear six. In all other respects she was a very praiseworthy sort of body; and especially as regards the care she took of the little princesses, her granddaughters. They were six pretty children; but the youngest was the prettiest of all. Her skin was as clear and delicate as a rose leaf, and her eyes as blue as the deepest sea; but she had no feet any more than the others, and her body ended in a fish's tail.

They were free to play about all day long in the vast rooms of the palace below water, where live flowers grew upon the walls. The large amber windows were opened, when the fishes would swim inwards to them just as the swallows fly into our houses when we open the windows; only the fishes swam right up to the princesses, ate out of their hands, and allowed themselves to be stroked.

In front of the palace was a large garden with bright red and dark blue trees, whose fruit glittered like gold, and whose blossoms were like fiery sparks, as both stalks and leaves kept rustling continually. The ground was strewn with the most delicate sand, but blue as the flames of sulphur. The whole atmosphere was of a peculiar blue tint that would have led you to believe you were hovering high up in the air, with clouds above and below you, rather than standing at the bottom of the sea. When the winds were calm, the sun was visible; and to those below it looked like a scarlet flower shedding light from its calyx.

Each of the little princesses had a plot of ground in the garden, where she might dig and plant as she pleased. One sowed her flowers so as to come up in the shape of a whale; another preferred the figure of a little mermaid; but the youngest planted hers in a circle to imitate the sun, and chose flowers as red as the sun appeared to her. She was a singular child, both silent and thoughtful; and while her sisters were delighted with all the strange things that they obtained through the wrecks of various ships, she had never claimed anything— with the exception of the red flowers that resembled the sun above—but a pretty statue, representing a handsome youth, hewn out of pure white marble that had sunk to the bottom of the sea, when a ship ran aground. She planted a bright red weeping-willow beside the statue; and when the tree grew up, its fresh boughs hung over it nearly down to the blue sands, where the shadow looked quite violet, and kept dancing about like the branches. It seemed as if the top of the tree were at play with its roots, and each trying to snatch a kiss.

There was nothing she delighted in so much as to hear about the upper world. She was always asking her grandmother to tell her all she knew about ships, towns, people, and animals. What struck her as most beautiful was that the flowers of the earth should shed perfumes, which they do not below the sea; that the forests were green, and that the fishes amongst the trees should sing so loud and so exquisitely that it must be a treat to hear them. It was the little birds that her grandmother called fishes, or else her young listeners would not have understood her, for they had never seen birds.

"When you have accomplished your fifteenth year," said the grandmother, "you shall have leave to rise up out of the sea, and sit on the rocks in the moonshine, and look at the large ships sailing past. And then you will see both forests and towns."

In the following year one of the sisters would reach the age of fifteen, but as all the rest were each a year younger than the other, the youngest would have to wait five years before it would be her turn to come up from the bottom of the ocean, and see what our world is like. However, the eldest promised to tell the others what she saw, and what struck her as most beautiful on the first day; for their grandmother did not tell them enough, and there were so many things they wanted to know.

But none of them longed for her turn to come so intensely as the youngest, who had to wait the longest, and was so reserved and thoughtful. Many a night did she stand at the open window, and gaze upwards through the dark blue water, and watch the fishes as they lashed the sea with their fins and tails. She could see the moon and stars, that appeared, indeed, rather pale, though much larger, seen through the water, than they do to us. If something resembling a black cloud glided between the stars and herself, she knew that it was either a whale swimming overhead, or a ship full of human beings, none of whom probably dreamed that a lovely little mermaid was standing below, and stretching forth her white hands towards the keel of their vessel.

The eldest princess was now fifteen, and was allowed to rise up to the surface of the sea.

On her return she had a great deal to relate; but the most delightful thing of all, she said, was to lie upon a sand-bank in the calm sea, and to gaze upon the large city near the coast, where lights were shining like hundreds of stars; to listen to the sounds of music, to the din of earriages, and the busy hum of the crowd; and to see the church steeples, and hear the bells ringing. And she longed after all these things, just because she could not approach them.

Oh, how attentively her youngest sister listened: And later in the evening, when she stood at the open window, and gazed up through the dark blue water, how she thought about the large city, with its din and bustle, and even fancied she could hear the church bells ringing from below.

In the following year, the second sister obtained leave to rise up to the surface of the water, and swim about at her pleasure. She went up just at sunset, which appeared to her the finest sight of all. She said that the whole sky appeared like gold, and as to the clouds, their beauty was beyond all description. Red and violet clouds sailed rapidly above her head, while a flock of wild swans, resembling a long white scarf, flew still faster than they across the sea towards the setting sun. She, too, swam towards it, but the sun sank down, and the rosy hues vanished from the surface of the water and from the skies.

The year after, the third sister went up. She was the boldest of them all, so she swam up a river that fell into the sea. She saw beautiful green hills covered with vines; castles and citadels peeped out from stately woods; she heard the birds singing, and the sun felt so warm that she was frequently obliged to dive down under the water to cool her burning face. In a small creek she met with a whole troop of little human children. They were naked, and dabbling about in the water. She wanted to play with them, but they flew away in great alarm, and there came a little black animal (she meant a dog, only she had never seen one before), who barked at her so tremendously that she was frightened, and sought to reach the open sea. But she should never forget the beautiful forests, the green hills, or the pretty children, who were able to swim in the water although they had no fish's tails.

The fourth sister was less daring. She remained in the midst of the sea, and maintained that it was most beautiful at that point, because from thence one could see for miles around, and the sky looked like a glass bell above one's head. She had seen ships, but only at a distance—they looked like sea-mews;

and the waggish dolphins had thrown somersaults, and the large whales had squirted water through their nostrils, so that one might fancy there were hundreds of fountains all round.

It was now the fifth sister's turn. Her birthday was in the winter, therefore she saw what the others had not seen the first time they went up. The sea looked quite green, and huge icebergs were floating about; each looked like a pearl, she said, only larger than the churches built by human beings. They were of the oddest shapes, and glittered like diamonds. She had placed herself upon the largest of them, letting the wind play with her long hair, and all the vessels scudded past in great alarm, as though fearful of approaching the spot where she was sitting, but towards evening, the sky became overcast, it thundered and lightened, while the dark sea lifted up the huge icebergs on high, so that they were illuminated by the red flashes of the lightning. All the vessels reefed in their sails, and their passengers were panic struck, while she sat quietly on her floating block of ice and watched the blue lightning as it zig-zagged along the silent sea.

The first time that each of the sisters had successively risen to the surface of the water, they had been enchanted by the novelty and beauty of all they saw; but being now grown up, and at liberty to go above as often as they pleased, they had grown indifferent to such excursions. They longed to come back into the water, and at the end of a month they had all declared that it was far more beautiful down below, and that it was pleasanter to stay at home.

It frequently happened in the evening that the five sisters would entwine their arms, and rise up to the surface of the water all in a row. They had beautiful voices, far finer than any human being's, and when a storm was coming on, and they anticipated that a ship might sink, they swam before the vessel, and sang most sweetly of the delights to be found beneath the water, begging the seafarers not to be afraid of coming down below. But the sailors could not understand what they said, and mistook their words for the howling of the tempest, and they never saw all the fine things below, for if the ship sank the men were drowned, and their bodies alone reached the sea-king's palace.

When the sisters rose up arm-in-arm through the water, the youngest would stand alone, looking after them, and felt ready to cry; only mermaids have no tears, and therefore suffer all the more.

"How I wish I were fifteen!" said she. "I am sure I shall love the world above, and the beings that inhabit it."

At last she reached the age of fifteen.

"Well, now you are grown up!" said her grandmother, the widow of the late king. "So let me dress you like your sisters." And she placed in her hair a wreath of white lilies, every leaf of which was half a pearl; and the old dame ordered eight large oyster shells to be fastened to the princess's tail, to denote her high rank.

"But they hurt me so," said the little mermaid

"Pride must suffer pain," said the old lady.

Oh! how gladly would she have shaken off all this pomp and laid aside her heavy wreath—the red flowers in her garden adorned her far better—but she could not help herself. "Farewell!" cried she, rising as lightly as a bubble to the surface of the water.

The sun had just sunk as she raised her head above the waves, but the clouds were still pink, and fringed with gold; and through the fast vanishing rosy tints of the air beamed the evening in all its beauty. The atmosphere was mild and cool, and the sea quite calm. A large ship with three masts was lying on its surface; only a single sail was hoisted, for not a breeze was stirring, and the sailors were sitting all about in the rigging. There were musical instruments playing, and voices singing; and when the evening grew darker, hundreds of gay-coloured lanterns were lighted, which looked like the flags of all nations streaming through the air. The little mermaid swam close to the cabin window, and as often as the water lifted her up, she peeped in through the transparent panes, and saw a number of well-dressed persons. But the handsomest of all was the prince, with large, dark eyes; he could not be above sixteen, and it was *his* birthday that was being celebrated with such magnificence. The sailors danced upon deck, and when the young prince came up above a hundred rockets were let off, that lit the air till it was as bright as day, and so frightened the little mermaid that she dived under the water. But she soon popped out her head once more, when all the stars in heaven seemed to be falling down upon her. She had never seen such fireworks before; large suns were throwing out sparks, beautiful fiery fishes were darting through the blue air, and all these wonders were reflected in the calm sea below. The ship itself was thrown into such bright relief that every little cord was distinctly visible, and, of course, each person still more so. And how handsome the young prince looked, as he pressed the hands of those present and smiled, while the music resounded through that lovely night!

It was late. Still the little mermaid could not take her eyes off the ship or the handsome prince. The variegated lanterns were now extinguished, the rockets ceased to be let off, and no more cannons were fired; but there was a rumbling and a grumbling in the heart of the sea. Still she sat rocking up and down in the water, so as to peep into the cabin. But now the ship began to move faster, the sails were unfurled one after another, the waves ran higher, heavy clouds flitted across the sky, and flashes of lightning were seen in the distance. A tremendous storm seemed coming on, so the sailors reefed in the sails once more. The large ship kept pitching to and fro in its rapid course across the raging sea; the billows heaved, like so many gigantic black mountains, threatening to roll over the topmast, but the ship dived down like a swan between the high waves, and then rose again on the towering pinnacle of the waters. The little mermaid fancied this was a right pleasant mode of sailing, but the crew thought differently. The ship kept cracking and cracking, the thick planks gave way beneath the repeated lashings of the waves, a leak was sprung, the mast was broken right in twain like a reed, and the vessel drooped on one side, while the water kept filling the hold. The little mermaid now perceived that the crew were in danger, and she

herself was obliged to take care not to be hurt by the beams
and planks belonging to the ship that were dispersed upon the
waters. For one moment it was so pitch dark that she could see
nothing, but when a flash of lightning illumined the sky, and
enabled her to discern distinctly all on board, she looked especially for the young prince, whom she perceived sinking into
the water just as the ship burst asunder. She was then quite
pleased at the thought of his coming down to her, till she reflected that human beings cannot live in water, and that he
would be dead by the time he reached her father's castle. But
die he must not, therefore she swam towards him through the
planks and beams that were driven about on the billows, forgetting that they might crush her to atoms. She dived deep
under the water, and then, rising again between the waves, she
managed at length to reach the young prince, who was scarcely
able to buffet any longer with the stormy sea. His arms and
legs began to feel powerless, his beautiful eyes were closed,
and he would have died had not the little mermaid come to his
assistance. She held his head above the water, and then let the
waves carry them whither they pleased.

Towards morning the storm had abated, but not a wreck of
the vessel was to be seen. The sun rose red and beaming from
the water, and seemed to infuse life into the prince's cheeks,
but his eyes remained closed. The mermaid kissed his high,
polished forehead, and stroked back his wet hair; she fancied
he was like the marble statue in her garden, and she kissed him
again, and wished that he might live.

They now came in sight of land, and she saw high blue
mountains, on the tops of which the snow looked as dazzlingly
white as though a flock of swans were lying there. Below, near
the coast, were beautiful green forests, and in front stood a
church or a convent—she did not rightly know which—but, at
all events, it was a building. Citrons and China oranges grew
in the garden, and tall palm-trees stood in front of the door.
The sea formed a small bay at this spot, and the water, though
very deep, was quite calm; so she swam with the handsome
prince towards the cliff, where the delicate white sands had

formed a heap, and here she laid him down, taking great care that his head should be placed higher than his body, and in the warm sunshine.

The bells now pealed from the large white building, and a number of girls came into the garden. The little mermaid then swam farther away and hid herself behind some high stones that rose out of the water, and covering her head and bosom with foam, so that no one could see her little countenance, she watched whether any one came to the poor prince's assistance.

It was not long before a young maiden approached the spot where he was lying. She appeared frightened at first, but it was only for a moment; and then she fetched a number of persons; and the mermaid saw that the prince came to life again, and that he smiled on all those around him. But he did not send her a smile, neither did he know she had saved him, so she felt quite afflicted; and when he was led into the large building she dived back into the water with a heavy heart and returned to her father's castle.

Silent and thoughtful as she had always been, she now grew still more so. Her sisters inquired what she had seen the first time she went above, but she did not tell them.

Many an evening, and many a morning, did she rise up to the spot where she had left the prince. She saw the fruit in the garden grow ripe, and then she saw it gathered; she saw the snow melt away from the summits of the high mountains, but she did not see the prince; and each time she returned home more sorrowful than ever. Her only consolation was to sit in her little garden and to fling her arm round the beauteous marble statue that was like the prince; but she ceased to tend her flowers, and they grew like a wilderness all over the paths, entwining their long stems and leaves with the branches of the trees, so that it was quite dark beneath their shade.

At length she could resist no longer, and opened her heart to one of her sisters, from whom all the others immediately learned her secret, though they told it to no one else, except to a couple of other mermaids, who divulged it to nobody, except to their most intimate friends. One of these happened to know who the prince was. She, too, had seen the gala on ship-board,

and informed them whence he came, and where his kingdom lay.

"Come, little sister," said the other princesses; and, entwining their arms, they rose up in a long row out of the sea at the
spot where they knew the prince's palace stood.

This was built of bright yellow, shining stone, with a broad
flight of marble steps, the last of which reached down into the
sea. Magnificent golden cupolas rose above the roof, and marble statues, closely imitating life, were placed between the pil-
lars that surrounded the edifice. One could see, through the
transparent panes of the large windows, right into the magnificent rooms, fitted with costly silk curtains and splendid
hangings, and ornamented with large pictures on all the walls;
so that it was a pleasure to look at them. In the middle of the
principal room, a large fountain threw up its sparkling jets as
high as the glass cupola in the ceiling, through which the sun
shone down upon the water, and on the beautiful plants growing in the wide basin that contained it.

Now that she knew where he lived, she spent many an evening, and many a night, on the neighbouring water. She swam
much nearer the shore than any of the others had ventured to
do; nay, she even went up the narrow canal, under the handsome marble balcony that threw its long shadow over the
water. Here she would sit, and gaze at the young prince, who
thought himself quite alone in the bright moonshine.

Many an evening did she see him sailing in his pretty boat,
adorned with flags, and enjoying music: then she would listen
from amongst the green reeds; and if the wind happened to
seize hold of her long silvery white veil, those who saw it took
it to be a swan spreading out his wings.

Many a night, too, when fishermen were spreading their
nets by torchlight, she heard them speaking highly of the
young prince; and she rejoiced that she had saved his life, when
he was tossed about, half dead, on the waves. And she remembered how his head had rested on her bosom, and how heartily
she had kissed him—but of all this he knew nothing, and he
could not even dream about her.

She soon grew to be more and more fond of human beings,

and to long more and more fervently to be able to walk about amongst them, for their world appeared to her far larger and more beautiful than her own. They could fly across the sea upon ships, and scale mountains that towered above the clouds; and the lands they possessed—their fields and their forests—stretched away far beyond the reach of her sight.

There was such a deal that she wanted to learn, but her sisters were not able to answer all her questions; therefore she applied to her old grandmother, who was well acquainted with the upper world, which she called, very correctly, the lands above the sea.

"If human beings do not get drowned," asked the little mermaid, "can they live for ever? Do not they die, as we do here in the sea?"

"Yes," said the ancient dame, "they must die as well as we; and the term of their life is even shorter than ours. We can live to be three hundred years old; but when we cease to be here, we shall only be changed into foam, and are not even buried below among those we love. Our souls are not immortal. We shall never enter upon a new life. We are like the green reed, that can never flourish again when it has once been cut through. Human beings, on the contrary, have a soul that lives eternally—yea, even after the body has been committed to the earth—and that rises up through the clear pure air to the bright stars above! Like as we rise out of the water to look at the haunts of men, so do they rise to unknown and favoured regions, that we shall never be privileged to see."

"And why have not we an immortal soul?" asked the little mermaid sorrowfully. "I would willingly give all the hundreds of years I may have to live, to be a human being but for one day, and to have the hope of sharing in the joys of the heavenly world."

"You must not think about that," said the old dame. "We feel we are much happier and better than the human race above."

"So I shall die, and be driven about like foam on the sea, and cease to hear the music of the waves, and to see the beautiful flowers, and the red sun? Is there nothing I can do to obtain an immortal soul?"

"No," said the old sea-queen; "unless a human being loved you so dearly that you were more to him than either father or mother; if all his thoughts and his love were centred in you, and he allowed the priest to lay his right hand in yours, promising to be faithful to you here and hereafter: then would his soul glide into your body, and you would obtain a share in the happiness awaiting human beings. He would give you a soul without forfeiting his own. But this will never happen! Your fish's tail, which is a beauty amongst us sea-folk, is thought a deformity on earth, because they know no better. It is necessary there to have two stout props, that they call legs, in order to be beautiful!"

The little mermaid sighed as she cast a glance at her fish's tail.

"Let us be merry," said the old dame; "let us jump and hop about during the three hundred years that we have to live—which is really quite enough, in all conscience. We shall then be all the more disposed to rest at a later period. To-night we shall have a court ball."

On these occasions there was a display of magnificence such as we never see upon earth. The walls and the ceiling of the large ball-room were of thick, though transparent glass. Hundreds of colossal mussel-shells—some of a deep red, others as green as grass—were hung in rows on each side, and contained blue flames, that illuminated the whole room, and shone through the walls, so that the sea was lighted all around. Countless fishes, great and small, were to be seen swimming past the glass walls, some of them flaunting in scarlet scales, while others sparkled like liquid gold or silver.

Through the ball-room flowed a wide stream, on whose surface the mermen and mermaids danced to their own sweet singing. Human beings have no such voices. The little mermaid sang the sweetest of them all, and the whole court applauded with their hands and tails; and for a moment she felt delighted, for she knew that she had the loveliest voice ever heard upon earth or upon the sea. But her thoughts soon turned once more to the upper world, for she could not long forget either the handsome prince or her grief at not having an immortal soul like his. She, therefore, stole out of her father's palace, where all within was song and festivity, and sat down sadly in her own little garden. Here she heard a bugle sounding through the water.

"Now," thought she, "he is surely sailing about up above—he who incessantly fills all my thoughts, and to whose hands I would fain entrust the happiness of my existence. I will venture everything to win him and to obtain an immortal soul. While my sisters are dancing yonder in my father's castle, I will go to the sea-witch, who has always frightened me hitherto, but now, perhaps, she can advise and help me."

The little mermaid then left her garden, and repaired to the rushing whirlpool, behind which the sorceress lived. She had never gone that way before. Neither flowers nor sea-grass grew there; and nothing but bare, grey, sandy ground led to the whirlpool, where the waters kept eddying like waving mill-wheels, dragging everything they clutched hold of into the fathomless depth below. Between these whirlpools, that might have crushed her in their rude grasp, was the mermaid forced to pass to reach the dominions of the sea-witch; and even here, during a good part of the way, there was no other road than across a sheet of warm, bubbling mire, which the witch called her turf-common. At the back of this lay her house, in the midst of a most singular forest. Its trees and bushes were polypi—half animal, half plant—they looked like hundred-headed serpents growing out of the ground: the branches were long, slimy arms, with fingers like flexible worms, and they could move every joint from the root to the tip. They laid fast hold of whatever they could snatch from the sea, and never yielded it up again. The little mermaid was so frightened at the sight of them that her heart beat with fear, and she was fain to turn back; but then she thought of the prince, and of the soul that human beings possessed, and she took courage. She knotted up her long, flowing hair, that the polypi might not seize hold of her locks; and, crossing her hands over her bosom, she darted along, as a fish shoots through the water, between the ugly polypi, that stretched forth their flexible arms and fingers behind her. She perceived how each of them retained what it had seized, with hundreds of little arms, as strong as iron clasps. Human beings, who had died at sea and had sunk below, looked like white skeletons in the arms of the polypi. They clutched rudders, too, and chests, and skeletons of animals belonging to the earth, and even a little mermaid whom they had caught and stifled—and this appeared to her, perhaps, the most shocking of all.

She now approached a vast swamp in the forest, where large, fat water-snakes were wallowing in the mire and displaying their ugly whitish-yellow bodies. In the midst of this loathsome spot stood a house, built of the bones of shipwrecked human beings, and within sat the sea-witch, feeding a toad from her mouth, just as people amongst us give a little canary-bird a lump of sugar to eat. She called the nasty fat water-snakes her little chicks, and let them creep all over her bosom.

"I know what you want!" said the sea-witch. "It is very stupid of you, but you shall have your way, as it will plunge you into misfortune, my fair princess. You want to be rid of your fish's tail, and to have a couple of props like those human beings have to walk about upon, in order that the young prince may fall in love with you, and that you may obtain his hand and an immortal soul into the bargain!" And then the old witch laughed so loud and so repulsively that the toad and the snakes fell to the ground, where they lay wriggling about. "You come just at the nick of time," added the witch, "for to-morrow, by sunrise, I should no longer be able to help you till another year had flown past. I will prepare you a potion; and you must swim ashore with it to-morrow, before sunrise, and then sit down and drink it. Your tail will then disappear, and shrivel up into what human beings call neat legs. But mind, it will hurt you as much as if a sharp sword were thrust through you. Everybody that sees you will say you are the most beautiful mortal ever seen. You will retain the floating elegance of your gait: no dancer will move so lightly as you, but every step you take will be like treading upon such sharp knives that you would think your blood must flow. If you choose to put up with sufferings like these, I have the power to help you."

"I do," said the little mermaid, in a trembling voice, as she thought of the prince and of an immortal soul.

"But bethink you well," said the witch; "if once you obtain a human form, you can never be a mermaid again! You will never be able to dive down into the water to your sisters or return to your father's palace; and if you should fail in winning the prince's love to the degree of his forgetting both father and mother for your sake, and loving you with his whole soul, and bidding the priest join your hands in marriage, then you will never obtain an immortal soul! And the very day after he will have married another, your heart will break, and you will dissolve into the foam on the billows."

"I am resolved," said the little mermaid, who had turned as pale as death.

"But you must pay me my dues," said the witch, "and it is no small matter I require. You have the loveliest voice of all the inhabitants of the deep, and you reckon upon its tones to charm him into loving you. Now, you must give me this beautiful voice. I choose to have the best of all you possess in exchange for my valuable potion. For I must mix my own blood with it, that it may prove as sharp as a two-edged sword."

"But if you take away my voice," said the little mermaid, "what have I left?"

"Your lovely form," said the witch, "your buoyant carriage, and your expressive eyes. With these you surely can befool a man's heart. Well? Has your courage melted away? Come, put out your little tongue, and let me cut it off for my fee, and you shall have the valuable potion."

"So be it," said the little mermaid; and the witch put her cauldron on the fire to prepare the potion. "Cleanliness is a virtue!" quoth she, scouring the cauldron with the snakes that she had tied into a knot; after which she pricked her own breast, and let her black blood trickle down into the vessel. The steam rose up in such fanciful shapes that no one could have looked at them without a shudder. The witch kept flinging fresh materials into the cauldron every moment, and when it began to simmer it was like the wailings of a crocodile. At length the potion was ready, and it looked like the purest spring water.

"Here it is," said the witch, cutting off the little mermaid's tongue; so now she was dumb, and could neither sing nor speak.

"If the polypi should seize hold of you on your return through my forest," said the witch, "you need only sprinkle a single drop of this potion over them, and their arms and fingers will be shivered to a thousand pieces." But the little mermaid had no need of this talisman; the polypi drew back in alarm from her on perceiving the dazzling potion that shined in her hand like a twinkling star. So she crossed rapidly through the forest, the swamp, and the raging whirlpool.

She saw her father's palace—the torches were now extinguished in the large ball-room—and she knew the whole family were asleep within, but she did not dare venture to go and seek them, now that she was dumb and was about to leave them for ever. Her heart seemed ready to burst with anguish. She stole into the garden and plucked a flower from each of her sisters' flower-beds, kissed her hand a thousand times to the palace, and then rose up through the blue waters.

The sun had not yet risen when she saw the prince's castle and reached the magnificent marble steps. The moon shone brightly. The little mermaid drank the sharp and burning potion, and it seemed as if a two-edged sword was run through her delicate frame. She fainted away, and remained apparently lifeless. When the sun rose over the sea she awoke, and felt a sharp pang; but just before her stood the handsome young prince. He gazed at her so intently with his coal-black eyes that she cast hers to the ground, and now perceived that her fish's tail had disappeared, and that she had a pair of the neatest little white legs that a maiden could desire. Only, having no clothes on, she was obliged to enwrap herself in her long, thick hair. The prince inquired who she was, and how she had come thither; but she could only look at him with her mild but sorrowful deep blue eyes, for speak she could not. He then took her by the hand, and led her into the palace. Every step she took was, as the witch had warned her it would be, like treading on the points of needles and sharp knives; but she bore it willingly, and, hand in hand with the prince, she glided in as lightly as a soap-bubble, so that he, as well as everybody else, marvelled at her lovely lightsome gait.

She was now dressed in costly robes of silk and muslin, and was the most beautiful of all the inmates of the palace; but she was dumb, and could neither sing nor speak. Handsome female slaves, attired in silk and gold, came and sang before the prince and his royal parents; and one of them happening to sing more beautifully than all the others, the prince clapped his hands and smiled. This afflicted the little mermaid. She knew that she herself had sung much more exquisitely, and thought, "Oh, did he but know that to be near him I sacrificed my voice to all eternity!"

The female slaves now performed a variety of elegant, aërial-looking dances to the sound of the most delightful music. The little mermaid then raised her beautiful white arms, stood on the tips of her toes, and floated across the floor in such a way as no one had ever danced before. Every motion revealed some fresh beauty, and her eyes appealed still more directly to the heart than the singing of the slaves had done.

Everybody was enchanted, but most of all the prince, who called her his little foundling; and she danced on and on, though every time her foot touched the floor she felt as if she were treading on sharp knives. The prince declared that he would never part with her, and she obtained leave to sleep on a velvet cushion before his door.

He had her dressed in male attire, that she might accompany him on horseback. They then rode together through the perfumed forests, where the green boughs touched their shoulders, and the little birds sang amongst the cool leaves. She climbed up mountains by the prince's side; and though her tender feet bled so that others perceived it, she only laughed at her sufferings, and followed him till they could see the clouds rolling beneath them like a flock of birds bound for some distant land.

At night, when others slept throughout the prince's palace, she would go and sit on the broad marble steps, for it cooled her burning feet to bathe them in the sea water; and then she thought of those below the deep.

One night her sisters rose up arm in arm, and sang so mournfully as they glided over the waters. She then made them a sign, when they recognised her, and told her how deeply she had afflicted them all. After that they visited her every night; and once she perceived at a great distance her aged grandmother, who had not come up above the surface of the sea for many years, and the sea-king, with his crown on his head. They stretched out their arms to her, but they did not venture so near the shore as her sisters.

Each day she grew to love the prince more fondly; and he loved her just as one loves a dear, good child. But as to choosing her for his queen, such an idea never entered his head; yet, unless she became his wife, she would not obtain an immortal soul, and would melt to foam on the morrow of his wedding another.

"Don't you love me the best of all?" would the little mermaid's eyes seem to ask, when he embraced her and kissed her fair forehead.

"Yes, I love you best," said the prince, "for you have the best heart of any. You are the most devoted to me, and you resemble a young maiden whom I once saw, but whom I shall never meet again. I was on board a ship that sank; the billows cast me near a holy temple, where several young maids were performing divine service; the youngest of them found me on the shore and saved my life. I saw her only twice. She would be the only one that I could love in this world; but your features are like hers, and you have almost driven her image out of my soul. She belongs to the holy temple; and, therefore, my good star has sent you to me—and we will never part."

"Alas! he knows not that it was I who saved his life!" thought the little mermaid. "I bore him across the sea to the wood where stands the holy temple, and I sat beneath the foam to watch whether any human beings came to help him. I saw the pretty girl whom he loves better than he does me." And the mermaid heaved a deep sigh, for tears she had none to shed. "He says the maiden belongs to the holy temple, and she will, therefore, never return to the world. They will not meet again while I am by his side and see him every day. I will take care of him, and love him, and sacrifice my life to him."

But now came a talk of the prince being about to marry, and
to obtain for his wife the beautiful daughter of a neighbouring
king; and that was why he was fitting out such a magnificent
vessel. The prince was travelling ostensibly on a mere visit to
his neighbour's estates, but in reality to see the king's daughter. He was to be accompanied by a numerous retinue. The
little mermaid shook her head and smiled. She knew the
prince's thoughts better than the others did. "I must travel,"
he had said to her. "I must see this beautiful princess, because
my parents require it of me; but they will not force me to bring
her home as my bride. I cannot love her. She will not resemble
the beautiful maid in the temple whom you are like; and if I
were compelled to choose a bride, it should sooner be you, my
dumb foundling, with those expressive eyes of yours." And he
kissed her rosy mouth, and played with her long hair, and
rested his head against her heart, which beat high with hopes
of human felicity and of an immortal soul.

"You are not afraid of the sea, my dumb child, are you?"
said he, as they stood on the magnificent vessel that was to
carry them to the neighbouring king's dominions. And he
talked to her about tempests and calm, of the singular fishes to
be found in the deep, and of the wonderful things the divers
saw below; and she smiled, for she knew better than any one
else what was in the sea below.

During the moonlit night, when all were asleep on board,
not even excepting the helmsman at his rudder, she sat on
deck, and gazed through the clear waters, and fancied she saw
her father's palace. High above it stood her aged grandmother,
with her silver crown on her head, looking up intently at the
keel of the ship. Then her sisters rose up to the surface, and
gazed at her mournfully, and wrung their white hands. She
made a sign to them, smiled, and would fain have told them
that she was happy and well off; but the cabin-boy approached,
and the sisters dived beneath the waves, leaving him to believe
that the white forms he thought he descried were only the
foam upon the waters.

Next morning the ship came into port, at the neighbouring
king's splendid capital. The bells were all set a-ringing, trumpets

sounded flourishes from high turrets, and soldiers, with flying colours and shining bayonets, stood ready to welcome the stranger. Every day brought some fresh entertainment: balls and feasts succeeded each other. But the princess was not yet there; for she had been brought up, people said, in a far distant, holy temple, where she had acquired all manner of royal virtues. At last she came.

The little mermaid was curious to judge of her beauty, and she was obliged to acknowledge to herself that she had never seen a lovelier face. Her skin was delicate and transparent, and beneath her long, dark lashes sparkled a pair of sincere, dark blue eyes.

"It is you!" cried the prince—"you who saved me, when I lay like a lifeless corpse upon the shore!" And he folded his blushing bride in his arms. "Oh, I am too happy!" said he to the little mermaid: "my fondest dream has come to pass. You will rejoice at my happiness, for you wish me better than any of them." And the little mermaid kissed his hand, and felt already as if her heart was about to break. His wedding-morning would bring her death, and she would be then changed to foam upon the sea.

All the church-bells were ringing, and the heralds rode through the streets, and proclaimed the approaching nuptials. Perfumed oil was burning in costly silver lamps on all the altars. The priests were swinging their censers; while the bride and bridegroom joined their hands, and received the bishop's blessing. The little mermaid, dressed in silk and gold, held up the bride's train; but her ears did not hear the solemn music, neither did her eyes behold the ceremony: she thought of the approaching gloom of death, and of all she had lost in this world.

That same evening the bride and bridegroom went on board. The cannons were roaring, the banners were streaming, and a costly tent of gold and purple, lined with beautiful cushions, had been prepared on deck for the reception of the bridal pair.

The vessel then set sail, with a favourable wind, and glided smoothly along the calm sea.

When it grew dark, a number of variegated lamps were lighted, and the crew danced merrily on deck. The little mermaid could

not help remembering her first visit to the earth, when she wit-
nessed similar festivities and magnificence; and she twirled round
in the dance, half poised in the air, like a swallow when pursued;
and all present cheered her in ecstasies, for never had she danced
so enchantingly before. Her tender feet felt the sharp pangs of
knives; but she heeded it not, for a sharper pang had shot through
her heart. She knew that this was the last evening she should ever
be able to see him for whom she had left both her relations and
her home, sacrificed her beautiful voice, and daily suffered most
excruciating pains, without his having even dreamed that such
was the case. It was the last night on which she might breathe the
same air as he, and gaze on the deep sea and the starry sky. An
eternal night, unenlivened by either thoughts or dreams, now
awaited her; for she had no soul, and could never now obtain
one. Yet all was joy and gaiety on board till long past midnight;
and she was fain to laugh and dance, though the thoughts of
death were in her heart. The prince kissed his beautiful bride,
and she played with his black locks; and then they went, arm in
arm, to rest beneath the splendid tent.

All was now quiet on board; the steersman only was sitting
at the helm, as the little mermaid leaned her white arms on the
edge of the vessel, and looked towards the east for the first
blush of morning. The very first sunbeam, she knew, must kill
her. She then saw her sisters rising out of the flood. They were
as pale as herself, and their long and beautiful locks were no
longer streaming to the winds, for they had been cut off.

"We gave them to the witch," said they, "to obtain help,
that you might not die to-night. She gave us a knife in
exchange—and a sharp one it is, as you may see. Now, before
sunrise, you must plunge it into the prince's heart; and when
his warm blood shall besprinkle your feet, they will again
close up into a fish's tail, and you will be a mermaid once
more, and can come down to us, and live out your three hundred years, before you turn into inanimate, salt foam. Haste,
then! He or you must die before sunrise! Our old grandmother
has fretted till her white hair has fallen off, as ours has under
the witch's scissors. Haste, then! Do you not perceive those red
streaks in the sky? In a few minutes the sun will rise, and then

you must die!" And they then fetched a deep, deep sigh, as they sank down into the waves.

The little mermaid lifted the scarlet curtain of the tent, and beheld the fair bride resting her head on the prince's breast; and she bent down and kissed his beautiful forehead, then looked up at the heavens, where the rosy dawn grew brighter and brighter; then gazed on the sharp knife, and again turned her eyes towards the prince, who was calling his bride by her name in his sleep. She alone filled his thoughts, and the mermaid's fingers clutched the knife instinctively—but in another moment she hurled the blade far away into the waves, that gleamed redly where it fell, as though drops of blood were gurgling up from the water. She gave the prince one last, dying look, and then jumped overboard, and felt her body dissolving into foam.

The sun now rose out of the sea; its beams threw a kindly warmth upon the cold foam, and the little mermaid did not experience the pangs of death. She saw the bright sun, and above were floating hundreds of transparent, beautiful creatures; she could still catch a glimpse of the ship's white sails, and of the red clouds in the sky, across the swarms of these lovely beings. Their language was melody, but too ethereal to be heard by human ears, just as no human eye can discern their forms. Though without wings, their lightness poised them in the air. The little mermaid saw that she had a body like theirs, that kept rising higher and higher from out the foam.

"Where am I?" asked she! and her voice sounded like that of her companions—so ethereal that no earthly music could give an adequate idea of its sweetness.

"Amongst the daughters of the air!" answered they. "A mermaid has not an immortal soul, and cannot obtain one, unless she wins the love of some human being—her eternal welfare depends on the will of another. But the daughters of the air, although not possessing an immortal soul by nature, can obtain one by their good deeds. We fly to warm countries, and fan the burning atmosphere, laden with pestilence, that destroys the sons of man. We diffuse the perfume of flowers through the air to heal and to refresh. When we have striven for three hundred years to do all the good in our power, we then obtain an immortal soul, and share in the eternal happiness of the human race. You, poor little mermaid! have striven with your whole heart like ourselves. You have suffered and endured, and have raised yourself into an aërial spirit, and now your own good works may obtain you an immortal soul after the lapse of three hundred years."

And the little mermaid lifted her brightening eyes to the sun, and for the first time she felt them filled with tears. All was now astir in the ship, and she could see the prince and his beautiful bride looking for her, and then gazing sorrowfully at the pearly foam, as though they knew that she had cast herself into the waves. She then kissed the bride's forehead, and fanned the prince, unseen by either of them, and then mounted, together with the other children of the air, on the rosy cloud that was sailing through the atmosphere.

"Thus shall we glide into the Kingdom of Heaven, after the lapse of three hundred years," said she.

"We may reach it sooner," whispered one of the daughters of the air. "We enter unseen the dwellings of man, and for each day on which we have met with a good child, who is the joy of his parents, and deserving of their love, the Almighty shortens the time of our trial. The child little thinks, when we fly through the room, and smile for joy at such a discovery, that a year is deducted from the three hundred we have to live. But when we see an ill-behaved or naughty child, we shed tears of sorrow, and every tear adds a day to the time of our probation."

The Fisherman and
His Soul[1]

The parents of Irish poet and playwright Oscar Wilde (1854–
1900) had a strong interest in collecting folklore, so perhaps it is
not so surprising that their son wrote fairy tales. As a philoso-
phizing aesthete, however, he wrote them for a double audience,
though perhaps privileging adults over children.

"The Fisherman and His Soul" was published in Wilde's
second collection of fairy tales, A House of Pomegranates, and
it is clearly in conversation with Andersen's "The Little Mermaid" and its self-sacrificing heroine. The focus in Wilde's
fairy tale is not the mermaid's thoughts and aspirations, but
those of the fisherman, whose role parallels that of the prince in
Andersen's tale, except that his love for the mermaid moves the
plot. Reminiscent of the Sirens' lure, Wilde's mermaid sings to
the fisherman every evening until love overpowers his desire
for a good catch of fish. But the fisherman is no captive. Love,
he proclaims, is better than wisdom and riches, and to be with
the mermaid he happily gives up his soul. Later, dramatically
severing that shadowy self from his body, the fisherman will
throw himself in the depths of the ocean, from which he
emerges yearly to hear of his soul's adventures in the human
world.

Wilde's tale is notable in at least two other ways. It combines eroticism with exoticism. The body of the mermaid—
whom the fisherman first sees lying asleep in his net—is a work
of art, exhibiting the beauty of ivory, pearls, and silver.[2] And,
as is the case for Wilde's fairy tales in general, there is no happy
ending to this tale, for which the fisherman's soul plays a part.
However, the love of the fisherman and mermaid leaves its
beautiful mark in the human world. We have opted to include

only the beginning of the tale, to highlight the fisherman's fall-
ing in love and the mermaid's description of her beautiful
world.

Every evening the young Fisherman went out upon the sea,
and threw his nets into the water.

When the wind blew from the land he caught nothing, or
but little at best, for it was a bitter and black-winged wind,
and rough waves rose up to meet it. But when the wind blew to
the shore, the fish came in from the deep, and swam into the
meshes of his nets, and he took them to the marketplace and
sold them.

Every evening he went out upon the sea, and one evening the
net was so heavy that hardly could he draw it into the boat.
And he laughed, and said to himself, "Surely I have caught all
the fish that swim, or snared some dull monster that will be a
marvel to men, or some thing of horror that the great Queen
will desire," and putting forth all his strength, he tugged at the
coarse ropes till, like lines of blue enamel round a vase of
bronze, the long veins rose up on his arms. He tugged at the
thin ropes, and nearer and nearer came the circle of flat corks,
and the net rose at last to the top of the water.

But no fish at all was in it, nor any monster or thing of horror, but only a little Mermaid lying fast asleep.

Her hair was as a wet fleece of gold, and each separate hair
as a thread of fine gold in a cup of glass. Her body was as
white ivory, and her tail was of silver and pearl. Silver and
pearl was her tail, and the green weeds of the sea coiled round
it; and like sea-shells were her ears, and her lips were like sea-
coral. The cold waves dashed over her cold breasts, and the
salt glistened upon her eyelids.

So beautiful was she that when the young Fisherman saw
her he was filled with wonder, and he put out his hand and
drew the net close to him, and leaning over the side he clasped
her in his arms. And when he touched her, she gave a cry like
a startled sea-gull and woke, and looked at him in terror with

her mauve-amethyst eyes, and struggled that she might escape. But he held her tightly to him, and would not suffer her to depart.

And when she saw that she could in no way escape from him, she began to weep, and said, "I pray thee let me go, for I am the only daughter of a King, and my father is aged and alone."

But the young Fisherman answered, "I will not let thee go save thou makest me a promise that whenever I call thee, thou wilt come and sing to me, for the fish delight to listen to the song of the Sea-folk, and so shall my nets be full."

"Wilt thou in very truth let me go, if I promise thee this?" cried the Mermaid.

"In very truth I will let thee go," said the young Fisherman.

So she made him the promise he desired, and sware it by the oath of the Sea-folk. And he loosened his arms from about her, and she sank down into the water, trembling with a strange fear.

Every evening the young Fisherman went out upon the sea, and called to the Mermaid, and she rose out of the water and sang to him. Round and round her swam the dolphins, and the wild gulls wheeled above her head.

And she sang a marvellous song. For she sang of the Sea-folk who drive their flocks from cave to cave, and carry the little calves on their shoulders; of the Tritons who have long green beards, and hairy breasts, and blow through twisted conchs when the King passes by; of the palace of the King which is all of amber, with a roof of clear emerald, and a pavement of bright pearl; and of the gardens of the sea where the great filigrane fans of coral wave all day long, and the fish dart about like silver birds, and the anemones cling to the rocks, and the pinks bourgeon in the ribbed yellow sand. She sang of the big whales that come down from the north seas and have sharp icicles hanging to their fins; of the Sirens who tell of such wonderful things that the merchants have to stop their ears with wax lest they should hear them, and leap into the water and be drowned; of the sunken galleys with their tall masts, and the frozen sailors clinging to the rigging, and the mackerel swimming in and out of the open portholes; of the little barnacles who are great travellers, and cling to the keels of the ships and go round and round the world; and of the cuttlefish who live in the sides of the cliffs and stretch out their long black arms, and can make night come when they will it. She sang of the nautilus who has a boat of her own that is carved out of an opal and steered with a silken sail; of the happy Mermen who play upon harps and can charm the great Kraken to sleep; of the little children who catch hold of the slippery porpoises and ride laughing upon their backs; of the Mermaids who lie in the white foam and hold out their arms to the mariners; and of the sea-lions with their curved tusks, and the sea-horses with their floating manes.

And as she sang, all the tunny-fish came in from the deep to listen to her, and the young Fisherman threw his nets round them and caught them, and others he took with a spear. And when his boat was well-laden, the Mermaid would sink down into the sea, smiling at him.

Yet would she never come near him that he might touch her. Oftentimes he called to her and prayed of her, but she would not; and when he sought to seize her she dived into the water as a seal might dive, nor did he see her again that day. And each day the sound of her voice became sweeter to his ears. So sweet was her voice that he forgot his nets and his cunning, and had no care of his craft. Vermilion-finned and with eyes of bossy gold, the tunnies went by in shoals, but he heeded them not. His spear lay by his side unused, and his baskets of plaited osier were empty. With lips parted, and eyes dim with wonder. he sat idle in his boat and listened, listening till the sea-mists crept round him, and the wandering moon stained his brown limbs with silver.

And one evening he called to her, and said: "Little Mermaid, little Mermaid, I love thee. Take me for thy bridegroom, for I love thee."

But the Mermaid shook her head. "Thou hast a human soul," she answered. "If only thou would'st send away thy soul, then could I love thee."

And the young Fisherman said to himself, "Of what use is

my soul to me? I cannot see it. I may not touch it. I do not know it. Surely I will send it away from me, and much gladness shall be mine." And a cry of joy broke from his lips, and standing up in the painted boat, he held out his arms to the Mermaid. "I will send my soul away," he cried, "and you shall be my bride, and I will be thy bridegroom, and in the depth of the sea we will dwell together, and all that thou hast sung of thou shalt show me, and all that thou desirest I will do, nor shall our lives be divided."

And the little Mermaid laughed for pleasure, and hid her face in her hands.

"But how shall I send my soul from me?" cried the young Fisherman. "Tell me how I may do it, and lo! it shall be done."

"Alas! I know not," said the little Mermaid: "the Sea-folk have no souls." And she sank down into the deep, looking wistfully at him.

The Golden Mermaid[1]

A "golden mermaid" in contemporary slang stands for a tall tale or "the biggest fish of all"; analogously, Andrew Lang's "golden mermaid" is too good to believe.

Guided by the magic wolf's instructions, the prince lures this golden mermaid by displaying "beautiful silken merchandise," with a merchant's logic applying to their first encounter. Though no human ever approached her before, the prince then manages to kiss and hold the golden mermaid, and even win her faithful affection. After this, obtaining a golden horse and a golden bird is easy. The "golden mermaid" in Lang's literary adaptation is a fantasy that replaces the princess that the unpromising hero inevitably marries in other tales. Both text and illustrations show her having no fishtail once she is on land, perfectly assimilated to live by the prince's side.

The popularity of Andrew Lang rests with the twelve volumes of fairy-tale books he published between 1889 and 1910; "The Golden Mermaid" is part of the third book in the series, The Green Fairy Book (1892).[2]

A powerful king had, among many other treasures, a wonderful tree in his garden, which bore every year beautiful golden apples. But the King was never able to enjoy his treasure, for he might watch and guard them as he liked, as soon as they began to get ripe they were always stolen. At last, in despair, he sent for his three sons, and said to the two eldest, 'Get yourselves ready for a journey. Take gold and silver with you, and a large retinue of servants, as beseems two noble princes, and go through the world till you find out who it is that steals my golden apples, and, if possible, bring the thief to me that I may punish him as he deserves.' His sons were delighted at this proposal, for they had long wished to see something of the world, so they got ready for their journey with all haste, bade their father farewell, and left the town.

The youngest Prince was much disappointed that he too was not sent out on his travels; but his father wouldn't hear of his going, for he had always been looked upon as the stupid one of the family, and the King was afraid of something happening to him. But the Prince begged and implored so long, that at last his father consented to let him go, and furnished him with gold and silver as he had done his brothers. But he gave him the most wretched horse in his stable, because the foolish youth hadn't asked for a better. So he too set out on his journey to secure the thief, amid the jeers and laughter of the whole court and town.

His path led him first through a wood, and he hadn't gone very far when he met a lean-looking wolf who stood still as he approached. The Prince asked him if he were hungry, and when the wolf said he was, he got down from his horse and said, 'If you are really as you say and look, you may take my horse and eat it.'

The wolf didn't wait to have the offer repeated, but set to work, and soon made an end of the poor beast. When the Prince saw how different the wolf looked when he had finished his meal, he said to him, 'Now, my friend, since you have eaten up my horse, and I have such a long way to go, that, with the best will in the world, I couldn't manage it on foot, the least you can do for me is to act as my horse and to take me on your back.'

'Most certainly,' said the wolf, and, letting the Prince mount him, he trotted gaily through the wood. After they had gone a little way he turned round and asked his rider where he wanted to go to, and the Prince proceeded to tell him the whole story of the golden apples that had been stolen out of the King's garden, and how his other two brothers had set forth with many followers to find the thief. When he had finished his story, the wolf, who was in reality no wolf but a mighty magician, said he thought he could tell him who the thief was, and could help him to secure him. 'There lives,' he said, 'in a neighbouring country, a mighty emperor who has a beautiful golden bird in a cage, and this is the creature who steals the golden apples, but it flies so fast that it is impossible to catch it at its theft. You must slip into the Emperor's palace by night and steal the bird with the cage; but be very careful not to touch the walls as you go out.'

The following night the Prince stole into the Emperor's palace, and found the bird in its cage as the wolf had told him he would. He took hold of it carefully, but in spite of all his caution he touched the wall in trying to pass by some sleeping watchmen. They awoke at once, and, seizing him, beat him and put him into chains. Next day he was led before the Emperor, who at once condemned him to death and to be thrown into a dark dungeon till the day of his execution arrived.

The wolf, who, of course, knew by his magic arts all that had happened to the Prince, turned himself at once into a mighty monarch with a large train of followers, and proceeded to the Court of the Emperor, where he was received with every show of honour. The Emperor and he conversed on many subjects, and, among other things, the stranger asked his host if he had many slaves. The Emperor told him he had more than he knew what to do with, and that a new one had been captured that very night for trying to steal his magic bird, but that as he had already more than enough to feed and support, he was going to have this last captive hanged next morning.

'He must have been a most daring thief,' said the King, 'to try and steal the magic bird, for depend upon it the creature must have been well guarded. I would really like to see this bold rascal.' 'By all means,' said the Emperor; and he himself led his guest down to the dungeon where the unfortunate Prince was kept prisoner. When the Emperor stepped out of the cell with the King, the latter turned to him and said, 'Most mighty Emperor, I have been much disappointed. I had thought to find a powerful robber, and instead of that I have seen the most miserable creature I can imagine. Hanging is far too good for him. If I had to sentence him I should make him perform some very difficult task, under pain of death. If he did it

so much the better for you, and if he didn't, matters would just
be as they are now and he could still be hanged.' 'Your coun-
sel,' said the Emperor, 'is excellent, and, as it happens, I've got
the very thing for him to do. My nearest neighbour, who is
also a mighty Emperor, possesses a golden horse which he
guards most carefully. The prisoner shall be told to steal this
horse and bring it to me.'

The Prince was then let out of his dungeon, and told his life
would be spared if he succeeded in bringing the golden horse
to the Emperor. He did not feel very elated at this announce-
ment, for he did not know how in the world he was to set
about the task, and he started on his way weeping bitterly, and
wondering what had made him leave his father's house and
kingdom. But before he had gone far his friend the wolf stood
before him and said, 'Dear Prince, why are you so cast down?
It is true you didn't succeed in catching the bird; but don't let
that discourage you, for this time you will be all the more
careful, and will doubtless catch the horse.' With these and
like words the wolf comforted the Prince, and warned him
specially not to touch the wall or let the horse touch it as he led
it out, or he would fail in the same way as he had done with
the bird.

After a somewhat lengthy journey the Prince and the wolf
came to the kingdom ruled over by the Emperor who possessed the golden horse. One evening late they reached the
capital, and the wolf advised the Prince to set to work at once,
before their presence in the city had aroused the watchfulness
of the guards. They slipped unnoticed into the Emperor's stables and into the very place where there were the most guards,
for there the wolf rightly surmised they would find the horse.
When they came to a certain inner door the wolf told the
Prince to remain outside, while he went in. In a short time he
returned and said, 'My dear Prince, the horse is most securely
watched, but I have bewitched all the guards, and if you will
only be careful not to touch the wall yourself, or let the horse
touch it as you go out, there is no danger and the game is
yours.' The Prince, who had made up his mind to be more
than cautious this time, went cheerfully to work. He found all

the guards fast asleep, and, slipping into the horse's stall, he seized it by the bridle and led it out; but, unfortunately, before they had got quite clear of the stables a gadfly stung the horse and caused it to switch its tail, whereby it touched the wall. In a moment all the guards awoke, seized the Prince and beat him mercilessly with their horse-whips, after which they bound him with chains, and flung him into a dungeon. Next morning they brought him before the Emperor, who treated him exactly as the Emperor with the golden bird had done, and commanded him to be beheaded on the following day.

When the wolf-magician saw that the Prince had failed this time too, he transformed himself again into a mighty king, and proceeded with an even more gorgeous retinue than the first time to the Court of the Emperor. He was courteously received and entertained, and once more after dinner he led the conversation on to the subject of slaves, and in the course of it again requested to be allowed to see the bold robber who had dared to break into the Emperor's stable to steal his most valuable possession. The Emperor consented, and all happened exactly as it had done at the court of the Emperor with the golden bird; the prisoner's life was to be spared only on condition that within three days he should obtain possession of the golden mermaid, whom hitherto no mortal had ever approached.

Very depressed by his dangerous and difficult task, the Prince left his gloomy prison; but, to his great joy, he met his friend the wolf before he had gone many miles on his journey. The cunning creature pretended he knew nothing of what had happened to the Prince, and asked him how he had fared with the horse. The Prince told him all about his misadventure, and the condition on which the Emperor had promised to spare his life. Then the wolf reminded him that he had twice got him out of prison, and that if he would only trust in him, and do exactly as he told him, he would certainly succeed in this last undertaking. Thereupon they bent their steps towards the sea, which stretched out before them, as far as their eyes could see, all the waves dancing and glittering in the bright sunshine. 'Now,' continued the wolf, 'I am going to turn myself into a boat full of the most beautiful silken merchandise, and you must jump boldly into the boat, and steer with my tail in your hand right out into the open sea. You will soon come upon the golden mermaid. Whatever you do, don't follow her if she calls you, but on the contrary say to her, "The buyer comes to the seller, not the seller to the buyer." After which you must steer towards the land, and she will follow you, for she won't be able to resist the beautiful wares you have on board your ship.'

The Prince promised faithfully to do all he had been told, whereupon the wolf changed himself into a ship full of most exquisite silks, of every shade and colour imaginable. The astonished Prince stepped into the boat, and, holding the wolf's tail in his hand, he steered boldly out into the open sea, where the sun was gilding the blue waves with its golden rays. Soon he saw the golden mermaid swimming near the ship, beckoning and calling to him to follow her; but, mindful of the wolf's warning, he told her in a loud voice that if she wished to buy anything she must come to him. With these words he turned his magic ship round and steered back towards the land. The mermaid called out to him to stand still, but he refused to listen to her and never paused till he reached the sand of the shore. Here he stopped and waited for the mermaid, who had swum after him. When she drew near the boat he saw that she was far more beautiful than any mortal he had ever beheld. She swam round the ship for some time, and then swung herself gracefully on board, in order to examine the beautiful silken stuffs more closely. Then the Prince seized her in his arms, and kissing her tenderly on the cheeks and lips, he told her she was his for ever; at the same moment the boat turned into a wolf again, which so terrified the mermaid that she clung to the Prince for protection.

So the golden mermaid was successfully caught, and she soon felt quite happy in her new life when she saw she had nothing to fear either from the Prince or the wolf—she rode on the back of the latter, and the Prince rode behind her. When they reached the country ruled over by the Emperor with the golden horse, the Prince jumped down, and, helping the mermaid to alight, he led her before the Emperor. At the sight of the beautiful mermaid and of the grim wolf, who stuck close to the Prince this time, the guards all made respectful obeisance, and soon the three stood before his Imperial Majesty. When the Emperor heard from the Prince how he had gained possession of his fair prize, he at once recognised that he had been helped by some magic art, and on the spot gave up all claim to the beautiful mermaid. 'Dear youth,' he said, 'forgive me for my shameful conduct to you, and, as a sign that you pardon me, accept the golden horse as a present. I acknowledge your power to be greater even than I can understand, for you have succeeded in gaining possession of the golden mermaid, whom hitherto no mortal has ever been able to approach.' Then they all sat down to a huge feast, and the Prince had to relate his adventures all over again, to the wonder and astonishment of the whole company.

But the Prince was wearying now to return to his own kingdom, so as soon as the feast was over he took farewell of the Emperor, and set out on his homeward way. He lifted the mermaid on to the golden horse, and swung himself up behind her—and so they rode on merrily, with the wolf trotting behind, till they came to the country of the Emperor with the golden bird. The renown of the Prince and his adventure had gone before him, and the Emperor sat on his throne awaiting the arrival of the Prince and his companions. When the three rode into the courtyard of the palace, they were surprised and delighted to find everything festively illuminated and decorated for their reception. When the Prince and the golden mermaid, with the wolf behind them, mounted the steps of the palace, the Emperor came forward to meet them, and led them to the throne room. At the same moment a servant appeared with the golden bird in its golden cage, and the Emperor begged the Prince to accept it with his love, and to forgive him the indignity he had suffered at his hands. Then the Emperor bent low before the beautiful mermaid, and, offering her his arm, he led her into dinner, closely followed by the Prince and her friend the wolf; the latter seating himself at table, not the least embarrassed that no one had invited him to do so.

As soon as the sumptuous meal was over, the Prince and his mermaid took leave of the Emperor, and, seating themselves on the golden horse, continued their homeward journey. On the way the wolf turned to the Prince and said, 'Dear friends, I must now bid you farewell, but I leave you under such happy circumstances that I cannot feel our parting to be a sad one.' The Prince was very unhappy when he heard these words, and begged the wolf to stay with them always; but this the good creature refused to do, though he thanked the Prince kindly for his invitation, and called out as he disappeared into the thicket, 'Should any evil befall you, dear Prince, at any time, you may rely on my friendship and gratitude.' These were the wolf's parting words, and the Prince could not restrain his tears when he saw his friend vanishing in the distance; but one glance at his beloved mermaid soon cheered him up again, and they continued on their journey merrily.

The news of his son's adventures had already reached his father's Court, and everyone was more than astonished at the success of the once despised Prince. His elder brothers, who had in vain gone in pursuit of the thief of the golden apples, were furious over their younger brother's good fortune, and plotted and planned how they were to kill him. They hid themselves in the wood through which the Prince had to pass on his way to the palace, and there fell on him, and, having beaten him to death, they carried off the golden horse and the golden bird. But nothing they could do would persuade the golden mermaid to go with them or move from the spot, for ever since she had left the sea, she had so attached herself to her Prince that she asked nothing else than to live or die with him.

For many weeks the poor mermaid sat and watched over the dead body of her lover, weeping salt tears over his loss, when suddenly one day their old friend the wolf appeared and said, 'Cover the Prince's body with all the leaves and flowers you can find in the wood.' The maiden did as he told her, and then the wolf breathed over the flowery grave, and, lo and behold! the Prince lay there sleeping as peacefully as a child. 'Now you may wake him if you like,' said the wolf, and the mermaid bent over him and gently kissed the wounds his brothers had made on his forehead, and the Prince awoke, and you may imagine how delighted he was to find his beautiful mermaid beside him, though he felt a little depressed when he thought of the loss of the golden bird and the golden horse. After a time the wolf, who had likewise fallen on the Prince's neck, advised them to continue their journey, and once more the Prince and his lovely bride mounted on the faithful beast's back.

The King's joy was great when he embraced his youngest son, for he had long since despaired of his return. He received the wolf and the beautiful golden mermaid most cordially too, and the Prince was made to tell his adventures all over from the beginning. The poor old father grew very sad when he heard of the shameful conduct of his elder sons, and had them called before him. They turned as white as death when they saw their brother, whom they thought they had murdered, standing beside them alive and well, and so startled were they that when the King asked them why they had behaved so wickedly to their brother they could think of no lie, but confessed at once that they had slain the young Prince in order to obtain possession of the golden horse and the golden bird. Their father's wrath knew no bounds, and he ordered them both to be banished, but he could not do enough to honour his youngest son, and his marriage with the beautiful mermaid was celebrated with much pomp and magnificence. When the festivities were over, the wolf bade them all farewell, and returned once more to his life in the woods, much to the regret of the old King and the young Prince and his bride.

And so ended the adventures of the Prince with his friend the wolf.

A Mermaid's Tears[1]

Kurahashi Yumiko (1935–2005) was an antirealist and contro-
versial Japanese novelist who published two volumes of fairy
tales: Cruel Fairy Tales for Adults, which draws on European
and Japanese tales as well as works by Oscar Wilde and Franz
Kafka, and Cruel Fairy Tales for Old Folks. These titles might
lead us to expect a parade of fairy-tale violence, but this is not
the case: as Kurahashi herself noted, "cruel" refers to how the
logic of magic is fully rational in its outcomes and does not
yield to sentiment. The tales' focus on the erotic has led to
comparisons with Angela Carter's The Bloody Chamber; however, unlike Carter, the Japanese writer held rather conserva-
tive positions on women and sexual politics.

Kurahashi's parodic rewriting of Hans Christian Andersen's
"The Little Mermaid" is the first story in Cruel Fairy Tales for
Adults. Its title, "A Mermaid's Tears," evokes the sorrow of
Andersen's heroine, but this mermaid's tears are not due to un-
requited love. Kurahashi follows Andersen's plot with striking
reversals, especially when it comes to the mermaid's body,
which in the Danish tale simply dissolves in pursuit of a soul.
With a fishlike upper body covered in scales and beautiful long
legs, Kurahashi's mermaid is an unusual interspecies hybrid
that some say was influenced by Magritte's painting L'Invention
Collective, which portrays a female fish–human being on the
beach with similarly rearranged body parts. This mermaid also
already has a soul; she acts on openly sexual desires with the
prince; and her final transformation involves a transformation
of his as well, although neither of them gives up the materiality
of their bodies. There are two hybrid and new beings in the
end: one in the human world, whose sexual and gendered plu-
rality remains socially concealed, and the other underwater,
keeping company with the sea witch.

While the story's moral encapsulates Kurahashi's ironic play
of inversions, the unconventional images of embodied hybrid-
ity that proliferate in her story also point to the multiple ways
in which women in the contemporary world are reinhabiting
the figure and body of the mermaid.

A long time ago, at the bottom of the deepest ocean, lived a
sea-king who had six beautiful daughters. Of all the king's
daughters the youngest was by far the most beautiful. Her eyes
were as clear and blue as the deepest sea, and she was covered
from her head to her chest with the most lustrous and exquisitely well-formed scales. She was quite unlike her older sisters, for not only could you see her navel, which is unusual for
mermaids, but it was thought that no human girl could possibly match her long and shapely legs. The youngest of the mermaid princesses was shy and thoughtful, and often seemed to
be preoccupied, but fish never close their eyes, so even when
she was completely lost in thought her eyes had a golden glow
and always remained wide open.

The mermaid princesses liked nothing better than to listen
to their grandmother's stories about the world above the sea.
"As soon as you are eighteen," she would say, "you will have
my permission to rise to the surface, and then you will be able to
watch ships and humans." The most remarkable of all the tales
that they heard about the world above the sea told of the sweet-
smelling flowers that bloom there, and of the "fish" with delightful voices that swim in the wind. And it was almost unimaginable
to think that a mermaid might sit on a rock soaking up the silvery light from a "night sun" that is invisible from the bottom of
the ocean.

When at last the eldest of the king's daughters reached the
age of eighteen, she was given permission to rise to the surface
of the ocean; however, as misfortune is sure to befall anyone
who catches sight of a mermaid, she was warned in the presence of her sisters not to be seen by humans.

When the eldest princess returned, her sisters were entranced by her stories. It was the youngest, however, who listened most eagerly to how she had sat on a beach with her wet scales shining in the moonlight as she gazed at the twinkling lights of a town; and to how during the daytime she had hidden behind a rock listening excitedly to music and the peal of bells coming from a nearby church; and how, on approaching a wood, she had seen the sweet-smelling flowers and watched the singing "fish" darting through the air. Listening to these stories, the little mermaid was beside herself with excitement, but it would be another five years before she would be allowed to visit the world above the sea.

The following year, the second of the sisters reached the age of eighteen and was given permission to rise to the surface. She was followed by the third, the fourth, and the fifth until, in just one more year it would be the turn of the youngest. But the youngest of the princesses couldn't wait a moment longer, and without waiting for permission she decided to rise up through the sea toward the surface.

She lifted her head above the waves just as the sun was setting and golden clouds glimmered in a rose-tinted sky; and right there before her very eyes lay a three-masted ship becalmed on the water. As darkness fell, lanterns of various colors were lit and the little mermaid could hear gay and festive music coming from on board. She swam close enough to the ship to be able to see a great number of elegantly dressed people through the cabin windows. The most remarkable of them all was an extraordinarily handsome young prince with eyes as clear and blue as the deepest sea and wavy, golden hair, the like of which had never been seen before at the bottom of the ocean. That day happened to be the prince's birthday and the celebrations had just begun. The little mermaid could not take her eyes off the handsome prince. How wonderful it would be if only I could be human, she thought, a beautiful human girl living among these finely dressed people and dancing with a prince. Forgetting that she was a mermaid, the princess pressed her head against the cabin window.

At that very moment she caught the prince's eye. He shouted, the music stopped, and his guests turned as one and stared in her direction. The ship heaved to one side, and as the lights went out, there were screams from on board. A dreadful storm had descended upon the ship, and the little mermaid realized that by ignoring her grandmother's warning, she had caused this terrible misfortune, and now there was nothing that she could do about it. The ship was tossed about by the raging ocean until, in the midst of terrible thunder and lightning, it was smashed to pieces and swallowed beneath the waves. The mermaid, thinking of nothing but trying to save the prince, swam with his lifeless body, desperately trying to keep his head above the water.

The storm had subsided before dawn, and the little mermaid had managed to swim with the prince to the safety of a sandy beach where she would be able to take care of him. Suddenly, she noticed a tower of flesh rising rigid and acicular above his belly. Instinct told her to put the supplementary thing into the part of her body that felt a lack. It was a perfect fit, and getting hotter and hotter inside she forgot that she was a mermaid and even believed for a moment that she was becoming human. In the warm glow of the morning sun the prince's face seemed to have regained a little color, and the mermaid would have liked nothing better than to have remained with him forever, but she leapt up horrified at the thought that on recovering his senses he would see the ugly upper part of her body. And so it was that with tears in her eyes the little mermaid returned to the bottom of the ocean.

Although she told her sisters about the adventure, the youngest of the princesses could say nothing about what she had done with the prince. And she could no more reveal her feelings about wanting to leave her sisters and her parents than she could about her wish to abandon the sea world altogether and become human. In fact, the youngest of the mermaid princesses, who had always been quiet and thoughtful, became more withdrawn than ever.

One day, she determined to visit the sea-witch who lived below the whirlpools in the darkest, fathomless depths of the ocean, where bleached human bones and the wreckage of ships lay scattered about.

"I know what you want," said the sea-witch as soon as she saw the little mermaid. "You've had your way with a human and now, instead of that fish's head, you want the long hair, slender arms, and ample bosom of a human girl, don't you?"

"That's right," cried the mermaid, "I'll do anything, anything at all, if only you'll grant my wish."

The witch nodded and, with a strange smile, demanded the mermaid's immortal soul. The little mermaid agreed at once. It didn't matter to her if she died, only that she should be with the prince. "Listen carefully," said the witch, "this will make you mortal just like humans, but if the prince were to love you more than his own life, you will regain your immortal soul. If, on the other hand, he should abandon you for another woman, you will once more become a mermaid, die, and turn into foam on the surface of the ocean." At that, the witch gave the little mermaid a magic potion that she had brewed in her cauldron. As she drank the potion, the mermaid's scales began to lose their luster and fall off, and in no time at all the upper part of her body was transformed into that of a young girl.

The little mermaid swam straight to the beach and waited. When evening came, the prince finally left the palace and, with a somber and pensive expression, walked toward the beach in the setting sun. He often walked along that same beach thinking vaguely about the girl who had saved his life on that stormy night, hoping that one day he would meet her again. Imagine his astonishment, then, to find a young girl standing there naked but for the golden glow of the setting sun. "It was you," he cried, embracing her. "It was you who saved my life." Once more they did what they had done on the morning after the storm, and at last the fog clouding the prince's memory began to clear.

Now there could be no doubt whatsoever that this was the girl who had saved his life. As soon as the prince got the little mermaid back to the palace he dressed her in the finest clothes and installed her in his bedroom. Ironically, she felt ill at ease; after all, she was quite unused to dancing and wearing beautiful gowns, and polite conversation with the crowds who thronged to the palace made her feel awkward. And so it seemed quite natural that she should spend more time lying naked in the arms of the prince than she did wearing the gorgeous dresses that she had until so recently longed to wear. The prince's lifestyle was starting to raise eyebrows. Not only was his behavior unacceptable to the king and queen, but it was also of great concern to their senior retainers. Consequently, the court went ahead with plans to find a suitable bride for the prince, and in time it was decided that the beautiful princess from the land across the sea should be his wife. The prince owed his life to the girl who had been introduced at court as "the fisherman's daughter," but the idea of actually marrying her had never entered his head; equally, he had no intention of removing her from the palace even when the time came to take a wife.

As soon as he laid his eyes on the beautiful princess from the land across the sea, the prince was besotted. Before long there would be a grand wedding, and the little mermaid realized that her time as a human would soon be over. On the evening of the wedding, the little mermaid returned to the sea, and as she swam in the moonlight, scales began to appear on her back and chest, and then, just as the witch had foretold, her head returned to its former piscine shape. At that very moment, the ship carrying the bride and groom sailed into view, and the little mermaid once more heard gay and festive music coming from on board. She peeped through the cabin window, and again misfortune befell the ship, which broke up in a dreadful storm and sank without trace. This time, however, the little mermaid embraced the prince and swam to the deepest part of the ocean. She lost consciousness as she was pulled downward by the roaring whirlpools, and when she regained her senses she found herself in the sea-witch's lair. The witch looked at her incredulously and asked if she had another wish. "Please join us together," said the little mermaid, "then we'll be able to live as one until the day we die. I'll give you the remaining halves of our bodies."

The witch considered this quite a bargain. After all, the lower half of the prince's body, the manly part, was as magnificent as it was desirable. And so she fused the upper half of the prince with the lower—human—half of the mermaid.

The people were delighted with the prince's miraculous return. In time, he succeeded the old king and ruled the country honorably, but he never married and nobody really knew why, nor whether he was truly happy. The lower half of the prince's body, the mermaid's half, still had its own soul, and the two souls continued to communicate. However, while the prince could satisfy the little mermaid's demands by comforting the most feminine part of her body, there was nothing that she could do for him in return. Whenever that part was comforted by the prince, it shed tears, which, in sadness or delight, immediately hardened into pearls, and it is pearls, they say, that continually flood the prince's bed.

Moral: *The nether parts are not for loving.*

Abyssus Abyssum Invocat[1]

"Some stories will never be right," Genevieve Valentine, a contemporary author of science fiction, fantasy, comics, and film criticism, writes in "Abyssus Abyssum Invocat."[2] This statement could refer to "The Little Mermaid," as the moment in Hans Christian Andersen's story when the mermaid falls in love is rewritten three times in this one. None of the scenarios, however, leads to a happy ending. Iconic images from Andersen's tale—the drowning prince, the pained woman found on the beach, the ship sinking in the storm—are reshuffled to link with the mythology of the Sirens' call and the mermaid as a death omen. Valentine's story amplifies the yearning and isolation of the little mermaid in the human world, turning it into an obsession that envelopes the two main characters, Miss Warren/the mermaid and Matthew/the prince.

In this short story, Matthew attends a small school on the shores of Cornwall, which is one of the clues to linking Valentine's story with a legend told about a famous mermaid carving in the Cornish village of Zennor. In the "Mermaid of Zennor" legend, a local man named Mathey also disappears after falling in love with a mysterious woman and her singing voice.[3] The Latin verse that gives the story its title translates as "deep calls to deep" in the King James Bible and is from Psalm 42. It perhaps evokes the idea of the mermaid seeking to acquire a soul, and it definitely raises questions about language, translation, love, and humans' attraction to mermaids.

The Prince

Once, a mermaid fell in love with a prince who fell from his ship in a storm; when he had ceased to struggle, the mermaid took his face in her hands, passed her fingertips over the lids of his closed eyes, pressed her mouth against his mouth. Then she delivered him to the surface, where he was safely found.

But the salt of a man's lips was sweeter than the salt sea, and the memory of it drove the mermaid nearly mad, until at last she left behind all she knew to find the prince again.

She gave her voice to the hag in the grotto; the hag gave her a knife and said, "Very well."

She swam until her home waters were far behind her, until the prince's castle was in sight and she could swim no farther; then she lay at the edge of the water, and cut at her flesh until it was cleaved in two.

She was not allowed to wash her hands clean (she was not allowed to ask anything again, of the sea); when the men found her in the morning, they saw a naked woman holding a knife, up to her elbows in blood.

They hanged her from the first tree they found, so young that it sagged under her weight.

It's grown crooked ever since; I can see it from my window, as I tell you this.

Miss Warren came to the school the winter the ice broke in filmy crusts across the rocks.

The rain was coming down in sheets, waves trying to devour the shore, and no one saw her arriving; she was just *there*, waiting for them in the schoolroom the morning after, as if she'd grown overnight from the boards.

She looked them over, one by one, as if searching for something, but she must not have found it, because they just studied geography, and she walked among them carefully, and silent as the grave.

The consensus after class was, it was no wonder young single ladies were now permitted to teach in Cornwall, if they were as plain as Miss Warren.

(Matthew said nothing—he was already sixteen, and would graduate by summer, what did he care if she was plain for a spring?

She had paused by his desk a long time, watching him draw

from the map, little strings of islands like a necklace of beads. He could feel her gaze on his neck; it never moved, all the time she stood there. Her hands were thin and white, and she held the fingers together, like a dove's tail.

There was a hitch when she breathed, as if her lungs were giving out.

He watched her walk back up to the board, watched the line of her arm all the while she wrote the names of cities on the blackboard, her little white wrist sliding in and out of her sleeve, her hair as colorless and fragile as a sheet of ice.)

The first story she writes at the start of spring, when the green is creeping back over the rocks wherever the ice scraped it away, and the ospreys wheel over the courtyard of the school.

She writes it on the ruins of the old stone wall, where she was high above the water and alone but for the ghosts of the oppidum, who had, in the Roman years, looked out onto the ocean and seen serpents in the spray.

(It's a relief from the press of anxious boys, their little wars and flares of temper.)

She gives it to Matthew, a single sheet of paper pressed into his workbook, where he'll discover it some time from now, turning a page to start a lesson, frowning at it, touching his left lapel as he always does when something has taken him by surprise.

(She wants him, by then, because he holds very still; because of the way he looks at dead things with an air of sorrow; she wants him because his hair is dark, and gleams like the hair of a drowned man.)

Matthew waited two weeks for some word from her, but nothing came. She gave lessons as though nothing had happened, and spent Saturdays in the schoolroom reading, and Sundays walking the path that led to the sea, stopping from time to time to turn her profile to the water as if she was looking behind her. But she was too far, and from where he stood at the window, he couldn't see anything for sure.

The next week he stayed behind on Saturday, after service, to get her alone.

(The story wasn't the sort of thing one brought up to the Schoolmaster.

It was the sort of thing you read over and over as you pretended to study at night, casting looks out the pitch-black window, as if you could peer past the candlelight and all the way down to the sea.)

She was reading from an atlas.

"Sit, if you like," she said.

Her voice was metallic at the edges, like a rusted bell, and she didn't look up to greet him, or use any words of kindness.

He thought how strange she was, how little she knew of manners or the customs of the school.

Still, he sat beside her.

"I found this," he said, and set the story on the open pages.

She looked at it. Then she turned a leaf; the paper vanished.

"Why did you give it to me?"

"I don't love you," she said. "You mustn't think that. You'll go mad if you do."

She had unfastened the topmost button of her collar, as if she couldn't breathe; he could see a sliver of shadow under the line of her dress.

"What did you think of the story?"

He thought about it.

(He had drawn the scene twice in his notebook, then burned the pages. They weren't the sort of thing you left for others to find.)

"It seems truer than the other stories they tell you," he said at last.

She raised an eyebrow, turned another page.

He said, "And I pitied her, for losing everything in pursuit of love."

She looked at him, just for a moment, as if she was surprised. Her eyes were green as glass.

The pages were a map of the West Indies and the sea that surrounded them. Amidst the roiling waves, someone had drawn a ship, splintering to pieces. Sirens circled the drowning sailors, the water beneath them nearly black. Safely at the edge of the tumult slid the legend, *Abyssus Abyssum Invocat*.

He sucked in a breath.

She looked sad, now; he didn't know what he had done.

"The deep calls unto the deep," she said.

The translation wasn't quite right—Millard and some of the other boys would have called her stupid or romantic, if they'd heard her, said it was the reason she taught geography and not Latin.

But her hair was the color of seafoam, and the lines of her profile were carved out by the last of the daylight, and the words sounded so like a prayer to her that he only nodded yes.

If he reached out a hand and held the edge of her cuff in two fingers, who else was there to see it; if they sat together until it was full dark, who was there to say?

The Ship

Once, a mermaid fell in love with the prow of a ship that fell from a ship in a storm; the mermaid pushed aside the bodies of the dead as she swam, and caught it up in her arms.

It had hair like her own, blown back, and it had arms like her own flexed in fists, and a face like her own set in a mask of triumph, and from the bottom of her gown bloomed two pointed feet, one on top of the other like the suffering Christ.

Within each thing on the land, the mermaid thought, *there must be such a spirit waiting to be freed*, and kissed the wooden lips.

She gave her voice to the hag in the grotto; the hag gave her a knife and said, "Very well."

She cut at her flesh until it was cleaved in two. Then she walked along the beach, the sand a hundred thousand little wounds against her feet, until she came to the first tree she saw, and sank down with weariness.

The bark came apart in her bloody hands, and beneath it

she saw the grain-wood of her beloved, and she began at once to weep for joy, and to kiss its smoothness. And the tree, from her beauty and from its loneliness, bent its branches down to meet her.

But the mermaid had been careless. Day is ever the enemy of the sea, and as dawn touched the shore, the mermaid was turned into a spray of seafoam; the tree, stained with blood and tears, died of grief, still reaching out for its beloved.

The tree has been crooked ever since; I can see it from my window, as I tell you this.

The second story comes in full spring, when the trees are leafing and the birds are roosting in nests that cling to the rocks.

(She has been back often to the wall, and rested her feet on the bodies of the dead that lie under this ground that is shallow enough to push them through the grass at any moment.

His was a careful sorrow, in a careful heart, and had to be tended as carefully as a grave.

She has let a dozen papers be ripped from her hands, until it was the right story.)

The water at the foot of the cliffs is green, green as the waters of home.

Since the first story, she has seen Matthew go out walking past the shelter of the school and stand along the path that goes down to the sea, holding perfectly still in a way she can't stop looking at.

She doesn't know how he can do it, with the wind here the way it is.

Sometimes he frowns; sometimes he closes his eyes.

His eyes are dark, as dark as if no happiness ever reaches them. She had thought it was a sorrow of his own, before he told her he had sorrowed for a mermaid in a fairy tale.

(Some stories have been ripped from her hands against her will; some stories will never be right.)

Matthew had looked for stories a hundred times before the next one came.

He knew it was the day when her hand trembled as she held

it out, her fingers resting an instant too long on the cover, as if she was thinking better of it until the very last.

As soon as they were dismissed, he turned and took the long way round to mathematics, just so he could hang back alone and read it as fast as he could, his fingers trembling.

(She never said what the mermaids looked like; for him they all had green eyes and hair the color of seafoam, their white wrists sliding in and out of the waves as they swam.)

He folded the story shut when he had finished, closed his eyes, pressed it to his chest like a talisman.

The paper carried a smell of the salted sea, and he breathed deep, felt his fingers ache as though he had torn at a tree.

He was late to mathematics; all the while the willow switch was stinging across his hands, he was looking out the window, where the tide was coming in.

He grew distracted. He watched the sea when he should have been at study; he looked at little trees until he swore he could see the branches curling in.

He kept the story folded in half inside his jacket pocket. When he was nervous, he touched his lapel until he could feel the paper pressing back.

During science, they looked at anatomies of insects and frogs and fish and birds, the skin peeled back like the skin of a fruit, everything carefully labeled.

He drew seals, bones and muscles and blubber cradling a pocket of organs. Beside them came drawings of men, the groups of muscles that powered the arms and the abdomen.

At night, he cut them each in half and set them side by side.

(Such a thing could be, he thought, if Nature was clever; he tried to determine how high the little mermaid had cleaved herself in two, before she could walk.)

Sometimes he looked out the windows of the library and said the words over and over to the glass, his lips barely moving, watching a figure in a slate-gray dress walk the narrow path that wandered too close to the sea.

But he wasn't afraid, watching her; if the waves rose and

claimed her, he would run down the rocks and dive into the sea, and seek her until he found her.

He imagined pressing his mouth to her mouth until she breathed; he thought, Abyssus Abyssum Invocat.

The atlas sits on her desk, beside her globe.

It's safe there, of course; none of the boys see much thrill in pilfering a text.

If Matthew wants to study in the room after the others are gone, who cares enough to stay behind? Who cares enough to watch him turning pages, examining the chains of islands to be sure he can recall them?

His notebook fills up with mermaids in ink. He knows more of the true shapes of things than the men who made the maps, and his sirens have a breath of life.

They have marlin tails and seal tails; their hair spreads out across the surface of the water as they gather around the bodies of the drowned.

(He never draws the shipwrecks; the ships don't matter, the ships are gone.)

All the mermaids have hair like seafoam; their lips are parted.

When she sees them, her hands tremble.

(She wants, for an awful moment, to reach for a knife and cut until she's cleaved in two.)

You can't do this, she writes in the margin. She writes, as small as she can, They were warnings; I told you, you would run mad.

The drawings are too close to life; her face is stamped on every one.

He leaves it on her desk two days later.

He's drawn a page so thick with waves the page is nearly black. Amid the storm, a mermaid—empty and white—has embraced a sailor with dark hair.

His limbs are loose in hers; he's stopped struggling; it's too late.

(Outside, when she looks, he's standing on the path to the sea, watching her window.)

She writes, *This is not for you.*

(The waves are too dark to write anything on; she writes it across the body of the mermaid, a tattoo that swallows up her torso, her hair, her open mouth.)

The Deep

Once, a mermaid fell in love with death.

Men fell from a ship in a storm. The mermaid caught one up in her arms, pressed her hand to his screaming mouth to feel the warmth of his lips. After he stopped struggling, she swam among them all, closing their eyes with the tips of her fingers, their lids so thick that she could no longer see their eyes.

She kissed their hands; she carried each of them as far down as she dared, watched them sink into the dark water with their legs trailing like seaweed behind them and their faces sleeping, sleeping.

They carried pink halos with them, where her nails had curled into the skin and drawn blood.

The mermaid could not forget the faces of the drowned men; their faces kept sleep at bay, they drove her mad, and she knew she would find no peace until she could release all the suffering of men.

And she said, "Very well."

She swam until her home was far behind her. She followed storms wherever they touched the water, and gathered the dead gratefully into her arms, and sent them to the depths with her salt kiss on their mouths.

When there are no storms, or when those who die have not grief enough, she swims as close to shore as she dares, and tastes the salt tears on the air, and waves all mourners welcome in the sea.

She has been searching since; I can see her beckoning me from my window, as I tell you this.

The last story is written in haste, in a schoolroom in a moment of quiet, and pressed between the pages of an atlas.

She wants to warn him, *Don't follow, don't follow*, but her hands betray her, and the story stops.

(Nothing she says will keep him away from the water, now. He has an interest in dead things, and his hair gleams like the hair of a drowned man.)

On the beach she strips down to nothing, walks into the waves.

(The tide is going out; the sea is pulling at her with every step.)

Against the rocks, the waves crash and shatter like bodies; hair like seafoam, white as bone, sharp as the water calling you home.

Don't follow, she thinks, just before the water closes over her head.

Miss Warren's disappearance caused a little uproar in the school.

She could not be found. There was nothing in her room to suggest she had lived there at all, save the atlas. At first there was some little scandal as if she'd eloped, but then they all remembered she was plain.

Matthew was not surprised to find her missing; he was only surprised she had gone alone.

(He had gone down to the edge of the water. One lace cuff had gotten trapped in the rocks. It lived in the pocket of his jacket, between a story that had warned him and a story that told him what had happened.)

For two days, he counted time. He did not weep. He was not afraid of little partings.

(He knew what she was; he had always liked dead things.)

On the morning of the third day, there was a storm; sheets of rain battered the windows and hid the shore from view.

He woke when it was still dark.

He wrote across the body of the sailor, Abyssus Abyssum Invocat.

He carried the book tucked close at his side, all the way down to the sea.

MERFOLK AND
WATER SPIRITS
ACROSS CULTURES

AFRICAN MERMAIDS AND OTHER WATER SPIRITS

African water spirits often personify the sources of water in which they live and sometimes bear the same name as the river in which they dwell. The Bini of Benin in West Africa, for example, honor Igbagho, a river goddess whose mermaid servants are tasked with guarding her sacred river. Igbagho also rules the underworld located beneath the water.[1] The Tshi-speaking peoples (Ahantas, Fante, Akyem, and Akuapem) of Ghana's Cape Coast honor two ferocious marine deities, Tahbi and Tabhi-yiri, who are husband and wife. Tahbi's form resembles that of a large and dark-skinned human, except for his left hand, which resembles a shark's fin. Tabhi-yiri's form resembles that of a mermaid. Malignant entities who drown humans, they personify the rough coastal waters of this area. Among the most widely known Yoruba river spirits is Ọṣun (also spelled Oshun). Ọṣun's sisters, Oya and Oba, are also river spirits, and all three are married to their brother Shango, a thunder god.[2] Ọṣun was offered human sacrifices "in times of need," such as when Jebu warriors went up against the British forces in May 1892.[3] She continues to be honored today, with an annual two-week-long festival dedicated to her.[4] Ọṣun, Oya, Oba, and Shango, along with many other siblings, are the children of Yemọja, whose name means "Mother of Fish." We include a mythological account about her, "Aganju and Yemaja," which was collected by Alfred Burdon Ellis (1852–1894), a British Army officer who spent the better part of two decades in Ghana.

For the Yoruba-speaking peoples of West Africa (mainly Nigeria and Benin), Yemǫja (also spelled Yemaja) is a primary water deity. Yemǫja, who is associated with family, women, motherhood, and the arts, makes her home in the Ogun River.[5] *When Yoruba peoples were captured during the transatlantic slave trade, they brought their worship of Yemǫja with them. Today, she is a transnational water goddess, known by the local transliteration of her Yoruba name. She is worshipped in Brazil (Yemoja, Lemanja, Janaina), Uruguay (Lemanja and Yemalla), the Dominican Republic (Lemanja and Yemalla), Haiti (La Sirène and Lasirène), Cuba (Yemaya, Yemoya, Yemoyah, Iemanja), and the United States (Yemaila, Yemana, Yemaja).*[6] *Yemǫja is sometimes associated with another notable transnational water goddess, Mami Wata*[7] *or "Mother Water," who is a veritable religious-cultural phenomenon, and we include tales about her in "African Water Spirits in the Caribbean."*

Far from being relics of the distant past, African water spirits continue to be strikingly relevant to those who believe in them. Attesting to this vibrancy of beliefs are the scores of news reports over the last several decades about sightings of mermaids and other water beings. In the summer of 2013, a Nigerian news site reported that police dispelled reports of a fish turning into a mermaid at Ibadan, the nation's capital. According to this report, "a middle-aged woman, identified as Ramota Salau," claimed that one of the fishes she was selling "suddenly turned into what was called an 'Omo Yemoja' or 'mermaid.'" Hundreds flocked to see the portentous being, but it turned out to be a baby octopus.[8] *In early 2012, a local news station reported that the community blamed the malfunction of Gwehava Dam in Gokwe (Zimbabwe), completed just two years earlier, on "angry spirits" who "exist in the form of a mermaid and a large strange snake that dwells within the surroundings of the dam." According to the report, "traditional leaders, the town council leadership and villagers who live close to the dam said that the town's water woes were set to continue unless certain rituals were conducted to appease the angry spirits."*[9] *That same year, mermaids were blamed for delays in the construction of a reservoir at Mutare, also in*

Zimbabwe. Another news source reported that Samuel Sipepa Nkomo, Zimbabwe's Water Resources minister, "told a Zimbabwean parliamentary committee that terrified workers are refusing to return to the sites, near the towns of Gokwe and Mutare." Nkomo explained, "We even hired whites thinking that our boys did not want to work but they also returned saying that they would not return to work there." He added "that mermaids were also present in other resevoirs."[10]

In South Africa, every decade or so, the residents of Suurbraak report that they have seen "the legendary 'mermaid' known as Kaaiman" in the Buffelsjags River." Suurbraak resident Daniel Cupido spoke about his encounter with Kaaiman in the late evening of January 5, 2008, as members of his family and some friends were relaxing near the river. After hearing what "sounded like someone 'bashing on a wall,'" Cupido and his friends investigated "the sound coming from the nearby low water bridge. At the bridge, he said he saw a figure, 'like that of a white woman with long black hair thrashing about in the water.' Thinking to save her, he waded toward her, but said he stopped in his tracks when he noticed a reddish shine in her eyes. He said the sight sent shivers down his spine." The creature matched the description of the Kaaiman as "a half-human, half-fish creature that lived in deep pools in the river. It is white in colour and has long black hair and red eyes." One member of the party said the woman they saw "had an eerie silver-white glow," and another said, "the figure was making 'the strangest sound, like a woman crying.'"[11] *These reports we have shared are just a sample of the news articles that evidence ongoing beliefs in mermaids and other water spirits in Africa.*

Aganju and Yemaja[1]

Before her amour with the hunter, Odudua bore to her husband, Obatala, a boy and girl, named respectively Aganju and Yemaja. The name Aganju means uninhabited tract of country, wilderness, plain, or forest, and Yemaja, "Mother of fish" (*yeye*, mother; *eja*, fish). The offspring of the union of Heaven and Earth, that is, of Obatala and Odudua, may thus be said to represent Land and Water. Yemaja is the goddess of brooks and streams, and presides over ordeals by water. She is represented by a female figure, yellow in colour, wearing blue beads and a white cloth. The worship of Aganju seems to have fallen into disuse, or to have become merged in that of his mother; but there is said to be an open space in front of the king's residence in Oyo where the god was formerly worshipped, which is still called *Oju-Aganju*—"Front of Aganju."

Yemaja married her brother Aganju, and bore a son named Orungan. This name is compounded of *orun*, sky, and *gan*, from *ga*, to be high; and appears to mean "In the height of the sky." It seems to answer to the *khekheme*, or "Free-air Region" of the Ewe peoples; and, like it, to mean the apparent space between the sky and the earth. The offspring of Land and Water would thus be what we call Air.

Orungan fell in love with his mother, and as she refused to listen to his guilty passion, he one day took advantage of his father's absence, and ravished her. Immediately after the act, Yemaja sprang to her feet and fled from the place wringing her hands and lamenting; and was pursued by Orungan, who strove to console her by saying that no one should know of what had occurred, and declared that he could not live without her. He held out to her the alluring prospect of living with two husbands, one acknowledged, and the other in secret; but she rejected all his proposals with loathing, and continued to run away. Orungan, however, rapidly gained upon her, and was just stretching out his hand to seize her, when she fell backward to the ground. Then her body immediately began to swell in a fearful manner, two streams of water gushed from her breasts, and her abdomen burst open. The streams from Yemaja's breasts joined and formed a lagoon, and from her gaping body came the following:—(1) Dada (god of vegetables), (2) Shango (god of lightning), (3) Ogun (god of iron and war), (4) Olokun (god of the sea), (5) Olosa (goddess of the lagoon), (6) Oya (goddess of the river Niger), (7) Oshun (goddess of the river Oshun), (8) Oba (goddess of the river Oba), (9) Orisha Oko (god of agriculture), (10) Oshosi (god of hunters), (11) Oke (god of mountains), (12) Aje Shaluga (god of wealth), (13) Shankpanna (god of small-pox), (14) Orun (the sun), and (15) Oshu (the moon).[2] To commemorate this event, a town which was given the name of Ife (distention, enlargement, or swelling up), was built on the spot where Yemaja's body burst open, and became the holy city of the Yoruba-speaking tribes. The place where her body fell used to be shown, and probably still is; but the town was destroyed in 1882, in the war between the Ifes on the one hand and the Ibadans and Modakekes on the other.

The myth of Yemaja thus accounts for the origin of several of the gods, by making them the grandchildren of Obatala and Odudua; but there are other gods, who do not belong to this family group, and whose genesis is not accounted for in any way. Two, at least, of the principal gods are in this category, and we therefore leave for the moment the minor deities who sprung from Yemaja, and proceed with the chief gods, irrespective of their origin.

MERFOLK IN
THE THOUSAND
AND ONE NIGHTS

In The Thousand and One Nights *or* The Arabian Nights *(from now on the* Nights*), Shahrazâd becomes a storyteller in order to stop the king from serially putting to death the women he marries, whom he considers inherently deceitful. Shahrazâd's voice may charm the king, although she is no mermaid, but it is the variety and wonder of her stories that eventually turn him away from his obsession with death and misogynist violence.*

The Nights *contains tales from the Indian, Persian, Arabic, and Jewish traditions that were transmitted in Arabic manuscripts for many centuries before Antoine Galland first translated them into a European language—French—in the early eighteenth century.[1] Now mostly known through movies featuring Aladdin, Ali Baba, and Sindbad, as well as for its iconic genies, magic lamps, flying carpets, and extraordinary riches, in the West the world of the* Nights *has become a fantasyland that often perpetuates a highly gendered Orientalism. Since many tales prominently feature merchants, sea voyaging is often part of the plot.*

"Jullanâr the Sea-born and Her Son King Badr Bâsim of Persia" is a mermaid-wife tale that has little in common with its European counterparts. This female protagonist, like Hans Christian Andersen's little mermaid, is silent—but only during the first year of her life in the palace of the White City, when she chooses not to speak, not only because she misses her merfolk

family but also because she is observing the king and deciding whether he is worthy of her. Jullanâr has beauty, virtue, and magic; she has strong family ties in the high seas and onshore, where she becomes the king's wife and the mother of the future king Badr Bâsim; and she is an expert diplomat, bringing about respectful relations between the two realms. First a virgin, then a mother, and in the conclusion of the tale, a warrior and wise counselor, Jullanâr is a leader who believes in cross-cultural communication and puts it in action.

Notably, the tale "'Abdallâh the Fisherman and 'Abdallâh the Merman," also from the Nights, presents a different take on merfolk and their interactions with humans. The relationship between the two 'Abdallâhs—one of whom is a fisherman, the other a merman—is based on trade and friendship, but even as they honor the promises they make to each other, they are never like family. In her tale, Jullanâr affirms, "There are so many kinds of people in the high seas and various forms and creatures on land, but the differences are not that great"; but on a grand tour of the underwater world, 'Abdallâh the Fisherman is quite dissatisfied with the food—raw fish only—and is publicly mocked because he is tailless.[2]

"Jullanâr the Sea-born and Her Son King Badr Bâsim of Persia" has two parts, with the second one focusing on Jullanâr's son, Badr Bâsim, and his quest for the sea princess Jauharah. This part of the story takes place in a dreamlike sequence involving bodily transformations, betrayals, and magic competitions. While the characters are underwater, their appearances, behaviors, and customs are completely humanlike. Jullanâr makes a deus ex machina appearance at the end.

What follows is the first part of the tale only. The names of characters in the Nights have different spellings in English-language translations (e.g., Jullanâr, Julnar), and we have chosen to let these differences stand.

Julnar the Mermaid and Her Son Badar Basim of Persia[1]

Many years ago there was once a mighty monarch in the land of Ajam called King Shahriman, who lived in Khorasan. He owned a hundred concubines, but none of them had blessed him by giving birth to a child. As time passed, he began to lament the fact that he was without an heir, and there would be nobody to inherit his kingdom as he had inherited it from his father and forebears. One day, as he was grieving about this, one of his mamelukes came to him and said, "My lord, there is a merchant at the door with a slave girl, who is more beautiful than any woman I've ever seen before."

"Send them in," the king said.

After they had entered, Shahriman saw that the girl had a marvelous figure and was wrapped in a silk veil lined with gold. When the merchant uncovered her face, the place was illuminated by her beauty, and her seven tresses hung down to her anklets in lovelocks. She had coal-black eyes, heavy lips, a slender waist, and luscious thighs. Just the sight of her could heal all maladies and quench the fire of hearts longing for love. Indeed, the king was amazed by her beauty and loveliness, and grace, and said to the merchant, "Oh sheikh, how much for this maiden?"

"My lord," answered the merchant, "I bought her for two thousand dinars from a merchant who owned her before I did. Since then I have traveled with her for three years, and she has cost me another three thousand gold pieces up to the time of my arrival here. Despite all these expenses, she is a gift from me to you."

As a reward for this gesture, the king presented him with a splendid robe of honor and ten thousand ducats, whereupon the merchant kissed his hands, thanked him for his generosity, and went his way. Afterward the king gave the damsel to the slave girls and said, "Go and bathe her. Then adorn her and furnish her with a bower, where she is to reside." In addition, he ordered his chamberlains to bring her everything she requested and to shut her doors after they left.

And Scheherazade noticed that dawn was approaching and stopped telling her story. When the next night arrived, however, she received the king's permission to continue her tale and said,

Now, the king's capital was called the White City and was located on the seashore. Therefore, the chamber in which the damsel was installed had windows that overlooked the sea. When Shahriman eventually went to visit her there, she did not speak to him, nor did she take any notice of him.

"It would seem that she's been with people who never taught her any manners," he said. Then he looked at the damsel and marveled again at her beauty, loveliness, and grace. Indeed, she had a face like the rondure of the full moon or the radiant sun shining on a clear day. And he praised Almighty Allah for having produced such a splendid creature, and he walked up to her and sat down by her side. Then he pressed her to his bosom, and after seating her on his thighs, he sucked the dew of her lips, which he found sweeter than honey. Soon after this he called for trays spread with all kinds of the richest viands, and while he ate, he also fed her by mouthfuls until she had had enough. All the while she did not speak a single word. Even when the king began to talk to her and asked her name, she remained silent and did not utter a syllable or give him an answer. Only her incomparable beauty saved her from his majesty's wrath. "Glory be to God, the Creator of this girl!" he said to himself. "She would be perfectly charming if she would only speak! But perfection belongs only to Allah the Most High." And he asked the slave girls whether she had spoken, and they said, "From the time of her arrival until now she has not uttered one word, nor has she even addressed us."

Then he summoned some of his women and concubines and ordered them to sing to her and make merry so that perhaps she might speak. Accordingly they played all sorts of instruments and games before her so that all the people present enjoyed themselves except the damsel, who looked at them in silence and neither laughed nor spoke. The king became extremely distressed because of this, and he dismissed the women and the rest of the company. When everyone was gone, he took off his clothes and disrobed her with his own hand. When he looked at her body, he saw that it was as smooth as a silver ingot, and his love for her was aroused. So he lay down next to her and began making love. Soon he took her maidenhead and was pleased to find that she was a pure virgin. "By Allah," he said to himself, "it's a wonder that a girl so fair of form and face should have been left untouched and pure by the merchants!"

From then on he devoted himself entirely to her and gave up all his other concubines and favorites. Indeed, he spent one whole year with her as if it were a single day. Still, she did not speak one word, until one morning he said to her, "Oh love of my life, my passion for you is great, and I have forsaken all my slave girls, concubines, and favorites, and I have made you my entire world and had patience with you for one whole year. So I now beseech Almighty Allah to do me a favor and soften your heart so that you'll speak to me. Or, if you are mute, tell me by some sign so that I'll give up hope of ever hearing you speak. My only prayer is that the Lord will grant me a son through you so that there will be an heir to the kingdom after me. May Allah bless you, and if you love me, you'll now give me a reply."

The damsel bowed her head awhile in thought. Eventually she raised it and smiled at him, and it seemed to him as if the rays of the sun had filled the chamber. Then she said, "Oh magnanimous lord and valorous lion, Allah has answered your prayer, for I am with child by you, and the time of my delivery is near at hand, although I am not sure whether the baby will be a boy or girl. But one thing is certain: if I had not become pregnant by you, I would not have spoken one word to you."

When the king heard her talk, his face shone with joy and

gladness, and he kissed her head and hands out of delight. "Praise the Lord!" he said. "Almighty Allah has granted all my wishes—your speech and a child!"

Then he got up, left her chamber, and seated himself on his throne. In his ecstasy he ordered his vizier to distribute a hundred thousand dinars to the poor and needy and widows as a way of showing his gratitude to Allah Almighty. The minister did as he was commanded, and then the king returned to the damsel, embraced her, and said, "Oh my lady, my queen, your slave desires to know why you were silent so long. You spent one whole year with me, and yet you did not speak to me until this day. Why?"

"Listen to me carefully, my lord," she replied, "for I want you to know that I am a wretched exile and brokenhearted. My mother, my family, and my brother are far away from me."

When the king heard her words, he knew how she felt and said, "There's no more need for you to feel so wretched; for I swear to you my kingdom and goods and all that I possess are at your service, and I have also become your husband. But as for your separation from your mother, brother, and family, I understand your sorrow, but just tell me where they are, and I will send for them and fetch them here."

"Gracious king, you must listen to the rest of my story," she answered. "First, let me tell you that my name is Julnar the Mermaid, and that my father was a descendant of the kings of the High Seas. When he died, he left us his realm, but while we were still upset and mourning him, one of the other kings arose against us and took over our realm. I have a brother called Salih, and my mother is also a woman of the sea. While all this was happening, I had a falling out with my brother and swore that I would throw myself into the hands of a man of the land. So I left the sea and sat down on the edge of an island in the moonshine, and a passerby found me. He took me to his house and tried to make love to me, but I struck him on the head so hard that he almost died. Once he recovered, he took me away and sold me to the merchant from whom you bought me. This merchant was a good man—virtuous, pious, loyal, and generous. If it were not for the fact that you fell in love with me and promoted me over all your concubines, I would not have remained with you a single hour. Rather, I would have sprung into the sea from this window and gone to my mother and family. Now, however, I've become ashamed to travel to them, since I am carrying your child. They would consider this to be sinful and would no longer regard me with esteem, even if I were to tell them that a king had bought me with his gold, given me his property, and preferred me over all his wives. —This then is my story."

And Scheherazade noticed that dawn was approaching and stopped telling her story. When the next night arrived, however, she received the king's permission to continue her tale and said,

Then the king thanked Julnar for telling him her story, kissed her on her forehead, and said, "By Allah, oh lady and light of my eyes, I can't bear to be separated from you for more than one hour. If you were ever to leave me, I would die immediately. What are we to do?"

"My lord," she replied, "the time of my delivery is near at hand, and my family must be present so that they can tend me. You see, the women of the land do not know how women of the sea give birth to children, nor do the daughters of the ocean know the ways of the daughters of the earth. When my people come, we will all be reconciled to one another."

"But how do people of the sea walk about in the water and breathe?" asked the king.

"We walk in the water and breathe as you do here on ground," she said, "thanks to the names engraved on the ring of Solomon David-son. But now, listen to me, when I call for my kith and kin to come here, I'll tell them how you bought me with gold and have treated me with kindness and benevolence. It will be important for you to show them that you have a magnificent realm and that you're a mighty king."

"My lady," he said, "do whatever you think is appropriate, and you can rely on me to carry out your commands."

Then the damsel continued telling him about her life. "Yes," she said, "we walk in the sea and perceive everything that is in the water. We even behold the sun, moon, stars, and sky, as though they were on the surface of the earth. But this does not bother us. There are many types of people in the high seas and various forms and creatures on land, but the differences are not all that great."

The king was astounded by her words, and then she pulled two small pieces of Comorin lign aloes from her bosom, and after kindling a fire in a chafing dish, she took some of the lign aloes and threw them into the fire. Right after that she whistled loudly and said something that the king could not understand. Suddenly a great deal of smoke arose, and she said to the king, "My lord, get up and hide yourself in a closet so that I may show you my brother, mother, and family without them seeing you. I have decided to bring them here, and you will soon see a wondrous thing and marvel at the strange creatures and forms that Allah Almighty has created."

So he quickly entered a closet and began watching what she would do. And indeed, she continued her incantations until the sea began to foam and froth, and all at once a handsome young man arose from it. He was as bright as the full moon with a handsome white brow, ruddy cheeks, and teeth like pearls. Moreover, he was very much like his sister in looks. After him came an ancient dame with speckled gray hair and five maidens, radiant moons, who resembled Julnar a great deal. The king watched them as they walked on the face of the water until they drew near Julnar's window and saw her. Once they recognized her, they entered the chamber through the window, and she rose to greet them with joy and gladness. Indeed, they embraced and wept profusely until one of them said, "Oh Julnar, how could you leave us four years and not tell us where you were? By Allah, we've been extremely upset since your separation, and we haven't been able to enjoy food or drink. No, not for one day. We have longed so much for you that we've not been able to stop weeping!"

Then Julnar began kissing the hands of her mother, brother, and relatives, and they sat with her awhile asking her to tell them what had happened to her and what she was doing there.

"When I left you," Julnar began, "I emerged from the sea and sat down on the shore of an island, where a man found me and sold me to a merchant, who brought me to this city and sold me for ten thousand dinars to the king of this country. Now, this king has treated me with great honor and given up all his concubines, women, and favorites for my sake. Moreover, he has devoted all this time and energy into looking after my welfare."

"Praise be to Allah, who has reunited us with you," said her brother. "But now, my sister, it's time for you to come back with us to our country and people."

When the king heard these words, he almost went out of his mind, fearing that Julnar might agree with her brother and he would not be able to stop her. He loved her passionately and was extremely afraid of losing her.

"By Allah," Julnar replied, "the mortal who bought me is the lord of this city, and he is a mighty king and a wise, good, and generous man. Moreover, he has a great deal of wealth and does not have an heir to his throne. He has treated me with honor, done all sorts of favors for me, and has never spoken one unkind word to me. He does nothing without my advice, and I have the best of all possible worlds with him. Furthermore, if I were to leave him, he would perish, for he cannot endure to be separated from me for more than one hour. Indeed, if I left him, I, too, would die because I love him so much. Even if my father were alive, I could not have a better life than the life I presently lead with this great and glorious monarch. And right now, to tell you the truth, I am carrying his child, and praise be to Allah, who has made me a daughter of the kings of the sea, and my husband the mightiest of kings of the land. Indeed, Allah has compensated me for whatever I lost."

And Scheherazade noticed that dawn was approaching and stopped telling her story. When the next night arrived, however, she received the king's permission to continue her tale and said,

Julnar paused for a moment and then continued explaining her situation to her brother and family. "As I mentioned before, this king does not have an heir, and so I have prayed to Allah to bless me with a son who would inherit everything that belonged to this mighty lord's realm."

Now, when her brother and family heard her speech, they understood her situation much better and responded, "Oh Julnar, you know how much we respect and love you. You are the dearest of creatures, and we only want you to lead a life without travail or trouble. Therefore, if you are suffering in any way, we want you to come with us to our land and folk. But if you are happy here and are honored the way you should be, we would not want to take you away or do anything against your wishes."

"By Allah," she said, "I have all the comfort, solace, and honor I need here."

When the king heard what she said, his heart was set at rest, and he thanked her silently for everything. His love for her grew immensely, and he now knew that she loved him as he loved her and desired to remain with him, and that he would get to see his child.

Then Julnar ordered her women to set the table with all sorts of viands, which had been cooked in the kitchen under her supervision, and fruit and sweetmeats. When that was done, she and her kinsfolk sat down and ate. But soon they said to her, "Julnar, we have never met your lord, and yet we have entered his house without his permission or knowledge. You have praised his excellent qualities and have set his food before us, which we have eaten. Yet, we have not enjoyed his company or seen him." So they all stopped eating and were angry with her. Suddenly fire spouted from their mouths, and the king was scared out of his wits.

But Julnar arose, and after calming them, she went to the closet where the king was hidden, she said, "My lord, have you seen and heard how I praised you to my people and have you noted that they would like to take me back to my land?"

"I heard and saw everything," he said. "May the Lord reward you for what you have said and done! By Allah, until this blessed moment I did not know how much you loved me!"

"My lord," she replied, "what is the best reward for kindness but kindness! You have been most generous with me and have treated me with love and respect. So, how could my heart be content to leave you, especially after you have been so good to me? But now I would like you to show how courteous you are. Please welcome my family and become friends with them. Thanks to my praise of you, my brother, mother, and cousins already love you and refuse to depart for their home until they have met you."

"As you wish," said the king. "Indeed, this has been my very own desire as well."

Upon saying this he arose, went over to them, and greeted them warmly. In turn, they stood up and received him with utmost respect. Then he sat down and ate with them, and he entertained them in his palace for the next thirty days, at which point they desired to return home. So they took leave of the king and queen, and after he showed them all possible honors, they departed for home. Some time after this Julnar gave birth to a boy, and he looked as radiant as the full moon. Of course, the king was beside himself with joy, for he had been longing to have an heir for many years. Soon they celebrated the event for seven days and decorated the entire city. Everyone was filled with joy, and on the seventh day Julnar's mother, Queen Farashah, her brother, and her cousins arrived, for they had learned about her giving birth to a son.

And Scheherazade noticed that dawn was approaching and stopped telling her story. When the next night arrived, however, she received the king's permission to continue her tale and said,

The king was most happy about their visit, and told them, "I promised not to give my son a name until you arrived and could know what he was to be called." So they named him Badar Basim, and all agreed that this was a fine name. Then they showed the child to his Uncle Salih, who took him in his arms and began to walk all around the room with him. Soon he left the palace with him and took him down to the ocean until he was hidden from the king's sight. Now, when Shahriman saw him take his son and disappear with him into the depths of the ocean, he gave the child up for lost and began weeping. But Julnar said to him, "Don't worry. There is no need to grieve for your son, for I love my child more than you, and he is with my brother. Therefore, you don't have to be afraid of the sea or of his drowning. If my brother had thought that the little one would be harmed, he would not have done this. Don't worry, he'll soon bring your son safely back to you."

After an hour went by and the ocean sea became turbulent, King Salih emerged and left the water. When he came up to them with the child lying quiet and his face as radiant as the full moon, he said to the king, "Perhaps you were afraid your son would be harmed when I plunged into the sea with him?"

"Yes," he said, "I was afraid and even thought that he wouldn't come back."

"My lord," Salih replied, "we penciled his eyes with an eye powder that we know and recited the names engraved on the ring of Solomon David-son over him, for this is what we generally do with our newborn children. Now you'll never have to fear his drowning or suffocation in all the oceans of the world. Just as you walk on land, we walk in the sea, and he, too, has our gift."

Then he pulled an engraved and sealed box from his pocket, and after he broke the seals and emptied it, all sorts of jacinths and other jewels fell out. In addition, there were three hundred emeralds and other gems as big as ostrich eggs that glistened more brightly than the sun and moon.

"Your majesty," said Salih, "these jewels and jacinths are a present from me to you. The reason we never brought you a gift before this is that we never knew where Julnar was residing, nor did we have any trace of her. But now that we know she is united with you and we have all become part of the same family, we have brought you this present, and every once in a while we shall bring you more of the same. These jewels and jacinths are like pebbles on the beach for us, and we know how good and bad they can be, and we know all about their power and where to find them."

When the king saw these jewels, he was completely amazed and dazzled. "By Allah," he said, "just one single gem of these jewels is worth my entire realm!" Then he thanked Salih the Merman, and turning toward Queen Julnar, he said, "I am abashed before your brother, for he has treated me most generously and bestowed this splendid gift on me."

So she, too, thanked him for his deed, and Salih replied to the king, "My lord, it is we who are obliged to you, for you have treated our sister with kindness, and we have entered your palace and eaten your food. Therefore, even if we stood on our heads in serving you, it would be nothing but a scant gesture for what you deserve."

The king thanked him warmly, and the merman and mermaids remained with him for forty days, at the end of which time Salih arose and kissed the ground before his brother-in-law, who asked, "What can I do for you, Salih?"

"Your majesty, you have done more than enough for us, and we only crave your permission to depart, for we long for our people and country. We shall never forget you, our sister, or our nephew and shall always be there to serve you. By Allah, it is not easy to part from you, because you have been so kind to us, but what can we do? We were reared in the sea, and we cannot get accustomed to the land."

When the king heard these words, he arose and said farewell to Salih, his mother, and his cousins, and they all wept together. Soon they said to him, "We must be off, but we won't forsake you, for we plan to visit you as often as possible."

Then they departed, and after descending into the sea, they disappeared from sight.

And Scheherazade noticed that dawn was approaching and stopped telling her story. When the next night arrived, however, she received the king's permission to continue her tale and said,

After this King Shahriman showed Julnar even more kindness and honored her with even more respect than before. Their son grew up and flourished, while his maternal uncle, grandma, and cousins visited the king whenever they could and stayed with him a month or two months at a time.

A PERSIAN SEA FAIRY

In Persian tales of magic, the character of the mermaid as it appears in European folktales—that is, a being whose body is half human and half fish—does not exist. On the shores of the Persian Gulf, some people believe that there are beings in the sea whose body is completely identical to that of a human. Most of these characters are seen as evil and harmful. But some of them, particularly those whose physical features are close to those of the pari (a beautiful winged creature somewhat like the European fairy), are believed to help humans in need. The following are some of the maritime creatures known in Persian folklore:

1. The sea fairy, who is beautiful beyond comparison and normally has long hair.
2. Bu Salāme, a male character whose name, meaning "The Father of Peace/Safety," is of Arabic origin. Contrary to the name's meaning, he is an evil and harmful character.
3. Kheżr and Elyās, who save seamen from drowning in storms. These two characters are not limited to maritime folklore, as they also help people on land.
4. Bābā Daryā ("Father of the Sea"), whose figure is that of a human being, although he is much more powerful. He is also one of the evil and harmful creatures.
5. Pāryune, a female character who lives at the bottom of the sea and whose long hair reaches down to her toes. She always sings lullabies for her children. If you don't disturb her, she is not harmful. But if divers or pearl fishers

accidentally step on the cradle of her children, she will cause that person to become either paralyzed or insane.

—MOHAMMAD JA'FARI QANAVĀTI,
Center for the Great Islamic Encyclopedia, Iran

Translated by ULRICH MARZOLPH,
independent scholar, Germany

The Sea Fairy[1]

Narrated by 'Ali Dashti, aged sixty-four, in 1997; recorded by Nāhid Jahāzi in Bushehr.

In the old days, the fishermen used to go out to sea in their sailboats. There were three fishermen who always went fishing together. One of them had bad luck. While the other two would catch plenty of fish, he only ever caught a small amount. Often, he did not even catch enough to make a living, so his living conditions were very poor.

One night, this fisherman and his two friends set out to sea, each one with his own boat. Although they threw their nets many times, they did not catch any fish. Moving to a new area, they still did not catch any fish. Again, they moved to another place. As they moved, the fisherman with the bad luck was separated from his friends and found himself alone.

Suddenly, he heard somebody calling him. He said to himself, "That must be my friends." He moved toward the voice, which got louder and closer. The voice said, "Throw your net right here!" Suddenly, the fisherman saw somebody come out of the water and sit down at the other end of his boat. The fisherman was frightened. But when he looked closely, he saw that the creature was a sea fairy, whose loose curly hair reached down to her feet. Out of fear, the fisherman did not throw his net and just watched her, dumbfounded and puzzled. The fairy said, "What's wrong? Why are you frightened? Don't be afraid. I have come to supply your daily income. Remember this place, and from now on, come here every night! But remember not to tell anybody this secret!" That said, the fairy went down into the sea.

The fisherman was dumbfounded and puzzled for a while.

When his wits returned, he ate the bread and dates that he had brought along and threw his net into the sea. In a little while, the net was full of fish, and what fish they were—all the best and most delicious kinds! When morning came, the two other fishermen showed up and noticed that, unlike usual, their friend had caught many fish. They asked him, "What happened? Usually, you don't even catch enough fish to make a living!" He said, "Nothing in particular happened. I just anchored and threw my net." Again, they asked, "And then what happened?" But the fisherman did not say anything, because the fairy had told him not to reveal the secret.

Time passed. Every night the fisherman went to the same place and caught fish, and plenty did he catch! His living conditions got much better. He sold his small boat and bought a larger one. He bought himself a carpet and whatever else he needed to furnish his house. Finally, he was living well. One winter day, all of the fishermen got together outside and talked to each other. Each one of them told a story. That one fisherman told the tale of himself and the sea fairy. Then they all went back to their houses. When the weather was good, the fishermen went out to the sea, including that fisherman. Actually, all of the others followed him so that they would also catch more fish. At that moment, the sea fairy came out of the water and said, "Did I not tell you not to reveal the secret? From now on you will catch just as much as you did before, and you will never be able to catch more than that!"

THREE KHASI NARRATIVES
ABOUT WATER SPIRITS

Water entities among the Khasi ethnic community of north-eastern India are able to traverse multiple realities, including the world of ancestors, the dream world, and the world of water nonhuman entities. When encounters between entities of water and human beings occur, multiple narratives are transmitted widely, which then generates a folklore of water.

The following section documents narratives of interaction with such entities and their consequences. The most common word among Khasi to denote a water entity is puri. *Among the Khynriam Khasis, the* puri *are narrated to be female and have the physical quality of being divinely beautiful. The Khasi describe an extremely attractive woman as* kum puri blei—as *beautiful as a divine* puri. *Narratives about human encounters with* puri *from Shillong city include the motifs of beauty and (sometimes fatal) seduction of Khasi men by* puri. *Illness is the most frequent indication of* puri *possession. Among the Pnar, water entities are named after the place with which they are associated and are referred to as goddesses. Encounters with them take the form of divine possession, where the goddess possesses a chosen medium in order to mediate human problems. Among the Bhoi and Nongtrai communities, these water entities are called* Niaring, *and* puri *is just an entity who inhabits* Niaring. Niaring *is water personified and alive, constituting high divinity and medium in rituals.*

In the third narrative, the places where the puri *enchantment took place are named. From the perspective of the victim, the* puri *came from his ex-wife's village, indicating that Kynsai (the victim) thought that the* puri *was "sent" to ensnare him and drive him to madness. Family conflicts seem to be ascribed to a supernatural cause.*

Please note that place and clan names are changed in the narratives themselves to protect the tellers' privacy.

—MARGARET LYNGDOH,
University of Tartu, Estonia

About K——, the River Goddess Who Exists in Jaintia Hills[1]

A family narrative as told by an anonymous teller on October 10, 2012, in East Khasi Hills.

It was a long time ago that some members of our clan—you know how it was, our Tapang Clan[2]—just a few of our families, moved from Nongtapang village to Shynrai village[3] in Jaintia Hills. It was from here that our family migrated to Shillong in search of better opportunities. But they tell a story about one faction of our family, about what happened long ago in Shynrai village and how it affects us even today. We don't talk about it, we are afraid to. It was said long ago that our ancestor, a woman from our clan, held the responsibility of worshipping a deity—I will not name it here, for I am afraid to even speak her name. One day, our Tapang ancestor visited the weekly market at what is now Jowai. As she was making her purchases, she encountered a woman whom she met only on the market days and with whom she shared only a cursory relationship. This woman had a grudge against our ancestress—where our ancestress went in the market, she [this other woman] followed. Our ancestress selected a kilo of vegetables from a vendor at the market, and just as she was about to put it inside her bag, this woman came to the vendor and said, "Give me that portion, I will pay more," and the vendor took the vegetables he was about to give to our ancestress and gave it to the other woman.

Our ancestress said nothing at this obvious slight. But this other woman was relentless and she followed our ancestress to every shop she went and repeated the slight. You see, it was an attempt to disrespect and dishonor her and you know, us Khasis, we believe very strongly in respect and honor.

Our ancestress said nothing, she did not even acknowledge the woman or rebuke her. Instead, she went back to Shynrai, her village, and she took a goat and went to the bank of this river, the River K——, and she sacrificed the goat and pleaded for justice from the K—— Deity. That evening, the husband of the woman who had dishonored our ancestress died. Next morning, her son died, and in evening, it was her daughter who died. It was then that this woman realized what had happened. She came to our ancestress to beg forgiveness and our ancestress relented. She went to the River and gave thanks, and said, "That is enough." The deaths then stopped in the other woman's family.

You see, when our great grandmother left Shynrai village to come to Shillong, she gave up the worship of this deity with the proper rites or rituals, and after her death, our grandmother dishonored K—— by eating beef. She suffered greatly, her neck turned around a hundred and eighty degrees. The ritual performer was able to heal her, but since then, we have paid the price of the dishonor. Our family is broken and there are always bad deaths, misfortunes, and sickness. This is the reason.

How Water Tied
a Covenant with Man and
the Divine Nature of Water[1]

*As told by Marcus Lapang in Korstep Village, Ri Bhoi District,
on November 2, 2005.*

In the olden days, the true name of water was Niaring. Niaring was the older sister of air. In those day, Niaring was confined to one place by the Supreme Being. In her place of confinement, the sounds of her sorrow, of her crying, could be heard. Then a Council of the Supreme Being was convened, and in that Council it was decided that Niaring should be freed to flow into the earth. So the *riew ramhah*,[2] appointed by the gods, began to clear the earth, thereby making channels for Niaring to flow into the world. These *riew ramhah* came into existence only to fulfill this task. Neither human nor spirit, they were never used by the Supreme Being again, and we do not know where they are today. The Khasi lands as we know them today are so hilly and uneven because Niaring had to be allowed to flow out into the world. After Niaring was freed, she tied a *jutang*, or covenant, whereby she agreed to help mankind in any way that she could, and to go wherever she was needed in the Khasi lands. Niaring promised that she would cleanse and purify the illnesses[3] she shelters and nurtures. In return, mankind agreed not to be cruel or violate her. Water came before Lukhmi, the spirit of paddy (or rice grain).

When Niaring became free, the sounds of her sorrow turned into music and joy as she flowed over the rocks and mountains, which then became her musical instruments. Every water body is the road, the pathway of the *ryngkew* (guardian deity of a place in nature) and *basa* (the deity of water). We see the water flowing, but we never see it return; still, it returns, it goes back. There are thirty kinds of entities, including fish, that live within Niaring, and she offered to cleanse any human afflicted by any of these entities. The *puri*, or water nymph/ spirit, is one of the entities belonging to Niaring. Niaring also harbors evil spirits inside her, and other nonhuman entities (*ki ksuid ki khrei*). This is the reason why Jhare[4] magical practitioners use Niaring to heal illnesses caught from water. In times of necessity, a white hen or white nanny goat must be sacrificed to Niaring. But this sacrifice should only be performed when the Jhare practitioner tells you to do so.

About a *Puri* Enchantment[1]

A family narrative as told by an anonymous interlocutor in East Khasi Hills about an event that occurred in the autumn of 2009.

So Kynsai went fishing or for a picnic (don't remember which) with his friends, and when they were driving back to Shillong, he asked his friends to stop near Um Tyngngar (a small stream near Mylliem in East Khasi Hills) to go pee. But he never came back. His friends searched for him everywhere but couldn't find him. It was really late, and when they couldn't find him, they came home and informed Kynsai's family. The next day, he was found by the villagers near the river without any clothes on, completely naked. He kept saying that someone was calling for him to go toward the river. He couldn't remember what had happened. He was awakened by the villagers and it was only then he realized he was naked. They covered him up and contacted his family to pick him up. Since then, he always gets possessed, even when he's at home or drinking with friends. Like a split personality thing. He becomes super violent and he's fighting the spirit. No names, please. It's in the family so I don't want to be named. Even Kynsai (the victim), for that matter, does not want to be named. Now I don't know. But now, he is married to another lady and he has a son, so he's not as conflicted and depressed as he was before. But alcohol still makes him a little crazy. And he keeps mentioning that the *puri* is from ——, the village of his first wife. But please do not mention the village name.

A MER-WIFE IN
THE INDIAN OCEAN

This tale is from the Andaman and Nicobar Islands, a union territory of India that is part of an extensive archipelago in the Eastern Indian Ocean. According to Frederik Adolph de Roepstorff, a British officer stationed in the Nicobars for thirteen years in the late nineteenth century, he had once related a story to the Nicobarese, who later adopted and reshaped it. The result was "Shoān, a Nicobar Tale," which de Roepstorff published in 1884. Because de Roepstorff does not offer the original story, we are unable to ascertain the extent to which the Nicobarese adapted it. Here, the King of Fishes, a whale, finds a human, Shoān, and gifts him to his daughter, Giri, a mermaid. While this story is similar to others in which a man falls in love with a mermaid, such as "The Mermaid of Kessock," its ending differs strikingly. Tales of human-mermaid marriages often end unhappily, most often because the mermaid abandons her human husband to return to the sea, but in this account, it is the human husband who leaves behind a bereaved mermaid wife. The catalyst for their separation is not the man's desire to abandon her, but a simple desire to procure a hand mirror for her so that she may see what his eyes behold every day—her beautiful face.

Shoān,
a Nicobar Tale[1]

Come all, Nicobarese and foreigners, old and young, men and women, boys and girls, youths and maidens, and listen to a story.

There was formerly a man by the name of Arang, whose wife had borne (him) three sons and three daughters.

He made himself a nice house, and possessed much property.

One day he went out on the sea with his eldest son, called Shoān. They wanted to fish with hook and line.

Strong wind got up and heavy sea sprung up.

Then it happened that one of the outriggers of the canoe broke and both sank into the sea. Arang was drowned, but the boy[2] crawled up on the back of the canoe and cried.

"What shall I do, my father is dead, what am I to do!"

"Wish[3]—it is the whale arriving."

"Why are you crying child?"

"Oh my father is dead, I cannot survive, how shall I get home (lit. there is no road), what *am* I to do, my father is dead!"

"Sit down on my back, I know the road," said the whale. "Oh no, I will not!" said the boy. "I am afraid, I do not know the road, as my father is dead."

But after a while Shoān did sit down on the back of the whale. Wish—off they were, quickly, swiftly.

The whale is a chief of the sea. At the sight of him all got afraid.

The flying fish flew in all directions, the turtle dived down suddenly, the shark sank down (below) his fin, the sea snake dug himself into the sand, the ilū[4] danced along the sea, the dugong[5] hugged her young one, the dolphins fled, for they were afraid of the whale.

Thus (sped) the two. Bye and bye they arrived at the country of the whale. It was a domed big stone-house. The walls were of red coral, the steps were made of tridachna.[6] In the house they saw the daughter of the whale, whose name was Girī.

"Do you like this boy?" said the whale.

"All right, let him stay," said Girī.

"Do you like to stay Shoān?"

"I am willing to stay here."

Then Shoān became the servant of Girī.

Girī's face was like that of a woman, below she was shaped with a fishtail, her breast was the colour of mother of pearl, her back like gold; her eyes were like stars, her hair like seaweed. Said Girī—"What work do you know?"

"I can collect cocoanuts in the jungle."

"Never mind, we have no cocoanuts, but what other work do you know?"

"I can make boats."

"We do not want boat, (but) what other work (do you know)?"

"I know how to spear fish."

"Don't! you must not do it, (for) we love the fish, my father is a chief among the fish. Never mind, comb my hair."

Shoān remained, he combed her hair, they (used to) joke together and they married.

Said Shoān—"How is it wife that you do not possess a looking-glass, although your face is so nice."

"I want a looking-glass, look out for one."

"In my parent's house in the village there is one looking-glass, (but) I do not know the road."

"Never mind I know the road, sit on my back and I will bring you near the land." "I cannot walk in your country, but do, (I pray you, return quickly.)"

"Certainly wife, you (had better) stop near the edge of the coral reef on this big stone, I will return quickly."

Then Shoān returned to his village. He came to (lit. saw) his father's house.

"Who is there?" (said his mother).

"It is I, Shoān."

"No (you are not), Shoān died with his father on the sea."

"Look at my face, I am Shoān, your son."

He came up into the house. When they heard (about it), all the people (of the village) came. They asked many questions and Shoān answered. He told the story about the whale, and the story of his marriage with Girī. The people laughed and said he was telling lies. Shoān got sorry and angry, and he ran away with the looking-glass. The people went after him and speared him and thus died Shoān.

Girī stops in the sea near the coral banks and she sings and calls. In the night when the moon is high, fishermen hear like singing and crying of a woman. They ask other people (about it) and wonder, for they do not know (about) Girī. Girī will not return alone, (that is why) she sings and she calls out: "Come (back) Shoān, come (back) Shoān."

A HAIRY CHINESE
MERMAID

While powerful dragons overseeing seas and rivers are strongly associated with Chinese mythology, aquatic beings that are both fish and human are also mentioned in some ancient texts, and mermaids continue to have a strong hold on the Chinese imagination. Hans Christian Andersen's "The Little Mermaid" has been extremely popular in China since its early-twentieth-century translations, influencing the development of children's literature in the country, and in 2016 the movie The Mermaid broke a number of box-office records.[1]

Nicholas Belfield Dennys—a colonial settler in Beijing, Hong Kong, and Singapore in the latter half of the nineteenth century—drew on earlier Chinese works to describe the mermaids in his book The Folklore of China. Compared to European mermaid-wife counterparts such as Mélusine, the mermaid in the first account summarized below has no tail and no ability to speak human language; an aquatic humanoid, she is covered in silky, rainbow-colored hair. The couple remains happily married, and she returns to the sea only after her husband dies, presumably of natural causes. She is not described as a beauty, and neither is the mermaid in the second account, whose appearance is, however, more "conventional."

Mermaids[1]

Some of my readers may perchance be interested to learn that the original home of the mermaid (Ch. sea-woman 海女 *hai nü*) is almost within sight of the room in which these notes are being written. The only specimen of a veritable mermaid I ever saw was Barnum's celebrated purchase from Japan, which, so far as could be judged, consisted of a monkey's body most artistically joined to a fish's tail. But the author of a work entitled *Yueh chung chieh wên*, or "Jottings on the South of China," compiled in 1801, narrates how a man of the district of Sin-an (locally *Sin-on*) captured a mermaid on the shore of Ta-yü-shan or Namtao Island. "Her features and limbs were in all respects human, except that her body was covered with fine hair of many beautiful colours. The fisherman took home his prize and married her, though she was unable to talk and could only smile. She however learned to wear clothes like ordinary mortals. When the fisherman died the sea-maiden was sent back to the spot where she was first found, and she disappeared beneath the waves." The narrator quaintly adds, "This testifies that a man-fish does no injury to human beings," and he moreover informs us that these creatures are frequently to be found near Yü-shan and the Ladrone Island—so that any adventurous Hongkong canoeist may still have a chance of making a novel acquaintance. Another case recorded by the same writer speaks of a mermaid of more conventional form than the lady already noticed. "The Cabinet Councillor Cha Tao being despatched on a mission to Corea, and lying at anchor in his ship at a bay upon the coast, saw a woman stretched upon the beach, with her face upwards, her hair short and streaming loose, and with webbed feet and hands. He recognised this being as a mermaid (or man fish) and gave orders that she should be carried to the sea. This being done, the creature clasped her hands with an expression of loving gratitude and sank beneath the waters."

MERMAIDS FROM JAPAN

Ningyo, *the Japanese word for mermaid, has no gender.*[1] *Stories about mermaids have been part of the Japanese tradition for centuries, ranging from sightings of "strange" creatures to encounters with beautiful, white-skinned eroticized* ningyo, *even before illustrations of European merfolk made their way to Japan in the seventeenth and eighteenth centuries.*[2] *That said, the "Japanese mermaids" that European and Americans lined up to see for a price in the early to mid-nineteenth century were of a different order.*[3]

The following Japanese tale appeared in the English edition of the Kokumin-no-tomo *(Nation's Friend), a magazine published in Tokyo in the 1890s. The tale features a mermaid wife who, like her European counterpart Mélusine, must leave the human world once her husband breaks his promise and sees her hybrid shape while she is taking her weekly saltwater bath. Like the very popular Japanese animal-bride tale "The Crane Wife,"*[4] *"The Mermaid" is a tale of gratitude, not of abduction, as in European selkie stories. But in all cases, the hybrid being is fully domesticated while in the husband's home. In this Japanese mermaid story, the wife cooks fish delicacies; later, when she leaves, she offers blessings to her husband.*

Hanashika, *to whom this tale is attributed, refers to a professional storyteller, often a* rakugo *(comical stories) performer. This* hanashika *appends two morals, which are both somewhat sexist and tongue in cheek. Notably, the tale contains a reference to the belief—demonstrated in the tale that follows this one, "Yao Bikuni"—that consuming a mermaid's flesh will grant immortality to humans.*

The Mermaid[1]

In days of yore, so runs the Japanese legend as interpreted in the *Nihon no Mukashibanashi* (Old Legends of Japan) there lived a man, a good-natured soul, who yearned to be married but had reached middle-age without finding a suitable partner of his joys and sorrows. His joys consisted mainly in fishing with rod and line from the rocks or the river-bank: his sorrows were most acute when he reached home tired at night and found no one to welcome him and to cook the fish that he had hooked.

One day he was sitting, rod in hand, on a rock meditating on his forlorn and solitary condition when suddenly he felt a tug at his line and found that he had hooked something out of the common. Fearing to break his line and lose both tackle and fish he warily played it for some time and at last succeeded in landing it on the rocks, when to his surprise he found that it was no real fish, but a mermaid with the face of a beautiful maiden, and a body which ended in the orthodox tail.

"Desinit in piscem mulier formosa superne." The mermaid's face was tearful, for the hook was in her cheek, and there was also the shame of being forcibly dragged out of her native element; and the angler was a man of tender heart.

Gently extracting the hook from her jaws, he held her in his hands and meditatively speculated on the money which he could gain by selling her to an itinerant exhibition, or the long life which he might obtain by eating her flesh, (it being, according to the Japanese legend, the peculiar property of mermaid's flesh to give perpetual youth and life to those who eat it).

But his soul revolted at the thought of eating this fair creature, that whimpered and cried like a human being, and so after another long gaze he threw it back into the waves, when the mermaid, waving its grateful adieux, speedily dived out of sight.

The man (his name does not appear in the story) then went on with his fishing. He caught an astonishingly large number of fish and at evening returned home satisfied not only on account of his great catch, but also because of the act of kindness which he had performed. That night as he was in his kitchen, with his sleeves tucked up, preparing his supper, he heard a gentle voice, as of a woman, calling to him from the front of the house. On going to open the door, he found a woman of ordinary appearance but with a sweet and loveable countenance, who told him that she was a homeless and belated traveller who begged a night's lodging. "Come right in," he said, "and make the best you can of my poor accommodation." Then, showing her into the parlour, he begged her to sit down and rest a little while he got ready the supper, and went off into the kitchen. But the woman followed him, and peering over his shoulder as he was scraping the fish said:

"Won't you let me earn my supper by helping you with the cooking?"

"No, no," replied the man, "it would be poor hospitality to make my guest work in the kitchen. Please go into the parlour and sit down. I'll be with you directly."

But the woman insisted that she had lived all her life by the seaside, that she knew all manner of beautiful recipes for cooking fish, and that it was but right that she should do something for her night's entertainment; and being a woman she got her way.

Never before had such delicious fish been served in that poor bachelor's house. He ate what was set before him and came again for a second help and a third, and then fell to expressing his regret that he could not hope to have such a supper every night. Then coyly and modestly the lady remarked that such a hope need not be beyond his powers of attainment; and when pressed for an explanation of this speech, she let fall a modest tear and said that she was a lone woman without parents and without a home. He was, as we have before said, a tender-hearted man, and the upshot of it all was that the lady consented to become the mistress of his house, his hand, and his heart.

But on conditions:—when in the first burst of joy, he was about to press his newly found treasure to his heart, "My dear" she said, holding out a warning hand, "My dear, you know I have lived all my life by the sea side, and I can't do without my salt-water bath once a week. Promise me that." He readily assented. "And promise me," she continued, "never to come in, nor to look, while I am taking my bath." It was such a simple request and such a natural one, that the lover (for he was that now) could but joyfully acquiesce and congratulate himself that he had obtained so great a treasure on such easy terms.

So they were married, and lived happily for many months. The fish were always excellently cooked now, and the husband grew sleek and comfortable, as men do when they have got wives at home who take good care of them. But the bath! It was her one pleasure and diversion, and she took the whole morning preparing for it, and stayed in for hours in the afternoon, and then spent the rest of the day in adorning her person after her bath. So that when bath day came around her husband had a poor time of it. Still he bore it patiently, satisfied with his bargain, till one fatal afternoon when he came home and found her as usual in her bath. The doors were shut, but there was a chink, and he was hungrily anxious to know how long it would be before he got his supper. So he just peeped in to see how long she was going to he, when to his suprise and horror, he saw no wife, but a mermaid swimming about in the bath-tub.

"Ah!" he said, with half a shudder, "now I understand why she is such a good hand at cooking fish. I hope she did not see me peeping at her, but all the same I don't think I shall be able to eat those fish as heartily hereafter."

Presently the door opened and his wife appeared. With a tearful face she knelt down before him and said, "You were kind to me long ago when you saved my life out fishing. In order to repay your kindness I came to help you and be your cook. You have treated me with unfailing kindness, and have honoured me by making me your wife. I cannot thank you enough for all you have done. But, alas! you have seen me in my true form, and now I can stay with you no longer. It grieves me to the heart, but I must bid you goodbye. Heaven bless you, and give you a long and prosperous life." And before he could speak she was away on the rocks and plunged into the sea.

Poor man! by one thoughtless act he had lost a good wife, and as his marriage with a mermaid had procured for him the gift of a long life, there were many lonely days of widowerhood in store for him.

The fable appears to have two morals. The one is that if a lady wishes to gain and to keep a good husband, she should feed him. The other is that if you with to retain the affections of a good wife you should not interfere with her toilet.

Yao Bikuni[1]

"Yao Bikuni" is a legend about longevity found throughout the main island of Japan. Yao literally means "eight hundred," and bikuni means "Buddhist priestess." The oldest written source for this legend dates back to the fifteenth century. Several variants exist, and many of them originated in a coastal area in Fukui Prefecture, where a stone monument commemorating this legend stands. They share the following basic plot: a little girl eats mermaid's flesh without knowing its effect and gets to live for eight hundred—or in some versions, two or four hundred—years.[2]

—MAYAKO MURAI, *Kanagawa University, Japan*
Translated by Mayako Murai

A long time ago, a gathering was held. A man went to the gathering and took home mermaid's flesh served as fish to give to his beloved daughter. The little girl, who later came to be known as Yao Bikuni, ate the mermaid's flesh, and, lo and behold, her life was extended to no less than eight hundred years!

Then, she said, "I no longer want to live in this world. All my family are gone, and I cannot keep up with what is going on around me. This is all because I have lived eight hundred years. So please bury me in the ground." She was going to be buried up on the mountain in Obama where Kuin Temple was. "Please bury me here, and plant a camellia tree where I am going to be buried. When this tree stops blossoming, I will die. As long as it is blossoming, I won't yet be dead." Yao Bikuni explained this, and people buried her there. Then water began to drip from the spot. "When this water stops dripping, I will also stop breathing," said she. Water is still dripping if you go there.

After a while, however, they moved the stone monument and the camellia that stood where Yao Bikuni was buried to another place. Maybe they were in an inconvenient place for the temple. Then, Yao Bikuni's camellia began to wither. People said, "This is not good," and moved the tree back to where it was. Since then, it has continued to blossom. So it is said that Yao Bikuni is still alive today, and will be until the day when the water stops dripping and the camellia stops blossoming.

WATER SPIRITS OF
THE PHILIPPINES

*The Republic of the Philippines is an archipelago of more than
7,600 islands, colonized by the Spanish from the mid-sixteenth
century to the late nineteenth century. In the Philippines, stories about the* sirena *have a colonial origin, but they circulate
in syncretic relation to stories about old-time water dwellers
such as the* catao *(or* kataw*),* litao*, and* magindara—*often
guardians of freshwater and the trees surrounding it. American
anthropologist Henry Otley Beyer (1883–1966), over several
decades, amassed a vast collection of materials about Filipino
culture and history. His great-granddaughter, Charity Beyer-
Bagatsing, found more than forty mermaid stories in his papers, three of which appear here. Beyer-Bagatsing notes,*

The *sirena*, or mermaid, and the facts surrounding this
mythical creature are of Spanish origin. Using the 160 volumes of the Beyer Ethnographic Series, I was amazed that
the maiden of the waters was predominantly unique to the
Ilokano volumes. I approached my Ilokana grandmother—
Pacita Malabad Beyer—with the question, "Why is the sirena only found in the Ilokano papers, barely mentioned in
the Tagalog papers, and not at all mentioned in the Visayan
and Mindanao papers?"[1] She replied, "The different rivers
in the Ilocos region, although calm and pristine on the surface, have strong currents and undertows beneath. Through
the years, I heard accounts of swimmers drowning or in a
half-dazed state after escaping the grip of an unknown force

that tried to drag them to the bottom of the river; having no other explanation for this phenomenon, the early Spaniards told the natives it might have been a mermaid or *sirena*." She also added, "The Ilokano term *litao*—the male deity of the waters—supports the Ilokano traditions and dialects; besides, the word *sirena* is a Spanish word and has no Ilokano equivalent."

The following *sirena* stories are my personal favorites. The first one, "The Mermaid Queen," is one of the oldest stories in the Ilokano volumes, dating back to the 1600s. The *sirena* is described as a kind lady with supernatural powers rather than a half human-fish creature. The second story, "The Litao and Serena," intertwines the Ilokano and Spanish beliefs into a love story that parallels the blending of the two cultures. Finally, "The American and the Sirena of Amburayan" came about during the American years [when the Americans occupied the Philippines], adding humor and notoriety to the infamous water nymph's character and persona.

The Mermaid Queen[1]

This story is from San Carlos, Pangasinan. In the olden days, Binalatongan's main product was mongo beans (balatong), hence its name. It was a wealthy settlement of two thousand houses where ordinary people wore the finest Chinese silk for daily use and gold flowed in the rivers surrounding the region.

The name of their sovereign ruler was Maginoo Palasipas, who was unhappy in spite of his vast wealth and power brought by his exemplary rulership. His greatest desire was to be conquered by the heart of a woman and share his kingdom with a soul mate. This woman had to be the fairest of the fair, whose beauty and character was unmatched by no other. His loyal datus sought the fairest maidens in the land and presented their beauty to the king. Tagalog chieftains sent envoys with a message offering their secluded royal daughters to be his bride. Chinese, Japanese, and Bornean merchants volunteered to sail back to their native lands to bring back princesses of pure royal blood. However, he refused all their offers and suggestions.

One evening, Maginoo Palasipas strolled by the riverbank and laid down on the dewed grass to admire the fullness of the moon. He heard a faint and mystical melody from afar. Following the sound of the music, he came upon a maiden sitting on a rock with her back turned. She was combing her thick ankle-length hair and had the most enchanting voice.

He noticed a crown of pearls adorning her head and she wore a silk robe embroidered with gold beads, pearls, and diamonds. The maiden instinctively turned around and he beheld the face of a goddess with flawless olive skin, blue-green eyes like the waters, and blood-red lips.

Instantly smitten, Maginoo Palasipas asked who she was. She answered, "I am the mermaid of Binalatongan."

Palasipas replied, "I have heard about your kindness toward my people. Thank you for guiding my fishermen back into shore during a storm, for rescuing Datu Angat's only son from drowning, and leaving a string of pearls to Datu' Bakat's widow after he was killed by raiding Tirong pirates."

By this time, Palasipas got down on his knees and asked the mermaid to be his wife and rule as the Queen of Binalatogan. The mermaid smiled, nodded her head, and gave her hand to the Palasipas. The mermaid renounced her sea life and thus began the long and glorious reign of the once-mermaid and the powerful Maginoo Palasipas.

The Litao and Serena[1]

Long ago, the beautiful Serena lived with her mother by the sea. At the end of the day, she would sit on a rock to comb her long tresses while singing so sweetly. One day a litao heard her voice and fell in love with this mortal maiden. The merman wasted no time expressing his feelings; serenading her under the shadows of the moonlight and leaving flowers and treasures at her doorstep.

Serena's mother grew fearful of the deity that sought her daughter's heart and forbade her from leaving the house. Two weeks went by and Serena grew increasingly bored, and angry from being kept indoors. One morning while her mother was distracted preparing breakfast, she opened the window and noticed a bright object sparkling by the water's edge.

Filled with curiosity, she crept outside and saw a diamond the size of a small coconut, dancing with the waves. As her fingers scarcely touched the waters, a huge bubble enveloped her and transported her to the litao's palace in the bottom of the sea. When she reached his abode, she gazed upward and saw the sun shimmering like a glorious diadem. A soft voice called her name, turning her head, she saw a half-fish and half-human creature whose eyes were filled with love and kindness.

He showed her his kingdom and by the end of the day, Serena was in love and agreed to live with him at the bottom of the sea. The litao explained she would have to drink a potion mixed with his blood to transform her into an immortal half-human and half-fish creature like himself. However, he withheld the dark secret of the price he had to pay for her immortality, which turned him into a mortal after a hundred years.

Piercing his wrist with a silver knife, he prepared the elixir and gave it to Serena to drink, and within a few minutes her transformation was complete. After sunset, they went up to the surface and visited Serena's grieving mother, who almost fainted from the shock of her daughter's new form. But seeing their great love for each other, she blessed their union and the sirens lived happily in their underwater paradise for one hundred years.

Their union produced seven beautiful daughters who now live in the various waters of the area. On the eve of the hundredth year, the litao whispered in her ear, "A hundred years with you is better than eternity without you." After disclosing his dark secret, he spent the rest of the evening consoling his distraught wife. Early the next day, the merman kissed Serena good-bye and swam near the entrance of their home where he turned into a rock.

Serena, full of anguish at the loss of her husband, went up to the shore and transformed herself into a human. Hearing the sounds of a procession, she walked toward town and followed behind the carriage of the Virgin Mary; walking sorrowfully with tear-filled eyes fixed to the ground.

People wondered who the mysterious lady was. After the procession, a curious few followed the lady with the fishlike odor as she walked toward the river. When she came to the water's edge, they surely thought she was going to drown herself. They watched in awe as the waters divided into two walls giving her passage into her underwater palace. The litao was soon forgotten by all except Serena, who is forever grateful for the gift of immortality her husband gave her long ago.

The American and the Sirena of Amburayan[1]

This story is about the siren living in the Amburayan River in Tagudin. During the construction of the bridge, which occurred during the American occupation, the chief architectural engineer was an American who made his home near the river.

The mermaid who had never seen a man with light blond hair, sky blue eyes, and skin that turned into gold from the sun's rays became obsessed with the young man. Each night she would sit under the window of his bedside singing and inviting him to meet her by the waters of the half-finished bridge. By the end of the week, the mermaid felt insulted and wondered why the object of her desires never came to the water's edge or even acknowledged her presence.

The mermaid was unaware of the fact that the American was very sensitive to foul smells, and the rotten fishlike odor permeating from the mermaid's skin made him sick to the stomach, causing him to pass out. One night, determined to find the cause of his fainting spells, he tied a bandanna to cover his nose and fully loaded his rifle. That same evening, the mermaid was intent on making the American her husband, changed herself into a human, and knocked on his door.

The American, upon opening the door, was astonished at seeing a beautiful, scantily clad, voluptuous woman with jet-black floor-length hair standing at his doorway. The mermaid gazed at her paramour, who stood speechless at the magnificent sight before him. She leaned close to plant a kiss on his lips, the American, who found no harm in accepting a kiss from this peculiar maiden, removed his bandanna to meet her eager red lips. In less than a second, he knew her to be the vile repugnant creature whose odor rendered him unconscious.

The mermaid, seeing the panic in his eyes, grabbed his legs and tried to drag him toward the water's edge. In the middle of their scuffle, he pulled the rifle trigger and the strange woman instantly vanished before the silver bullet could pierce her scaly body. The American, frightened by this experience, quit his position, took the first ship back to the United States, and never returned to the Philippines.

A Mermaid in Mabini[1]

Regie Barcelona Villanueva's grandfather, who grew up in Mabini, told him this tale about the mermaid of Mabini in Iloco, which Villanueva translated into English, and to which he added historical details. The events related in this account— a well-known, but until recently unpublished, legend—took place in 1832 in Mabini, a municipality in the province of Pangasinan in the Philippines. At that time, river fishermen believed that mermaids were pests that needed to be eradicated, which of course is in sharp contrast with other views of mermaids as lovely and gentle, or sexualized objects of desire. Residents refer to this mermaid as an engkantada *(enchanted and enchantress, a being with magical powers), an apt description given that she has power over the waters of the sky and land. Significantly, this legend informs present-day Lent-related processions, which diverge from Church-sanctioned devotional practices, in Mabini: people believe that the mermaid joins the parade in the form of a woman. As such, it speaks to the power of folklore.*

In 1832, a great flood devastated the town Balincaguing (later called Mabini), to the extent that the Catholic Church, convent, and all other houses erected therein were under water.

There was once a hole directly beneath the present altar of the town church. Some people discovered it during the time of the flood, and it's been said that there was an underground river. The underground river, then, led you to the river where fishermen catch fish. One time, an "engkantada," which was a mermaid, laid eggs in the underground river. But due to unfavorable circumstances, the mermaid's eggs were found by a group of fishermen. Since they were convinced that the eggs were from a mermaid, they stole them and aborted the hatching of the eggs, believing that mermaids are a plague.

Because of the mermaid's wrath toward the cruel group of fishermen, she summoned the water in the sky and in the nearby river to devour the town. That time, the town was completely obliterated. Those who survived the catastrophe were told by the mermaid that they would never forget her wrath because she would forevermore take the life of one man every year in the river.

Mabinians believe that the mermaid usually takes that life during the festival of the Cabinuangan neighborhood (which is the village next to the river), when one man drowns from bathing or swimming in the river.

Also, even now, Mabinians still believe that the mermaid transfigures into a woman every Lenten season and joins the "libot" (procession). People also believe that the prettiest and fairest lady at the tail of the parade is the mermaid.

—*As told by Regie Barcelona Villanueva*

The Mermaid[1]

This next folktale is from the island provinces of Cebu and Bohol in the Central Visayas region of the Philippines, and appears, as translator Erlinda K. Alburo notes, in a volume collecting for the most part oral and unpublished materials.[2] Cebuano is one of the most widely spoken languages across the Philippines. Like some of the other accounts in our volume, this Cebuano story tells of the metamorphosis of a human into a water spirit; however, the catalyst in this case is not love or a curse, but a pregnant woman's craving for milkfish. Pregnancy cravings are taken seriously in many cultures, lest the unborn child be harmed or physically marked in some way.

Once there lived beside the sea a couple named Juan and Juana. For a long time they were childless. When Juana was at last with child, they were quite happy.

But in her pregnancy, Juana would become very restless if she did not have milkfish to eat every day. So one afternoon, when Juan failed to catch any milkfish, he became very sad.

Suddenly, Juan heard his name called. He was greatly surprised when he looked down and saw a shiny milkfish wearing a crown.

The milkfish identified himself as the King of Fishes and he asked Juan: "Why do you fish only for milkfish?" Juan told him the reason, and his sorrow at the moment.

The King of Fishes pitied Juan and promised "I'll give you plenty of milkfish every day. But in return, you are to deliver your coming child to me when it turns seven years old."

Because it was already getting dark and since milkfish was becoming scarce that season, Juan finally agreed.

The King of Fishes was true to his word. Even after Juana had given birth, Juan continued to bring home milkfish from the sea.

Their child was a lovely girl with very black hair. They loved her and were very happy with her. They called her Maria.

When Maria turned seven, Juan went out to see the King of Fishes and begged him: "Have pity on us. Can't you possibly release me from my promise? We love Maria very much, and we can't bear to part with her." But the King of Fishes was firm, saying: "A promise is a promise." With a heavy heart, Juan went home.

Since that day, the couple and Maria never went near the sea.

But one day, while Juan was on the farm and Juana was doing the laundry in the river, there came a big wonderful boat. The people immediately flocked to the shore to see it. Maria was alone at the time and was looking out the window. She became curious and joined the rest on the shore.

While she was watching the wonderful boat, a big wave rushed up and dragged her to the sea.

Immediately, the neighbors told her parents of the incident. Juan and Juana ran to the shore but they were too late. Maria was gone!

Every evening after that, the couple would stand by the shore and stare at the deep. They kept hoping that Maria would return. Years passed and still they failed to see her.

But one moonlight night, there appeared before the old couple a lovely creature. She had very long black hair, but—while half of her body was that of a beautiful girl, the other half was that of a milkfish.

Then they knew that it was Maria, now a mermaid.

A MER-WIFE IN
NORTHERN AUSTRALIA

Like the European mermaid, the Karukayn of northern Australia is human on top and fish below; however, with some effort, her fishtail is detachable, revealing human legs underneath. This story takes place in Gurindji country and concerns a young Gurindji man who sees two Karukayn sunning on the shore and decides to take one as his wife. However, catching her poses challenges: the area is teeming with freshwater crocodiles, and, as he discovers, the Karukayn is not docile, and puts up a struggle when he attempts to remove her tail. The man's determination and ingenuity in overcoming these obstacles add an element of humor to the tale. As in many other mermaid-wife tales, the union of a human with a Karukayn proves only temporary, cautioning against marriage outside one's social group.[1]

Part of the Gurindji repertoire of yijarni, which translates as true stories, this tale speaks to beliefs that are not necessarily confined to the past, and the fear of being pulled underwater by a mermaid is real. The book's epigraph is in the voice of Mr. Ronnie Wavehill, the teller of this mermaid story: "I'm telling the stories they told me: my father, my father's father, my mother's father and whoever else. They told me, 'Keep these stories here and pass them on to anyone, whitefellas and all. Tell the stories! Don't keep them to yourself!' So it's true what I'm telling you today, it's still true today."

Karukayn (Mermaids)[1]

Another story I'm going to tell you is about mermaids. It's about one who got taken from the water by a man. He was single and he used to go hunting by himself. One day he was out in the high country, looking around for rock wallabies first. Then he went back home. The next day he went hunting again.

'I might go hunting down by the river tomorrow,' he was thinking. 'Might get some fish or crocodile . . . might get a go-anna — or anything like that there, riverside — turtle, or fish.' He went along the banks, further and further, until he came out at a little spot and there he found them lying in the sun.

'Here's something!' he was thinking. He spotted them from a long way away off: a couple of freshwater crocodiles warming themselves in the sun. Looking upstream, he muttered, 'True! Crocodiles!' As he looked he thought, 'What on earth are those two black things lying there?'

Two dark things were lying there amongst the crocodiles: two water-girls. Those two black bodies were mermaids. While he was watching them, one of them sat up and took a look around each way. She had really long hair, all the way down to here. *(He points to his hip.)* Both of them did, just like those bush girls. He could make out the long hair even as she was sitting.

'Hey, they're women! These are water-girls these two — *karukayn*, wait a minute here . . . How to get around to them? Hang on . . .' Still watching, he saw one lying down and the other sitting up.

'Two watchimicallits — two of those girls.' He went right around, downstream. 'Well, how can I get through — maybe this way? Or where?' He came to a sudden stop, but just then a gust of wind blew and the girls could smell that someone was there, and they dived into the water. The crocodiles went in after them.

'Well hang on. I'll still wait for them,' he was thinking. 'I'll wait it out and come back for them. After how long? Maybe three days? Three days and I'll come back for them then.'

'I'll come back right here to the same place. I know where they are now, these *karukayn*. I've found them now and I'll grab one of them and make her my wife.'

He went back now, back to the camp, but he never told anybody, this man, about how he found those two mermaids. He just kept that news to himself. He stayed there.

In the meantime he went hunting for kangaroo. 'Leave it for now,' he was thinking. 'Let them forget about it first, and then . . . When to go back? Maybe after three days?'

So he just kept going hunting and returning home to sleep, day after day. Then he decided, 'Tomorrow I'll go back.'

'I'll see them there downstream at the same crossing,' he decided. Well, back he went, right back to the same place. Quietly all the way, he went back to the same place where he had seen them before. He spotted them: 'True, true! Here they are.' They were still there. 'Well, there you go!'

This time he went a really long way around, like from here to where the school is (about 100 metres). He kept his distance, that old man, well . . . young man. He was a grown man alright, but still young.

Into the water, down he went, very slowly. Then he got some river grass with mud still on it and put it on his head like a big hat. The grass was hanging down over his face: 'This will keep them from spotting me . . . Can't let them find me.'

He started moving very slowly towards them along the side of the riverbank. Only that nose of his was sticking out of the water, just enough to let him catch some air. Breathing carefully he went crawling along the riverbank, closer and closer. One of the women was sitting up. He didn't move, and then she lay down again. Then very slowly, still lying low, he went crawling along again.

One girl was looking all around where they were sitting, but she never thought to look to her north to the water. She kept looking from that sunny spot up and through the bush to the east. There was no reason to look to the water! They wouldn't find him sitting in the water. 'She won't be looking over this way.'

The crocodiles were there too. He kept moving quietly, closer and closer, really slowly. He had that hat-like thing on his head, the mud with the grass he'd pulled out. He was just hiding behind the grass hanging down over his face. What if a little wave came along and washed away his disguise? He went floating along, quietly, that man, with only his eyes peeping through the grass hanging down.

He kept going along . . . the other mermaid sat up. That first one was still there looking over her shoulder—he was keeping very quiet—one *karukayn* was lying down a bit closer. He kept moving on in the water—slowly all the way.

Almost . . . he was just about there—but what if the water took his grass disguise away now? That grass could go with a little wave—and then the two of them would see there's a man underneath—a man sneaking along in the water. One mermaid sat up and was glancing over her shoulder, scanning around, and then she lay down again. He kept moving—not far now—he was in shallow water. He took hold of the grass and slowly took it off; he got up and started walking.

Right! Spotted by the crocodiles! The crocodiles went scuttling down the bank and dived into the water. The two girls leapt up and then he did too. He ran and started grabbing at them.

'Here now, here.' That young fella went for one girl, but she pushed him away; pushed him back. He grabbed her body then and dragged her up the riverbank: dragging her up towards the top. She was struggling and wanted to get into the water, diving here and there, but he was strong, and he picked her up and carried her in his arms to the top of the bank.

He got firesticks and started rolling them between his hands to get the fire going to smoke her tail off. To hold her he made a shallow hole in the ground where he kept her tied down and propped up. The fish tail can come off as one piece. Mermaids get it when they go in the water and it makes them swim fast like a fish. With the working of the firesticks, the flames appeared and he put some river gum leaves on top; they're good for smoking. Meanwhile below, the fire caught alight.

He put a cover of river gum leaves on the fire and held her in the smoke. She was writhing around: wrestling with him, trying to get away. But he was strong, that man. She couldn't get away from him. He put her lying face down to let the smoke go all around her. He kept smoking her, while she was yelling out and squirming around. He kept smoking her properly, all around, turning her this way and that. Then the tail started to come off. Those *karukayn* tails, they're like a fish tail, but they're detachable, you can take them off just like clothes. Well, he took the tail off and found she had legs underneath, just like a person. Like the legs that people have, she had legs, but the tail was on the outside to make her move quickly through the water. He pulled it off.

He kept smoking her all round, smoking her head and her ears; he kept turning her around to make sure she was alright, smoking everything. Okay, she should be right now. She could stand up and walk. He took her hand and led her off to the camp.

He took her back and they saw him. 'Hey, he's got a woman!' 'Where's he been keeping that woman?' 'I thought he's supposed to be a single man, that bloke,' they all talked at once.

'Wow, light skin like a *pilyingpilying!*' That woman had long hair all the way down her back: past her back. She had long hair like a bush girl.

'I found her.'

'Where?'

'She's a mermaid.'

'Really? Where did you get her?'

'Over that way,' he said.

'Many more there?'

'Nah, only two. One of them dived into the water. This is the younger one, the other one was . . . you know. I got the young one.'

'Ah, yeah, okay.'

'Well, keep her now and don't take her back near the water now; no river or spring, anywhere like that . . .'

'Nah, I'll keep her with me.'

Well, he took her everywhere, all around, but not down to

the river, till she understood. He kept her with him all the time, until she was used to him. She recognised him as her husband and they stayed together for some time.

They still used to tell him, 'Well don't take her back to the water you know, that kind of woman might leave you.'

'No, it's okay. I can take her to the river if I want to, no reason not to. She accepts me as her husband: this is my wife.'

'Is that right!' they said. 'We're talking to you from experience, you know. They used to get that kind of girl before. You want to keep her in the bush all the time, until she's had a baby. You know she doesn't have any kids yet! Don't take her to the river, or else she'll leave you.'

'No, she won't leave me: she's accepted me. You've seen us go everywhere together. She can't leave me now, why would she? She's my wife.'

'We're talking to you for your own good, young man, we're just telling you how it is. We've seen this kind of thing before. If you take her down to the river, she'll leave you; she'll just dive off into the water.'

'Rubbish, you can ask her yourself. I can take her anywhere, even down to the water,' he said.

'Well okay, but we're just giving you good advice. It's alright, we'll not mention it again.'

They went down to the river then, that man and his mermaid wife, just to look around, just go hunting, and they got a goanna. They made a camp by the side of the big river and cooked it.

That girl was looking at something. 'That might be my place . . .' She was looking at the spot down under the water. 'Down there, that could be my home.' It might have been near where he grabbed her in the first place.

A little while later the man was walking around the camp, when suddenly the woman began running. Run-run-running she went, and dived into the water—no sign of her any'where. He was broken-hearted.

'Well.' There was nothing he could do. He started looking down into the water, where she disappeared into the water, leaving him for good.

The man still stood there. 'She might come up yet.' He looked and looked, but she'd disappeared into the water, gone for good.

He started to realise that they'd been right. 'Don't take her to the river, even if she's happy with you. You don't know that she won't return to the water.' He was heart-broken and left feeling helpless. That's all.

—RONNIE WAVEHILL
—*translated by* ERIKA CHAROLA *and* RONNIE WAVEHILL

A CHAMORRO GIRL
BECOMES A MERMAID

This tale is from Guam, an unincorporated U.S. territory in the Pacific Ocean (Micronesia). Sirena is a well-known and beloved figure in Chamorro culture. While it is true that Guam was once colonized by the Spanish, and thus some might argue that the Sirena story is ultimately based on Spanish tales about las sirenas, *it diverges from typical European tales of mermaids in that it is not a story about a human-mermaid encounter, but a cautionary tale about the negative consequences of not attending to one's responsibilities. In this intergenerational plot focused on the young girl Sirena, the grandmother's wish means to alleviate the mother's curse.*

Sirena[1]

A CHAMORRO GIRL

An ancient grand-mermaid sits on top of her pearly throne, brushing her long white hair. Upon her lap perch two little mergirls, their sparkling tails twisting and twirling.

"Oh, Auntie Sirena, tell us how the mermaids first became!"

"Haven't you heard that story enough? I must have told it to you a hundred times already!" the ancient one chuckles.

"Oh please, Auntie Sirena! We'll be oh-so-good if you will tell of our great-grand-mermaid Sirena, your mama!" the youngest pleads. Her large, charcoal-black eyes fill with shy tears, her black hair settles around her face. A butterfly fish peeps out from behind her ear, looking at the old mermaid reproachfully.

"All right, sit down and behave. I'll tell you the tale of Sirena," laughs the grand-mermaid. Looking at the two little mergirls with their rapt eyes, she slowly nods. And so the story begins . . .

On the faraway island of Guam lived Sirena, a graceful Chamorro girl. Sirena had silky hair and big dark eyes that surveyed her world in constant wonder. Her face was round and lovely; her hair was long and black. When Sirena laughed, her face smoothed into bliss and it seemed that nothing could be as sweet and innocent as this young girl.

As lovely as Sirena was, she was also very careless. She was constantly reminded by her mother to work hard. Sirena was good at weaving and could cook savory fish and find the most fragrant flowers and vines. Her flaw was that her whole self was always yearning for the water.

Sirena would start her work, weaving, cooking, or fishing, but soon her thoughts would turn to the river. She would run off to play in the cool water, her hair glistening in the warm tropical sun. Her mother was very patient with Sirena and usually excused these errors. She was fond of Sirena and knew that her beautiful daughter was still blessed with the naiveté of youth.

However, one day her mother was in a particularly bad mood. She had so much work to do. Her cousin was preparing a huge feast, and the mother's job was to cook heaps of tapioca, fish, and coconut crab. All of Sirena's brothers and sisters were busy. Sirena was splashing in the river when her youngest sister came down to fetch water.

"Sirena, you'd better get up there and help. Mama needs you. She is already angry because she can't find you," her sister warned. She giggled at Sirena's nonchalant glance, then bent to dip her urn into the cool water. Once the vessel was filled to the brim, she gave Sirena an entreating tap on her shoulder, but Sirena brushed her away.

Sirena's sister ran back up the shaded path to their thatched dwelling. She knew her mother would be angry.

"The water looks especially nice," Sirena thought. I will have one quick swim before wasting the whole day cooking." Sirena swam and then reluctantly trudged up to her house. Inside her mother was shouting at her brother to get breadfruit from their auntie across the bay.

"Sirena, there you are! I've been looking all over for you! Come, take this basket from your brother and fill it with breadfruit from auntie's. Hurry, come directly back." Her mother looked stern and angry. "Do not swim!"

Sirena took the basket. She raced from her house down the trail to her auntie's. Her feet padded quickly along the soft, sandy path until she reached a small resting hut that looked out on the river. There Sirena sat down and waited for her heartbeat to slow down as she took deep breaths of the warm tropical air.

Suddenly, a flock of birds screeched. Sirena looked up. Right in front of her, the birds dipped and dove into the river, beckoning her to play. The sun shone off the clear waters sparkling like laughter. Fearless fish jumped and let the bright sun leap off their silver scales.

"Oh, if I play only a moment, then it won't matter," Sirena said to herself. She ached to step into the water! She put down her basket and ran to the glistening waters. They lifted her up and carried her out to deeper slopes where her feet barely touched the sandy bottom. Sirena splashed and swam. She didn't notice that the birds had flown away.

Sirena was diving from a small rock when she looked up with alarm. The sun had disappeared behind the horizon, and dusk was coating the island. Sirena was very afraid of the night spirits that might leap out of the river. She sped up the beach to her empty basket. In the dim light, it looked emptier than ever! A frightened, hopeless tear slid down her cheek.

"Mama will be so mad when she finds out I didn't get the breadfruit! She needed it for the cooking. Now she will be so disappointed in me!" Sirena cried. Her soft, whimpering voice received no pity from the night as it spread its lightless cloak over the sad girl.

Fear of the darkness soon caused her to forget her woes. Sirena turned her back to the river and darted up to her house. At first she cowered in the dark, but then she tiptoed up the doorway when she saw a branch of the flame tree tremble. Was it a taotaomo'na about to snatch her?

"Sirena!" Her mother's face loomed out of the darkness. Her angry eyes burned with wrath. "Shame, shame, shame on you! Careless, idle child! Your own sister of six can do better! Shame, Sirena! I had to walk over to your anutie's house myself for the breadfruit. Sirena, if you ever go in the water again, you will become an ugly, fat fish!" her mother screamed.

Sirena knelt trembling in a corner, her godmother's hand on her shoulder. "No, please, no!" Sirena wailed when she heard her mother's curse.

Sirena leaped from the house and began to streak down the path toward the water.

"Wait, Sirena, wait!" the godmother called. Tears coursed down the godmother's wrinkled face. She knew the power of a mother's curse. If Sirena touched the river, she would become a fish with slimy gray scales, staring eyes, and an ugly, wordless gaping mouth.

"Oh, spirits in your haunts, hear me! Save Sirena! Let her not become a disgusting fish! Save her beautiful face and her joyful spirit! Let the power of this curse be dimmed! She is but a foolish child, help her!" the godmother prayed.

Tears streamed down the mother's cheeks and her body shook with sobs. Too late she realized what she had said.

Sirena stopped at the water's edge. She saw the full orange moon rising above the distant horizon. Not a sound echoed from the watery silence. Sirena wept in fear and in pain. She didn't want to leave her family—her mother and her god-mother. She didn't want to leave the soft grass and the waving palms. But her whole body wanted, needed the water. Its songs and hypnotic rhythms were a part of her as much as the fragrant flowers and tender breezes of her tropical birthplace. Sirena knew in her heart that she could not survive a day without swimming freely in the river.

As her godmother was chanting and her mother weeping, Sirena ran into the water. She dove from the shallows and swam down the river until she reached the deep sapphire depths of the ocean.

At once she began to change. She felt her legs binding, twisting, and turning, but not into ugly gray scales. Instead, an iridescent tail stretched down from her waist. Sobs shook her body, but her clear voice and beauty remained unchanged.

Sirena looked one last time at her beloved island. She whispered her last good-bye, a call that her mother heard with sadness and her godmother heard with a painful but understanding smile.

Some say that to this day, Sirena's whispered call continues to echo across the vast, rippling sea.

"And so our story ends," whispers the old grand-mermaid to the two sleepy mergirls.

"What a sad story. I like it, but it makes me cry," murmurs the one, curling up in a pile of soft seaweed.

"I think so, too. Too bad it's only pretend," sighs the other.

The grand-mermaid smiles at her two yawning granddaughters. "Legend is the only truth, my children."

THE FEEJEE MERMAID
HOAX

In his autobiography, written in 1854, Phineas Taylor Barnum outlines his efforts to cash in on "the general incredulity in the existence of mermaids" by exhibiting what he claimed was a mummified mermaid, known as the "Fejee mermaid" (also Feejee or Fiji), to the public.[1] Barnum gives the following account of his acquistion of the mermaid:

Early in the summer of 1842, Moses Kimball, Esq., the popular proprietor of the Boston Museum, came to New-York and exhibted to me what purported to be a mermaid. He stated that he had bought it of a sailor whose father, while in Calcutta in 1817 as captain of a Boston ship (of which Caption John Ellery was principal owner), had purchased it, believing it to be a preserved specimen of a veritable mermaid, obtained, as he was assured, from Japanese sailors.

Barnum wrote letters to three newspapers in New York, dated within a week or two of each other, and gave them to his friends to mail them from different locations. The first two letters gave local news, but also mentioned an agent of an important London museum, Dr. Griffin, who had purchased a mummified Fejee mermaid. The third letter asked the editors if they would consider asking Dr. Griffin to see the mermaid before he left for England. Barnum then ordered his employee, Mr. Lyman, to pretend to be Dr. Griffin and show the mermaid to the owner of a major hotel in Philadelphia. As Barnum explains, "*Suffice it to say, that the plan worked admirably, and the Philadelphia press aided the press of New-York in awakening a wide-reaching and increasing curiosity to see the mermaid.*"

On August 8, Barnum exhibited the Fejee Mermaid to the public for the first time. His assessment of how the mermaid was received is phrased in a manner befitting a man who was a master at pulling off hoaxes:

The public appeared to be satisfied, but as some persons always *will* take things literally, and make no allowance for poetic license even in mermaids, an occasional visitor, after having seen the large transparency in front of the hall, representing a beautiful creature half woman and half fish, about eight feet in length, would be slightly surprised in finding that the reality was a black-looking specimen of dried monkey and fish that a boy a few years old could easily run away with under his arm.

The first of the three letters that Barnum asked his friends to send for him was to The New York Herald. *That letter inspired the following article, "The Mermaid," which was published on July 17, 1842. Notably, the editorial took up half of the paper's front page and included an engraving of the "mermaid." Only the first paragraph discusses the "Fejee mermaid"—the rest is essentially a chronology of mermaid sightings.*

The Mermaid[1]

Our readers will recollect that a few weeks since, we published a letter from a correspondent in Montgomery, Alabama, giving a description of a mermaid, which he had seen there in possession of an English gentleman, who had brought it from the Fejes Islands. A young artist at the south has had a peep at this strange animal, and has sent us a perfect drawing of it, from which we have had the above engraving executed for the gratification of our readers. The artist assures us that the drawing is perfectly correct, with the exception of the hair, which he has taken the liberty to make a little longer than the original would warrant.

The Mermaid has long been considered by many as a fabulous animal; but some naturalists have declared that there is too much evidence of the existence of these animals to warrant them in pronouncing the mermaid to be a mere creature of fancy.

We discover in the ourang outang the connecting link between the human and animal race. The flying squirrel or bat is the link between birds and quadrupeds, the platipus, has the body of a seal and the webbed feet and bill of the duck; the flying fish connects the bird and sealy inhabitant of the deep, and why may we not suppose that there is also a connecting link between fish and the human species?

Had not fossil remains of the great Mastedon been discovered, few would be found at the present day who would believe that such an animal had ever existed. We have seen many sea captains and sailors, whose honesty could not be questioned, who would take their bible oath that they have seen among the rocks of barren islands, animals with a body and head resembling a woman, and the lower extremity bearing the scales, fins and tail of a fish. Doubtless there are twenty such men now in this port.

When the animal of which the above is a picture, shall arrive here, we hope our citizens and the professors of natural history especially, will have an opportunity of testing this question in such a manner as to put the subject forever hereafter to rest. We learn that the gentleman who owns this animal is about taking it to London as a present to the British Lyceum of Natural History.

With regard to the real or fabulous existence of this animal, we find that in the year 1187, as Laray informs us, such a monster was fished up on the coast of Suffolk, and kept by the governor for six months. It bore so near a conformity with man, that nothing seemed wanting to it but speech. One day it took the opportunity of making its escape, plunging into the sea, was never more heard of.

In the year 1430, after a huge tempest, which broke down the dikes in Holland, and made way for the sea into the meadows, &c., some girls of the town of Edam, in West Friesland, going in a boat to milk their cows, perceived a mermaid embarrassed in the mud, with very little water. They took it into their boat, and brought it with them to Edam. It fed like one of them, but could never be brought to offer at speech. Some time afterwards it was brought to Herlem, where it lived for some years, though still showing an inclination to the water.

Another creature of the same species was caught in the Baltic, in 1531, and sent to Sigismond, king of Poland, with whom it lived three days, and was seen by all the court. Another very young one was taken near Rocca da Cintra, as related by Damien Goes. The king of Portugal and the grand master of the order of St. James, are said to have had a suit at law to determine which party these monsters belonged to.

In the year 1560, near the island or Manar, on the western coast of Ceylon, some fishermen brought up at one draught of a net, seven mermen and mermaids of which several Jesuits, and among the rest, F. Hen. Henriques and Dimas Bosquer, physicians to the viceroy of Goa, were witnesses. The physician, who examined them with a great deal of care, and made dissection thereof, asserts, that all the parts, both external and internal, were found perfectly conformable to those of men.

We have also another account of a merman seen near the great rock called the Diamond, on the coast of Martinico. The persons who saw it gave a precise description of it before a notary. They affirmed that they saw it wipe its hand over its face, and even heard it blow its nose.

In Pontoppidan's Natural History of Norway, also, we have accounts of mermaids; but not more remarkable, or any way better attested than the above.

More modern instances are the following:—In 1613 a mermaid was taken in the harbor of Cherbourg, after a violent storm, and was carried by the mayor of that place as a present to the French court; but, dying before it reached Versailles, it was afterwards shown publicly in the streets of Paris.

In the year 1758, a mermaid was exhibited at the fair of St. Germaine's in France. It was about two feet long, very active, sporting about in the vessel of water in which it was kept, with great agility and seeming delight. It was fed with bread and small fish. Its position, when at rest, was always erect. It was a female, with ugly negro features. The skin was harsh, the ears very large, and the back parts and tail were covered with scales. M. Gautier, a celebrated French artist, made an exact drawing of it.

Another mermaid, which was exhibited in London in 1775, was said to have been taken in the gulf of Stanchio, in the Archipelago, or Ægean Sea, by a merchantman, trading to Natolia, in August, 1774. It was, therefore, an Asiatic mermaid. The description is as follows:—Its face is like that of a young female—its eyes a fine light blue—its nose small and handsome—its mouth small—its lips thin, and the edges of them round like that of the codfish—its teeth are small, regular and white—its chin well shaped, and its neck full. Its ears are like those of the eel, but placed like those of the human species, and behind them are the gills for respiration, which appear like curls. Some are said to have hair upon their head; but this has only rolls instead of hair, which, at a distance, might be taken for short curls. But its chief ornament is a beautiful membrane or fin rising from the temples,

and gradually diminishing till it ends pyramidically, forming a
fore-top like a lady's head-dress. It has no fin on the back, but a
bone like that of the human species. Its breasts are fair and fall;
the arms and hands are well proportioned, but without nails on
the fingers; the belly is round and swelling, but there is no navel.
From the waist downward, the body is in all respects like the
codfish; it has three sets of fine, one above another, below the
waist, which enable it to swim erect on the sea.

MERMAIDS AND MO'O
OF HAWAI'I

While water beings are plentiful in Hawaiian culture, Hawaiian stories about half-human, half-fish entities are rare. More common are stories about the class of Hawaiian reptilian water deities, predominantely female and generally noted for their great size, called mo'o (the Hawaiian word for lizard). Their lizard forms symbolize regeneration (shedding of skin and regrowing tails) and continuity (their backbones with their visible vertebre and distinct markings), and their association with water also symbolizes continuity (water flow and the water cycle). Mo'o held important roles in Hawaiian culture, religion, and society, as guardians of place, ancestral guardians, and in certain cases, as deities associated with war and politics. They continue to be relevant for many Hawaiians today.

According to Mary Kawena Pukui, a renowned expert on Hawaiian culture, mermaids are kin to mo'o.[1] Although Pukui did not elaborate on this connection, it is clearly based on certain affinities. Both mermaids and mo'o possess fishlike qualities: mermaids have fishtails, and dwell in fresh or salt water, while mo'o generally live in or nearby bodies of fresh water or fishponds (sometimes rain forests, and more rarely, on a seashore or in a sea cave). Mo'o also exude walewale (a thick watery substance), like certain fish species.

Notably, mo'o personify the life-giving and death-dealing qualities of water, and as such they can be beneficent or malevolent. Mo'o are thought to have the power to attract fish and lead them elsewhere, and this power of attraction seems to extend to humans. Like the sirens of European lore, female moʻo have the reputation of being incredibly seductive. In their human forms, they are generally stunningly beautiful, and the humans they set out to seduce are unable to resist them. The moʻo's beauty, like still waters whose placid surface is lovely to behold, may hide a dangerous nature, just as still water may hide dangerous undercurrents.

Hawaiian deities personify nature and natural phenomena. The moʻo clan's kinship and antagonism with other deities, especially the family of volcanic deities, speaks to Hawaiian understandings of balance in nature, and the ways in which opposing elements (like water and fire) are in eternal struggle and complementarity.

Most importantly, these deities, water spirits included, are part of a living tradition that finds its narrative expression in moʻolelo and kaʻao as well as song, hula, and chant. It is important to note here that in moʻolelo and kaʻao there is no sharp distinction between belief narratives and histories, or between belief narratives and wonder genres. Conceptually, moʻolelo—which as a word connects to oral tradition, family, land, and more[2]—encompasses what in English would be termed myth, legend, wonder tale, history, and life writing. Within this capacious genre, a single moʻolelo might incorporate and weave together elements from two or more of these genres, and that is perfectly acceptable. Moreover, kaʻao— "legend, tale, novel, romance, usually fanciful; fiction" in the Hawaiian Dictionary[3]—also overlaps with the moʻolelo, as historical figures and events can be transformed over time by multiple retellings into a more fantastical kaʻao.[4] In the Hawaiian and other genre systems of larger Oceania, cosmic genealogies, myths, and legends constitute history according to these people's worldview; not to be confused with fiction, they constitute different narrative approaches to that history.

The Mermaid of
Honokawailani Pond[1]

Typically in mermaid lore, it is a human male who falls in love with a mermaid, but in this story from Hawai'i, a young woman falls in love with a male water spirit who lives in a deep pond. Because of her love for him, she renounces her humanity and her ties to the human world to undergo the transformation from human to wahine-hi'u-i'a (literally, fishtailed woman).[2]

I am a native of 'Ewa of which it is said "Maka 'Ewa'ewa" (Averted Eyes). But my aloha wells up for the elders and friends who have passed on, who did not look the other way when strangers arrived, and who demonstrated to all their open heart full of boundless aloha.

One thing I fondly recall when I think about it now that my head is covered in gray hair that becomes ever sparser as time passes is my grandmother combing my long hair, which had grown quite long, with a small comb and rubbing it with coconut oil. My hair nearly reached my ankles at that time.

During one of these sessions to beautify my hair, my grandmother told me a story about a girl of her time whose hair nearly reached her feet, made shiny with coconut oil and fragrant with perfume. According to my grandmother, this young woman was incomparably beautiful, and her reputation as a beautiful woman was known from one side of 'Ewa to the other.

Upland of our family compound (in this time, upland of the electric building of the Hawaiian Electric Company) was a pond called Honokawailani. This pond was always full of water from beneath the earth. When it was high tide, the freshwater of Honokawailani rose like that of the sea, and the water of the pond rose and became a stream. The water was a dark blue-green until the sun hit it, and then made it transparent. The pond was thick with water lilies on every side and here and there within it. Its lushness was striking.

It was the meeting place for all the youths from Waimalu to Manana when I was a child. We would go to Honokawailani to swim and play in water. And it was common for small children to hide in the bushes at the side of the pond and spy on the activities of the youths who had gathered.

That pond is still here today as a kind of memorial for those days. However, it is not beautiful as it was in our days, and even perhaps many years before my birth. In these days, it is crowded with dayflowers and various weeds. Come to think of it, it is very sad.

And about this pond Honokawailani, I learned a story told by my grandmother about the girl with the long hair.

One day, according to my grandmother, the young girl left her family to go with her friends. When they finished amusing themselves there for the day, and had reached home, only then did they notice that one of them was missing. This happened to be that girl. Immediately, they quickly called around, and the families came together to search for the girl. But they found no trace of her.

Then, the expert trained in the art of deep-seeing met with the parents. This expert could seek and find the answers to puzzling questions and find things that had disappeared. The expert told the parents to stand with him. Then, they all looked up and exhorted the Great Mana to spread forth and assist them with their (the parents') cherished one that they had deeply loved as they raised her.

That same evening, the mother was startled out of a deep sleep by the sound of her daughter's voice saying "Honokawailani." The second time this word was said, she understood it was the name of the pond.

She got up in a hurry, gave thanks for this revelation, covered her shoulders with a shawl, and went outside. With dawn on the horizon of the Leeward Side she began her journey toward Honokawailani.

Along the way, the sky cleared, and the uplands were also clear of clouds. She rushed along, hurrying toward the slope before her because it was the place where she could turn to one side and look down at Honokawailani. She reached the top of the slope and stood there. After a while, she spied her favorite child among the many water lilies that surrounded her. Her daughter waved. Her need to be next to her daughter made her run quickly toward the pond's edge. A path opened between the many water lilies so that the girl could float closer to her mother. The mother pushed through many water-lily pads, moving between the dayflowers and water-lily buds that were just beginning to unfurl. The girl held up her hand as if to say, "Come no farther."

The woman saw her child's long hair and said, "Let's go back, and I will comb . . ." The girl gently shook her head, looking at her with cool eyes. The mother spoke again with tears in her eyes, "Oh child of my heart, let us return home. I see that your sweet face looks at me with such aloofness."

Upon hearing these words, the girl shook her head forcefully and the mother understood that her child could not speak to her. Suddenly, she retreated backward into the water lilies. The mother immediately cried out in pain, "With love your mother has cared for you every day and you said, 'I need you.' I searched for you until I found you, to find out how you were, and instead look at you, no concern for the way you cause me pain."

Just as the mother finished speaking, a young man appeared at the girl's side. The young woman waved good-bye to her mother, and then jumped up high so that her mother could see the answer to her questions, and thus not feel sad. Behold, a fishtail had replaced her legs.

The mother looked around, but her daughter had vanished beneath the water lilies. She was a mermaid! And this boy, he was her daughter's sweetheart.

"And there she is until this day," said my grandmother.

Kalamainu'u,
the Mo'o Who Seduced
Puna'aikoa'e[1]

In this tale, Kalamainu'u encounters Puna'aikoa'e, a ruling chief of O'ahu, while she is surfing. She finds him attractive and lures him to another island, where she keeps him prisoner in her cave.[2] This story was told to explain the appearance of two images of female deities associated with war and politics: one was carved with a missing eye (Kalamainu'u) and the other with a flattened nose (Haumea)—injuries they received in a battle over Puna'aikoa'e.

When the time came to complete the closing ceremony for the dedication of the war temple, the expert to whom that duty belonged was ready. Two or three images of female deities draped in yellow kapa stood in the places designated for them. One was called Kalamainu'u (Kihawahine). She was a mo'o. Another was called Haumea (Kāmeha'ikana) because she had physically entered a breadfruit tree, perhaps by virtue of her divine nature. It was said that her husband, Makea, had been killed and his corpse hung on a breadfruit tree, the very breadfruit tree she had entered.

Makea was not the real name of the man who died but Puna'aikoa'e, an ali'i of O'ahu. While he was touring the island with his entourage, they reached Kukui at Waimānalo in Ko'olaupoko from the direction of Waikīkī. Because it was a good time for surfing there, the ali'i and his companions went surfing. But when they arrived at the surf spot, they were surprised to see a stunningly beautiful woman, and their hearts were startled by desire. She told Puna'aikoa'e, "This is not the best place to catch swells." "Where then?" asked Puna. "It's further out, and I know it well." It seemed as if there were covetous thoughts in her heart as she observed him, and likewise for him when he looked at her, because their gazes locked. When desire is equal, nothing will stand in its way. They paddled their boards for some time, asking each other questions to get to know one another, and swam on. After a while the woman said, "Just beyond here is the good surf spot where we can catch waves." They continued paddling until they left the surf break behind, carrying on until the upland cliffs could no longer be seen, and further still until the island itself completely disappeared from sight. He had long since stopped looking behind him. All that remained before him was what his eyes beheld. The people ashore cried out for him, but amazingly, they didn't go on canoes to search for him. But then again, this is a story. Indeed, it would've been the right thing to do if she'd been a real woman.

They go ashore at Molokai

They abandoned their boards on the shore and went inland to the woman's cave dwelling. When he entered the cave, however, he saw no signs of human presence and heard no voices, just an oppressive quiet and eerie solitude. His dwelling there was like being imprisoned. He obeyed all the woman's commands to placate her in order to remain alive. She took good care of him, giving him food and making certain his every need was met. She took him as her husband. He lived with that kupua wife for such a long time that he barely looked human anymore.

He hears voices shouting boisterously

One day when he emerged from their cave and stood outside, he heard voices resounding from a distance. He greatly wished to discover why but it was impossible because he was bound by his wife's edict. He must never leave secretly, or he would die. Thus, he lived most long-sufferingly. He went back into their cave and he asked her, "What kind of revelry did I heard seaside of us just now?" The woman answered, "It could be surfing or possibly the game of the rolling stone disks. Perhaps it is something else, and someone is defeating another person, and that is the revelry you heard." "I would love very much to see these things you speak of." The woman spoke again. "If you wish to go, then tomorrow is a good time for me to let you go there and so that you can see."

He goes down toward the sea to witness the recreational pursuits

When the next day dawned, he left and descended toward the sea, reaching the crowd. He saw a great number of entertaining activities. While he was having a good time, a local man named Hinale, who was his wife's brother, noticed him. When Hinale saw him, he was quite astonished at the strangeness of his features. When the pastimes ended, the man took him to his house to enjoy a meal and rest. While they were relaxing, Hinale asked him, "Where do you hail from now and what kind of house do you live in?" Puna'aikoa'e replied, "I am dwelling upland in a cave." At this declaration, Hinale became pensive. Hinale was preoccupied because he had heard about the disappearance of Puna'aikoa'e, an ali'i of O'ahu. Kalamainu'u had taken him.

This conversation made Hinale's heart fill with compassionate affection for his brother-in-law. So he asked, "How did you arrive there?" He told him the story. Hinale replied, "Your wife is not human, if that is your wife, for she is a kupua. You should return early. If you creep in silence, then you will discover her true nature as her mouth snatches in secret spiders and their webs. Even so, she will know you have returned. She will also know about our conversation. It is because of my great affection and compassion for you that I tell you this.

Your former wife is an older sister of all your sisters-in-law. I advise you to plan for the moment when her [Kalaimanuʻu] anger has waned. When she is pleased with you, simply moan, 'I have such an intense craving for water.' She will ask, 'What water do you crave?' You should answer, 'The water of Poli-ahu at Maunakea.' However, you should pierce her water gourd until it is riddled with holes so that it delays her. Then go to the old woman's crater, the woman whose eyes have become diseased. She alone is your salvation. You and your wife are well known. But when your life is safe, she will seek mine. I care deeply about your life because you need to return to your former wife."

His return to their cave dwelling

As he neared the cave, he secretly crept in silence and he saw her indeed, her mouth reaching here and there for spiders on their webs. When he saw this, he then understood Hinale's statements. He then backed up until he was far away and made noises to announce his arrival.

When she heard him, she went back to being human. He entered, and she spoke harshly to him, "It seems that you are secretly creeping in silence to see the worst of people. You retreated not too long ago and then made noises to announce your presence, perhaps because you thought I wouldn't know better? Maybe I should eat your eyeballs. It's possible that Hinale gave you some advice and when you heard it, you came back to observe my nature." Before he had left, she had ordered him to speak loudly so that she could hear him as he was arriving if he returned early.

As that beloved husband stood in the sea spray of her anger, he refrained from saying a word until the storm of anger that prickled the gills and the wind ruffling the neck feathers had completely died down, until her displeasure was finally spent like a whirlwind that meets an obstacle and then dissipates. Thus, they cast away their discord and dwelt with each other very peacefully. In fact, that woman would have wagered her bones on his words because she almost trusted him more than before.

"Lovers are wooing in the woods"

Kalamainu'u's taking leave of Puna

Once Puna felt everything had gone back to normal and he saw that his wife was once again fulfilling all his desires, he let out a loud sigh because he was thirsty. It was not a real thirst, just a ruse to carry out Hinale's advice to be freed from living in captivity with that monster. When his wife heard his moaning, she quickly asked, "Why are you sighing?" He replied, "I just felt thirsty as we were sitting here and relaxing—the thirst rose forth for no reason." "The water of where," asked the wife. "For the water of Poliahu, at Maunakea." She said, "What is your reason for craving that water?" Puna replied, "I yearn for water mixed with ice, which I have always drank since I was a child. My grandparents would only fetch water for me from that place. If I traveled, that water would be brought as well. Whenever it was about run out, it would be fetched again. It was like this until the day that I became yours. You have water and I drink it, but it tastes nothing like water mixed with ice. However, I do not want to send you to fetch it because of the distance, which would be unfair to you, my wife." The wife bowed her head down. When she raised her eyes, she said, "You do not crave water, you just want to wear me out with work. But I should fetch it lest you say I ignore your words."

Just before he mentioned his craving for water, he had pierced the bottom of her water gourd until it was riddled with holes to delay her, just as Hinale had advised him, which would give him time to escape. His wife rose to go. That same day, he left to board a canoe for Maui. From Maui, he took another canoe to Hawai'i and landed at Kona. From there, he sailed to Ka'ū. Once he landed at Ka'ū, he made his way to Pele's crater, and climbed up its rim. The people of the crater recognized him, and their welcoming call resounded, "Here is the husband of our older sister." Hearing their welcome, he quickly joined them. He spoke of his voyage there and shared his story.

Pele listened attentively to his words. She said, "It will not be long before this woman arrives to fetch you and wage battle. But we will not yield you lest you die, because she is incredibly angry with you. Furthermore, she abducted you for no reason, you who are our older sister's husband. If she had proven her beauty by seeking her own husband, no one would annoy her without cause, but she stole our older sister's husband, whom she had earned with her beauty. You will stay with us until the opportunity arises to return you to your first wife."

Kalamainu'u's battle with Pele

While Kalamainu'u was tarrying at Polihau to retrieve water, she was completely wearied by the fact that the water gourd would not fill up completely. It was filling but because its bottom had been pierced, the water would seep out. Because the gourd would not fill with water, her thoughts were entirely focused on her task. However, at one point, as she stood up, she happened to look behind her and saw that her husband had run away. The monster was furious. She called together all the mo'o of Molokai, Lāna'i, Maui, Kaho'olawe, and Hawai'i because she knew her husband was with Pele and the others at Kīlauea.

After the mo'o gathered, they departed for Kukuilau'āni'a and climbed Kīlauea. When she stood at the crater's rim, she demanded the crater dwellers release her husband, but they refused. They asked her, "Do you have a husband here? This is our older sister's husband. You will get nothing at all because you are a vile woman." This speech by Pele and her ilk made Kalamainu'u furious. She said, "If you do not release my husband, I will command my people to fill this lava crater, and your fiery nature will soon be extinguished." Just as she had threatened, the mo'o filled the lava crater with their slime, and the Pele clan barely avoided catastrophe.

The craters of the Pele clan were nearly extinguished, only Kamohoali'i's crater remained. From there, the fire reignited until it was endlessly immense and the mo'o slime was nullified. Kalamainu'u and her legion of mo'o were unable to remain in the vicinity. The fire's heat came forth so aggressively everywhere that most of the mo'o were killed. They perished in the crevices that opened as they fled. As for Kalamainu'u, she dove in the pond named after the mo'o Aka (Loko Aka). She was defeated, husbandless, and barely escaped with her life.

Kalamainu'u's punishment for Hinale

When Kalamainu'u reached Molokai, she pursued Hinale, intending to kill him because she was furious for the part he played in Puna'aikoa'e's escape, but because he was so quick, he escaped. Hinale, fully aware of his dangerous predicament with his sister, immediately fled to the ocean, and entering it, turned into a fish. Because Hinale dove into the sea, Kalamainu'u dived in after him. She looked for him in the places he usually frequented, among the short coral heads and the long coral heads. But she did not find him because he resembled a fish—the hīnālea that sells for a quarter at 'Ulakōheo fish market.

Kalamainu'u continued searching, but it was all for naught. 'Ōunauna (hermit crab) was greatly annoyed by her frequent passage back and forth in front of his home. He asked, "Whatever are you searching for, Kala?" Kala replied, "I am looking for Hinale." 'Ōunauna said, "You will not capture Hinale unless you listen to what I have to say. If you do not listen, nothing will be gained. You will be thwarted in the same way that Pele and her clan shamed you and you will be husbandless. That is what might happen if you refuse to listen to me." Kalamainu'u replied, "I shall listen to what you have to say if I feel it to be right, but if nothing is gained, you will die an outcast's death by my hand." 'Ōunauna said, "You must go

and fetch the 'inalua [a climbing vine with oval leaves and blu-
ish one-seeded fruits used to make the funnel-mouthed fish
trap] then weave a fish trap and tether it in the sea. Leave it for
a long time, and later when you dive, you will see that he has
entered the fish trap and you will capture him."

Kalamainu'u went to fetch the 'inalua, then returned to
weave it, and when the fish trap was done, she left it for a long
time in the ocean. But when she dove to check the trap, Hinale
was not inside it but swimming near it. She rose to the surface
to catch her breath. When she dove again, he was still not in
the fish trap. She did this over and over again until her nose
and eyes were inflamed because she had dived repeatedly in
the water. Still nothing was gotten.

She was infuriated. Filled with wrath, she searched for
'Ounauna. "Here you are," said 'Ounauna. Kalamainu'u answered angrily, "Here you are. I will kill you today if I have
my way. I made the mistake of believing your advice. Instead,
you intended my death. How could you possibly capture him
when I was unable to do so—me, the one with more power?
You are truly worthless, 'Ounauna, you miserable beach
crawler. This conversation is finished. I am going to kill you.
Know that your days of crawling on the beaches and the tide
pools are over."

'Ounauna replied, "Before my demise, perhaps we should
talk and then these bones of mine will be handed over for
death, but should you find the conversation useful, there will
be no death. I want you to tell me exactly how you carried out
the task so that I can understand the reason why you were unable to capture Hinale." Kalamainu'u replied, "I do not want
to talk with you again right now. You heard my decision."
'Ounauna said with fervor, "Please, just tell me a few words
about it, perhaps I forgot to tell you something." Kalamainu'u
replied, "I will talk to you, but I still intend to kill you because
your advice has wearied me." 'Ounauna answered, "I do not
want to hear your complaints. I want you to tell me exactly
what you did. Besides, if I die, who else would entertain you in
this place?"

Kalamainu'u replied angrily, "Mistaken indeed, I returned

home and then left to go inland to gather the 'inalua. When I returned, I wove the funnel-shaped fish trap and then I turned the entrance outward. I tethered it in the sea in an appropriate place and left it for a long time. I was surprised when I dived to discover that Hinale was not inside. I thought it was not the right place, so I moved it. But each time I dived, it was the same. So, I continued until I was exhausted. Therefore, I came to kill you. Your death would serve as balm to ease my head-ache because your tedious tasks wore me out."

'Ōunauna said, "That's it indeed, I forgot to tell you to get some things. They are easily gotten. Go dive for the long-spine sea urchin, the short-spine sea urchin, and then get a sand crab. Mash everything together until it is mixed, then thrust it inside of the funnel-shaped fish trap. You must turn the open-ing, which was turned outward, so that it faces inward, then take it away into the sea and set it up in a suitable location. Leave it for a while. When you dive, he will be inside because he will have seen that his cousins are dead, and this is why he will have entered the trap. He will escape quickly, but you will have caught him before then." In this way, he was captured, or so it was said.

Today, this continues to be the technique for trapping the hīnālea fish. A chant was composed about this method, given here:

Kala passes to and fro,
Come evening, the beautiful one will be bad-tempered,
Yearning eyes settled upon Puna,
Puna'aikoa'e the husband,
Walinu'u the wife,
Kala took Puna,
Harsh was the language at Maunaloa,
Filled with wrath was the tree-smiting lizard,
At her vain attempts to capture Hinale.
Why is your reason [for going to and fro], Kala?
Hinale
You will not catch Hinale [like this].
Look for the 'inalua,

Squeeze the long-eyed sand crab, [with]
Hawae sea urchin in the deep sea, [and]
The wana sea urchin moving swifly in sea-floor hollows.
You have adversaries, Kala
Pu—na escaped.

Pele and her band return Punaʻaikoaʻe

After this battle between the Pele clan and Kalamainuʻu because Punaʻaikoaʻe escaped with Hinale's guidance, Puna was reunited with his wife. This is a woman of many names.

Perhaps that was the way to become a deity in those times. It was also said that those deities fought in their human form—Walinuʻu, the first wife of Punaʻaikoaʻe, with Kalamainuʻu (Kihawahine) and with Haumea (Kāmehaʻikana). That man of theirs was the reason for their battle, perhaps out of jealousy. Because of that battle, Kalamainuʻu became blind in one eye and Walinuʻu's nose was flattened when it was broken, which is reflected in their images when they stand in the House of Papa—probably Papa who was the wife of Wākea.

Punaʻaikoaʻe's capture under his new name of Makea

A new aliʻi succeeded Punaʻaikoaʻe after he had vanished because he was gone for such a long time from the moment he had gone missing. While those two were living in upland Kalihi, when they wanted fish, Walinuʻu would go crabbing at the Koʻolau Cliffs, Heʻeia, and several other places. But by and by on another occasion, when she went crabbing in the usual places, Punaʻaikoaʻe got up and went to the middle of a banana patch to lay down where it was cool. As he was resting in the coolness of that mountain banana patch, he was overcome with sleep. While he was asleep, a guard seized him, thinking he was a banana thief. They removed his loincloth and tied his hands. They led him to the sea of Honolulu where they probably drowned him, and then brought him back upland where they hung his corpse from the branch of a breadfruit tree.

It is said that on the northwest side of the Wahikahalūlū Pond precipice, on the ridge between it and Pūehuehu, just mountainside of Kamano, right in front of the cliff perhaps, is the place where that very breadfruit tree stands.

Walinuʻu's return and her fainting

While Walinuʻu was gathering seaweed and catching crabs in the usual places down from Kalihi, she heard rumors of unfortunate events concerning her husband. Because of this bad news, she stood and tied a fisherwoman's skirt around her hips, which is made from the morning-glory vines that grow on the beach. This skirt was a temporary one that women wore when they went crabbing, and discarded afterward, and in this way, they didn't ruin their regular skirt.

Because of this worrisome news, she did not think about changing into her regular skirt and went inland wearing her morning-glory skirt. She saw her husband's body hanging from the breadfruit tree surrounded by a crowd. Anguished, she wailed for her husband and beat her chest in grief. From her reaction, everyone realized that she was the dead man's wife. Although she was grief stricken, because her husband was innocent, she came up with a plan to punish the person who caused his senseless death. For that reason, she split the breadfruit tree until it opened. The entire crowd, awestricken, fell to the ground when they saw this incredible feat. She dropped her morning-glory skirt to the ground where she had been seated and stood up naked. Then she entered the breadfruit tree, which fused closed after her as it was before. It became something much talked about, well known even where the aliʻi lived. As for the morning-glory skirt that she had left behind, it took root and thrived, and perhaps still grows there today.

The demise of the ali‘i responsible for the death [of Makea]

When Makea's corpse began to leak greasy fluids, the dogs crowded below the breadfruit tree began to lick it, including the dog of the ali‘i who owned the banana patch for which her husband had been killed. When the dog went home, he wagged his tail when he saw the ali‘i, and they began to romp around happily. But suddenly, as they played, the dog bit his royal owner's throat, and killed him. This dog's behavior that caused a death was quite strange. It seems that food was the cause of death. One would have thought that only Makea was meant to die, but in the end, both men lost their lives. That is what happens to whoever seeks the death of someone innocent as Herod did by taking the head of John the Baptist.

WATER BEINGS OF
SOUTH AMERICA

The different groups of Amerindians living in Guyana are de-scended from the original inhabitants of upper South America or the Caribbean, and water spirits abound in the folklore of Amazonian tribes. The Warrau (also Warau, Warao, or Guarao) of Guyana speak of the Ahúba, which are two fish (a male and a female) with human heads who rule over other fish, and who, according to Warrau belief, live in subterranean water sources that flow to the sea. The Ahúba are considered evil because they eat the bodies of humans drowned in shipwrecks. The Ho-inarau and Ho-aránni (male and female sea spirits) and the Naba-rau and Naba-ranni (male and female river spirits), on the other hand, may appear like either humans or fish. These water spirits and the Warrau once enjoyed good relations, and even took each other's females for their wives. This was not a perfect situation, because Warrau women isolated themselves when menstruating, which annoyed the water spirits because they greatly enjoyed intercourse with menstruating women. When their peaceful relations terminated, the water spirits, both males and females, began to seduce or abduct human spouses instead.

Water spirits called Oriyu are familiar to both the Warrau and the Arawak (a tribe of South America and the Caribbean; called Taino in the Caribbean). In one tradition, the Oriyu came about when gigantic lizards lost a battle against an Ama-zonian tribe and escaped to the river, where they became Oriyu. Male and female Oriyu enjoy intercourse with humans and seek them out, but they forbid their human lovers to speak about these trysts with other humans. The price humans pay for divulging their relations with Oriyu includes the threat of premature death, or the refusal of the Oriyu to have anything more to do with them.[1]

The Fisherman's Water-Jug and Potato[1]

While this story, from Guyana, concerns an Oriyu and the fisherman she agrees to marry, it is also a story about the origins of a huge catfish termed the low-low (Silurus) and a smaller catfish termed imiri (Sciadeichthys). Here, the broken-oath motif drives the plot, but it is the Oriyu's mother-in-law, not the Oriyu's husband, who breaks the promise she extracted from them.

There was once a fisherman who went fishing daily, and whose catch was invariably large. One day, when out in his corial something pulled at his line but he missed it: three or four bites followed, yet he caught nothing. Once more he tried. Something tugged at the hook; he hauled in the line, and what should he drag up to the surface but Oriyu herself! There she was, the real Spirit of the Water, with all her beautiful hair entangled in the line. It was but the work of a minute to get her into his boat, and she was indeed beautiful to look upon. So beautiful was she that he carried her home to his mother, and made her his wife, the only condition that Oriyu stipulated being that neither her prospective husband nor her mother-in-law should ever divulge her origin. Being so accustomed to the water, Oriyu proved an excellent helpmate: out she would go with her husband, in his boat, and look into the depths for fish. These she could see when no one else could, and she would advise him not to throw his line in here, but over there, and so on. And thus day after day they returned home, always bringing the old mother-in-law plenty of fish. As you can well imagine, this happiness did not last very long; it came to an end through the old woman, when in liquor, loosening her tongue and letting out the secret of Oriyu's origin. Oriyu said

nothing at this time, so grieved she was, but she waited her opportunity to take her husband with her to her former home
under the waters. So on the next occasion that the crabs began
to "march" from out the ocean to the shore, the family made
up a large party, and all took their places, with their quakes,
in a big corial. As they were coming down the river, Oriyu all
of a sudden told her companions that she and her husband
were about to pay a visit to her people below, but that they
would not be gone long, and that in the meantime she would
send up something for them to eat and drink, but they must
share everything fairly. Without more ado she and her man
dived into the water. After awhile up came a large jar of cassiri, and a lot of potatoes, a very welcome addition to the few
provisions they had on board. When they had each had their
fill of the cassiri, and had eaten the potatoes, they threw the
jug and the useless skins back into the water, where the Oriyu
turned the former into the giant low-low [*Silurus*] and the latter into the squatty little imiri [*Sciadeicthys*]. This is why we
old Arawaks always speak of the low-low as the fisherman's
water-jug, and of the imiri as his potatoes.

Oiára, the Water-Maidens[1]

*In the second narrative, a synopsis by the American Herbert H.
Smith (1851–1919), who lived in Brazil from 1880 to 1886, we
learn that the peoples of the Lower Amazon tell stories about
seductive water spirits they call Oiára. Apparently, female
Oiára are not friendly water spirits, for they use their pleasing
songs and beauty to entice men and drag them beneath the
water. In some traditions, Oiára are male entities described as
having a human upper half and a river-porpoise lower half, or
as being able to alternate between their human and river-
porpoise forms. Unlike their female counterparts, the males
are content with seducing women and then letting them go
free.*

Stories of water-maidens are common on the Lower Amazons.
The Indians say that these maidens are exceedingly beautiful;
they have long, black hair, in which they entwine the flowers
of the *moreru*.[2] They entice the young men by their beauty,
and by the sweetness of their songs; once in their embrace,
they drag them down into the water, and nothing more is ever
heard of them.

Although these tales are current among the Indians, I am in-
clined to think that they were introduced by the Portuguese.
But there was, undoubtedly, an aboriginal myth which bore a
considerable resemblance to the Old World stories, which have
been tacked to it. The myth, as given by Dr. Couto de Magal-
hães, represents the Oiara (or Uauyará) as a male, not a female:

"The fate of the fishes was confided to Uauyará; the animal
into which he transformed himself was the river-porpoise. No
one of the supernatural beings of the Indians furnishes so
many legends as this. There is not a settlement of the province
of Pará where one may not hear a series of these stories, sometimes grotesque and extravagant, often melancholy and tender.

The Uauyará is a great lover of our Indian women; many of them attribute their first child to this deity, who sometimes surprises them when they are bathing, sometimes transforms himself into the figure of a mortal to seduce them, sometimes drags them under the water, where they are forced to submit to him. On moonlight nights the lakes are often illuminated, and one hears the songs and the measured tread of the dances with which the Uauyará amuses himself."

The Pincoya[1]

Francisco Javier Cavada (1864–1950), a Chilean priest and scholar from the city of Ancud in Chiloé, writes about the Pincoya as a water spirit in the Chiloé Archipelago, which was colonized by the Spanish in the late 1560s and has been controlled by the Chilean government since 1824. The first peoples of Chiloé were originally the Chono, the Huiliche, and the Cunco, and while their descendants tell tales about las sirenas, they also continue to speak of the Pincoya and her husband, the Pincoy, who is also her brother. There are important differences between las sirenas and the Pincoya-Pincoy water spirits, and, as Bernando Quintana Mansilla's work shows, between the Pincoya and the Pincoy. To begin with, unlike typical mermaids, the Pincoya does not have a fishtail but appears completely human, while her husband has a human face and the body of a large seal with silver fur. Moreover, the Pincoya is not associated with seduction, but with the fruitfulness of the sea. She controls edible marine resources and is able to increase or decrease the number of fish and shellfish at will. The Pincoy, however, is attracted to human women and sometimes seduces them.

The Pincoya is a type of nereid or sea fairy, that, together with the Pincoy, her husband, attracts an abundance of fish and shellfish to the place or area of the sea where they live.

To summon abundance, the Pincoya puts shellfish in the sand while taking care that her face is turned toward the sea. When she wants the seafood to become scarce or ngal, she turns her face toward the mountain.

Some regularly set out in their boats to search for these sorcerers to take them to other places where they desire abundance; but it is necessary that girls with a happy disposition and cheerful smiles accompany these men because the Pincoyes are always in a good mood.[2] Both are blond and attractive.

It is said that when fishermen fish too often in a single spot, the Pincoya gets angry and leaves those places, which then become barren.

Some confuse the Pincoya with the Serena (Sirena); but they are mistaken because the Serena does not live only in the sea, but also in lakes and even pools, where she has been seen combing her luxuriant blond hair with a golden comb and holding a mirror in her hands.

The pools in which some Serena live have a whitish and milky water.

Whoever sees a Serena in one of these pools or ponds will have a short life.

The Mermaids[1]

Julio Vicuña Cifuentes (1865–1936), a preeminent Chilean folklore scholar and founding member of the Sociedad del Folklore Chileno, raised the question of whether beliefs about las sirenas (mermaids) were the result of Chileans being introduced to Greek Siren stories. What is striking about Cifuentes's treatise is that as he was writing it, he read Francisco Javier Cavada's essay on Chiloé water spirits, which changed his mind, but rather than rewrite his work, he added to it. Thus, not only do we gain deeper insight into his thinking process, but we can better appreciate the degree to which the familarity (or unfamiliarity) with just one local tradition can critically influence scholarly understanding of folklore. In fact, Vicuña Cifuentes ends his treatise by citing the opening paragraph of Cavada's essay. To avoid repetition, we have omitted that passage because we include Cavada's account in full.

Our folk are not unfamiliar with the legend of the Mermaids. It is known of them at least that they are monstrous half fish, half women; that with their sweetest songs mislead mariners, especially fishermen, as mermaids prowl in preference near the coast. Some tales without interest reference this point, connected to the disappearance of young and good-looking individuals, who were "perhaps" abducted by mermaids; but the complete absence of details that reveal the nationalization of the legend suggests that it has no roots in our tradition.

However, in my childhood, I remember hearing in La Serena the following tale, which relates an incident that supposedly happened in that same city.

Many years ago, an old woman lived with her daughter, whose name was Serena, a girl of tough and headstrong character. One day, she wanted to go for a bath at the river, but her mother was sick and could not go with her. As the old woman

tried to stop her, the daughter, who lacked any natural affection, hit her, wounding her in the face. Then the mother cursed
her. But the girl ignored the curse and went alone to the river
as she had planned. The river had grown, and engulfed the
daughter in its turbid current, dragging her to the sea; and
when the mother, hours later, went to look for her, seized by
anguished despair, some fishermen who had huts in the same
area of the river told her they had seen pass, with its head
above the waters, a horrendous monster, half woman, half
fish, which waved its arms and tail as if it wanted to fight the
current to reach the shore. Later, on several occasions, the
fishermen of those coasts saw the monster, and upon spotting
her, collected their nets, not because of fear that the strange
animal would fall on them and break them, but because they
knew that the fish would abandon the waters when it appeared.

I recall that I observed to my informant that the name of the
cursed daughter must be Sirena, and not Serena, as he pro-
nounced it. The good man affirmed it was so, probably because this name was familiar to him, and the other was not.

I do not know what diffusion this tale has achieved, forged,
apparently, not as an independent legend, but to explain the
origin of mermaids, by someone who knew of the Greek fable.

Since I have written this account, I have come across information that I will transcribe immediately, which modifies in
part my judgment about the absence of details that reveal the
nationalization of the fable concerning the mermaids. Undoubtedly, at least in the Chilean tradition, the legend is suffi-
ciently rooted, as it has led to several local superstitions.

AFRICAN WATER SPIRITS
IN THE CARIBBEAN

These tales come from the Caribbean islands of Trinidad and Tobago. Originally inhabited by Native peoples, Trinidad and Tobago were colonized by the Spanish in 1498. In 1797, they were ceded to the British, but at various points in time they have also been controlled by the Dutch, the Coulanders, and the French. Due to slavery and indentured servitude, Africans and Indians are the two largest ethnic groups in these islands: the French brought slaves of African origin with them in the late eighteenth century, while a great number of East Indians were imported as indentured laborers after slavery was abolished in the British Empire in 1833. Snakes abound in both Africa and India, and there are many stories of water spirits whose forms incorporate both human and serpentine features. This holds true also for Trinidad and Tobago. Between these two islands, more than forty species of snakes have been identified; among these is the green anaconda, also known as the water boa. The dread that the peoples of Trinidad and Tobago feel for this snake is justified, as it is one of the largest in the world. In 2013, an anaconda that was seventeen feet, nine inches long and weighed 220 pounds was caught in Caroni, Trinidad. The fear of being attacked and swallowed alive by such an anaconda, justified or not, is understandable.

Mami Wata, or "Mother Water," a powerful, transnational water deity, may appear either as a beautiful woman or as an anaconda from the hips down. Wherever Mami Wata is worshipped, her devotees generally call her their linguistic equivalent of "Mother Water" or "Mother of Water," such as Maman de l'Eau, Maman Dlo, Mamy Wata, Mammy Wata, etc. In her human-anaconda form, she is described as dreadful to behold. In her mermaid form, be it piscine or reptilian, Mami Wata dwells in the waters of the forests she protects, but just as often, she might pass you by in her human form as she walks down the street in high heels, dressed to the nines and wearing stylish sunglasses.[1] She takes seduction to a whole new level, using her beauty and promises of wealth to attract followers, and is not above sleeping with her devotees or taking them as spouses.[2]

Significantly, she has the power to transform a human into a water spirit by changing the lower half of their body to that of a fish. Beautiful young women should beware, for Maman Dlo might transform them so that they can act as her assistants, as seen in "Ti Jeanne," a story about a young woman named Ti Jeanne who has a life-changing encounter with Maman Dlo. If a man damages the forest or pollutes its waters, however, Maman Dlo might "punish" him by taking him as her husband—an arrangement that does not end with his death. But as the tale "Mama Dlo's Gift" shows, this water spirit is also capable of kindness to those who honor her. This tale also mentions Oriyu, the Amazonian water spirit.

Ti Jeanne[1]

Maman Dlo, whose name is derived from the French "maman de l'eau," which means "mother of the water" is one of the protectresses of the forest and its rivers, waterfalls and pools.

It was towards the end of the rainy season. Ti Jeanne, who lived with her grandmother in Blanchisseuse, went to the river pool with her basket of laundry.

She tied up her skirt around her waist, waded into the water, and her round, brown arms moved rhythmically up and down as she beat the laundry against a stone. Her voice rang out in the forest, mingling with the song of birds high up in the trees, the screech of parrots and the more mysterious sounds of the forest. Whap, whap went the wet laundry.

"La rene, la rene, la rene rivé," sang Ti Jeanne.

"Qu'est-ce qu'elle dit?" asked the kiskidee, who never really understands anything. Ti Jeanne worked away in the solitude of the ravine, the sun travelled its course across the sky, and when the last piece of laundry was washed and wrung and laid out to bleach on the stones, Ti Jeanne sat down, splashing her feet in the water, and looking at her reflection in the water of a small, clear pool, turning this way and that to catch a glimpse of her pretty features.

"Who's that singing so fine?" came a hissing, creaky voice from the dark greenery. "Who's that splashing in the water? Who's that looking at herself?"

Ti Jeanne got scared, because she heard the voice but couldn't see who it belonged to. Not daring to move, she asked in a feeble voice:

"Who you talkin but not showin youself?"

A throaty chuckle came from the dark, then a rustle. Ti Jeanne saw circular ripples on the water emerging from under the foliage, and then the face of an old old African woman emerged from the water. She had tattoos, and wore large earrings and strands and strands of necklaces made of colourful beads.

"Ti Jeanne, Ti Jeanne," the woman sang in her rusty old voice, "Ti Jeanne, so beautiful, washerwoman, blanchisseuse! Ti Jeanne, mmh, mmh."

As her song changed to a humming sound, rising and falling, the old woman rose and rose, and Ti Jeanne, who was by now totally entranced in spite of her fear, saw that the hag had the body of an anaconda.

"Maman Dlo," Ti Jeanne whispered. "Maman Dlo, I didn't mean to be rude. I didn't hurt anything." For the girl knew that punishment awaits the one who offends the forest creatures, the plants or the animals, and she was in great fear to be talked to by the great water spirit.

"Vanity, vanity, my child," said Maman Dlo, who was now fully seven feet erect on her snakebody, swaying from side to side. "Looking at yourself in the water's reflection. But beautiful you are, sssssssso beautiful! Mmh, mmh!"

Ti Jeanne, entranced, started to swing along with Maman Dlo. As she listened to her song, the girl got up from her seat, and slowly walked into the water. Maman Dlo's tail flapped furiously, creating bigger and bigger splashes, waves, and foam started to rise. Ti Jeanne's chemise fell from her, her hair grew long, covering her round shoulders and her bare breasts, and when the girl's lips reached the water's surface, the bubbles covered the pool as if hundreds of laundresses had been working.

Maman Dlo had enchanted Ti Jeanne, who was to live with her and serve her forever after. She gave the girl a fishtail, and Ti Jeanne was to become one of the most beautiful of the fairy maids, playing with the other river spirits and protecting the forest, its waters and pools for a long time to come.

When the villagers came to look for her, they found only the laundry she had washed, and next to it on the riverbank the chemise she had been wearing and seven shiny fishscales.

Ti Jeanne in later times also chose a husband from amongst

the village folk, but that is another story and shall be told another time.

* * * * *

"Mama Dlo" or "Mama glo," whose name is derived from the French "maman de l'eau," which means "mother of the water," is one of the lesser-known personalities of Trinidad and Tobago folklore.

A hideous creature, her lower half takes the form of an anaconda. She is sometimes thought to be the lover of Papa Bois, and old hunters tell stories of coming upon them in the "High Woods." They also tell of hearing a loud, cracking sound, which is said to be the noise made by her tail as she snaps it on the surface of a mountain pool or a still lagoon.

Mortal men who commit crimes against the forest, like burning down trees or indiscriminately putting animals to death or fouling the rivers, could find themselves married to her for life, both this one and the one to follow.

Sometimes she takes the form of a beautiful woman singing silent songs on still afternoons, sitting at the water's edge in the sunlight, lingering for a golden moment, a flash of green—gone. If you meet Mama Dlo in the forest and wish to escape her, take off your left shoe, turn it upside down and immediately leave the scene, walking backwards until you reach home.

Maman Dlo's Gift[1]

From the time of her earliest memories, she always entered the forest quietly, silently stepping, slowly moving through the dew-wet underbrush, trying not to tread too hard.

She paused, not so much to listen but to learn, to learn the feel of the day, for every day was different in her forest. Her forest—it lay along a steep valley through which rushed a river called "Shark," halting only in selected places to make pools deep and sure with eddies that swirled backwards in their own placid repose, slick on the surface, secret in their tumultuous depths, where enormous, ancient trees stood sentinel. All fast asleep in ageless repose, same height, same girth, same breadth as though created simultaneously by some mighty hand that reached out from eternity and sowed their dreams in unison so long ago, before words like day or night were made to punctuate the passage of time.

Time had been invented by one of her ancestors, she was sure. Before she entered her forest, she left it, together with her shoes, down by the road. Papita had told her about the Caribs of long ago, their family, the old people who owned all the land. She had told her about the river and of the Oriyu, the water spirits. She always felt that she had just missed them and that, had she come a little earlier, she would have seen them. But she was always just in time to see the ripples they left on the water fade away into placidity. Sometimes, she heard a loud slap upon the surface of the pool. Once, she saw an enormous shape turn around and around in the water like a wheel. Today, she saw the face. A shimmer just beneath the surface of the pool, it seemed to call out with open mouth. A song, she thought. Now she knew for certain that there was a Maman Dlo living in Shark River.

After that, she would bring flowers and pretty buttons, a

buckle from a shoe, a dolly's head, quite pink, with staring eyes of blue and tiny holes where hair would have been implanted. She brought little gems made of red and green glass, pins and pretty bow clips. One morning, as she slipped in silence through the woods, the river, coursing with a roar through the rocks and bolders, gray and striped with white lines, she saw something glimmer in the water. It was a lovely comb made of shell and silver, gold-tipped. She stood there entranced, the river foam, a lacy frock around her legs. She picked up the comb and ran it through her hair. At once, she heard music, a song, sighing, which filled her heart with yearning—for what? She had no idea. She knew she must keep this gift a secret.

She would spend her days sitting in the sunshine where the water fell from high up to crash upon the rocks, its spray a brilliant rainbow iridescent about her, combing her long, black hair and listening to Maman Dlo's comb. She learnt that Amana was her true name and that she had a sister who was called Yara, "beautiful river," which flew into a bay not too far away. Others were called Marianne, Madamas and Paria. She heard the sirens' song of sailors who had been dashed to death upon the rocks at Saut d'Eau, and learned not to dread the deafening silence of the forest.

She saw the stranger come into her forest. He grew afraid at her sight, his eyes were startled. She did not smile but combed her hair, listening to the melody of Maman Dlo's song. The river's spray made iridescent colours swirl about her. He ran away. They laughed at him. He would return.

In the time that followed, whenever she combed her hair with the magic comb, she heard a voice that warned her of her curiosity for the stranger and cautioned her to dismiss him from her memory. Maman Dlo's voice came to her like a mother's plea to remain pure and not fall victim to curiosity. But she longed to meet the stranger and would dream him with her in the river.

One day, Maman Dlo rose up from the water to tell her "no." She saw her terrible beauty, her feminine form conjoint with that of a massive anaconda that swirled about and slapped the water with its tail, making a sound like the cracking of huge branches. "No," Maman Dlo breathed, "don't go." But go she did and as time went by, her comb no longer sang its silent song. Mr. Borde and herself would build a house at Cachepa Point and live a happy life.

Close upon a century later, as a very old woman, she sat to the back of a pirogue which was plunging through a turbulent sea towards Yara Bay in the hope of beaching at the river's mouth. The outboard engine whined and coughed, and the huge waves threatened to swamp the overcrowded boat. She sensed the terror in the group and took an old, broken comb with an unusual shape out of her pocket. Standing up in the plunging boat and steadying herself, she called to the tillerman to point the bow at the river's mouth and asked the passengers to pray. In a voice at first old and frail, then strong and commanding, she began to sing:

"Maman Dlo, oh Maman Dlo, save us from this terror sea. Be calm, be calm," she told the waves, "Be slow, lie low."

The swirling waters seemed to pause and flatten into an insulent roll that fell away at her call.

"Ma Dolly calmed the sea," they would later say. "She calmed the sea at Yara Bay."

WATER BEINGS OF
INDIGENOUS
NORTH AMERICA

There are more than a thousand different groups of Indigenous peoples in North America—573 federally recognized tribes in the United States to date and 617 First Nation communities in Canada.¹ These numbers do not include the many tribes that are not, as yet, federally recognized. While each group has a name for itself, they are often referred to collectively in the United States as Native Americans and in Canada as Aboriginal peoples. In Canada, the term "Aboriginal peoples" comprises three distinct groups: First Nations peoples, Inuit, and Métis. Water beings abound in the traditions of many of these peoples; some are known only to specific tribes or areas while others are, to a certain extent, cross-cultural. In the case of water spirits common to two or more groups, it is important to note that views toward these entities may differ in terms of whether a group considers them helpful or harmful to humans. This holds true for the water spirits—water snakes and mermaids—who appear in the stories in this section. The horned serpent is an example of such a cross-cultural water entity. In some instances, the horned serpent may choose to appear as a man. Like water-snake beings, mermaids may also be perceived as benign or malevolent, and their lower bodies may be fish or snakelike.

The Horned Serpent Runs Away with a Girl Who Is Rescued by the Thunderer[1]

In this tale from the Seneca of western New York State, the horned serpent is a dangerous male who preys on naïve women, setting out to make a young woman his wife. When he is in his human form, certain aspects of his person and dress are reminiscent of a snake and thus hint at his real identity, but the girl is oblivious to them. Unbeknownst to the girl, a Thunderer, a sky being who considers horned serpents his enemies, also wants her for his wife. This cautionary tale also explains why Seneca men keep black snakeskin in their medicine bundles.[2]

There was a Thunderer named Hi"no[n] who often hovered about a village where he sought to attract the attention of a certain young woman. He was a very friendly man and would have nothing to do with witches. He hated all kinds of sorcery and his great chief up in the sky whom we call Grandfather Thunder hated all wizardry and sorcery too. All the Thunderers killed witches when they could find them at their evil work.

Now, this Hi"no[n] was very sure that he would win the girl he wanted and he visited her lodge at night and took a fire brand from the fire and sat down and talked with her, but she kept saying, "Not yet, perhaps by and by."

Hi"no[n] was puzzled and resolved to watch for the coming of a rival. He told the girl's father that he suspected some witch had cast a spell on her or that some wizard was secretly visiting her. So they both watched.

That same night a strange man came. He had a very fine suit of clothing, and the skin had a peculiar tan. It was very clean, as if washed so that it shone with a glitter. Over his back and down the center there was a broad stripe of black porcupine quills with a small diamond-shaped pattern. He had a long neck and small beady eyes, but he was graceful and moved without noise. He went directly to the lodge and taking a light sat at the girl's bedside.

"Are you willing?" he asked her. "Come now, let us depart. I want you for my wife. I will take you to my house."

The girl replied, "Not yet, I think someone is watching, but in three days I will be ready."

The next day the girl worked very hard making a new dress and spent much time putting black porcupine quills upon it as an ornamentation. It was her plan to have a dress that would match her lover's suit. Upon the third day she finished her work and went to bed early. Her apartment was at the right side of the door and it was covered by a curtain of buffalo skin that hung all the way down.

Hi"no" again called upon her, taking a light and seating himself back of the curtain. "I am willing to marry you," he said. "When will you become my wife?"

"Not yet," she replied. "I am not ready now to marry."

"I think you are deceiving me," answered Hi"no", "for you have on your new dress and have not removed your moccasins."

"You may go," the girl told him, and he went away.

Soon there came the stranger and he too took a little torch and went behind the curtain. Soon the two came out together and ran down the path to the river.

"I shall take you now to my own tribe," said the lover. "We live only a short way from here. We must go over the hill."

So onward they went to their home, at length arriving at the high rocky shores of a lake. They stood on the edge of the cliff and looked down at the water.

"I see no village and no house," complained the girl. "Where shall we go now? I am sure that we are pursued by the Thunderer."

As she said this the Thunderer and the girl's father appeared running toward them.

"It is dark down there," said the lover. "We will now descend and find our house."

So saying he took the girl by the waist and crawled down the cliff, suddenly diving with a splash into the lake. Down they went until they reached the foot of the cliff, when an opening appeared into which he swam with her. Quickly he swam upward and soon they were in a dimly lighted lodge. It was a strange place and filled with numerous fine things. All along the wall there were different suits of clothing.

"Look at all the suits," said the lover, "when you have found one put it on."

That night the couple were married and the next day the husband went away. "I shall return in three days," he announced. "Examine the fine things here, and when you find a dress that you like put it on."

For a long time the girl looked at the things in the lodge, but she was afraid to put on anything for everything had such a fishy smell. There was one dress, however, that attracted the girl and she was tempted to put it on. It was very long and had a train. It was covered all over with decorations that looked like small porcupine quills flattened out. There was a hood fastened to it and to the hood was fastened long branching antlers. She looked at this dress longingly but hung it up again with a sigh, for it smelled like fish and she was afraid.

In due time her husband returned and asked her if she had selected a suit. "I have found one that I admire greatly," said she. "But I am afraid that I will not like it after I put it on. It has a peculiar fishy smell and I am afraid that it may bring evil upon me if I wear it."

"Oh no!" exclaimed her husband, "If you wear that suit I will be greatly pleased. It is the very suit that I hoped you would select. Put it on, my wife, put it on, for then I shall be greatly pleased. When I return from my next trip I hope you will wear it for me."

The next day the husband went away, again promising soon to return. Again the girl busied herself with looking at the trophies hanging in the lodge. She noticed that there were many suits like the one she had admired. Carefully she examined each and then it dawned upon her that these garments were the clothing of great serpents. She was horrified at the discovery and resolved to escape. As she went to the door she was swept back by a wave. She tried the back door but was forced into the lodge again by the water. Finally mustering all her courage she ran out of the door and jumped upward. She knew that she had been in a house under water. Soon she came to the surface but it was dark and there were thunder clouds in the sky. A great storm was coming up. Then she heard a great splashing and through the water she saw a monster serpent plowing his way toward her. Its eyes were fiercely blazing and there were horns upon its head. As it came toward her she scrambled in dismay up the dark slippery rocks to escape it. As the lightning flashed she looked sharply at the creature and saw that its eyes were those of her husband. She noticed in particular a certain mark on his eyes that had before strangely fascinated her. Then she realized that this was her husband and that he was a great horned serpent.

She screamed and sought to scale the cliff with redoubled vigor, but the monster was upon her with a great hiss. His huge bulk coiled to embrace her, when there was a terrific peal of thunder, a blinding flash, and the serpent fell dead, stricken by one of Hi^{n}no^n's arrows.

The girl was about to fall when a strong arm grasped her and bore her away in the darkness. Soon she was back at her father's lodge. The Thunderer had rescued her.

"I wanted to save you," he said, "but the great horned serpent kept me away by his magic. He stole you and took you to his home. It is important that you answer me one question: did you ever put on any dress that he gave you? If you did you are no longer a woman but a serpent."

"I resisted the desire to put on the garment," she told him.

"Then," said he, "you must go to a sweat lodge and be purified."

The girl went to the women's sweat lodge and they prepared her for the purification. When she had sweat and been purged with herbs, she gave a scream and all the women screamed for she had expelled two young serpents, and they ran down and slipped off her feet. The Thunderer outside killed them with a loud noise.

After a while the young woman recovered and told all about her adventure, and after a time the Thunderer came to her lodge and said, "I would like to take you now."

"I will give you some bread," she answered, meaning that she wished to marry him. So she gave him some bread which he ate and then they were married.

The people of the village were now all afraid that the lake would be visited by horned serpents seeking revenge but the Thunderer showed them a medicine bag filled with black scales, and he gave every warrior who would learn his song one scale, and it was a scale from the back of the horned serpent. He told them that if they wore this scale, the serpent could not harm them. So, there are those scales in medicine bundles to this day.

Of the Woman Who Loved a Serpent Who Lived in a Lake[1]

The Passamaquoddy's traditional territory is along the coasts of Maine (United States) and New Brunswick (Canada). As they are a coastal people, tales about water spirits are plentiful in their culture. Men who marry beautiful women only to discover that something about them is amiss is a common motif in folktales and legends. In this account, a village beauty marries five men within a single year, each man dying shortly after the wedding. Her sixth husband suspects that she has a secret and is determined to uncover it. Not only does he learn that his wife has taken an enormous water-serpent spirit as her lover, but he discovers that fangs are not the only way to transmit venom.[2]

Of old times. There was a very beautiful woman. She turned the heads of all the men. She married, and her husband died very soon after, but she immediately took another. Within a single year she had five husbands, and these were the cleverest and handsomest and bravest in the tribe. And then she married again.

This, the sixth, was such a silent man that he passed for a fool. But he was wiser than people thought. He came to believe, by thinking it over, that this woman had some strange secret. He resolved to find it out. So he watched her all the time. He kept his eye on her by night and by day.

It was summer, and she proposed to go into the woods to pick berries, and to camp there. By and by, when they were in the forest, she suggested that he should go on to the spot where they intended to remain and build a wigwam. He said that he would do so. But he went a little way into the woods and watched her.

As soon as she believed that he was gone, she rose and walked rapidly onwards. He followed her, unseen. She went on, till, in a deep, wild place among the rocks, she came to a pond. She sat down and sang a song. A great foam, or froth, rose to the surface of the water. Then in the foam appeared the tail of a serpent. The creature was of immense size. The woman, who had laid aside all her garments, embraced the serpent, which twined around her, enveloping all her limbs and body in his folds. The husband watched it all. He now understood that, the venom of the serpent having entered the woman, she had saved her life by transferring it to others, who died.

He went on to the camping ground and built a wigwam. He made up two beds; he built a fire. His wife came. She was earnest that there should be only a single bed. He sternly bade her lie by herself. She was afraid of him. She lay down, and went to sleep. He arose three times during the night to replenish the fire. Every time he called her, and there was no answer. In the morning he shook her. She was dead. She had died by the poison of the serpent. They sunk her in the pond where the snake lived.

How Two Girls
Were Changed to
Water-Snakes[1]

This Passamaquoddy story concerns two girls who become water snakes. Certain details suggest that it is colored by Christian values. While the reason for the young women's transformation is left unexplained, the storyteller's criticism of their improper behavior—disappearing every Sunday to go swim naked in a lake, where they engage in other inappropriate activities—suggests that their metamorphosis into water snakes comes about because they, too, are evil, like snakes. For many Christian denominations, Sundays are reserved expressively for the worship of God. The idea of snakes as evil derives from the Old Testament story that Satan, in the form of a serpent in the Garden of Eden, tempted Eve to eat the forbidden fruit from the Tree of Knowledge of Good and Evil, and she in turn, convinced Adam to also partake of it. Despite the Christian-inflected moral overtones, the description of the girls changing into snakes speaks to traditional understandings of water spirits: their human bodies slowly elongate until they become serpents with a human head, their long black hair intact. Once these girls are seen in their serpent form, they are forevermore obliged to remain that way.

Pocumkwess, or Thoroughfare, is sixty-five miles from Campobello. There was an Indian village there in the old times. Two young Indian girls had a strange habit of absenting themselves all day every Sunday. No one knew for a long time where they went or what they did. But this was how they passed their time. They would take a canoe and go six miles down the Grand Lake, where, at the north end, is a great ledge of rock and sixty feet of water. There they stayed. All day long they ran about naked or swam; they were wanton, witch-like girls, liking eccentric and forbidden ways.

They kept this up for a long time. Once, while they were in the water, an Indian who was hunting spied them. He came nearer and nearer, unseen. He saw them come out of the water and sit on the shore, and then go in again; but as he looked they grew longer and longer, until they became snakes.

He went home and told this. (But now they had been seen by a man they must keep the serpent form.) Men of the village, in four or five canoes, went to find them. They found the canoe and clothes of the girls; nothing more. A few days after, two men on Grand Lake saw the snake-girls on shore, showing their heads over the bushes. One began to sing,

> "N'ktieh iében iut,
> Qu'spen ma ké owse."

> We are going to stay in this lake
> A few days, and then go down the river.
> Bid adieu to our friends for us;
> We are going to the great salt water.

After singing this they sank into the water. They had very long hair.

A picture of the man looking at the snake-girls was scraped for me by the Indian who told me this story. The pair were represented as snakes with female heads. When I first heard this tale, I promptly set it down as nothing else but the Melusina story derived from a Canadian French source. But I have since found that it is so widely spread, and is told in so many different forms, and is so deeply connected with tribal traditions and totems, that there is now no doubt in my mind that it is at least pre-Columbian.

Ne Hwas, the Mermaid[1]

In the Passamaquoddy language, niwesq, here transliterated into ne hwas, denotes spirit. The niwesq of this story is a human from the waist up and a water snake from the hips down. This account is a variant of the previous story, but lacks its Christian overtones. Unlike in the previous tale, the girls are not depicted as evil. Instead, a mother tells her two daughters never to go into the lake lest they encounter misfortune, but what she means by that is not specified. The girls ignore her, and as a result, bear the consequences of not heeding their mother's warning. In the end, however, they prove to be dutiful daughters.[2]

A long time ago there was an Indian, with his wife and two daughters. They lived by a great lake, or the sea, and the mother told her girls never to go into the water there, for that, if they did, something would happen to them.

They, however, deceived her repeatedly. When swimming is prohibited it becomes delightful. The shore of this lake *sands* away out or slopes to an island. One day they went to it, leaving their clothes on the beach. The parents missed them.

The father went to seek them. He saw them swimming far out, and called to them. The girls swam up to the sand, but could get no further. Their father asked them why they could not. They cried that they had grown to be so heavy that it was impossible. They were all slimy; they grew to be snakes from below the waist. After sinking a few times in this strange slime they became very handsome, with long black hair and large, bright black eyes, with silver bands on their neck and arms.

When their father went to get their clothes, they began to sing in the most exquisite tones: —

> "Leave them there!
> Do not touch them!
> Leave them there!"

Hearing this, their mother began to weep, but the girls kept on: —

> "It is all our own fault,
> But do not blame us;
> 'T will be none the worse for you.
> When you go in your canoe,
> Then you need not paddle;
> We shall carry it along!"

And so it was: when their parents went in the canoe, the girls carried it safely on everywhere.

One day some Indians saw the girls' clothes on the beach, and so looked out for the wearers. They found them in the water, and pursued them, and tried to capture them, but they were so slimy that it was impossible to take them, till one, catching hold of a mermaid by her long black hair, cut it off.

Then the girl began to rock the canoe, and threatened to upset it unless her hair was given to her again. The fellow who had played the trick at first refused, but as the mermaids, or snake-maids, promised that they should all be drowned unless this was done, the locks were restored. And the next day they were heard singing and were seen, and on her who had lost her hair it was all growing as long as ever.

Legend of the Fish Women
(Mermaids)[1]

*This legend belongs to the Ahwahnechee people,[2] whose tradi-
tional territory is Ahwahnee,[3] the area known today as Yosemite Valley in the Sierra Nevada Mountains in California.
Although the mermaids of Ahwahnechee folklore are beautiful,
the Ahwahnechee do not find them desirable. Like sirens, these
"fish-women" use their voices and beauty to lead men to their
death by enticing them close enough to drown them, and for this
reason, the Ahwahnechee consider them malevolent spirits.[4]*

Long ago when the Ah-wah-nee-chees were a young nation the
Merced River was the home of the Fish-women (Mermaids).
These were beautiful creatures, having the tails of fish and the
upper bodies of women. They could not leave the water, but
would often sit on the rocks in the shallows, or around the edges
of the deep pools, combing their long black hair, and chanting
luring songs to the warriors of Ah-wah-nee. But, charming as
they were, the warriors would have nothing to do with them.

One day while two braves were fishing in the deep pools of
the river, with a net made of milkweed thread, the net became
tangled with the rocks on the bottom of the pool. One of the
braves dived down to loosen it, and the Fish-women, darting
out from their hiding places under the rocks, tied the threads
of the net to his toes, and held him under the water until he
was drowned. Then they carried the brave away to their land
beneath the river, and neither he nor the Fish-women have ever
been seen since.

The Woman Who Married
the Merman[1]

This story, from the Coos people of coastal Oregon, is about a young woman who discovers she is inexplicably pregnant after having gone swimming in the ocean. She gives birth to a boy. Not long after, a water spirit (whether of the fish or serpent variety remains unexplained) who appears in human shape reveals that he is the father of her child. He convinces her to live in the water with him. As the woman's child grows, he asks for arrows, and she shares that his uncles have many arrows. (Arrows carry a symbolic meaning in this account, and their use in hunting prey is important.) When she asks her brothers for arrows, she gifts them with otter skins and promises to send a whale, thus becoming their provider. By this time, the storyteller notes, her shoulders were changing into tsaLtsiL (blubber) and turning black, which suggests that she was transforming into a whale. The woman, her husband, and her child eventually cease to visit her brothers, presumably because they are afraid of being killed by arrows.[2]

There was a village (called) Takimiya. There lived five young men, and they had one younger sister. They lived in Takimiya. She was the head (of the family). From everywhere they wanted to buy her. But she did not want a husband. She would always swim in the water, and (one day) she became pregnant. Every one asked her, "Who made you pregnant?" She did not know it. "Nobody touched me." So a young boy was born, and he would always cry. No matter who took care of it, the child would still cry. Thus spoke to her her elder brother: "Put the child outside. Who is it? You are just holding it."

So the next day she put the child out again. It did not cry

any longer. She had it there for a long time, and then went to see it. It is said that her child must have been eating something fat. It had a mouth (full of) grease. The child was eating seal-meat strung on a stick. She examined the mouth. She saw no one anywhere. Then again she brought the child in. The child again began to cry. The child did not (let) anybody sleep. It cried one (whole) night. So thus said her elder brother: "Take the child outside. (See) what it will do there. You shall watch it there." The child was growing very (fast). So again she left it (outside). Now she was watching it there. She was leaning sidewise alongside of her child. So she left it there a whole day.

Then she went there when evening came. She was sitting sideways. Nowhere did she see anybody. All at once a man was standing there. "You are my wife. Do you know it? Our (dual) child is my child." The woman became ashamed. "You get ready, we two will go home." The woman said nothing, and began to think. "I wonder what my folks will say."—"You will not get lost. You will again come back. You will see your folks." Thus she was thinking: "All right!"

Now they went. "We two will go down into the water."— "Won't I be out of breath?"—"You will be all right. If we two go down, you will hold on to my belt. You will keep your eyes shut; and when I tell you so, then you shall look." It seemed as if they went through (some) brush. She knew that they were going in the water. They went through. There was no water in the village. Her husband was a rich man's son. There were five boys, and he was the youngest.

The boy grew very (rapidly). The boy always wanted to (have) arrows. His mother made him small arrows. Thus she would say to the child: "Your maternal uncles have many arrows." So thus spoke the boy: "How would it be if we two should go after arrows?" Thus said the husband: "Your mother will go alone for the arrows. You will stay (here). We two will go (some other) time."

Then the next day she got ready and went. She wore five sea-otter hides. The flood-tide (came) early in the morning. They saw a sea-otter swimming in the river. They hunted the sea-otter in canoes. She was swimming along the beach. They were shooting at her with arrows. It seemed that they hit the sea-otter; but she would come out again, and the arrows were nowhere to be seen. The sea-otter went up the river. They followed her in canoes. Many people were shooting at her. The sea-otter turned back and went (away) again. Still they were shooting at her. No one hit her. Again the sea-otter went out into the ocean. The elder brother kept on following the sea-otter. It is said that she went ashore somewhere. The elder brother went around the ocean beach. Suddenly he saw (what appeared to be) a person. The person was playing on the beach in the water. He went there. He came closer, and, verily, it was a woman. As he looked at her, he recognized her. Verily, it was his younger sister. Indeed, it was she. "It's I, my younger brother. I was travelling there. Here are all the arrows. You were shooting them at me." Many were the arrows. The man was ashamed when he saw all the arrows. "My child sent me here just to get arrows. I came here. My child always wants arrows." She was drying the sea-otter hides. Then they two went home. "Don't think about it. I will go home. I give you these sea-otter hides. You can trade some things for them. My husband is a person, he is a chief's child. We do not live very far from here. His house is close by. You can see in the ocean this stone house whenever it is low tide." He saw his elder sister as she went down into the water. The water reached to her stomach. She held up both her hands and dove into the water. Thus she said to her younger brother, before she went down into the water: "To-morrow early in the morning you will find a whale at your landing-place."

The next day he got up a little before daylight. Verily, a whale had been washed ashore. They cut that whale into pieces. They distributed it among their friends. So, indeed, she returned (to) her husband and child. Her shoulders were turning into *tsaltsiL*, and (became) black. Again they went back, her husband and child. Afterwards little serpents came in and out to the ocean. And the woman did not come ashore: she was not seen again. The little serpents came after arrows,

jumping (over one another). The people shot arrows at them.
They were merely giving them arrows. They did not come
back again. Afterwards two whales came ashore,—one (in
the) summer, and (one) also (in the) winter. They sent two
whales ashore. They gave (them) to their relatives by marriage.

Notes

Notes preceded by an asterisk are taken from the original source material.

Oannes

1. E. Richmond Hodges and Isaac Preston Cory, *Cory's Ancient Fragments of the Phoenician, Carthaginian, Babylonian, Egyptian and Other Authors* (London: Reeves & Turner, 1876), 56–57.
2. *The Persian Gulf.

Kāliya, the Snake

1. Cornelia Dimmitt, ed., J.A.B. van Buitenen, trans., *Classical Hindu Mythology: A Reader in the Sanskrit Purānas* (Philadelphia, PA: Temple University Press, 1978), 114–16.

Odysseus and the Sirens

1. Alexander Pope, trans., *The Odyssey of Homer* (London: Bernard Lintot, 1725–1726).
2. Marina Warner, *Fantastic Metamorphoses, Other Worlds* (Oxford: Oxford University Press, 2002), 7. Sirens became nymphs who, depending on the tradition, acquired their hybrid bodies as punishment or reward, and had names connected with speech and voice.
3. When the words "mermaid" and "siren" appeared in Chaucer, they consolidated the confusion of the two beings: "Though we mermaydens clepe hem here . . . Men clepe hem sereyns in Fraunce" ("Though we call them mermaids here . . . Men call them sirens in France." From Geoffrey Chaucer's *The Romaunt*

of the Rose (ca.1366) in the entry for "siren" in the *Oxford English Dictionary*. The OED also reports, "Sur la ripe est vn ceroyne, On the bank is a meremayde" as the earliest use (ca. 1350) of "mermaid."

The Tuna (Eel) of Lake Vaihiria

1. Teuira Henry, *Ancient Tahiti*, Bernice P. Bishop Museum Bulletin 48 (Honolulu: Bishop Museum, 1928), 615–19.

2. *Received from Madame Butteaud, née Gibson, a descendant of the Hina of the legend.

3. Teuira Henry (1847–1915), a respected scholar of Tahitian literature and culture, found this account among the extensive ethnographic materials that her grandfather, Reverend John Muggridge Orsmond (ca. 1784–1856), compiled and analyzed after his arrival in Mo'orea in 1817 and throughout his life. Henry dedicated her life to transforming these ethnographic materials into a monograph, which includes her own notes and comparative study of Polynesian literatures and cultures.

Merfolk in the Waters of Greenland and Iceland

1. Courtesy of Terry Gunnell's translation: "In the autumn, Grímr went fishing with his farmhands and the boy Þórir lay in the prow and was in a sealskin bag which was tied up at the neck. Grímr caught a *marmennill,* and when he got him up, Grímr asked, 'What can you tell us about our fates? Where in Iceland ought we to settle?'" In *Landnámabok* [The Book of Settlements], ed. Jakob Benediktsson (Reykjavík, Iceland: Hið íslenzka fornritafélag, 1968), 97.

2. Some folklorists classify this story as a folktale belonging to tale type ATU 670, in which a human protagonist understands the language of animals and uses this to his advantage. Others (see Michael Chesnutt, "The Three Laughs: A Celtic-Norse Tale in Oral Tradition and Medieval Literature," in *Islanders and Water-Dwellers. Proceedings of the Celtic-Nordic-Baltic Folklore Symposium held at University College Dublin [16–19 June 1996]*, eds. Patricia Lysaght, Séamas Ó Catháin, and Dáithí Ó hÓgáin [Dublin: DBA Publications Ltd., 1999], 37–49) group it under the umbrella title of "The Three Laughs," with widespread versions going back to the Middle Ages. Only in the Icelandic and other Norse traditions of "The Three Laughs" is the

seer not a human or a leprechaun, but a hybrid sea being. See note 1, "A Freshwater Mermaid in Grimms' Fairy Tales," for an explanation of folktale classification.

The Marvels of the Waters About Greenland

1. *The King's Mirror (Speculum regale-Konungs skuggsjá)*, Scandinavian Monographs 3, trans. Laurence Marcellus Larson, 135–37 (New York: The American-Scandinavian Foundation, 1917).
2. *The belief that mermaids lived in the Arctic waters was one that was long held by European navigators. Henry Hudson reports that on his voyage into the Arctic in 1608 (June 15) some of his men saw a mermaid. "This morning one of our companie looking over boord saw a mermaid, and calling up some of the companie to see her, one more came up and by that time shee was come close to the ships side, looking earnestly on the men: a little after a sea came and overturned her: from the navill upward her backe and breasts were like a womans, as they say that saw her; her body as big as one of us; her skin very white, and long haire hanging downe behind of colour blacke: in her going downe they saw her tayle, which was like the tayle of a porposse and speckled like a macrell." Asher, *Henry Hudson*, 28.

The Merman

1. Jón Árnason, ed. *Icelandic Legends*, trans. George E. J. Powell and Eiríkur Magnússon, (London: Richard Bentley, 1864), 103–106.

Two Mermaids and a Selkie from the Scottish Highlands

1. In the first half of the twentieth century, Ronald Macdonald Robertson collected tales from Scottish fishermen and peasants in places that, he wrote in his preface to *Selected Highland Folktales*, "possessed a charming old-time atmosphere, in an alluring land of wilderness and wonder."

The Mermaid of Kessock

1. Ronald Macdonald Robertson, *Selected Highland Folktales* (Isle of Colonsay, Scotland: House of Lochar, 1961), 156–57.

The Grey Selchie of Sule Skerrie

1. Ronald Macdonald Robertson, *Selected Highland Folktales* (Isle of Colonsay, Scotland: House of Lochar, 1961), 166–67.

The Mermaid's Grave

1. Alexander Carmichael, *Carmina Gadelica*, vol. 2 (Edinburgh: Norman McLeod, 1900), 305.

A Seal Woman or Maiden of the Sea from Ireland

1. It is classified as ML 4080 in Reidar Th. Christiansen's *The Migratory Legends: A Proposed List of Types with a Systematic Catalogue of the Norwegian Variants* (Helsinki: Academia Scientiarum Fennica, 1958).
2. In other versions, her sealskin is taken from her; and when she is not a seal woman but a merrow (mermaid), it is her magic cap (see Thomas Crofton Croker, *Fairy Legends and Traditions of the South of Ireland* [London: Murray, 1828].)

Tom Moore and the Seal Woman

1. Jeremiah Curtin, *Tales of Fairies and of the Ghost World Collected from Oral Tradition in South-West Munster* (Boston: Little, Brown and Company, 1895), 150–54.

Dangerous Mermaids in Two Child Ballads

1. Child was the first American folklorist to be named professor of English at Harvard, and his ten volumes gathered over three hundred ballads. The ones we selected are classified as Child 42A and Child 289B respectively. "Clark Colven" has variant spellings, as in "Clerk Colven" (Child 42B). Child presented several versions of each ballad and also compares "Clark Colven" to a number of Scandinavian, Icelandic, French, and Italian ballads that either replace the mermaid with an elf or feature no mermaid at all in the death of the man. Another version of "The Mermaid" introduces some humor, as the cook compares the other men's sadness about leaving their wives to his being "sorry for my pots and pans."

2. In another version of "Clark Colven," the mermaid comes to Clark Colven's deathbed and asks him to choose between dying and living with her in the water.

Clark Colven, Child 42A

1. Francis James Child, ed., *The English and Scottish Popular Ballads*, vol. 1, part 2 (Boston: Houghton, Mifflin and Company, 1884), 387–88.

The Mermaid, Child 289B

1. Francis James Child, ed., *The English and Scottish Popular Ballads*, vol. 5, part 9, (Boston: Houghton, Mifflin and Company, 1894), 150.

A Bavarian Freshwater Merman

1. Franz Xaver von Schönwerth, a government official, admired the Brothers Grimm and published books about Bavarian folk customs. This tale was untitled in the archives and did not see print until the twenty-first century, when researcher Erika Eichenseer compiled hundreds of stories, mostly tales of magic, from Schönwerth's papers, and scholar Maria Tatar published a selection of them in 2015.

In the Jaws of the Merman

1. Franz Xaver von Schonwerth, *The Turnip Princess and Other Newly Discovered Fairy Tales,* ed. Erica Eichenseer, trans. Maria Tatar (London and New York: Penguin Books, 2015), 140.

A Freshwater Mermaid in Grimms' Fairy Tales

1. The Grimms collected "The Water Nixie" (Grimm 79) from Marie Hassenpflug, while "The Nixie in the Pond" (Grimm 181) was drawn from *Zeitschrift für deutsches Alterthum* (1842), a journal founded by Moritz Haupt in 1841, focusing on older German literature, customs, and beliefs.

   These stories are not legends, but folktales that rely on readers' suspension of disbelief. Folklorists have classified folk

and fairy tales according to "tale types," which identify charac-
teristic plot and thematic elements in variants and versions collected internationally. This is an imperfect system, but it helps
scholars to place a tale within an extended family of stories that
share affinities based on common episodes and conflicts. It is
common for scholars to identify folk and fairy tales according
to their tale type name and number. "The Nixie in the Pond,"
like Straparola's "Fortunio," also in this volume, belong to ATU
316, The Mermaid in the Pond. ATU stands in for Aarne-
Thompson-Uther, the editors of the latest edition of *The Types
of International Folktales*. The Brothers Grimms' tales have received so much critical attention that they too have their own
numbering system, such as Grimm 79 and 181 above.

The Nixie in the Pond

1. *The Complete Fairy Tales of the Brothers Grimm,* trans. Jack
    Zipes, vol. 2 (New York: Bantam Books, 1987), 224–28.

Three Estonian Water Spirits

1. This legend is classified as ML 4050 in Reidar Th. Christian-
    sen's *The Migratory Legends: A Proposed List of Types with a
    Systematic Catalogue of the Norwegian Variants* (Helsinki: Ac-
    ademia Scientiarum Fennica, 1958).

Three Tales (Untitled)

1. ERA II 18, 481/2 (1). Source in the collections of the Estonian
    Folklore Archives in Tartu. Trans. Ülo Valk.
2. Oskar Loorits, *Endis-Eesti elu-olu I: lugemispalu kaluri ja
    meremehe elust. Eesti Rahvaluule Arhiivi Toimetused* [*Every-
    day Culture of Old Estonia I: Readings About the Life of Fish-
    ers and Sailors*] 19 (11) (Tallin: Kultuurkoondis, 1939; Tartu:
    Eesti Kirjandusmuuseum, 2002), 37. Trans. Ülo Valk.
3. Oskar Loorits, *Endis-Eesti elu-olu I: lugemispalu kaluri ja
    meremehe elust. Eesti Rahvaluule Arhiivi Toimetused* [*Every-
    day Culture of Old Estonia I: Readings About the Life of Fish-
    ers and Sailors*] 19 (11) (Tallin: Kultuurkoondis, 1939; Tartu:
    Eesti Kirjandusmuuseum, 2002), 123. Trans. Ülo Valk.

Two Greek Mermaids

1. In modern Greek, mermaids are called *gorgones*, but they should not be confused with another set of ancient Greek mythological creatures, the Gorgons. See Nicolaos Politis, Νεοελληνική Μυθολογία [*Modern Greek Mythology*] (Athens: Perri Bros Booksellers, 1871), 61–65, for further information.

2. *The Romance of Alexander,* a collection of legends about Alexander the Great, dates back to the third century and is attributed to Pseudo-Callisthenes.

New Tunes

1. Nicolaos Politis, Παραδόσεις [*Legends*], vol. 1 (Athens: Grammata, 1904), 226–27. Trans. Marilena Papachristophorou.

2. The storyteller shifts to the present tense to underscore the immediacy of Alexander's action and the speed with which he accomplishes what is presented as an impossible task. At the very end of the tale the present tense instead indicates the reoccurrence over time or iterative nature of humans' encounters with this mermaid.

The Mermaid

1. Georgios Rigas, Σκιάθου Λαϊκός Πολιτισμός [*Skiathos' Popular Culture*], vol. 2 (Thessaloniki: The Society for Macedonian Studies, 1962), 36–42. Trans. Marilena Papachristophorou.

2. Here, the storyteller pulls the audience in by placing the dialogue between the Mermaid and the captain in the present tense. Shifting from past to present tense and back to the past tense is not unusual in oral storytelling, with the immediacy of a dialogue or action often presented in the present. In the Greek text, "Mermaid" is capitalized, and the translation reproduces this.

Merfolk from the South of Italy

1. Gigli recounts in his introduction how in the late 1880s he conducted an ethnographic study of traditional beliefs, customs, and narratives in the southern Italian peninsula surrounded by the Adriatic and the Ionian seas. Later folklore scholars are skeptical of his scholarly methods, however. Like Italo Calvino, who nonetheless adapted several of Gigli's tales in *Fiabe Italiane*

[*Italian Folktales*] (1959; New York: Harcourt, 1980), they consider him to be more of a creative interpreter of the songs and tales he collected.

Knowing this does not make the clearly fictional tale "Storia di una Sirena" any less interesting, Calvino also reminds us of a Tuscan proverb: "La novella nun è bella se sopra non ci si rappella" ("The tale is not beautiful if nothing is added to it"). When Calvino adapted Gigli's tale, he composed lines for the sirens' songs and tweaked the ending so as to have the fairy and the rescued beauty flying away on the back of an eagle. The translation in this volume stays pretty close to Gigli's text, but takes one liberty having to do with the word *sirena*, which translates into both the English words "siren" and "mermaid." Cristina Bacchilega chose "mermaid" in most cases, except for the occasions in which the emphasis on song evoked the mythological Sirens.

2. The two Sicilian tales are translated into English from *Fiabe e Leggende Popolari Siciliane*, which the renowned Giuseppe Pitrè (1841–1916) collected and edited in 1888. The volume was recently reprinted with Bianca Lazzaro's expert translations of tales and legends from Sicilian into Italian. Pitrè published over three hundred other Sicilian tales and other volumes of Sicilian lore, and in 1904 an extensive study of Cola Pesce folk and literary legends. A brilliant folklorist and comparatist who made a living as a medical doctor and also taught at the University of Palermo, Pitrè took down tales in dialect as well as each teller's name and other information. For other Cola Pesce tales in English, see Jack Zipes, ed. and trans., *Catarina the Wise and Other Wondrous Sicilian Folk & Fairy Tales*, illustrated by Adeetje Bouma (Chicago: University of Chicago Press, 2017).

A Mermaid's Story

1. "Storia d'una Sirena," *Superstizioni, Pregiudizi e Tradizioni in Terra d'Otranto: Con un'Aggiunta di Canti e Fiabe Popolari* [*Superstitions, Prejudices and Traditions from the Land of Otranto: With the Addition of Popular Songs and Tales*], ed. Giuseppe Gigli (Florence: G. Barbèra, 1893), 231–38. Translated by Cristina Bacchilega.

Cola Pesce

1. Bianca Lazzaro, Italian translation of the Sicilian "Cola Pisci," in Giuseppe Pitrè, *Fiabe e Leggende Popolari Siciliane [Sicilian Folktales and Popular Legends]* (Roma: Donzelli Editore, 2016), 860–61. Translated by Cristina Bacchilega.
2. From Pitrè's notation: Collected by the lawyer Franz Cannizzaro in the coastal area of Loccalumera, now part of the larger Messina.

The Sailor and the Mermaid of the Sea

1. Bianca Lazzaro, Italian translation of the Sicilian "Lu Marinaru e la Sirena di lu Mari," in Giuseppe Pitrè, *Fiabe e Leggende Popolari Siciliane [Sicilian Folktales and Popular Legends]* (Roma: Donzelli Editore, 2016), 641. Translated by Cristina Bacchilega.
2. From Pitrè's notation: Told in Palermo by Giovanni Minafò, a fisherman of the Borgo precinct. The same tale tradition was also collected in Siculiana, in the Agrigento area.

Legend of Melusina

1. Thomas Keightley, *The Fairy Mythology, Illustrative of the Romance and Superstitions of Various Countries* (London: H. G. Bohn, 1850), 480–82.
2. Jean d'Arras probably drew on Celtic and other myths of hybrid and thus monstrous female creatures (see Frederika Bain, "The Tail of Melusine: Hybridity, Mutability, and the Accessible Other," in *Melusine's Footprint,* 17–35; and Gregory Darwin, "On Mermaids, Meroveus, and Mélusine: Reading the Irish Seal Woman and Mélusine as Origin Legend," *Folklore* 126, no. 2 (2015).
3. *i. e. Cephalonia.
4. *It is at this day (1698) corruptly called La Font de Séc; and every year in the month of May a fair is held in the neighbouring mead, where the pastry-cooks sell figures of women, *bien coiffées,* called Merlusines.—*French Author's Note*
5. *A boar's tusk projected from his mouth. According to Brantôme, a figure of him, cut in stone, stood at the portal of the Mélusine tower, which was destroyed in 1574.
6. *At her departure she left the mark of her foot on the stone of one of the windows, where it remained till the castle was destroyed.

Fortunio and the Siren

1.   *The Great Fairy Tale Tradition: from Straparola and Basile to the Brothers Grimm*, trans. Jack Zipes (New York: Norton, 2001), 138–145.

2.   *Giovan Francesco Straparola, "Fortunio and the Siren"— "Fortunio per una ricevuta ingiuria dal padre e dalla madre putativi si parte; e vagabandondo capita in un bosco, dove trova tre animali da' quali per sua sentenza è guidardonato; indi, entrato in Polonia, giostra, ed in premio Doralice figliuola del re in moglie ottiene" (1550), *Favola* IV, *Notte terza* in *Le piacevoli notti*, 2 vols. (Venice: Comin da Trino, 1550/53).

The Day after the Wedding, from *Undine*

1.   Friedrich de La Motte Fouqué, *Undine and Other Tales*, trans. Fanny Elizabeth Bunnett (London: Samson Low, Son, and Marston, 1867), 45–50.

The Little Mermaid

1.   *The Fairy Tales of Hans Christian Andersen*, trans. Mary Howitt, illustrated by Helen Stratton (Philadelphia: Lippincott, 1899), 125–140.

2.   For a contemporary queer adaptation of "The Little Mermaid," see Maya Kern's *How to Be a Mermaid*, available as a webcomic at mayakern.com and in print in Cristina Bacchilega and Jennifer Orme, eds., *Inviting Interruptions: Wonder Tales in the 21st Century* (Detroit: Wayne State University Press, forthcoming).

The Fisherman and His Soul

1.   Oscar Wilde, *A House of Pomegranates*, illus. C. Ricketts and C. H. Shannon (London: James R. Osgood McIlvane, 1891) 73–147.

2.   Lucy Fraser's *The Pleasures of Metamorphosis: Japanese and English Fairy Tale Transformations of "The Little Mermaid"* (Detroit: Wayne State University, 2017), provides a developed discussion of this exoticism.

The Golden Mermaid

1. Andrew Lang, ed. *The Green Fairy Book* (London: Longmans, Green and Co., 1892), 340–49.
2. Scottish comparative mythologist and journalist Andrew Lang (1844–1912) wrote about fairy tales and mythology, introduced the 1884 *Grimms' Household Tales* in Margaret Hunt's translation, and produced a few tales of his own, such as "The Princess Nobody" and "Prince Riccardo." Concerning the fairy tales he published, it should be noted that his wife, Leonora, and several others translated and adapted many of the stories.

    Following "The Golden Mermaid" tale in Lang's book is a terse notation: "Grimm." Is this simply a reference to a somewhat similar story appearing in *Grimms' Fairy Tales*, or is "The Golden Mermaid" more specifically an adaptation of "The Golden Bird" (Grimm 57)? The latter is quite unlikely given their plot differences, but we do not know which text Lang and his collaborators had in mind.

A Mermaid's Tears

1. Kurahashi Yumiko, "Two Tales Translated from Cruel Fairy Tales for Adults," trans. Marc-Sebastian Jones and Tateya Koichi, *Marvels & Tales* 22, no. 1 (2008): 173–77.

Abyssus Abyssum Invocat

1. Genevieve Valentine, LightspeedMagazine.com, February 2013, www.lightspeedmagazine.com/fiction/abyssus-abyssum-invocat.
2. Genevieve Valentine's first novel, *Mechanique: A Tale of the Circus Tresaulti*, won the Crawford Award for Best Novel, as well as a nomination for the Nebula Award; *The Girls at the Kingfisher Club*, her 2015 novel, retells the "Twelve Dancing Princesses" fairy tale.
3. The legend of the Mermaid of Zennor, first published by Cornish folklorist William Bottrell in 1873, has been adapted in poems, novels, songs, and opera. The so-called "mermaid's chair"—a medieval chair that features the mermaid carving—is a tourist attraction in Zennor.

African Mermaids and Other Water Spirits

1. Funmi Osoba, *Benin Folklore: A Collection of Classic Folktales and Legends* (London: Hadada Books, 1993), 97.

2. Osoba, *Benin Folklore*, 46.

3. Osoba, *Benin Folklore*, 30, 77.

4. "A Yoruba Festival Tradition Continues: 50 Photos Celebrating the River Goddess Oshun," *OkayAfrica*, October 6, 2015.

5. Adetunbi Richard Ogunleye, "Cultural Identity in the Throes of Modernity: An Appraisal of Yemoja Among the Yoruba in Nigeria," *Inkaniyiso: The Journal of Humanities and Social Sciences* 7, no. 1 (2015), 60–68.

6. Ogunleye, "Cultural Identity in the Throes of Modernity," 61.

7. Solimar Otero and Toyin Falola, eds., *Yemoja: Gender, Sexuality, and Creativity in the Latina/o and Afro-Atlantic Diasporas* (New York: State University of New York Press, 2013), xvii–xxxii.

8. Daniel, "Police Dispel Reports of Mermaid in Ibadan, Says Fish Was Baby-Octopus," Information Nigeria, July 24, 2013, www .informationng.com/2013/07/police-dispel-reports-of-mermaid -in-ibadan-says-fish-was-baby-octopus.html.

9. Staff reporter, "Mermaid and Incensed Spirits Myth Haunts Zimbabwe Town," *Bulawayo 24 News*, February 6, 2012, bula-wayo24.com/index-id-news-sc-national-byo-11827-article-mer maid+and+incensed+spirits+myth+haunts+zimbabwe+town +.html.

10. Dan Newling, "Reason for Zimbabwe Reservoir Delays . . . Mermaids Have Been Hounding Workers Away!," *Daily Mail Online*, February 6, 2012, www.dailymail.co.uk/news/article -2097218/Reason-Zimbabwe-reservoir-delays--mermaids -hounding-workers-away.html.

11. Aldo Pekeur, "Mysterious 'Mermaid' Rises from the River," Independent Online News, January 16, 2008, www.iol.co.za /news/south-africa/mysterious-mermaid-rises-from-the-river -385945.

Agangu and Yemaja

1. A. B. Ellis, *The Yoruba-Speaking Peoples of the Slave Coast of West Africa* (London: Chapman and Hall, 1894), 43–45.

2. *The order, according to some, was Olokun, Olosa, Shango, Oya, Oshun, Oba, Ogun, Dada, and the remainder as above.

Merfolk in *The Thousand and One Nights*

1. Antoine Galland's *Les Mille et Une Nuit* [sic], which appeared between 1704 and 1717 and was comprised of twelve volumes, is now understood to be more of an enlarged adaptation than a translation. This publication met with an enthusiastic response in Europe, and the *Nights* made its debut in English translation shortly after Galland's first volumes were published.

2. The name of both protagonists is 'Abdallâh, marking them both as Muslim ('Abdallâh literally means "God's slave") and identifying them as typical folk characters in this tradition, comparable to the English "Jack." In this story, the children of the sea, like humans, obey God's laws, but their practice in dealing with the dead are opposite. It is precisely this irreconcilable difference that makes the two 'Abdallâhs go their separate ways.

Julnar the Mermaid and Her Son Badar Basim of Persia

1. *Arabian Nights: The Marvels and Wonders of the Thousand and One Nights*. Adapted from Richard F. Burton's Unexpurgated Translation by Jack Zipes (New York: Signet Classic, 1991), 223–63.

The Sea Fairy

1. From Mohammad Ja'fari Qanavāti's personal collection. Translated by Ulrich Marzolph.

About K——, the River Goddess Who Exists in Jaintia Hills

1. Collected and translated by Margaret Lyngdoh.
2. Clan name changed.
3. Place names changed.

How Water Tied a Covenant with Man and the Divine Nature of Water

1. Coll. and trans. Margaret Lyngdoh.
2. Literally, the people of the Ramhah deity.
3. In the narrative of the origin of ailments among humans, illnesses are also nonhuman entities, the children of the ill-fated

queen Maharajari, who was murdered during childbirth by her husband through treachery. Some of these children sought shelter inside *Niaring*.

4. Jhare is a magical practice in the North Khasi Hills. Everything in nature, including afflictions and illness, has a secret name, the knowledge of which gives the practitioner power and authority over the object or illness.

About a *Puri* Enchantment

1. Collected and translated by Margaret Lyngdoh.

Shoān, a Nicobar Tale

1. Frederik Adolph deRoepstorff, *A Dictionary of the Nancowry Dialect of the Nicobarese Language; in Two Parts: Nicobarest-English and English-Nicobarese*, ed. Mrs. deRoepstorff (Calcutta: Home Department Press, 1884), 251–54.
2. * Tentioāhlare—to go on board.
3. * Wŭs—an onomatopoetic word denoting the rush of water at the approach of the whale.
4. * Ilū—a fish, in form not unlike the "belone rostrate" (gar-fish). When hunted or hunting, it glides or skims very gracefully along on the surface of the water, its tail just touching it.
5. * Hiput—the Dugong, is common about the Nicobars. It is hunted, and the Nicobarese have much to say about the great care it takes of its young one, and of the funny way it seizes its calf when in danger.
6. * Ok kandu—The shell of the "tridachna gigantia". This shell grows to an enormous size. I have seen one 5' across, but I am told that they are found even bigger.

A Hairy Chinese Mermaid

1. In *A Manual of Chinese Quotations* under "Precious Things," we find "The mermaid wept tears that became pearls." The saying is thus annotated: "The mermaid was entertained hospitably when in the upper world by a certain person, and, in order to show some return, wept into a vessel, her tears being turned into precious stones." J. H. Stewart Lockhart (Hongkong: Kelly & Walsh, 1893), 280. While in European tales and legends the

mermaid is often attracted to precious objects and jewelry, the transformation in this Chinese saying links with the mermaid's tears becoming pearls in Japanese lore as well.

Mermaids

1. Nicholas Belfield Dennys, *The Folk-Lore of China* (Hongkong: China Mail Office, 1876), 114–15.

Mermaids from Japan

1. *Ningyo* combines the Chinese characters 人魚 for "human" and "fish."
2. See the comparative work of Japanese Studies scholar Lucy Fraser.
3. As noted in his 1876 account of Chinese mermaids, Nicholas Belfield Dennys recalls seeing "Barnum's celebrated purchase from Japan, which, so far as could be judged, consisted of a monkey's body most artistically joined to a fish's tail." *The Folklore of China* (Hongkong: China Mail Office, 1876), 114. Apparently exhibited in Japan as well (see Fraser), *ningyo no miira* or mummified mermaids were popular attactions in London and New York.
4. See Mayako Murai's book, *From Dog Bridegroom to Wolf Girl: Contemporary Japanese Fairy-Tale Adaptations in Conversation with the West* (Detroit: Wayne State University Press, 2015).

The Mermaid

1. N. A., *The Far East. An Exponent of Japanese Thoughts and Affairs*, vol. 2, no. 12, 714–17 (Tokyo: The Nation's Friend Publishing Co., December 20, 1897). Nicholas Belfield Dennys, *The Folk-Lore of China* (Hongkong: China Mail Office, 1876).

Yao Bikuni

1. Kōji Inada, and Ozawa Toshio, eds., *Nihon Mukashibanashi Tsūkan 11: Toyama, Ishikawa, Fukui* (Kyoto: Dōhōsha, 1981), 187–89. Translated by Mayako Murai.
2. The version translated here was told by a female informant from Obama City in Fukui Prefecture and recorded by Kasai Noriko.

Water Spirits of the Philippines

1. Tagalog, Ilokano, Visayan, and Mindanao are different ethno-linguistic groups native to the Philippines.

The Mermaid Queen

1. Henry Otley Beyer Collection held by Charity Beyer-Bagatsing.

The Litao and Serena

1. Henry Otley Beyer Collection held by Charity Beyer-Bagatsing.

The American and the Sirena of Amburayan

1. Henry Otley Beyer Collection held by Charity Beyer-Bagatsing.

A Mermaid in Mabini

1. Courtesy of Regie Barcelona Villanueva.

The Mermaid

1. Erlinda K. Alburo, ed. and trans., Ramon L. Cerilles, Marian P. Diosay, and Lawrence M. Liao, researchers; Fred C. Dimay, illus., *Cebuano Folktales 2* (Cebu: San Carlos Publications, University of San Carlos, 1977), 16–18.
2. Erlinda K. Alburo, *Cebuano Folktales* (Cebu: San Carlos Publications, University of San Carlos, 1977), iii.

A Mer-Wife in Northern Australia

1. At translator Erika Charola's suggestion, we have changed the title from "Karukany" to "Karukayn"; as she explains it, "the bilingual Gurindji-English book has a readership more likely to be familiar with Gurindji orthography, in which a palatal 'n' is represented by 'ny,' but the pronunciation is much closer to 'karukine.'"

Karukayn (Mermaids)

1. Told by Ronnie Wavehill and translated by Erika Charola and Ronnie Wavehill. In *Yijarni: True Stories from Gurindji Country*,

edited by Erika Beatriz Charola and Felicity Helen Meakins,
(Canberra: Aboriginal Studies Press, 2016), 13–20.

Sirena

1. *Marianas Island Legends: Myth and Magic*, retold by Macey
   Flood; comp., Bo Flood; illus., Connie J. Adams (Honolulu: The
   Bess Press, 2001), 43–47.

The Feejee Mermaid Hoax

1. P. T. Barnum, *The Life of P. T. Barnum Written by Himself*
   (New York: Refield, 1855), iv, 231, 232, 233.

The Mermaid

1. *The New York Herald*, July 17, 1842.

Mermaids and Moʻo of Hawaiʻi

1. Mary Kawena Pukui with Laura C. S. Green, col., trans., *Folktales of Hawaiʻi: He mau Kaʻao Hawaiʻi* (Honolulu: Bishop
   Museum Press, 2008), 48.
2. Moʻo and ʻōlelo combined denote "series of talks," a union re-
   flecting a long history of oral tradition (Mary Kawena Pukui and
   Samuel H. Elbert, *Hawaiian Dictionary* [Honolulu: University of
   Hawaiʻi Press, 1986], s.v. "moʻolelo"). Moʻo has many meanings,
   including lizard or reptile, thus referring to reptilian water deities.
   It is also brindled, speaking to the ways that the (Hawaiian)
   lizard—with its backbone and brindled markings—stands for
   continuity in the sense of an unbroken sequence. Similarly, other
   meanings of moʻo also refer to that which is part of a larger whole
   or series such as a grandchild or great-grandchild, a smaller piece
   of kapa or bark-cloth, a smaller land division within a larger land
   division. And most significantly, the Hawaiian word for genealogy, like the genre known as moʻolelo, incorporates the term
   moʻo—moʻokūʻauhau—"the story or telling of genealogy."
3. Pukui and Elbert, *Hawaiian Dictionary,* s.v. "kaʻao"; see also
   Lorrin Andrews, *A Dictionary of the Hawaiian Language* (Honolulu: Island Heritage Publishing, 2003), s.v. "kaʻao."
4. For more on moʻolelo and kaʻao, see Marie Alohalani Brown,
   Facing the Spears of Change: The Life and Legacy of John

Papa ʻĪʻī (Honolulu: University of Hawaiʻi Press, 2016), 15–20, 27–29.

The Mermaid of Honokawailani Pond

1. Sara Keliʻilolena Nākoa, "Ke Kiʻowai ʻo Honokawailani," in *Lei Momi o ʻEwa*, eds. William H. Wilson (1979), M. Puakea Nogelmeier (1993), and Sahoa Fukushima (Honolulu: Tongg Publishing, 1979; Honolulu: Ka ʻAhahui ʻŌlelo Hawaiʻi and Short Stack by Native Books, 2016), 6–9.
2. Sarah Nākoa, the teller of this tale, which she heard from her grandmother, was raised in ʻEwa, on the west side of Oʻahu. Nākoa was familiar with this pond, and like others in the area, had swam in its waters. *Lei Momi o ʻEwa (Pearl Lei of ʻEwa)* is a collection of stories that Nākoa told in Hawaiian. Nākoa's Hawaiian was strikingly elegant, and consequently Hawaiian-language instructors in Hawaiʻi use *Lei Momi o ʻEwa* in their classes. The story was translated by Marie Alohalani Brown; it is the first time that this tale has been translated into English for publication.

Kalamainuʻu, the Moʻo Who Seduced Punaʻaikoaʻe

1. John Papa ʻĪʻī, "Na Hunahuna no ka Moolelo Hawaii," *Ka Nupepa Kuokoa*, September 4, 11, and 18, 1869, trans. Marie Alohalani Brown.
2. John Papa ʻĪʻī (1800–1870), a noted nineteenth-century Hawaiian statesman, is the teller of this tale.

Water Beings of South America

1. A British citizen of English and Hungarian descent, Walter E. Roth (1861–1933) was a physician, educator, and museum curator who became interested in the indigenous peoples of the places in which he was stationed, Australia and Guyana.

The Fisherman's Water-Jug and Potato

1. Walter E. Roth, "An Inquiry into the Animism and Folk-Lore of the Guiana Indians," *Thirtieth Annual Report: Smithsonian Institution of the Bureau of Amerian Ethnology to the Secretary of the Smithsonian Instutions, 1908–1909* (Washington, D.C.: Government Printing Office, 1915), 245–47.

Oiára, the Water-Maidens

1. Herbert H. Smith, *Brazil: The Amazons and the Coast* (New York: Charles Scribner's Sons, 1879), 572.
2. *Pontederia. Dr. Barboza Rodriguez says that the oiára has the tail of a porpoise.

The Pincoya

1. Francisco Javier Cavada, "La Pincoya," in *Chiloé y los Chilotes* (Santiago: Imprenta Universitaria, 1914), 101–10. Translated by Marie Alohalani Brown.
2. The implication here is that girls with happy dispositions will attract abundance because their disposition is pleasing to the Pincoyes.

The Mermaids

1. Julio Vicuña Cifuentes, *"Las Sirenas," Mitos y Supersticiones Recogidos de la Tradición Oral Chilena con Referencias Comparativas a los de Otros Países Latinos* (Santiago de Chile: Imprenta Universitaria, 1915), 85–87. Translated by Marie Alohalani Brown.

African Water Spirits in the Caribbean

1. Misty L. Bastian, "Married in the Water: Spirit Kin and Other Afflictions of Modernity in Nigeria," *Journal of Religion of Africa* 27, no. 2 (May 1997): 116–34, 123.
2. Bastian, "Married in the Water," 124.

Ti Jeanne

1. Alice Besson, *Folklore and Legends of Trinidad and Tobago* (Port-of-Spain, Trinidad: Paria Publishing Co., 2001), 49–51.

Maman Dlo's Gift

1. Gérard A Besson, *Folklore and Legends of Trinidad and Tobago* (Port-of-Spain, Trinidad: Paria Publishing Co., 2001), 52–53.

Water Beings of Indigenous North America

1. Bureau of Indian Affairs; First Nations Peoples in Canada. See Bureau of Indian Affairs, "About us," https://www.bia.gov /about-us; Facing History and Ourselves, "Who are the Indigenous Peoples of Canada," https://www.facinghistory.org/stolen -lives-indigenous-peoples-canada-and-indian-residential-schools /historical-background/who-are-indigenous-peoples-canada; Facing History and Ourselves, "First Nations," https://www .facinghistory.org/stolen-lives-indigenous-peoples-canada-and -indian-residential-schools/historical-background/first-nations.

The Horned Serpent Runs Away with a Girl Who Is Rescued by the Thunderer

1. Arthur C. Parker, *Seneca Myths and Folk Tales* (Buffalo, NY: Buffalo Historical Society, 1923), 218–22.
2. The collector is Arthur C. Parker (1881–1855), a folklorist and archaeologist of both Seneca and Scots-English ancestry. In his discussion of Seneca storytelling customs, Parker notes that "no fable, myth-tale, or story of ancient adventures might be told during the months of summer," by order of the "little people' (djogë'o), the wood fairies," in part because "all the world stops work when a good story is told and afterward forgets its wonted duty in marveling. Thus the modern Iroquois, following the old time custom, reserves his tales of adventures, myths and fable for winter when the year's work is over and all nature slumbers." *Seneca Myths and Folk Tales*, xxvi.

Of the Woman Who Loved a Serpent Who Lived in a Lake

1. Charles G. Leland, *Algonquin Legends of New England or Myths and Folk Lore of the MicMac, Passamaquoddy, and Penobscot Tribes*, third ed. (Boston: Houghton, Mifflin, and Company, 1884), 273–74.
2. Folklorist Charles G. Leland (1824–1903) collected this tale and the two others that follow it from the Passamaquoddy (an Anglicization of Peskotomuhkat, their autonym) in 1882.

How Two Girls Were Changed to Water-Snakes

1. Charles G. Leland, *Algonquin Legends of New England or Myths and Folk Lore of the MicMac, Passamaquoddy, and Penobscot Tribes,* third ed. (Boston: Houghton, Mifflin, and Company, 1884), 268–69.

Ne Hwas, the Mermaid

1. Charles G. Leland, *Algonquin Legends of New England or Myths and Folk Lore of the MicMac, Passamaquoddy, and Penobscot Tribes,* third ed. (Boston: Houghton, Mifflin, and Company, 1884), 270–71.
2. This teller of this story is Mrs. W. Wallace Brown, the wife of an Indian agent, known for her knowledge of Passamaquoddy customs in Maine.

Legend of the Fish Women (Mermaids)

1. Herbert Earl Wilson, *The Lore and Lure of the Yosemite* (San Francisco: A. M. Robertson, 1922), 125–26.
2. Alternatively termed Awahnichi.
3. Alternatively termed Awani.
4. The collector of this tale is Herbert Earl Wilson (1891–1980), a long-term resident of Yosemite Valley who gave talks and wrote books about Yosemite history and folklore.

The Woman Who Married the Merman

1. Leo J. Frachtenberg, *Coos Texts,* vol. 1 (New York: Columbia University Press, 1913), 157–61.
2. Harry Hull St. Clair II (1879–1953), who received a master's degree in linguistics under the famed anthropologist Franz Boas, collected this tale from the Coos people of coastal Oregon in 1903.

Index

Note: Page numbers after 298 refer to Notes.